THEY
FALL

I0778312

THEY FALL

CLAIRE FRAISE

Sabertooth
Press

To you, reading this book right now.

I wrote this for you. I hope I did the characters justice. I hope I did YOU justice.

Thank you for coming on this journey with me to the very end. It's been an honor to tell this story.

I hope you like the ending.

3 MONTHS LATER

PART 1
The dead men gave a groan

1

Shiloh

Something's wrong.

I sit up in bed, my breath clouding inches from my face. Mom turned the heat high before going to bed. It shouldn't be cold enough for my breath to fog.

A thud comes from outside my bedroom door. I whip my head around.

It could be nothing. I strain to listen through the thundering pulse in my ears.

Another thud. Closer this time.

I fling the comforter off my body, snatching my phone from the nightstand and flipping it open. I use the screen to see where I'm going, but it can't cut through the deep shadows pooling in the corners of my room. I'm used to the nightmares. They come every night. Ghosts in the walls. Shadows that move when they shouldn't. Cold spots that make my breath fog indoors. But this is real. This isn't a nightmare. I'm awake.

And I know that feeling.

I run across my room and throw on the lights, pressing my back into the closed door and breathing hard as I peer into the spaces where the shadows were. Everything is in place.

A floorboard creaks down the hall. I whirl around and open the door, aiming my phone screen at the hallway. The weak beam cuts through the shadows, lighting up—

Nothing. Mom's door is closed. So is Max's. They're both sleeping like normal people do in the middle of the night.

I'm fine. Everything's fine.

There's another creak. This time from the kitchen. Footsteps. There are footsteps on the floor.

There's a ghost in the house. Of course there is. I knew it would only be a matter of time before they came looking for me, given how many enemies we made. I installed a new deadbolt on the front door last week, but that won't keep the actual dead out. They can come through wood, through plaster, through flesh. My phone beam trembles as I creep forward. Cold presses through my socks like I'm standing on ice. Something moves in the shadows in the kitchen. The beam catches it. Someone is standing at the sink.

I charge down the hallway and slap the light switch. The figure turns around, and all the panic in me dies.

"I had to get some water," Max says, clutching his *Cars* cup with both hands. My legs almost give out.

Oh thank God.

I close my phone, willing my heart to stop hammering. "Jesus, buddy, you scared the crap out of me."

"Why are you awake?" He scrunches up his forehead. "Did something happen?"

Did something happen? Where do I even start with that one?

"Uh, no. I just thought I heard a noise."

His eyes go huge. "Was it a ghost?"

"Nope." *Please, no more ghosts.* I walk over to him and push his cowlick out of his face. "Just you."

But he's already scanning every corner, muscles tensing like he's getting ready to run. I've spent so many nights the past couple of months crawling under the covers with him, trying to convince him that things were okay again and no bad men were coming to get him, but he doesn't trust it. I can't blame him. He watches me to see when I'm scared, like I'm some kind of scariness guide. The responsibility is crushing if I stop too long to think about it. I'm sure not acting strong for him tonight.

I reach for his hand. His fingers are ice in mine.

"Bring your water," I say. "Let's get you back to bed."

"Can I sleep in your room tonight?"

"Yeah." I want that probably as much as he does. "Course you can."

He drinks the entire cup of water and puts a hand on his head.

"Brain freeze," he says. "Goddamn it."

I grin. He grins up at me because he made me grin, and I put the empty cup in the sink before walking him back to my room. I slip under the covers and lift them up for Max to crawl in next to me, his small head nestling on the pillow.

Max has fallen asleep when the house makes another sound. I tell myself it's just settling, but what if it's not?

There hasn't been a ghost in here for three months, not since I put all the magnets everywhere. I should feel less scared with Max next to me, but all I can think about is how if one of those things gets in here, I'm the only thing standing between it and him. What if I'm not enough?

Another creak. *It's just the house.*

But after everything I've seen, how can I trust that anymore?

❦

I go back to sleep, but when my alarm goes off in the morning, I feel minutes from death. Max groans and covers his ears. I prop myself on my elbow. There's a pounding in my head that hasn't gone away in months. Amazing what not sleeping enough can do to a person.

I take a cursory glance around the room. The first light of morning filters through my curtains, just enough to scare away the shadows. My desk looks like a desk. My lamp looks like a lamp. Even my old Justin Bieber poster on the inside of my closet door that Jonah makes fun of me for still having looks, well, like Justin Bieber.

I kill the alarm, then nudge the lump next to me. "Buddy, it's time for school."

He burrows deeper. I smile at him. Oh, I can have some fun with this.

I sit up, melodramatically glancing around the room. "Oh my God, where did Max go?"

His giggle wraps around me like a warm hug. The corners of my mouth tug up.

"He was here a second ago."

He laughs harder. I flop onto my side, leaning on my elbow and tugging at the sheets.

"Max, you know what happens to kids who skip school, right?" I wriggle my hand under the covers to ruffle his messy hair. "Their brains shrink, and you know what happens to people without brains?"

He pulls down the sheet enough for me to see his eyes. Big and brown, but not that sad. "What?"

"They have to eat them!"

I poke at his sides. He erupts into laughter, trying to squirm away from me. I bear down, tickling his ribs, and he squeals. "You'll turn into a zombie and go hunting for brains!"

"I don't want to be a zombie."

I cross my eyes and do my best growl. *Braaaaiiiins.*

"Stop it!"

I pause to catch my breath, smiling so wide my face hurts. "Go get ready for school, then."

He scrunches up his nose. "Fine."

I kiss the side of his head, and he careens across the hallway to his room. He has enough energy to make me feel awake, so I drag myself out of bed, throwing on a pair of gray sweatpants and a navy zip-up hoodie, which is pretty much my uniform these days. It's too cold to consider wearing anything else. I examine my face in the full-length mirror hanging over my door. The state of the union is … not great. I tug at the circles under my eyes. My skin is so pale that it's turned sort of gray, like I haven't seen the sun in months. Not much I can do about that when it's zero degrees out there.

After running my fingers through my sandy hair and brushing my teeth, I go to the kitchen. It feels even colder in here than it did in my room. It always does. I flip on the kettle and drop two pre-sliced bagels into the toaster, glancing over my shoulder every two seconds like I'd find a real ghost behind me.

"Max!" I shout. "You better be getting dressed!"

"Yup!"

I go through the stack of letters on the doormat. Water bill. Internet bill. Pizza delivery menu. Red ink stamps the propane bill—OVERDUE. I wince. It's not an exaggeration to say it's costing us a fortune to heat this house. Mom got a job two months ago selling vacuum cleaners over the phone, but she can't get out of bed on some days, so the job doesn't bring in much. I've been dipping into my savings to cover the bills and groceries, but it won't last us forever. I will have to get a job soon. I hope I can get all my community service done first, because between school and community service and taking care of Max and making sure Mom eats …

Is Mom awake yet?

I head to her room and go to open the door, but my hand stops on the knob. Barging into this room still feels weird.

I need you to take your clothes off.

Enough. I force my hand to twist the knob.

"Mom?"

It takes me a second to see her, buried under so many blankets and pillows that she's just a lump in the bed. Her back is turned. She's wearing the same pajamas she's been wearing for days. Her blonde hair has gotten longer and is falling in knotted clumps over her shoulders. I don't remember the last time she brushed it. She has given up on it. Like she's giving up on life.

"Mom?" I ask again, stepping closer. "Are you awake?"

Mom nods. I can hear soft voices coming from her phone. I sit on the bed and peer over her shoulder at the weathercaster on the screen, who's pointing at a blue-and-purple-shaded map of the town.

"Today is looking like it's going to be a cold one," he says, as if that weren't already obvious, "with temperatures peaking at 9 degrees."

I want nothing more than to pluck that phone from her hand and tell her to stop watching. All she does is sit in here and watch the news.

But I force myself to take a deep breath and say, as gentle as I can, "Want me to bring you some tea?"

She rolls over to look at me. There are pillow creases on the side of her face.

"It's getting colder again." She presses her thumb on the dimple in my chin. "I was talking to the mailman yesterday, and he was telling me that this is a record snowfall for the state. The last time Bethany even got close to being this cold for this long was forty years ago, and even then it was ten degrees warmer."

"It's winter," I say. "It gets cold in winter."

"You don't think it has something to do with ..." Mom widens her blue eyes. "Ghosts?"

"No." I cringe at how fast the word comes out. "No, Mom, not everything has to do with ghosts."

Mom chews on her bottom lip. I try to push down the queasy feeling I get every time I lie to her. The cold has everything to do with the ghosts, but telling Mom that will make her panic, and there's nothing I can do to get rid of them, so what's the point?

"Will you please stop worrying about it and go outside today?" I say.

Her experience of becoming a ghost has made her borderline agoraphobic. I told her we should at least move to the apartment now that her divorce is underway, but because I don't have my driver's license yet, it's hard to live in Mount Keenan when I have to get to school every day, and Mom can't handle driving. Every day, there's another story about a freak traffic accident, or some strange object falling onto someone and killing them. Bethany is becoming a bad luck town.

I don't want to get angry at her, especially since it's my fault she became tied up in all this, but she's gotten so paranoid that she can barely even take care of herself, and some days, I'm convinced she takes something. I'm not sure what, but she's turned into a shell of a person. It's like she's standing on the edge of a cliff, getting ready to jump, and I'm at the bottom, and all I can do is watch. So I try to take care of her as best as I can.

Pressing down on the bad feeling in my stomach, I get up. "I'm going to bring you tea and a bagel. I'll be back in a minute."

She says nothing. I close the door, blinking back the tears.

I'm okay. This is fine.

I will not fall apart.

I'm pouring boiling water over a tea bag when the toast pops up and I almost jump out of my skin. Pulling out both bagels, I slather them with a generous helping of butter. I bring Mom her breakfast, which I set on the nightstand because I'm not holding out hope that she will eat. When I get back to the kitchen, Max still isn't there.

I yell into the hall. "Max!"

"I'm *coming*."

His little feet pound on the wood as he runs, sliding into the living room in his socks like that guy in *Risky Business*. For today's outfit, he has chosen a pair of bright red sweatpants and a yellow T-shirt with a *Transformers* character on it. I press a closed fist to my mouth, trying to hide my smile.

Max examines my face. "What are you smiling for?"

"You look like ketchup and mustard."

"At least cars will see me against the snow and won't run me over."

Well, that shuts me up. Too many people have gotten hit by cars these past couple of months.

I slide him his bagel on a plastic plate. He grins ear-to-ear before taking a giant bite, butter smearing across his face and crumbs falling out of his mouth.

I brace my forearms on the counter. "Worth getting ready for, huh?"

He nods, his mouth full as he grasps the bagel with both hands. I drop a tea bag into a mug and curl my hands around it, hanging my head and inhaling the steam as if it could warm me from the inside.

The gas bill. Seven minutes left before we need to leave. Lunches. I need to make lunches. *Shit.* I forgot to write the essay that's due in English today.

I'll give Max money for lunch. Not much I can do about the essay. Or the gas bill, at least not until after school. I take small sips of tea and lean against the counter as Max finishes his bagel, swallowing it in one giant gulp and pushing his plate away like he finished a feast. God, I'm so grateful for this kid. I may have done a lot of things wrong in my life, but protecting him is the one thing I got right.

I put his plate in the dishwasher and drain the rest of the tea, giving him the biggest smile I can muster. "Ready?"

Getting dressed up in his winter gear is something Max needs my help with. If it were up to him, he'd run out the door in a sweatshirt and then complain he's cold all the way to school, but it's not up to him so he stands still as I wrestle his arms through the sleeves of his coat and yank a wool hat over his head. A tuft of blond hair sticks out the front. He sees me smiling at him and shoves it back under the cap.

Yanking on my snow boots, I strap my backpack to my shoulders and take Max's hand. I can barely feel his fingers through my gloves as I slide back the deadbolt and kick the door open.

Icy air slams into me. I turn my face away, squinting

against the glare reflecting off the snow. Looks like we got two more inches of it last night. Maybe three. I swear I shoveled the steps yesterday, but now the path is gone. Of course it is. But that doesn't make me even close to as mad as the flowers on the doormat.

I glare at the bouquet. The wrapping looks cheap. Like something you could buy at a supermarket, which is fine, and would even be nice if anyone else sent them.

Gritting my teeth, I snatch up the flowers and ball up the cheap cellophane before shoving them into the trash can in the driveway. I stand there, staring at the closed lid as I try to catch my breath.

"Uh," Max's voice brings me back because, for a second, I forgot he was there. "What was that?"

"Nothing," I say. "Just some junk."

"Flowers are junk?"

They are when they're from your dad.

But he doesn't need to know about Dad's attempts to win Mom back. It's better if he doesn't know the pathetic lows the man we get half of our genetic makeup from will stoop to.

I lead Max out onto the road. A blue salt crust covers patches of asphalt, but the road is still a sheet of ice. I'm actually grateful for the new snow. It means we're not slipping and breaking our necks like last week when Mr. Peterson went down and broke his hip.

I can't believe Dad sent Mom flowers. Again. I mean, I can believe it, but this is the third bunch this week. At least Mom never sees them. That's the one good thing about her not leaving the house.

What the hell does he want? That's a dumb question. I know exactly what he wants. To worm his way back into our lives and have her call off the divorce, but she's not talking to him. She's holding strong in that, if nothing else. It's a good thing, too, because if I saw his face here ... well, I don't know what I'd do, but I'd want to throw a chair at it.

A plow grinds past, throwing up a pile of snow. Max bounces on his toes, grinning up at me.

"I'm going to drive one of those when I grow up," he says.

"I think that's a great idea."

He still sees the snow with that innocent wonder that died in me at five. After three months of this, I would've thought he'd be over it, but no. He still gets excited enough to want to walk on the strip of grass by the road so that he can be the first one to leave footprints in the untouched powder.

At the end of our road, a stop sign creaks. I try not to look at it. The wind is howling strong enough to move that sign, but I know enough to know that something else could be doing it and I try hard to push the thoughts from my mind.

I saw the ghosts from the hospital window. I've never seen so many of them in my life. The entire parking lot was glowing as they wove in between streetlamps, made signs flicker, and caused the sliding doors of the emergency room to glitch. I swear I can feel eyes on me as we drag our feet toward the school. Francesca made me promise we'd stop messing with the ghosts, but I think of Mr. Peterson's hip, the pile-up on the interstate last week that killed two drivers, the frozen branch that fell on that old lady last Tuesday, that freak tractor accident from three weeks ago ... Francesca said we had to leave them alone because they aren't hurting anybody, but they're hurting people all right.

I just have to hope they'll go away on their own. I'm done with all that ghost crap. I'm not about to risk my life again because it's a little cold.

But I tighten my grip on Max's hand. I can't help it.

Once we reach the school, I stop in front of the doors. Because our town is so tiny, the elementary, middle, and high schools all operate out of different wings of the same building, which makes bringing Max to school convenient but doesn't make me any less stressed about it. Even the small goodbyes feel big now.

The awning of the elementary wing drips with icicles. Kids bounce past us in their bright coats like nothing's wrong.

"I'll be here to pick you up at two forty-five," I say. "Okay?"

Max waves at a boy racing toward the entrance. I'm glad he's so much more well-adjusted than I am.

"Max, can you listen to me, please?"

He focuses back on me. "Yes. Okay."

A little girl coughs as she walks past us, with her tongue sticking out like little kids do. She wipes the back of her hand against her gummy nose and I cringe. Everyone seems to have caught something from this cold snap. Bugs are everywhere. Just like ghosts. Weakening immune systems and freezing pipes.

"Promise to wash your hands?" I ask.

Max nods. "I promise."

Good. I hope this will stick better than my 'don't talk to strangers' advice. I hug him. He hugs me back, and I rest my chin on his shoulder for what doesn't feel like long enough before he pushes me away. I guess I'm hugging him too long to be cool.

"I love you," I say. "Have a good day, okay?"

Giving me a thumbs-up, he runs toward the school. My heart pounds like a ticking bomb. I wish I could calm down. I wish I felt ready to send him back into the real world. I wish I could be ready to go back into the real world, too. I should be strong enough to do this. It's school, for crying out loud, I have gone to way scarier places. But watching him walk away feels harder than anything I had to go through with Leonard.

I can't protect Max from everything. I have to trust him to take care of himself, but I've spent so long with this hard death grip on him, trying to make sure he's safe, that I don't know if I'll ever be able to loosen it.

Breathe. He's fine. Kids go to school every day. Nothing's chasing him.

I spot a glimpse of something black, half-buried in the snow. Stepping closer to it, I realize it's a crow, lying dead with its claws in the air.

Poor guy. It's just lying there with its feathers flattened against the white. I don't know why, but it feels important. Like some kind of message I don't understand.

Get out of here.

I step around the building toward the main doors of the high school, stopping when I spot a familiar head of black hair walking up the steps.

2
Shiloh

I run to catch up to him. "Jonah!"

He turns around in time just for me to barrel into him, flinging my arms around him so hard that he has to step backward to catch me. One of his sleeves flaps empty. He still wears his sling at school, and I immediately pull back, not wanting to hurt him.

"Miss me much?" he asks.

"Please." I look up into his eyes, digging my chin into his chest. "You didn't come last night."

Jonah comes over and sleeps in my bed with me most nights. I either let him in through the front door or he climbs through my window, which is pushing the limits of what he can do physically these days, but he likes it because he says it makes coming over feel like a secret mission. In the temporary foster home his social worker put him in, he's crammed in with six other kids under the age of twelve and landed the bottom bunk in a room where three of the boys won't leave him alone. The parents are good people trying to do a good thing, but they're so overwhelmed that they don't notice Jonah slip out after they finish putting the kids to bed and walk thirty minutes to my house. He can sleep through the night in my bed. I can, too. If he's with me, I don't need to call him in the middle of the night and keep him on the phone, listening to his breathing on the other end of the line until I stop seeing ghosts in the shadows.

Mom caught us once. She's not a fan of the arrangement, but she's not exactly what I'd call aware. As far as she knows, he hasn't been back since.

"Fred was up late, so I couldn't slip out." He presses his lips to my temple. "Nightmares?"

Technically no, but he doesn't have to know about catching Max in the kitchen and thinking I was going to die.

"Max stayed in my room," I say. "He protected me."

"I wouldn't cross that kid."

I hug him tighter. After everything, having him solid and whole against me feels like a miracle. Like maybe we did make it through the nightmare after all.

The bell rings. He offers me a gloved hand. I knit my padded fingers through his and walk with him into the school.

Inside, other kids strip off wet coats and hats and shove them into lockers. Puddles cover the floor from people tracking in snow. I side-eye Jonah and tighten my grip on his hand to steady him in case he slips. He doesn't like it when I make a big deal about him, especially since he walks through the snow just fine on his own all the time, but it's hard not to worry about somebody once you realize how easy it is to lose them.

Jonah has lost so much weight since he was discharged from the hospital. You can't tell how bony he is when he's wearing his coat, but it's easy to see it in his face. I swear he's almost as skinny as Miles used to be, and looks almost like a different person. After surgery, his doctor told him to rest since he broke his arm in three places, so he spent a month lying on the couch watching movies and grumbling through his PT exercises. He cleaned himself up after he got the all clear to come back to school. Even asked me to cut his hair. He let me get near his head with scissors, which I'd never have thought possible given how things were with us after the foolery, but the drug, by some miracle, has cleared his system. He told me a couple of weeks ago that he never gets bad thoughts about me anymore so, you know, that's cool.

I stop at my locker, using my teeth to yank off the damp finger of my gloves so I can enter the combination. Jonah balls up his jacket and shoves it into my locker. He's wearing a gray long-sleeve shirt under the new peace sign T-shirt I bought him for Christmas. I tried so hard to find a tie-dye one like his old one, but from a distance, this one could almost pass for the Nirvana smiley, so it's more fitting. His black sling has two signatures on it (written in silver Sharpie). Mine, and some pretentious asshole by the name of Lord Byron.

I take out my biology lab notes. Jonah leans over my shoulder, staring at his reflection in the tiny mirror taped to the panel. He yanks off his beanie, raking a hand through his choppy black hair and grinning down at me.

I look up at him. "You got something to say?"

"Nope." That grin is trouble. "Just, this is real professional work here, Scooby. I look like I got in a fight with a weed whacker."

I roll my eyes. "I don't know what you expected, letting me cut your hair."

"Maybe I should return the favor." He tugs the beanie off my head, making my baby hairs all stand up. "I bet I could give you a sick hawk."

"What the hell is a hawk?"

"Short for mohawk."

I snort, unable to hold back the laughter. "You didn't seriously just shorten mohawk."

"It's a thing."

"It's not a thing." I smile wider. "A hawkmo is a thing."

"Now you're just making shit up."

"I'm serious," I say, though the laughter makes it hard to sound convincing. "It's the opposite of a mohawk."

"What, so you shave a stripe down your head?"

I laugh and nod. He flattens my baby hairs to reveal my part. "You'd look so hot with one of those."

"Don't even think about coming near my head with scissors."

"I'd need a razor for that job."

"You're such a dork."

"Yeah." He wraps his free arm around my shoulders from behind, meeting my gaze in the mirror. "But I'm your dork."

He turns me around and drops the hand to my waist, pulling my hips against his. A tiny breath slips through my lips. He drags his hand along my hip and up to my face, moving a strand of hair behind my ear before pressing his lips to mine. Everything else goes away. The squeaking wet shoes on linoleum. The slamming lockers. The voices. There's only the soft pressure of his mouth. His long fingers push into my hair. The solid warmth of him against me. I smile against his lips. After all the foolery and the attacks and everything that tried to tear us apart, kissing him feels like winning a war.

He leans back to look at me, and oh my God, a tremble courses through me. He smiles, like he noticed.

"You know, the world is a dumpster fire, but you're my favorite person in it," he says. "For real."

I smile so big. I love it when he gets like this. His tone may be half-joking, but that's the only way he knows how to be serious.

I must be getting sappy, because so much red floods into his cheeks.

"Don't look at me like that," he says. "Stop it."

My grin only grows. I swear my face is starting to hurt from smiling so much.

"I love you," I say. "A lot."

He smiles, cupping my face and leaning in close to me. "I love you, Shiloh. More than anything."

It's a miracle my heart doesn't stop beating. He leans down to kiss me again when the warning bell rings out, and he swears under his breath and steps away.

"Well, looks like you got to get your books."

I could stand here in this hallway with him all day because it's the only time in my life where I don't feel like the responsibility is crushing me and I don't have to keep looking over my shoulder scared something will jump out and get me, but life's not fair like that.

I try to get my head on straight as I turn back to my locker, staring at the mess as I try to remember which class I have next and which book I came here to get. Jonah reaches over my shoulder and digs through the pocket of his jacket to get his dab pen. He presses his back against the locker next to mine, placing it between his lips and inhaling deeply. I do my best to ignore it. I don't like smoking. Or drugs. Or anything that changes the way the brain works because of, well, how I grew up, but Jonah has been doing a lot of that since his accident to manage his pain. I don't want to push him to quit. I mean, he almost died. He did lose Aunt Moe. How he's still smiling every day is beyond me, so I'd be an asshole to crap on anything that is helping him. But knowing that doesn't make me less grossed out.

I eye him. "Is your arm hurting?"

Jonah shrugs. "I'm working on my audition for a medical drama."

"Be serious."

His grin falters. "Doesn't hurt any more than usual."

His usual is bad. I can tell that much from the way the creases appear at the corners of his eyes when someone knocks into him or how his smile strains when he has to lift his book bag.

I close my locker and turn to look at him. "How bad?"

Jonah stares at me as he takes a long drag from the pen, then turns to exhale away from my face.

"I'm fine," he says. "Really."

He's obviously not, but this is what he does. Pushes me away as soon as he gets uncomfortable. I thought we were over this, but apparently, we're not.

"Jonah."

He turns my hand over and presses his lips onto the soft part of my thumb. "I promise I'm fine, but if anything changes and I'm suddenly not fine, I'll tell you."

I don't believe he will, but what am I supposed to say? Pushing him harder will make him pull away even more, so I sigh. "Do you promise?"

"I'll go so far as to pinky swear."

I hate that the corner of my mouth tugs up. I hate that he is doing this to me, like giving a dog a treat to distract it from barking out the window, but I hate even more that it's working.

I curl my pinky into his. He gives me a small smile and steps away from me when someone slams into him while they're walking by. His face goes tight with pain.

The guy walking past, Kyle something, glares at me. He's shorter than Jonah but thicker, like he goes to a gym and knows how to use the equipment.

"Guess they'll let anyone back in school these days," Kyle mutters. "Even murderers."

Jonah moves so fast that I barely register it. One second he's next to me, the next he's got Kyle by the collar and is slamming him into the lockers with his good arm. The metal rattles. Other kids scatter.

"What did you just say?" Jonah's voice is deadly quiet.

Blood rushes in my ears. No. Not this again.

Kyle shoots Jonah a disbelieving look. "The fuck are you going to do, gimpy?"

Jonah's grip tightens. "You think you can talk shit?"

"Jonah, stop." I step forward, grabbing the back of Jonah's arm. "This is stupid."

Jonah gives me a quick glance over his shoulder. A couple of seconds go by. His chest rises and falls. I open my mouth to tell him to walk away when he pulls his arm back and slams his fist into Kyle's jaw.

Shit.

Kyle's head whips back. Jonah jerks away from me and swings at Kyle. Phones light up as people start to film. Kyle's fist slams into Jonah's bad shoulder and they crash into the lockers with a boom of bodies against metal, their wet boots squeaking on the slick floor. Kyle's elbow lands on Jonah's ribs with a dull thud that I can feel in my chest.

Enough of this. I shove forward, trying to squeeze between them when a voice stops me.

"Break it up! NOW!"

Principal Orr's commanding voice slices through the chaos. Call-Me-Bill rushes between Kyle and Jonah and physically separates them. Jonah runs a hand down his face, gripping his jaw. His lip is bleeding.

Principal Orr glares at Jonah. I guess she has her suspicions about who started it.

"Both of you. My office. Now."

Kyle rolls his eyes, muttering something under his breath as he trudges after Call-Me-Bill. Jonah's eyes find mine. I try to think of something to say to him, but before I can, he looks at his shoes and nods, walking away.

The whispers of the other kids are loud around me. Eyes everywhere. I can barely breathe, let alone think past the pounding in my chest. My phone buzzes. I'm desperate for something to look at, so I flip it open to find a text from Miles. Or technically Lord Byron, which is what Miles insisted his code name be because if anyone saw me texting someone named Miles, there would be some questions because he's supposed to be dead.

I open the text. It's a link to an article. The words are tiny on the flip phone screen.

GRAPHIC: Rare 2-headed calf born on farm - SECOND TIME!
January 5, 2020
BETHANY, Ohio — A rare event occurred on an Ohio farm last night when a calf was born with two heads. This marks the second occurrence this season on the same farm, leaving the owners in disbelief over the extraordinary birth.
[READ MORE]

In the picture, each of the calf's heads is facing in different directions. One has its tongue out. One has a white spot above its nose. Poor thing. Or things.

But if Miles is texting me this, I know what it means.

I grip my phone and shove my way through the gossiping kids to the girls' bathroom. It's empty. I hope it stays that way. I go into one of the stalls and close the toilet, sitting on the lid and calling Miles.

3
Shiloh

"Hello?"

I smile at the sound of his voice crackling through my phone's tinny speaker. Miles talks deeper now, but his voice still has that boyish pep that it's had for as long as I've known him. I don't know when his new voice started sounding more like him than his old one, but it does.

I readjust my grip on the phone and lean forward, my elbow digging into my knee. "Hey."

"Why are you calling me?" Wind howls into his receiver, making me wince and move the speaker away from my ear. "Aren't you supposed to be in school?"

"I am. Technically." More wind. "Where are you right now?"

"The labyrinth."

"In this weather? Are you insane?"

"I'll send you a picture."

The phone buzzes. I open his selfie, and the cold knot in

my stomach loosens at the sight of his goofy grin. He looks good. Quitting the police force has allowed him to shed that clean-cut look and trade it for something more ... well, Miles. His hair has grown out a couple of inches and swoops over his forehead in a way that's not unlike the Justin Bieber poster in my room. There's some stubble poking through his jaw now. During our nightly phone call yesterday, he told me he decided he's going to grow a beard. His pale skin is flushed from the cold but his coat is unzipped, revealing the ugliest green turtleneck sweater I've ever seen.

He's making a peace sign and cheesing into the camera, standing in what looks like an empty field covered in snow. I'd never have been able to tell it was the labyrinth if it weren't for the telephone pole behind him. I know he likes going there because it's unicursal and helps him reach his spiritual center and blah blah blah, but I can't understand the point of walking a path if the path is covered in snow.

I raise the phone back up, keeping my voice low enough that it barely echoes off the bathroom tiles. "God, which elderly woman did you have to mug for that sweater?"

"Your grandma."

"You going to the bookstore?"

"On my way there now."

He's been back at his old job for around two months now. It's not exactly his old job since Ed, the owner, doesn't know Miles is the same person in this new body as the scrawny high school kid he used to be. Call me crazy, but I don't think it's healthy to hold on to the past like he is. But it's such a sensitive subject, and I know Miles hasn't forgotten the part I played in his death, so it's not my place to say anything. I just worry about him. Like I worry about everything these days.

There's a rustle on the phone. I imagine him switching hands. "So what's up, Shiloh?"

I had called him to talk about the article he sent me, but there's enough pressure in my chest that it makes the words hard to get out. "Jonah got into a fight."

"*Again?*" Miles sighs. "Is he okay?"

"He's fine," I say, wincing at the bitterness in my own voice. "At least he says he is. He flipped out on this kid and ... I don't know, Miles, he's walling me out, and with him about to turn eighteen in a couple of months ... has he talked to you at all?"

"You're the only person I talk to these days."

The phone warms against my ear as I process this. Hold on. "Jonah hasn't texted you at all?"

"He stopped replying."

Wow. I mean, it's not like Jonah's amazing at keeping up with people over text, but I thought things would be different with Miles. They're best friends. Or used to be.

I drag the toe of my sneaker over a piece of wet toilet tissue, smearing it onto the tile. That's so ... *crappy* of him. I know he struggled to adjust to Miles being in the body of his enemy, or whatever he used to call Officer Randall Zweering, but he should be over that by now.

"I'm worried about him," I say. "And I think it's weird he's pushing us away."

Miles lets out a choked laugh. "I'm sorry, am I speaking to Shiloh Oleson right now?"

I make a face. Water rushes through the pipes behind me. "What's that supposed to mean?"

"You're one to talk," he says. "Of course I think it's weird not to talk about things, but you used to do the same thing to me, so you of all people should understand what he's going through."

Oh. I didn't even think of that. I did do that, and Miles pressuring me to open up did nothing to make me want to open up.

"I'm scared the foolery isn't gone."

"You know that's not true," Miles says. "He told you he doesn't get those thoughts anymore."

Jonah did tell me the foolery has cleared his system and he no longer daydreams about killing me—which, you know, is great—but I don't know anymore. I bend over my lap, gripping the phone so tight my fingers throb.

"Be patient with him," Miles reassures me, and I cling to the sound of his voice. "He's always been this way. When something bad happens, his walls go up."

"Losing Aunt Moe was bad."

"Not much worse than his mom overdosing and leaving him." God, when he puts it like that … I hear Miles sigh. "He's been through a lot of hard things for a guy his age."

Jonah once told me that after his mom overdosed, he started hurting himself. Is that happening again, and I don't know? I tug at my hair so hard my scalp burns. Picturing him feeling that sad and alone makes me want to punch something. He said he never told Miles about it, so mentioning it now feels wrong, but I need to do something right now or I might explode.

"I get that it sucks," Miles says, "but as someone who has seen Jonah through a lot of periods like this, you have to let him ride it out and be there for him when he's ready to talk."

I wrap my arm around my stomach. Everything he's saying makes sense, but sitting around and doing nothing hurts so bad.

"On another note," Miles says. The sudden change of subject jars me back to attention. "Did you read the article I sent?"

Right. The article about the two-headed cow. The reason I called him in the first place.

I open my mouth, but he's talking before I can get a word out.

"There's something wrong in Bethany," he says.

I sigh. "Miles ..."

"I know what you're going to say. *Miles, stop with the conspiracy theories. Miles, you need to go out and make some new friends. Miles, it's not healthy to sit alone in your apartment and doom-scroll through Facebook.*" I raise my eyebrows. That was actually pretty close to what I had been about to say. "Which is totally fair, but this is bigger than that. I've been gathering data. We know the weather's all kinds of wrong because of the ghosts. Ghosts pull energy, which is why it's so cold. Plus, they are attacking people. Like that man with the tractor."

I shudder, remembering the picture that was going around school of the man with all that blood in the snow. "That was never proven to be ghost-related."

"Okay," Miles admits, "but the mower blades ate that guy right up and the engine wasn't even on, which isn't something that is supposed to happen. And it's not just accidents. Other things happening too. Like those mutations."

I remember the picture of the two-headed calf with one of its tongues coming up through one of its noses.

"Mutations happen," I say, picking at a loose thread on my sweatpants. "It's normal."

"Do you know how rare they are?" Miles asks, his voice speeding up. "That was the second two-headed calf in a few months born to the same farmer. So many farmers I talked to lost entire fields last fall. Tons of trees have died too."

"How can you tell? Trees never have leaves in the winter," I argue, leaning onto the metal pipes behind me and focusing on how they dig into my spine.

"The trees are dead," he says. "Break off a branch and you'll see."

"But that doesn't mean anything. The cold could be killing them."

"People are losing their pets," Miles continues, on a roll now. I wince, thinking of Max's gecko. Randall Zweering's lizard better not die. Max would be devastated. The thing is already going blind, and Max has started feeding it worms with chopsticks. "But what's worrying me is all the people who are dying."

I straighten. Hold on. "How many people are dying?"

"Too many to be normal." Miles sounds like he's building a case. "The average annual mortality rate in the US is around 0.9% of the population. Using that and applying it to our town of 2,643 people, we'd expect around twenty-three deaths a year, or one death every fifteen or sixteen days." He pauses, breaths hitching. "But someone's dying here every day."

Something twinges in the pit of my stomach. Every day? That can't be right. "Are you sure?"

"Read the paper."

I roll my eyes. Not because I don't care, but because of how condescending he sounds.

It's true I haven't been keeping up with the news. Sure, that might make me lazy or ignorant or even scared, but I've been so busy trying to keep Max from getting scared, to unglue Mom from her TV, to try to make Jonah smile, to remember to text Francesca, and to never miss a phone call with Miles, that I literally have no space for anything else in my head. And maybe, just maybe, I thought that if I ignored everything long enough, it would go away on its own. Summer would come and things would get warm again and my whole world would for once be okay.

But Miles never uses this voice. He sounds like the world is coming to an end and nobody will believe him.

So I sigh. I may not be reading the paper, but I would know if there had been a graphic accident *every day*. "Ghosts are not killing one person every day."

"No," Miles admits. "They're dying of heart attacks, pneumonia, cancer, lung disease—"

"All normal things to die from."

"Not in this number. Most of them are old, but babies are dying too, and people who are already sick."

"Miles—"

"I know something's not right," he says. "And I have a gut feeling that it has something to do with the ghosts."

I bite down on the pad of my thumb, staring daggers at the *A* + *R* carved into the back of the stall door. He's not lying. I may not want to believe him, but Miles wouldn't lie about something like this.

So I make sure to keep my voice gentle. "What could the ghosts have to do with this?"

"I don't know," Miles admits. "But I think it's time to call in the big guns."

Seconds tick by. A panicky feeling rises through me as I realize what he means. I stop trying to be gentle.

"No."

"Shiloh, come on," Miles says. "You know as well as I do that Francesca is the only one who can stop this."

"She's not some ghost-hunting tool for you to use."

"Oh, like you didn't use her when Max went missing?"

I grip the phone so hard the pads of my fingers burn. "That was different."

"Why? Because it was *your* brother?"

The words hit hard. No sugar-coating. Just the truth meant to land.

I want to snap back at him, to tell him he's wrong, but I can't. Because he's not.

He doesn't let up. "Just because you don't know the people who are dying doesn't make it not real."

I look down. My thumbnail has torn a crescent into the skin of my palm. I didn't even notice I was clenching my fist.

"You think I want to call her?" Miles continues, quieter now. "You think I want to open that door again? After everything? But people are *dying*, Shiloh. And Francesca can stop it. Or at least slow it down."

"You can't even be sure this is tied to the ghosts."

"I really think it is," Miles says. "Everyone's dying of natural causes, but some of these people are getting this gray rash before they die."

A chill runs down my spine. "How would you even know that?"

"Facebook," he admits, and I roll my eyes. "People are taking pictures and posting. There's even a doctor at the hospital who's commenting."

The walls of the toilet stall seem to close in around me.

"I'm sending you a picture of the rash." Miles pauses. "Did you get it?"

The picture is of a hand marked by a rash. It starts near the wrist and creeps upward in branching lines like pale gray roots winding over bones and veins just under the skin.

I can barely hear Miles from the speaker held away from my ear. "Every person who gets that rash dies, no matter what they die from. People might be dying from heart attacks, but it has to be connected to the ghosts. I know it does."

The tiny picture blurs. Pretending this isn't happening isn't going to stop it from happening.

I raise the phone back up to my ear, swallowing hard against the bile rising in my throat. "Opening the gate almost killed Francesca. It's a miracle she's even alive."

"But Shiloh," he stammers, "she's the one who—I mean, she opened it. She brought the ghosts here. So technically, it's her responsibility to send them back."

I go still. "She didn't mean for it to happen."

"I know," he says quickly. "But that doesn't change the fact that people are dying because of what she did."

I grit my teeth so hard my jaw aches. I want to reach through the phone and shove the words back into his dumb mouth. "What, would you rather Leonard still be roaming around, haunting us?"

"That's not what I'm saying," he says. "I'm just—people are dying, Shiloh. Every day. She needs to come home and fix it."

"Leave her alone," I snap. "I mean it. Don't call her. It's not just her responsibility. We opened the gate. All of us."

Miles goes quiet. The silence stretches long. On the other end of the line, an engine roars by. He must be close to town by now.

"I'm sorry," he says, and just like that, I feel like a jerk. He has nothing to be sorry about. I'm the one who snapped. "This whole thing has me scared."

"Yeah," I say. "Me too."

"I want this to be over."

He's not alone on that one. "I know, but we can't hurt Francesca again."

Miles doesn't argue. In the stall next to me, a toilet flushes. I jolt. I hadn't realized anyone else was in here.

"Wait." I can hear a smile in Miles's voice. "Are you in the bathroom right now?"

"I'm at school."

"Oh my god, have you been sitting on a toilet this whole time?" He laughs. Actually laughs. "That's so gross, Shiloh. Do you want me to hang up?"

"The lid is down, you giant idiot."

The bathroom door opens and closes. I should be in English. I'm supposed to be listening to my teacher talk about *Of Mice and Men* right now, but instead, I've been in here for —what? Ten minutes? Fifteen?

Crap. "I got to go."

"Don't get caught skipping," he says, still sounding too amused. "That would be so embarrassing."

I smile, but it slips almost as fast as it comes. There's something sad in his voice. Suddenly, I remember how much he used to love school. Writing poems for the paper. Participating in class discussions. He'll never be able to go again.

Because of me.

I press my fingers to my temples and breathe. I can't go there. There's nothing I can do about that now, other than what I am already doing, which is to be a good friend to him and not think about it because otherwise, the guilt will consume me.

"Have a good day at work," I say. "Talk tonight?"

"Absolutely."

He hangs up. I snap the phone shut and curl it into my hand, pressing it against my chin for a second. The plastic is warm now from my grip.

I hope Miles doesn't call Francesca. He better not. By some miracle, she's finally okay and has recovered fully from her injuries. Columbus isn't perfect, but at least she's safe there. Healing. She likes her school. She actually smiles now. The last thing she needs is for us to drag her back into this mess.

I know Miles doesn't want to hurt her either, but I don't get what he thinks is going to happen. Does he think she can just open a gate to the other side like it's no big deal?

It won't be that easy. He has to know that.

I miss her. I'm glad she's happy living with her dad, even though she was nervous about moving in with him. At least she remembers to reply to my texts. I gave her my old iPod before she left so we could still talk. It doesn't take calls, but it works. Sort of.

I wish I could hear her voice right now, but she's in school, and I can't FaceTime from a flip phone, so I type in a quick message:

how's it going?

I stare at the screen for a second, then shove the phone in my pocket. I wish I could calm Miles down. I wish I could make it warm again. I wish I could keep pretending he's wrong about the ghosts.

If I were Francesca and could open the gate myself, I'd do it. Even if it wrecked me. But I'm not her, and I won't ask her to do that again.

I'll fix this. Somehow.

But I'm not going to fix anything with my stomach in this many knots, so I sling my backpack over my shoulder, take one last breath in the stall, and drag my feet to class.

4
FrANCeSCA

Something tickles me from inside my pocket. I take out Shiloh's iPod with a mittened hand and find a message on the screen:

> how's it going?

I smile. I enjoy getting messages from Shiloh. She is quite good at remembering to message me, although I do not extend the same courtesy to her. My memory is about as good as a frog's, which is a mean thing to say about frogs.

I find a funny photograph of a penguin wearing a pair of sunglasses and send it to her. She sends me back an emoticon of a yellow face laughing and crying at the same time, then writes:

> looks warmer than here

My stomach sinks. Is Bethany still very cold?

Somebody bumps into my wheelchair, hard enough to jolt my spine. I suppose that is my cue to get out of everybody's way. Slipping the iPod into the pocket of my purple coat, I curl my fingers around my wheels. The rims feel like solid ice through my mittens and when I push on them, the effort lights small fires in my arms. But I keep going up the ramp to the entrance.

There are quiet titters around me as I roll past the other students, but I have grown accustomed to that sort of thing, so it does not bother me much. When my father insisted I move with him, I did not argue. I was not thrilled about the idea, but I could not live in the trailer without the use of my legs. The one thing I had been looking forward to was changing schools. I was silly, really, to think anything would be different. The children here may not know about me burning George Haggarty or my way of seeing souls, but they do know my hair is white and I am in this chair, which appears to be enough reason to whisper. I am beginning to believe that being unkind is not so much a problem with the other children in Bethany as it is with the living in general.

I have not told Shiloh the entire truth about my life here. As far as she knows, I am happy, but she has so many other things to worry about, so I could not bring myself to tell her that I am not. I have not even told her about my legs. I would like to be happy as well. But simply because I want something does not make it magically happen.

Once I press the automatic button, the glass doors spread to allow me inside, releasing a gust of warm air. The sharp pine scent of floor cleaner mingles with the sweetness of somebody's strawberry-scented perfume as they pass. So many voices overlap each other that I could stop rolling forward so that I could cover my ears. Students run past me, their backpacks slapping down onto their backs with loud thumps. I wheel myself across the smooth linoleum that reminds me of frozen pond water from all the melting snow everybody has carried inside. I offer smiles to any eyes that meet mine. This school is so much bigger than the one in Bethany, but the stares follow me just the same. The rapid symptoms of aging have not reversed in the months since they began. My wrinkled skin and ivory curls make me look like I have been dancing with death, which is not exactly normal for a sophomore. I have found that children stare at things they find not normal.

But speaking of dancing with death ... I search the busy hallway for the one other person who makes my days here tolerable.

As if on cue, something tickles the base of my neck, as though a daddy longlegs is walking across my skin. A big smile spreads across my lips.

I raise my head to discover a shimmering figure hovering over my shoulder. Evangeline's tidy ringlets bounce around her face, tied back with a large bow. Her pale blouse has puffed-up sleeves, and the gossamer fabric appears to shimmer and shift like morning mist catching sunlight.

She smiles down at me. "Good morning."

I know I am in the middle of the hallway and there are students brushing around me, but I do not care. I stopped caring what the living think of me long ago. I belong with the dead. There are days when I cannot wait to join them on the other side.

With Evangeline.

So I do not even try to look away or pretend that I do not see her. Perhaps other children will wonder what I am doing, or why I am talking to somebody who is not there, but most of them are much too preoccupied with their phones to notice me talking to what appears to be empty air.

I reach up to dip my finger into the coolness of her curls. "Where did you go last night?"

"To explore the planetarium," Evangeline says, her voice sounding like a twinkling melody and eating candy at the same time. Souls do not sleep, so she rarely spends the entire night with me, meeting me instead every morning once I arrive at school. "It was unbelievable. The stars felt close enough to touch."

I suppose she could fly all the way up to the top of the planetarium if she wanted. I wonder if she could touch stars if she tried. What would happen if a soul soared into the air and kept going? Would they make it to the stars? Or would some earthly magnetism pull them back?

I do not believe I will ever want to go anywhere but here, so long as I can keep looking into Evangeline's eyes. Not even the stars twinkle so beautifully.

Evangeline flips over the top of my chair and stops in front of me. The air grows thick with that peculiar static feeling that Evangeline's presence brings. A girl with a head of brown curls that bounce like springs stares at me as she brushes past, but I hardly pay her any mind. Evangeline places her transparent hands on either side of my face, sending a chill through me, like she is pressing snow onto my skin. It is not the same as the soft hands she had when she was inside Talulah Monroe's body, but I can feel her there the same. I can feel her when I am not looking at her. Touching my arms. Brushing strands of hair out of my face. Even when I am sleeping, on nights she decides to stay with me, pressed up against me like a bag of ice shoved underneath the blankets. I need to put on wool socks on those nights because not even the blankets can keep me warm, but I do not want her to be anyplace else.

I had been afraid that being together in the way Evangeline and I had been before would be difficult now that she is dead and I have remained mortal, but I have not found it difficult at all.

"Did you see how I arranged all of the kitchen magnets into the shape of a heart when you were sleeping?" she asks. "I did it right at the top so your father cannot reach them. He is such a short man."

I nod, giggling through my words. "You must be careful, or my father will begin to think I am doing those things."

"So what if he does?" she asks. "It's not a bad thing for him to stay a little afraid of you. It means he'll always give you the biggest piece of chicken."

Of course she would say that. She is far more comfortable breaking the rules than I am.

"So," she says. "Do we have history first this morning?"

"Unfortunately."

"I can't wait for you to start talking about my time." She claps her hands. "Maybe you could bring me in as a special guest. Pretend you are channeling me, like in one of those scary movies your brother likes to watch."

Even thinking about those movies makes me shudder. "I could vomit peas on the class."

A boy peers at me as he walks past, because I suppose in his world he just overheard me talking to the air. I raise my eyebrows and stick my face out at him, causing him to scurry away like he would catch something from even standing close to me. I slump back into my chair in satisfaction. My father is too afraid of me to put me in a mental hospital. He believes I will find a way to get to him from there, so being kind to me is something that protects him. As long as he does not threaten me with padded walls or try to shove medications into me, there is no reason for me to pretend I am normal.

I meet Evangeline's eyes proudly. She does not look happy with me, which is unusual because she is always happy with me.

"Are you all right?" I ask.

She nods, and the troubled expression clears, replaced by a mischievous smile.

"I think you'd better hurry," she says, "or you will be late."

Evangeline slips around behind me and slams into the back of my chair without warning, sending the chair flying across the smooth floor so quickly that my hair billows away from my face. An involuntary laugh bubbles out of me as other children stumble out of the way. I slow the chair as it approaches the door and force myself to stop laughing as I wheel myself into the classroom. I roll the chair up to a table squarely at the front of the class, where the morning sun streams through dusty windows and makes little dancing sparkles on the surface of my desk. Our history teacher is still finishing his breakfast: a donut with strawberry frosting that clings to the corners of his mouth and gets stuck in his beard. The sugary smell makes my stomach growl. I am rather jealous. I would very much like one of those.

Perhaps I could ask Evangeline to steal it from him when he is not looking. Or perhaps I could scare him into giving it to me if I pretended to recite incantations or rolled my eyes backward in my head and demanded the donut to stop.

The corners of my mouth tug up at the thought before I push it away. Why would I want to scare Mr. Drubich? He is a perfectly kind man who deserves to eat his own donut.

Maybe I could scare my father into buying one for me after school.

After opening my pink binder and unzipping my pencil case, I rest my forearms on the desk and wait for class to begin.

A thin girl slides into the desk beside me. Elliot. The metal legs of her chair scrape against the floor, and she gives me a soft smile. Her skin is pale and covered with a smattering of freckles, and she is dressed in a striped long-sleeve shirt and a pair of torn jeans with a chain looped down from the pocket that look far too big on her. The chain makes quiet tinkling sounds when she moves. She has dyed her hair a brand-new color. Yesterday, the ends were pink, but now, all of her hair is pink. It is pin-straight and reaches down to her waist.

She raises a hand. The black lace of her glove is torn.

"What's up, Francesca?"

I tilt my head up. "Only the ceiling, as far as I can tell."

Elliot laughs. Evangeline waves to get my attention from where she is hovering near the chalkboard, trailing her ghostly fingers through the white dust where Mr. Drubich has written "The Treaty of Versailles" in rushed script.

"I like your sweater," Elliot says, and I turn my head to look at her again. "The purple makes your hair look sick."

I cannot tell if she is poking fun at me or not. "Is that a bad thing?"

"Huh? No. I mean, sick as in cool. Your hair looks cool."

I would not describe my hair as cool, and I certainly would not describe it as sick, but Evangeline likes it, which is good enough for me. "Thank you."

"I dyed my hair last night." Elliot fidgets with the hole in her glove. "I was thinking … if you ever wanted to try something different, you could come over and I could dye yours."

Evangeline draws a heart in the air with the chalk dust and claps both hands to her chest. A smile plays on my lips.

I turn back to Elliot. "I am sorry. What did you say?"

"Uh, I was asking if you wanted to hang out this weekend."

Really? Nobody has ever asked me to hang out with them before. Usually, when other children invite me places, it is because they are planning something unkind, like the time in fourth grade when Sara Fitzpatrick invited me to her birthday party to tell me at the door that monsters were not allowed inside.

Elliot does not appear to be an unkind person, but I am not good at knowing these things. I gave up on wanting anything more from the living. They have never accepted me before. I do not know why they would begin to do so now.

"That is kind of you to offer," I say cautiously, watching her face for any sign that this is a trick. "Perhaps another time?"

Elliot leans back in her chair. "Sure. Just let me know."

I stare down at the notebook on my desk, my heart still pounding. Admittedly, it would be nice to have a new friend who was alive, but I already have Shiloh, and she is enough because I know she would not hurt me.

Evangeline pauses in front of my desk, the early morning light beaming through her form and making her appear nearly invisible. She touches my hair, throwing my white curls up off my shoulders and making me let out a surprised sound. Elliot raises one eyebrow. I give her an apologetic smile.

Mr. Drubich clears his throat and demands the attention of the class, his chalk scraping against the board in a way that makes my teeth feel funny. The radiator near the window hums quietly, and the scratching of two dozen pens against paper fills the room like busy insects as Mr. Drubich begins his lesson.

Evangeline gives me a small smile and presses her cool lips to mine so quickly that they are gone before I can be certain they were there. She flashes me a two-fingered salute, her form shimmering before she shoots out through the wall. The temperature around my desk returns to normal. As much as she says she would like to keep me company, she also says she does not deserve to spend her afterlife trapped in a classroom, and I do not blame her for that one bit. I will see her again in an hour. I must simply make it through this class.

5

Shiloh

Jonah's not waiting for me after class like he usually does. I dig my phone out of my pocket to find a text from him on the screen.

Come to upside down tree

My fingers tighten on the straps of my backpack as I push through the other kids, weaving between bodies and slamming shoulders without meaning to. Outside, the wind hits me like a slap. I zip my jacket up to my chin and lower my head against the cold, trudging through snow as I make my way to the tree.

The tree is looking rough. The wind's been ripping at the branches for months without letting up and it shows, making it look like a weeping willow version of a sad Charlie Brown Christmas tree. Some trees look sad in winter. This one looks like it's actually mourning something.

I push through the branches, the bark scraping my palm. Jonah is leaning against the trunk, the wind whipping his dark hair across his face.

He looks up when he hears me. My breath stutters.

His right eye is swollen. An ugly bruise is already darkening along his cheekbone, and blood has crusted under his nose. His good arm shakes a little as he takes a hit from his JUUL. Oh God.

I go up to him and brush my thumb under his eye, trying to swallow the lump in my throat.

"Looks like a shiner," I say.

He catches my hand. Turns it over and lays a kiss on my palm. "No one talks shit about my girl."

My stomach flips over, but I ignore it. That fight wasn't about me. He knows it. I have a feeling I know exactly what this is about, and he can't keep getting hurt when he's barely healed from the last time.

I keep my hand in his. Not just because I want to—I do—but because I left my gloves in my locker, and right now, his hand is the only thing keeping mine from going numb.

"So," I say, my breath fogging in the cold air. "Are we going to agree that was dumb? Or am I supposed to lie to you and tell you what you did was okay?"

"Lie to me." He grins. "You're so cute when you lie."

I roll my eyes. "What did you get?"

That crooked smile I love so much crosses his lips before he drops his eyes to his boots. "Suspended."

"You're *suspended*?"

"For three days." He slumps against the tree like he's trying to melt into it. "Then detention for another week. Orr said one more strike and I'm out for good. Only reason I'm not expelled is because of, well ..." He shrugs one shoulder and nods toward the sling. "Kyle only got detention, which is so not fair."

"You threw the first punch."

Something flickers across his face that I can't read. Sadness? Betrayal?

I keep my voice low. "Your social worker ... is she going to—"

"Flip out?" He runs a hand through his hair. It's windblown and soft and makes him look younger somehow. "Yep. And Cindi, too."

My stomach turns. Trouble with his placement is the last thing he needs right now. He's so close to aging out, and Bethany isn't exactly full of open doors.

A car door slams in the parking lot. Someone laughs.

"You could have let it go," I say, my breath forming clouds between us.

"Could have." He gives me a half-smile. "Didn't want to."

"Jonah—"

"Shiloh, don't." His voice is quiet but firm. "I know it was dumb. I should've let it go. But I heard what he said about you and I just ..."

He clenches his hand into a fist. His knuckles are angry and red.

I sigh. "I think you were looking for a reason to punch him."

He says nothing. I know he doesn't want to hear that, but he has to know it's true. He doesn't care about Kyle.

"You're punishing yourself for something," I say, hoping I'm right and knowing deep down that I am. "And I wish you'd stop."

The bell rings inside the school. Jonah drops my hand.

"Guess you'd better get to class," he says.

I hate this. I hate every part of it. But what am I supposed to do?

Miles was right. He pushed me too hard, too fast, and I shut him out.

Be there.

So I rise onto my toes and press my mouth to his. Quick. Soft. The lamest kiss in the history of kisses. But it's all I can manage.

"I'll text you when I'm done," I say, pulling back. "You coming over this afternoon?"

He nods once, then taps my shoulder with the back of his hand. The way he leans back against the tree—slow and careful, like every part of him hurts—kills me.

"Get out of here, Scoob."

No part of me wants to leave him alone like this, especially when I know he has nowhere to go except back to that house, but I can't stay, and I can't fix him. Looking at him is making my eyes sting. Crying would be stupid. Jonah is literally doing this to himself, but I don't think he even knows he is.

So I give him a close-lipped smile and nod, then duck under branches and make my way back to the school.

In the cafeteria, I take a bite of my peanut butter sandwich at a corner table alone, trying to ignore the overwhelming smell of tater tots and industrial floor cleaner that seems permanently baked into the linoleum. I scan the article Miles sent me about that two-headed calf for the umpteenth time. The plastic chair digs into my thighs.

Miles sounded so serious on the phone. He was talking the way he does when he thinks the world's about to end.

Am I being an idiot by pretending nothing is wrong in Bethany?

I've got to stop kidding myself. The ghosts are everywhere. I can't see them because Miles begged to keep the ghost glasses because he lives alone and would drop dead of a heart attack if he heard something in his apartment that he couldn't see, but I don't know what I'm supposed to do about it. I can't see ghosts. I'm useless. All I can do is stick magnets under my bed and pray they don't come into the house and that none of the ones hanging around will drop something on my head on my way to first period.

But calling Francesca is out of the question.

I open YouTube and click on the first video that comes up: a compilation of people falling off trampolines. The video quality sucks. Watching anything on a flip phone sucks. But it's better than staring at the wall.

I'm watching a big guy do a backflip and land straight on his neck when my phone rings. The caller ID shows a 740 number I don't recognize.

I swallow my bite of sandwich. The peanut butter sticks to the roof of my mouth. It takes a second to clear my throat enough that I can answer the call.

"Hello?"

Static crackles on the line, then a woman's voice cuts through. "Hello. This is Nurse Thompson from Bethany Elementary. Is this Heidi Oleson?"

My heart drops. I've never been allowed to be Max's emergency contact. I'm not his mom, but four months ago, as soon as I got a phone, I called the school pretending to be her and told them I had a new number. As far as they know, Mom is still his emergency contact. But all calls go to me.

I press my finger hard against my ear, trying to block out

the clatter of lunch trays and squeaking chairs in the cafeteria. "Yes."

"I'm calling to let you know that Max isn't feeling well," she says, and I can barely feel the phone in my hand anymore. "He's been resting in the nurse's office, but I think it would be best if he went home for the day. Could you come pick him up?"

The world around me fades. I manage to say I'll get my daughter to come before hanging up, shoving my half-eaten sandwich into my backpack and pushing my way out of the cafeteria.

Everything feels thick. Slow. Like I'm running through water. I slam through the front doors, cold air slicing across my face, then cut around the side of the building to the elementary school wing.

I try to sign in. The pen feels heavy in my hand. The words don't sound right in my mouth. Only when I reach the nurse's office do I stop to breathe.

The walls are pale blue. The kind of color that's supposed to be calming but isn't. The smell of antiseptic and cherry cough drops is sharp. Max is on the bed, lying on a sheet of crinkly paper. His blond hair sticks up like it always does, but now it's damp with sweat.

The nurse says something. I go straight to Max.

I drop to my knees next to him, pushing his cowlick out of his face to feel his forehead. Burning up. He's burning up.

"What's wrong, buddy?" My voice comes out steady. I don't know how. "What hurts?"

He tries to answer, but all that comes out is coughing. Harsh. Wet.

I look back at the nurse. "What's wrong with him?"

She adjusts her glasses, blinking like she expected someone else to be here. "He came in complaining of a sore throat. He's been coughing, and he's running a high fever. I'd guess it's that bug that has been going around."

A bug? What bug?

He was fine this morning, eating his bagel and keeling over in laughter as he rolled around on my bed.

I turn back to him. The harsh lights cast sickly shadows under his eyes.

"You're going to be okay, buddy," I say. "We're going home. Can you stand up?"

He nods. The paper under him crinkles as he moves. I reach for his hands to help him up, but the second my fingers touch his skin, the world falls away.

Because I see it.

On the tops of his hands is the same gray rash from the picture Miles showed me.

6
Shiloh

I bring Max home. We start out walking, but he barely makes it through the doors before his legs give up and I scoop him into my arms. He fits perfectly against my chest like he was always meant to be carried this way. My shoulders scream under the weight of our backpacks, but I don't let go. Just count each step. Each breath. Whisper in his ear that we're almost there all the way home as he sobs against my neck.

Inside our house, Mom sits on the couch, wrapped in a blanket. I carry him past her, right to his room.

"Shiloh?" Mom asks. "What are you doing home?"

I prop him up on his bed. The mattress sags under him, springs groaning in protest. "Can you sit up for me, bud?"

He nods. Barely. His cheeks are pink from the cold.

Lifting his back off the pillows, I fight his arms into clean pajamas. He doesn't help. Just lets me move him. Mom stands in the doorway like she's scared to come in.

"Shiloh? Is something wrong?"

"His pajama pants," I snap, pointing to the closet. "Can you get them?"

She shuffles across the carpet like she's sleepwalking. I pull the pants onto Max, then help him lie down so I can fold the blankets over him. No gaps. He can't get cold.

I dig out my phone and peel back Max's sleeve to snap a picture of the rash climbing up his arm. The flash flares. I type out a message to Miles:

> is this the rash you were talking about?

Max wheezes. The comforter rises and falls too fast. The rash has already crept higher. It's gray and ugly, like mold on something that used to be alive.

"Shiloh?" Mom asks again. "Is he not feeling well?"

I give her a smile. It's fake and probably terrifying, but it's all I've got.

"He's fine," I lie. "Just cold."

Her hands curl around the edge of her blanket. "Is it the flu?"

"The nurse said it's a bug that's been going around." Another lie. God, I'm stacking them like bricks. "I'll call the doctor."

Her breaths come shallow and fast, like she's the one about to pass out. Of course it's not enough for me to have to hold it together for Max. I have to stay strong for her, too.

"Mom," I say. "Can you breathe with me?"

I suck in air through my mouth and lift my brows like I'm cueing her. She exhales. There we go. Good. Stay with me.

Max coughs and I turn to him, pressing my hand to his forehead. Still burning up.

"Talk to me, buddy," I say, my voice catching. "How do you feel?"

"Funny."

"What kind of funny?"

"Sleepy funny."

His arms twitch under the covers. The blue checkered fabric rustles with each tremble.

I grip the neckline of my sweatshirt, digging my fingers into the fabric like it can anchor me. The walls close in, pulsing with his breathing. I need air. I need Mom to stop staring at me like I'm about to cry because if she keeps looking at me like that, I might.

"Mom, could you get Max some water?"

She nods like I've handed her a life raft, then vanishes down the hallway, slippers whispering over the wood floor like a ghost.

I listen to the sink run. Try to make my lungs remember how to work. Miles once quoted something—was it from Wordsworth?

The child is father of the man.

I guess that goes for moms, too. Except I made her like this. She died when she came looking for me, and the person who came back wasn't her. Not fully. But she was never fully present before that, even on her best days.

My phone buzzes. I pull it out so fast I almost drop it, my fingers slick with sweat. I can't seem to get a grip on anything.

LORD BYRON

Whose arm is that?

The room tilts. Max's dinosaur posters smear into a mess of greens and oranges. The air turns solid. I gag on it. Miles's voice from earlier echoes in my head. Every person who gets that rash—

No.

Miles calls me. I go to my room before I pick up. Miles doesn't even wait.

"Whose arm?"

I close my eyes. I'm going to be sick.

"Max's."

"*Shit.*"

I can't do this. I can't breathe. My heart's pounding so hard it drowns everything else out.

"I can't lose him, Miles, I can't—"

"Just breathe."

"What's happening to him?" I rasp. "You said everyone who got that rash—what, *dies*?"

"Shiloh—"

"Why? What are the ghosts doing to him?"

"I ... don't know."

The unfairness of it hits like a punch. Max isn't supposed to die. He's just a kid. He doesn't deserve this. "Well, how the hell are we supposed to find out?"

"I don't know that either."

"*Miles.*"

"Don't panic," he says again. "Focus on breathing."

Easy for him to say. It's not *his* brother.

I bite down on the pad of my thumb. "How long?"

"What?"

"The people on Facebook. How long did they have?"

Silence. Long enough to make my stomach twist.

"A day," he says. "If that."

The phone's shaking in my hand now. Or maybe it's me. A day? That's it?

I dig in, desperate. "What if he just has a cold?"

But I know. I know. The rash. The way he's fading. This is not just a cold.

And Miles knows it, too. "You need to call Francesca."

I pace across my room. My foot snags on the pile of laundry I've been ignoring. "No."

"But—"

"*No*," I snap. "We can't ask her to come back here. She barely made it out alive last time."

"You think we can fix this ourselves with grit and a can-do attitude which, let's be honest, neither of us has?" He sighs. "I wish it were different, I do, but you have to call Francesca. She's our only hope."

I slam my fist into the door. Pain cracks through my knuckles, but I barely feel it. "What if she won't help?"

"She will," Miles assures me. "You know she will. Call her."

The line goes dead. I stare at the phone in my hand. Silence presses in.

Screaming through gritted teeth, I throw the phone onto the bed and dig my fingers into my hair, spinning in a slow, helpless circle. I don't *want* to call Francesca. It's wrong. So selfish. A couple of hours ago, Miles told me people were dying, and I didn't say anything. I didn't *want* to. Not until it was Max.

But Max always comes first. Before me. Before anything. Before anyone.

If I do nothing, he dies. No doctor can help him if it's ghost-related. And Mom can't even leave the house.

It's me. I'm all he's got.

There's no guarantee that opening another gate will hurt Francesca, but there is a guarantee that Max will die if I sit around hoping he will get better on his own.

So I call her. The ringing echoes in my skull like it's empty.

Until she answers. "Hello?"

"Hey," I say, screwing up my face around the words because I hate myself for what I'm about to say. "I ... uh, need your help."

7

JONAh

Shiloh's typing bubble appears, then goes away. I sigh. The bunk bed creaks as I stretch my legs out, the ancient springs groaning under the thin mattress. I'm still wearing my jacket because it's freezing in this house, even with a blanket over my legs that reeks of baby powder and sick.

I take a swig from my flask, sighing as I feel the heat radiate through my chest. It's about damn time. My nose and cheekbone are throbbing where that asshole landed his punch, and every beat of my heart sends a fresh throb of pain through my face.

I shouldn't have punched him. I knew it was wrong. The look on Shiloh's face ... shit, it was dumb, but the pain in my face is nothing compared to my arm right now. I ease it out of the sling, which helps a little. I barely ever take it out except for when I'm doing PT or sleeping, but the house is empty right now so there's no risk of getting nailed by one of the kids' remote-controlled nightmares or whatever the hell they're always launching at me. It would be depressing if it weren't so … no, it's just depressing.

Shiloh's message finally comes through, the glow from the screen lighting up the slats of the bunk above me.

> francesca said she'll help us save max but she said we have to help her "escape her dad's house"

Escape? What are we, in some kind of spy movie?

> What does that mean?

I stare at Shiloh's shrug emoji like it might reveal some deeper truth. Frankie probably doesn't mean escape in the way we think about it. She learned her words from ghosts so she talks kind of funny. The girl could have learned Shakespeare from actual Shakespeare.

That's not how it works. You know that's not how it works.

I take a long pull from the flask, which is a piece of garbage I bought at some gas station years ago. Cheap vodka burns like battery acid as it goes down. I type a response with my pointer finger, not putting down the flask even though my fingers keep hitting the wrong keys. Whatever. Close enough.

> I yhink she means we gotta pick her up but escaoe sounds cooler

> maybe

> im on my way to miles house

Of course she asks that. She always does.

Something hot and angry coils in my chest. I know she means well, but the way she sometimes treats me like some rescue dog makes me want to put my fist through a wall.

And what's all this about "we're leaving at 6"? She made this plan with Miles without me?

I punch in a reply:

I toss my phone toward the foot of the bed. I press the back of my head into the headboard, feeling the wood dig into my skull as I take another long pull from the flask. The burn feels good going down. It's better than thinking, anyway.

Aunt Moe would hate seeing me like this.

But Aunt Moe's not here anymore.

I grip the flask so hard my knuckles burn, the cheap metal warm and slick from my palm. I have to stop drinking this shit. I have to stop drinking, period. I got maybe ten minutes before I need to head to the bus stop if I'm going to get to Miles's place for six, and if Shiloh sees I've been drinking ... well, let's just say she'll have opinions. I try not to drink when I know I'm going to see her. I know it's weird for her, what with her dad, so I get why she doesn't like it, but I'm not like her dad.

She's got no right to judge me. I got suspended. It was my

own fault, sure, but still. What right does she have to judge me for the one thing that can give me a second of goddamn peace?

Her name pops up on my phone lying on the bed, the screen's blue glow harsh in the dim room. I stare at the phone until the notification goes away. At least when I'm texting her I don't have to see her face, so my brain can't give me any ideas about killing her. Small fucking victory. I usually don't have a problem with this when I'm sober. I have an easier time separating what thoughts are mine from the thoughts that come from that drug. I told her I don't get those thoughts anymore—telling her I still daydream about killing her is kind of a buzzkill—but it's not completely true. I've just gotten better at ignoring them.

Like I deserve any credit for not wanting to kill my girlfriend. Boyfriend of the Year material right here.

God, I love that girl so much it scares me, which makes it even more messed up that there's still this dark thing inside me that whispers about hurting her. It just proves what I've known all along. I'm damaged goods. A walking disaster chugging bottom-shelf vodka when I should be doing anything else.

I drag myself up from the bed, the springs squealing in protest as I shove the flask under my mattress where none of those asshole kids can find it. The room spins like a carnival ride when I stand. Great. Exactly what I need.

I slide my arm back into the sling, wincing once or twice until I can get it snug, then head down the stairs, each step creaking like it's giving away my location in this empty house. There are no screaming kids. No foster mom watching my every move like I might snap and go full-on psycho. Just silence and the hollow echo of my footsteps on the weathered floorboards. Cindi is going to flip out when she sees I snuck out, but I can't even summon up a fuck to give. She's not my mom. She's not Moe. I got to hope her do-gooder sense is strong enough that she won't send me packing so close to my birthday, but either way, I'm done ass-kissing.

I catch my reflection in the cracked hallway mirror, the glass spider-webbed in one corner. My eye is bruising up good. Shiloh's going to frown when she sees it. Add it to the list of ways I'm screwing everything up.

I struggle into a heavier coat and tug a hat deep over my head before stepping outside. I can't zip the coat one-handed, so I hold it closed around me. My breath comes out in puffs as I trudge toward the bus stop, my boots crunching through sand and salt on the gritty sidewalk. The sky's turned that sickly greenish-gray color it gets before it snows. Wind whips down the street, carrying the smell of exhaust mixed with the smoke from someone's fireplace. Some asshole left their Christmas lights up. The plastic bulbs rattle in the wind.

The bus stop bench is slick with ice, so I lean against the sign and watch cars crawl past. Everything feels dull around the edges, courtesy of the vodka burning a hole in my stomach.

The bus ride passes in a blur that makes my head spin worse than ever. Twenty minutes and one near face-plant on the sidewalk later, I round the corner to Miles's apartment.

Under the glare of a nearby streetlamp, I spot Miles and Shiloh loading what looks like an empty pizza box into Miles's beige sedan. Shiloh's wearing her teal and black color block jacket I love and an old gray beanie she stole from me a couple months ago that I let her keep because it looks so cute on her. Her blonde hair falls into her face when she slams the trunk closed.

It'd be so easy to grab some. Yank back hard enough to snap her neck.

Jesus. Where did that come from?

The booze. It came from the booze. Shiloh is the only good thing in my life, yet here I am, conjuring up ways to destroy her like some kind of rabid animal.

Miles is telling her something, probably explaining some conspiracy theory he has about ghosts or whatever. The two of them have gotten close these past couple of months since he stopped being Miles. I swear she talks to Miles more than I do nowadays, but that's because I talk to no one. Maybe she should go back to him instead of sticking with me. At least he'd be good to her. He's suddenly twenty-six, but if there's any situation in which a ten-year age gap is acceptable it's this one, and not the one where I was in hooking up with those women at Duncan's, which was messed up.

I stop walking. Shiloh spots me and comes running over like I mean something, her boots skidding on patches of ice before she barrels into my good side and wraps her arms around my neck. I hug her against me. The whole thing makes me feel so goddamn shitty that it takes everything in me not to cry.

Pull yourself together. She doesn't need you to be depressing on top of everything else.

I put on my biggest smile, tugging at the top of her hat so that it stands up on her head. "Hey, cone-head."

She tugs the hat back down and zips my jacket up for me, but the moment is over as soon as it started. Her eyes change.

"Have you been drinking?"

Of course she can tell. Her safety growing up depended on being able to tell, and here I am walking around drinking like it means nothing.

But there's no use lying to her. "Yeah."

"Why?"

Oh, the number of answers I can come up with to that question. "Because life is depressing."

The wind whips strands of hair across her face. "Are you drunk?"

"I didn't have that much."

She frowns. She obviously doesn't believe me. And she shouldn't. I'm lying right to her face.

I'm used to disappointing people. I was a disappointment to my dad. My mom, too, or why else would she have bounced on me? To say I disappointed Moe would be the understatement of the year, but Shiloh was the one person I swore I was never going to disappoint. Seeing her look at me like this right now breaks my heart.

She goes to turn away from me. I catch her wrist a little too rough.

She yanks her hand out of mine. "Let me go."

I do. Immediately. Step back and shove my hand deep into my pocket where it can't do any more damage.

"I'm sorry," I say. "I wasn't thinking."

She wraps her arms around herself. Miles comes up next to her, knitting his eyebrows together. Fan-fucking-tastic. Now I've got both of them worried.

But Miles just points at his eye. "Nice work."

I appreciate the attempt at humor. "I didn't know you knew how to be sarcastic."

He doesn't smile. Shiloh must have told him about my performance at school today. I don't want to talk about this anymore.

So I say. "We going to do this or what?"

Turns out Francesca using the word 'escape' wasn't her being dramatic. Her dad's actually keeping her locked up. I can't say I'm surprised. Parents are generally trash at being decent human beings.

I lean over the center console, gagging at the smell of Miles's pine tree air freshener dangling from the mirror. Shiloh stares ahead from the passenger seat. Miles is driving like an old lady. He never did pass his test, but he never had to. His new body came equipped with both a license and a car.

Shiloh won't look at me. Serves me right. I slump back against the cold seats and spend most of the drive on my phone, doom-scrolling through Instagram until my thumb freezes mid-scroll. A girl from school posted a screenshot of a post from the Bethany community Facebook group. The words blur for a couple of seconds before they snap into focus.

Posted by Anonymous Member – January 6, 2020
I've kept quiet about this for too long but you deserve to know the truth about our sheriff. You want to keep defending him, but how can you after seeing what he's done to his family?
These photos speak for themselves. This is what his daughter has had to deal with for years, and you all wonder why she's been so quiet? I don't know how much longer we can let someone like this keep representing our town. A man who does this should be locked up, not sitting in an office with a badge.
SHARE THIS. People need to see the truth. It's time for this town to wake up.

The girl captioned it with "😵 praying for u girl 🙏." I run

a Google search. My stomach lurches when I find exactly what I was dreading. Oh no.

Shiloh.

Her photos are in the post. The ones she took of what her dad did to her that I've never seen but heard about. Shiloh never talks about her dad. She never talks about what he did to her. When something does slip out, like when she's telling me about a nightmare she had, I keep it together for her or try to crack a joke because if I can make her smile, then she stops thinking about all the family crap.

She told me about those photos last month. Said she gave them to the FBI when Max went missing and was scared that she was going to have to bring them out in court if her dad challenged her mom to get custody in the divorce. But now those photos are out there for anyone to see.

I swipe through. There's one of her kitchen floor covered with broken glass. In another, Shiloh has her back to the camera and her bare skin covered with belt marks. Whoever posted this blurred her face, but it doesn't matter. Everyone knows it's her. She made sure to get her face in the originals in case she needed proof. The post already has hundreds of likes.

I clench my jaw until it hurts. What is this? Did someone leak the evidence photos from her case? What kind of person posts that on their Facebook feed?

I can barely stomach the comments.

Janice Wood: *Omg I knew something wasn't right with him but THIS?! How can anyone ignore this??*

Mark Peterson: *How did you get these pics?*

I could kill Sheriff Oleson. Shiloh could, too. She doesn't need me to kill him for her.

"You good, man?" Miles asks. The dashboard lights cast green shadows across his face in the rearview mirror.

I reach over his shoulder to show him the screen. He pushes my arm away.

"I'm driving."

"Just look."

He does. It takes a couple of seconds for him to realize what he's looking at, and when he does, his knuckles on the steering wheel go even whiter.

Shiloh's eyes bore into the side of my face. "What are you looking at?"

I go to hand her my phone. Miles grabs my wrist hard enough to hurt.

"Are you sure she should see that?"

I want to punch him. Those are *her* pictures. Of course she should see that.

"See what?" Shiloh asks, her voice sharp.

Shaking Miles off, I give Shiloh my phone. I want to say something. Do something other than sit here staring at her like a moron. The blood rushes from her head so fast I think she might pass out.

She wraps her arms around herself, fingers digging into her sides like she's trying to crawl out of her skin. Blood rushes in my ears, drowning out the rumble of the engine. I know Shiloh doesn't like being touched when she's thinking about her dad, but it takes everything in me not to tell Miles to pull over this piece of junk so I can open the passenger door and hug her right now.

"How could they release those without my permission? Is that even legal?" She turns around in her seat to look at me. "Everyone is going to see those."

I inch forward to the edge of the seat, fabric creaking under me. I've seen the scars in those pictures. One time in the middle of the night a couple months ago, we lay on her bed and she told me where each one of them came from. She couldn't look at me when she said any of it, and it filled me with so much rage thinking about how small that man had made her feel. So I traced her scars with my fingers. Planted kisses on each one. I told her one of them looked like that squirrel from *Ice Age*. It didn't, but I made her laugh, so I was proud of myself for that one.

Those scars belong to her. No one else has the right to look at them, let alone turn them into some kind of social media freak show.

She drops her eyes to her lap. "They're going to call me a liar."

"The pictures don't lie," I say. "Everyone in the comments is on your side."

She points at the screen. "One man doesn't think they're real."

"Who cares what he thinks?" The words come out harder than I mean them to but who cares, I'm angry. "I'll end him if he says a word to you. I'm not even kidding. I'll slit his throat and piss down the hole."

Miles glares at me in the rearview, clearly horrified at my dumb empty threat. But the corner of Shiloh's mouth twitches.

I know I'm still buzzed. I know I messed up today, but I'll be damned if I mess this up because she needs me right now.

"Your dad is the asshole," I say, looking at the side of her head even though she won't meet my eyes. "He's the one who should be ashamed, not you, and if this does one thing, it'll end his career forever. No one's going to elect him again. No judge in the world will side with him in court."

She still won't look at me. God, I hate seeing her like this.

"Shiloh, do you hear me?" I press. "Some good will come from this."

She nods and hands me back my phone. I want nothing more than to reach forward and wrap my arms around her, but I can't do that from back here and I've only got one working arm anyway, so I just reach forward and grip her shoulder. She lets out this tiny sigh that breaks something in me. I should be better for her. I should be sober for this. I should be anything but what I am. But all I can do is hold onto her shoulder while she checks her phone every thirty seconds all the way there.

8

FrANCeSCA

When my father picks me up from school, I tell him nothing about my plans to escape.

This is not difficult to do. He does not speak to me at all unless necessary. I believe it is because I told him I did not want to know him anymore that night he came to pick me up from the police station, and he took my words quite literally.

He helps me out of my chair and lifts me into the passenger seat. I can do this on my own because I still have some upper arm strength, but it takes me a while and he is too impatient, so I allow him to carry me. On the drive home, he stares at the road as I try not to feel sick from the chemical lemon scent of his brand-new car.

Evangeline tickles the underside of his nose, causing him to sneeze. I try my best not to laugh so that he does not think I am somehow causing it with my mind.

He stops the car in front of his house, which I suppose is my house now, especially since he has now sold the trailer, but I have trouble thinking of it that way. The perfectly trimmed hedges stand like green soldiers, and he carries my backpack and wheelchair up the steep front stairs. Richie emerges to collect me. Opening the passenger door, I reach for his outstretched hands, and he lifts me into his arms like a doll with no stuffing.

He still wears an eyepatch over one eye. He ended up needing to have his eye removed because of something that Shiloh did ... or perhaps Jonah did? I am not entirely clear on the specifics because Shiloh was quite shy telling me about them, but if I had to guess, I would say she is the reason behind it. Richie has an eye that is not real that he can take in and out, and sometimes he does it to upset me, but he prefers the eyepatch when he is out because he finds it more comfortable. I also think he believes girls prefer him that way than to have a face in which only one eye moves. Ashley Christensen stopped wanting to be his girlfriend after he lost his eye. I have trouble looking at him sometimes without laughing at how much he resembles a pirate.

He glances down at me. "School okay?"

Unable to resist, I say, "Arr."

Evangeline keels over in laughter. Richie rolls his one eye.

He carries me through the kitchen where my stepmother is sitting at the kitchen table with her daughter. The air smells of cookies and artificial cleaner, which is the product of my stepmother's never-ending battle against dirt. I wave at my half-sister Isabella, who sits coloring with broken crayons, and she waves back before her mother taps the table. Elena does not like it when I speak to Isabella, which does make me quite sad. My father may not have been thrilled to have me come live with him, but his wife might as well have made a doll with my resemblance and stuck pins in it. I was hoping that the soul of my mother would be able to follow me here, but she faded back to the other side rather quickly after I opened the gate, which was disappointing because I would have liked to talk with her some more.

Richie navigates around a stray plastic unicorn, its horn chipped and faded from too much love, and opens the door to my bedroom.

This room was my father's office until I moved in. He has done his best to make it a place I would like to live, hanging a poster of rainbow ponies on the wall and placing a vase of pink carnations on the table that droop their heads as though they are as uncomfortable here as I am. He may be doing nice things for me because he is afraid I can move kitchen magnets or make him sneeze with my mind, but at least he is doing nice things for me.

I am glad that the house has a toilet on the first floor so nobody has to carry me up to the bathroom every time I need to go (I can manage to use the toilet on my own, thankfully), but it is quite humiliating when my father or Richie must carry me upstairs when I want to take a shower every other day or so. I cannot get to the mirror or the bathroom sink, and although I have never been one to spend much time in front of the mirror, I do still like to make sure I do not leave any lasting damage to other people's eyes when I leave the house.

Richie puts me down on the bed. I grip my legs and swing them around the side, and he holds my wheelchair in place as I climb into it. His eyebrows scrunch together like caterpillars meeting in the middle.

"You think you're ever gonna walk again?" he asks.

Slumping into the chair's canvas back, I sigh. "I am not sure."

"The doctors said they don't know why it happened," Richie says. "You think it's, like, in your head or something?"

"Perhaps," I say. "But something being in your mind does not mean it is not real."

Richie frowns. Any more thinking and he will begin to get uncomfortable, so he backs out of the room with a wave and closes the door behind him.

I fill my school bag with as many shirts and skirts as I can fit into it. I do not know how long I will be in Bethany, but it does not hurt to be prepared. It is difficult getting the drawers to open when my wheelchair is up against them, and at one point I nearly overbalance, but I manage to get the job done.

Once I am finished, Evangeline clears her throat to get my attention from where she had been waiting near the window. "You going to do your homework?" she asks.

"I do not see the point, as I will not be at school in the morning."

She smiles. "How ever will you pass the time until your friends arrive?"

My stomach goes all topsy-turvy. "Perhaps you could help me?"

She rushes at me so fast that she becomes a blur, and I giggle at the sudden movement. Her misty hands find my face. I close my eyes at the sensation and when her lips meet mine, it feels as though I am pressing my mouth against newly fallen snow, cold that sparkles and burns in the most wonderful way. The sensation spreads through me like peppermint in my veins. I laugh against her mouth. The surrounding air grows thick with electricity, making the tiny hairs on my arms stand up as though they are reaching out for her touch. Kissing may feel different than it did when she was inside Talulah's body, but I must say, it is not any less enjoyable.

The sun dips behind the rooftops, casting long purple shadows across my bedroom floor. Shiloh sends a message to tell me she is on her way. I hope she gets here quickly because if what she said was true, Max does not have long for us to save him. I cannot begin to imagine what losing him would do to Shiloh. Her heart would shatter into a million tiny pieces. I simply do not believe she would survive it.

But she will not have to. I know it in my bones.

Close to an hour later, a small beige sedan comes around the corner and stops at the curb. The headlights beam like fireflies through the frost-edged window, and I press my nose against the glass as Shiloh steps out of the car. Oh my goodness. I have not seen any of my friends in months, and I did not realize how much I missed them until this moment. Miles steps out as well. I have seen pictures of Miles on the telephone, but in person, he looks quite a lot taller and thinner than I remember him being. He looks like a grown-up in his wool coat with brass buttons that catch the light. Jonah comes around the other side and opens the trunk.

I press my hand to the window, my breath fogging the glass. Miles and Shiloh run across the yard, their boots crunching on the frozen grass.

Unlocking the window, I push up on it with all my might. It opens with a soft whine, like a fairy yawning, and lets in a rush of crisp air that stings my nose.

Shiloh beams from ear to ear. "I'm so happy to see you."

I press my finger to my lips and turn my head to look over my shoulder. The television makes muted sounds from the living room, but my father is not far away, and even the thumping of my heart feels loud enough to echo through the house at the moment.

So I keep my voice to a whisper as I say, "I am happy to see you as well."

Shiloh beckons for me to climb out. I lift my bag onto the windowsill where Miles takes it before it can hit the ground. Then I slide onto the floor, my legs dragging beneath me. Shiloh does not know. I never told her about my legs, but now the truth is about to become quite evident whether I am ready or not. I stretch my arms up, but I am not strong enough to lift myself without using my legs, which might as well be made of lead for how impossible they are to move.

"Need a hand?" Shiloh asks.

I nod. She and Miles pull on my wrists, causing my skin to burn where they are gripping it. I whimper, so Miles reaches through the window frame and grabs hold of my underarms, his sleeve rough against my chin.

"A little help here, Francesca?" he asks through gritted teeth.

I do try, but my legs will not cooperate. Grunting with the effort, he lifts me through, and for a heartbeat I could be flying, until gravity remembers I exist and yanks me to the ground. I grunt from the impact.

Shiloh glares at me. "What the hell?"

My stomach flip-flops like a fish caught in a net. I am glad that it is nighttime, because I can feel my face burn. "Could you bring my wheelchair?"

"You can't walk?" she asks. "Since when?"

I had known she would not be happy when she learned this. Thinking she is disappointed in me makes me feel like creepy crawlies are writhing up my arms, but this is not the proper time to have this conversation.

"Please." I point up at the open window. "Could you get my chair?"

Shiloh presses her lips together and stares at me for a suspended second before reaching through the open window to try to grab the wheelchair. The metal frame scrapes against the windowsill, scratching the white paint. Her face scrunches with the effort. The chair is too large for the opening, its bulk refusing to yield to the narrow space.

"Does it fold?" Shiloh's voice is strained like a thread about to snap. "Or come apart?"

"Yes, it folds up neatly and the arms come off, but it still will not fit through the window," I say from my position on the cold grass. "You will need to take the wheels off. Can you climb into my bedroom?"

"Uh ..."

Shiloh grips the edge of the sill and jumps up, but does not jump high enough, so Miles has to give her a leg up. She crawls into my room and lands on my floor so lightly that I hardly hear it. Miles picks me up so I can tell Shiloh what to do.

Shiloh crouches on the hardwood floor, the shadows from the streetlight outside casting strange patterns across her face as she studies the wheelchair and avoids my eyes. I can tell she is upset with me. I do not believe it is fair for her to be, but fairness does not control people's emotions. Shiloh pushes her thumb into the center of the wheel and manages to get it loose. The bitter air blows through my open jacket. I wish she would hurry. Jonah is standing by the car, the brim of his red baseball cap pulled deep onto his head. I am not sure what he is supposed to be doing, but he is not being particularly helpful.

Pointing at him, I raise my eyebrows. "What is Jonah doing?"

Miles shrugs while he is still holding me, as though telling me not to worry.

This must be part of the plan. Perhaps the part Jonah concocted himself. He does come up with quite strange plans.

Shiloh yanks off the wheel, catching her balance with her

hand on the floor. The small thud echoes in my ears. The muffled drone of the television filters through the walls. What would my father would do if he discovered Shiloh inside my bedroom? He usually does not come in here until it is time for me to come to dinner and I have already eaten dinner. Shiloh yanks off the other wheel.

My heart hammers so loudly I can hardly breathe as Miles sets me back down on the grass. Shiloh passes the wheels through the open window, each one making a soft scraping sound as she slides it across the sill. She does not look at me as she lifts my chair through the window. The corner hits the frame with a *thump*.

I widen my eyes at Shiloh. The television's drone cuts off, leaving the house in an eerie silence.

"Francesca?" my father calls out.

Uh oh.

My father's footsteps echo down the hallway, growing louder the closer they approach. Evangeline swoops into the kitchen. A tremendous crash of pots and pans echoes through the house, the metal clanging against tile like angry bells. The footsteps pause, then resume with renewed purpose past my room to the kitchen. The distraction will not be enough. I must hurry.

Shiloh gives the chair one desperate push. It scrapes loudly against the frame, causing flakes of white paint to drift down like snow onto the frozen grass, but it does not budge.

Miles rushes up to the window. Shiloh grimaces as she tries to lift one of the corners.

"Tilt it!" she barks.

Miles readjusts his grip. "You tilt it."

"I'm *trying* to tilt it," she yells through gritted teeth, ramming her shoulder into the side of the chair.

Miles hardly has time to stumble out of the way before the

chair flies onto the grass, the metal rods creaking with the impact. Miles knits a hand through his hair, shaking his head at Shiloh before he points at Jonah and gives him a thumbs-up. Jonah grabs what appears to be a box of pizza from the car and runs up the steps to the front door. The doorbell rings. Shiloh leaps onto the ground.

The door to my room swings open with such force it bounces against the wall. I throw my hands up to cover my face as a figure comes running in. But it is not my father.

Jonah grabs my desk chair and jams it under the door handle. My father pounds against the door.

"Francesca!"

"Hey," Jonah says with a quick grin, jumping through the open window with far too much enthusiasm but landing on his feet. He has an ugly mark on his face, like someone hit him. "Good to see you."

The doorknob rattles. Miles sweeps me up onto his shoulder and runs away just as my father bursts into the room. His face is red with rage as he crashes up to the window.

"Francesca, come back inside right now!"

Jonah tilts his baseball cap at the man. "Call Pepe's for pizza-perfect service and all your window demolition needs!"

My father makes an enraged sound, which I would have guessed could have come out of an angry gorilla. He tries to climb out of the window I came through, but he is quite a heavy man, so it takes him a minute to realize he is not going to fit through.

This buys us the time we need. Shiloh works quickly at the car, shoving my folded wheelchair into the trunk before helping Miles position me sideways and lower me onto the backseat so quickly that I fall a couple of inches and my stomach lurches. It all takes such a long time that we may as well be moving in slow motion. Shiloh slides in next to me as Evangeline streaks through the air. My father shouts from the window, begging me to come back, but the car peels away before he can get down the front steps.

I catch sight of Richie's face in the front window of the house. He is standing perfectly still, watching us drive away. Unlike my father, he makes no move to stop us or raise an alarm. I press my palm against the glass, and to my surprise, Richie raises his hand in return. I hold his gaze until the car turns the corner and the house disappears from view.

9

FrANCeSCA

Shiloh turns on me. "Why didn't you tell me that you still couldn't walk?"

I drop my eyes to my lap, watching my fingers twist together like worms. The heat from the car vents suddenly makes my winter coat feel too warm and scratchy against my skin. "I am sorry."

"You said you could walk again," she snaps. "I asked you the day after you left, and you told me the feeling in your legs came back."

"I did get some of the feeling back," I say, moving my toes inside my boots where the wool socks have bunched. "I can wiggle my toes sometimes."

"You can't even stand on your own."

"I know."

"Why did you lie to me?"

Her words hit me like a blow to the stomach. I rub my nose with my hand, trying to think of something to say to her, but I cannot come up with a single proper excuse other than I did not want to make her sad.

Shiloh runs a hand through her hair, tugging at the ends. "You need to *tell* me things like that."

"There is nothing you could have done to help."

"At least I would have known."

"What would that have changed? You would have only had one more thing to be upset about."

She stares at me, a deep crease running between her eyebrows. The streetlights cast moving shadows across her face as we pass them. I am expecting her to say something mean, or come up with another reason I have wronged her, but instead, she slides over on the back seat and hugs me.

I am not expecting the gesture. It takes a moment or two for my body to respond, but when it does, I breathe out a sigh. Her body is warm and wiry against mine, and pressure builds behind my eyelids for a handful of seconds before she releases me.

She wipes her nose with the sleeve of her coat. "I take it things weren't as great for you in that house as you made out?"

I do not feel like dwelling on sad feelings. I am with my friends now, after all, and I am leaving that place.

Miles's car smells quite stale, like old French fries forgotten under the seats and sweaty gym clothes. Also very strongly of pine air freshener, which I am sure he installed to mask the staleness, but instead gives me a stomachache simply inhaling it. Jonah looks uncomfortable as well. I watch him dry-swallow what must be painkilling pills and mutter something to Miles, who pulls into a drive-through McDonald's and gets him a large black coffee. Shiloh gives him a look that does not seem friendly. Once we get driving again, warm air blasts out of the heating system and my neck begins to feel damp.

I grip Shiloh's hand, my cold fingertips boring into her warm knuckles. "How is Max?"

She pales, but says nothing. Jonah turns to look at her from the passenger seat.

"How fast is the rash progressing up his arm?" Miles asks Shiloh, his voice tight like a rubber band.

"It's not like I clocked it," she snaps. "How do I even measure that?"

"According to all the posts I read on Facebook, the progression is important, because it spreads at roughly the same rate as the person's illness develops." Miles's fingers drum an anxious rhythm on the steering wheel that matches the muffled thump-thump of slush under the tires. "I'm surprised more doctors aren't talking about it. Or maybe they are, and I don't know they are because they're in the hospital saving people's lives instead of—"

"Doom-scrolling through Facebook?" Jonah finishes.

Miles glares at him. "The rash usually presents itself a day before death."

"But ..." I pinch my temples. "Are you absolutely certain this is because of the souls?"

Miles nods. Jonah flattens his hand, tilting it from side to side like he is not so sure, then drains the coffee and goes to throw the cardboard cup out of the window. Shiloh reaches forward and takes the carton from him, scrunching it up and dropping it in the rear footwell instead.

Miles frowns at the crumpled cup but says nothing about it. "I don't see any other explanation. Everything started when the ghosts came over, so we need to send them back."

I do not know what to say. The only sound other than the engine rumbling beneath us is Shiloh's shallow breathing as she bounces her knee and wrings her hands together. I wrap my hands around my stomach to try to press down the uneasy feeling rising through my body as I watch the tall buildings turn into trees, which turn into fields on the other side of the window as we travel farther away from Columbus. The spindly fingers of bare trees scratch at the clouds. Snow and ice cling to each bare branch, glittering like crushed diamonds whenever our headlights sweep across them. Every couple of minutes, the temperature gauge drops another degree, and a cold feeling like an ice cube presses against the base of my skull, accompanied by an odd, barely noticeable tugging sensation beneath my skin. In the front seat, Jonah has closed his eyes. He looks a tiny bit more peaceful. The painkillers must have begun working.

Snow gleams against the headlights as the tires crunch on the icy road. Flakes swirl and eddy in their glare. I bury my hands in the sleeves of my purple coat, pulling the fabric taut as if to anchor myself more firmly within it. I peer at the piles of powder that have built up on the side of the road, filthy with the salt and gravel that have been put down.

The air thrums with quiet energy. A low-frequency vibration that hums right below the threshold of hearing.

Is all of this ... did this all happen because of *me*?

I press my nose to the glass, my breath creating fog that spreads like spilled milk across the window. Shiloh is watching me. Perhaps she is waiting to see if I react to the number of souls that are here, but it is nearly impossible to see anything past the glare of the car's headlights. The snow outside whirls like confetti in a snow globe, each flake catching in the headlights like tiny mirrors, and that is all I can see until I catch sight of something.

There is a man hovering several inches above the snowbank. He is dead, and not recently so, as he pulses brighter than any ghost I have ever seen. His glow is harsh, nearly painful to look at, and pierces the darkness like a searchlight through fog. He looks to be in his forties, with deep crow's feet and a jagged scar running along his weathered jawline. His worn denim overalls, frayed at the cuffs and peppered with stains down the front, hang loosely from his gaunt frame. His left leg twists backward at a sickening angle like a doll's limb that has been pulled out and twisted inside of the socket, and a large bone fragment juts through his flesh.

The car whips past him. Our eyes meet. His head swivels to follow me.

I crane my neck to see the man glide out into the center of the road, his feet never touching the ground as he watches the car. The thrumming grows stronger, my mouth aching like something is vibrating in my teeth. I press my hand to my lips. The car rounds a long bend on the road and the man disappears.

I turn around and slump back in my seat, still tapping my fingers against my lips. I have come to know many souls in my life, but I can say with certainty that I would not like to make the acquaintance of that one.

I do my best to ignore the thrumming as Miles drives off Route 13 and enters Bethany. The town is deserted. Yellow light spills onto the sidewalks from the flickering streetlamps, casting long shadows that dance like ribbons across the drifts. The bakery sits closed, its windowpanes glazed with frost, although I can still make out the cookies arranged in the display. The florist's neon CLOSED sign flickers against the falling snow, painting brief splashes of electric pink across the untouched drifts. There is nobody walking around even though it is not quite nine o'clock, and many lights are already off in the houses. Their dark windows remind me of hollow eye sockets.

The emptiness feels wrong. Bethany has always been full of gentle spirits, but I can see none of them now.

Shiloh watches me. Her eyebrows are drawn together in that way she does when she thinks I have gone peculiar in the head.

"Do you see them?" she asks me. "The ghosts?"

Um … the shadows seem deeper than usual, like they are hiding something, but I do not see anything inside of them. Only the faint outlines of trees.

Something twists inside me, growing tight like an overinflated balloon. "No."

"Nothing at all?"

"There are no souls here." I can hardly get the words out. "None that I can see."

Shiloh frowns, then smacks Miles on the shoulder. He cups his arm.

"*Hey!*"

"I thought you said this place was crawling with ghosts," she says. "When's the last time you checked with the glasses?"

"Yesterday." Miles rubs his arm. "I swear, I spotted five of them right outside the bookstore."

"Perhaps they are hiding?" I offer.

"Why would they be hiding?" Shiloh asks. "What would make them hide today that wasn't around yesterday? What do ghosts even have to hide from?"

"Us, perhaps. Or at least me."

The words sound silly as soon as they leave my mouth, and Shiloh's expression confirms it. Of course. The souls do not know we are here. They have no clue who we are or what we are planning to do.

My stomach drops. *Evangeline.* Where is Evangeline?

She must be following behind us. This is not entirely unusual. She often trails vehicles from above, preferring to stretch her arms in the open air rather than be confined within moving walls. But nothing feels usual about the strange vibrations that are humming through my body right now, so I roll down the window and I poke my head out into the bitter cold. The wind whips snowflakes against my face like tiny frozen needles. Evangeline is looking down at me from where she sails above us, her ethereal form rippling like silk against a sky filled with snow. Oh, thank goodness.

I pull myself back into the warmth of the car, my cheeks tingling as they thaw and we enter the community park. The sudden draft has woken up Jonah. He groans and lifts his head. The baseball diamond peeks through the snow like sand underneath white lace, revealed by all of the footprints that have trampled across the field.

Miles stops in a parking space. A streetlamp flickers once with an electric buzz before the bulb dies.

The snow makes it light enough to see quite well without any help from the overhead lights, so I roll down my window and search every corner of the park. I glimpse a flash of silver that makes my heart leap, but it is only the metallic swing set glinting as the wind moves it. How peculiar that something so ordinary could play tricks on my eyes.

"I cannot see anything, but I can feel something," I say, watching my breath make ghosts of its own in the air. The sensation reminds me of when my mother used to play her records too quietly in our old house, and I would strain to catch the melody from my bedroom. "I am not sure what it is, only that it hurts my head trying to find out."

"Okay." Shiloh pauses. "So where do you think all the ghosts are?"

I wish I had an answer for her. Something is very wrong. The souls are here. I can feel them, but I do not know where they could be. Souls do not have anything to hide from. That one man I saw earlier certainly did not appear to be afraid of anything.

Jonah's hand falls away from his face. "Holy shit."

Shiloh looks at him. "What?"

"How did I not think of this before?"

"Think of what before?"

Jonah turns to look at me, gripping the back of his seat. The way he stares at me makes me want to shrink into my coat until I disappear completely.

But the corner of his mouth tugs up. "I got no idea what's going on, but I bet I know someone who does."

10

JONAh

The wind chimes are going nuts right now. Each clang sends a chill down my spine that I pretend not to feel because that's what I do now, I guess. I try hard not to think about what, or who, could be playing with them.

Just like I try not to look at my old house across the street, buried in snow like a corpse in the dirt. No toys scattered across the yard now. No overgrown grass I'm going to get in trouble for forgetting to mow (again). No dog barking to welcome me home. The new owners tore down the chain-link fence and slapped a fresh coat of paint on the house like it could cover up what happened there. Like they could paint over death.

The death I caused.

Aunt Moe told me she didn't blame me when I saw her ghost. She said everything would be fine, but nothing is fine. Kaylee's learning to walk somewhere in Texas with Moe's parents and will never remember her mom. Bessie's going blind in animal control, according to Shiloh's depressing updates. Shiloh chose to do her community service gig there because, apparently, I need to get updates from my girlfriend because I'm too much of a coward to go see Bessie for myself.

Shiloh swears what happened to Moe wasn't my fault, and logically, I know she's right. I didn't kill Moe. Leonard did. But knowing that doesn't stop the voice in my head from waking me up at two in the morning and asking why I didn't stop him. Why I couldn't save her. Why I'm still around.

Shiloh would tell me to stop doing this to myself. I wish I knew how. The bottom-shelf vodka helps.

Shiloh's hand finds my arm, her touch warm even through my jacket. "You okay?"

This girl. I swear.

I messed up earlier by showing up drunk, and now she's comforting me? How did I get so lucky?

I nod, brushing her ice-cold nose with my thumb. "Peachy."

She gives me one of those tight smiles that says she knows I'm full of shit, but she's letting it slide.

Giving her hand a squeeze, I walk past the wind chimes and up to Ella Ruggles's door, knocking hard. I shove my hand back in my pocket because, oh my God, it's cold as balls out here. Even my toes are wet from the snow seeping through my old boots. I stomp my feet a couple times to warm them up, but it does nothing.

Miles and Shiloh join me on the porch. Something scratches inside the walls of the house. Please let it be rats.

A light turns on. I have to stop myself from fist-pumping as Ella Ruggles's face appears in the crack in the door. Her eyes go wide when she spots me.

"Oh hell." She goes to slam the door, but I catch it before

she can. Probably not my smartest move, considering the last time we were here.

"Wait," I say. "Please, we need to talk to you."

"Have you come to bring me my monocle back?" Behind her, something dark slides across the wall. "The one you stole from me?"

"No," I say, and she curses. "But I'll do you one better. Can we come in?"

She presses her lips into a line as she thinks. A bolt slides back before the door opens all the way, and she steps aside to let us in.

I kick some of the snow off my boots before going in. I don't know how, and I don't know why, but it feels like the temperature drops ten degrees the second we step inside, like the house is trying to freeze us out. The lights are off so I can't see much of what's around, but I can see the dark stains spread across the ceiling in patterns that look like screaming faces if you stare too long. I can also say this place looks emptier than I remember. The rugs are still here. So is that giant iron bird cage, but there's no bird in it.

I jerk my chin at the cage. "Where's your bird?"

The old woman shuffles into the shadows. "Dead."

Of course it is.

Miles has Francesca in his arms. Shiloh pushes her wheelchair into the house. She finds my eyes and points at the pile of white powder in the corner, the one that looks suspiciously like cocaine. Not that I've seen a lot of cocaine in my life, and for sure not that much. There's enough in each pile and spread around the floor that if it is cocaine, she could afford to heat this place.

I dig my toe into the closest pile. The crystals slide down and reveal themselves to be … salt? I shrug my shoulders in a sort of who'd-have-thought way, but Shiloh's already walking past me into the living room. Damn it.

The old woman flips on the light in the living room. Miles helps Francesca into her wheelchair. Shiloh closes the door and we all go after the woman.

I remember this room. The old furniture. The ugly paintings of super old dudes. The iron chandelier that belongs in a haunted house from the movies. Ella gestures at an ugly red couch with curved wood legs that are carved like animal paws. We all sit—except for Francesca, who's already sitting.

Ella stays standing. I must say, the months have not been kind to her. She already had a batshit old lady thing going on, but now she looks like she's tipped right off her rocker. She's got to be wearing every piece of clothing she owns. Of course she is. The heat isn't fucking on. Her white hair is covered by a hat that looks like it was knit by some senior citizen on speed. It's way too long and flops to one side of her head like an old nightcap. She's wearing so many jackets under her tattered felt bathrobe that she could be three hundred pounds, and she looks like it might be hard for her to find her own elbows. She's also got on these purple fluffy slippers that look like she killed two characters from Monsters Inc. and stuffed them on her feet. She braces her hands on her hips and peers at us, baring what's left of her teeth.

"I cannot say I'm all that happy to see you children." Her eyes fall on Miles. "And whoever you are."

Miles opens his mouth, probably to introduce himself, when the door we just walked through slams shut on its own. The words die on his tongue. Unfazed, the woman pulls a bundle of sage from her pocket and lights it. The smoke curls up.

"Ghost repellent," she says. Seems pretty ineffective, but who am I to judge?

The old woman's neck cranes at an impossible angle as she watches something move across her ceiling like the biggest invisible spider I ever didn't see. God, she is seriously messing with my head.

Her attention snaps back to us. Her beady eyes travel over me in a way that makes goosebumps break out even under my coat.

"So," she says. "What do you want?"

Shiloh leans onto her elbows. "We need your help."

"I recall you telling me something similar the last time I saw you."

"Ghosts have invaded the town," Shiloh says. "They came over from the other side."

"You don't say." The woman gets a lungful of smoke and coughs. "I took my precautions. Got awful tired of things being thrown at me."

Giving the woman a funny look, Shiloh stands and tries to peel up the couch cushion she'd been sitting on. The cushion won't budge.

Shiloh gives the thing one more tug. "Did you glue these together?"

"Super glue. Everything in this house has been glued down."

I look at the books on the shelf. The random metal elephants and trinkets. There had to be an easier way to ghost-proof her house. Like, say, burning it to the ground.

"You kids stole my monocle, so you left me no choice," Ella says, apparently reading my mind. "Why else would I keep it so cold in here?"

"Ghosts take energy from heat," Miles says. "If you keep it cold, there's less energy for them to power themselves with, so they will be weaker. The difference is marginal. One would need to weigh it against the very real chance of contracting hypothermia."

A slow smile spreads over the woman's mouth, revealing her teeth again, which are not good. "Your new one has knowledge."

"Not enough," Shiloh says, and I have to fight back a laugh. Sick unintentional burn. "We don't know how to send the ghosts back."

Ella scoffs. "Do you think I wouldn't have already done that if I knew?"

"We understand why it's so cold, but the mutations, and the deaths …" Shiloh swallows so hard her throat bobs. "Why are so many people dying?"

Ella's wrinkles deepen. She points the ember of the sage bundle at Shiloh.

"You. Would you be a dear and bring me the hourglass I keep in the kitchen?"

Uh … no? Like hell is Shiloh going in there by herself.

But of course Shiloh stands up and goes into the kitchen. I feel like I should go after her, but I just scoot to the edge of the couch so I can at least keep her in sight. This woman can't expect Shiloh to know where she keeps things like an hourglass in her kitchen, but because Shiloh is Shiloh, she comes back in under a minute with exactly what she was sent to get.

She puts the hourglass on the coffee table. The old woman sits down on the floor behind it, taking her time and grunting with the effort. I'd grunt too if I were wearing two hundred pounds of clothing. And if I were five hundred years old, like she is.

She hands the burning sage to Miles, whose eyes almost pop out of his head (probably because of the fire risk). She'd go up in flames if anything touched her clothes. They'd say she was one of those weird cases of spontaneous human combustion. She wipes the sleeve of her bathrobe across the thick layer of dust on the surface, sending it onto the rug.

"I'm no expert in any of these things," she says, "but this is, in my opinion, the only way to explain what I've seen."

Bracing her elbows on the table, she takes the hourglass in both hands, launching into another one of her creepy lectures:

"The world of the dead exists as a separate realm from ours," she says, then suddenly snaps her head to the left. "Quiet! I'm talking!"

I lean forward to look at Francesca, raising my eyebrows and pointing at the space to ask if there's a ghost there. She shakes her head. Holy crap. This woman might actually have gone insane.

Ella turns back to us like nothing happened. "These dimensions exist side by side, like mirror pictures of each other."

"The cling wrap." Shiloh nods. "I remember."

Ella bows her head, then jerks it sideways to stare at an empty corner. "I have never been there, but the general school of thought is that this realm mirrors our own, in shape and size, and the dead remain there unless ..." She stops mid-sentence, muttering something that sounds like counting under her breath. "Unless they are able to find a hole in the barrier."

Francesca just stares at her. I guess she's not about to reveal that she has actually been to the other side.

Ella flips the hourglass over. Sand pours down into the bottom and we all sit there watching it for almost a minute until it's about half done. Then she turns the thing on its side.

"I told you about *mana*?" She raises her eyebrows at me, her fingers tapping out an odd rhythm on the table.

I got no memory of that, but I check with Miles, and he nods. "Yes."

"That's the energy that ghosts are made of," Miles explains.

"And souls." Ella jabs a finger into her chest. "There is a finite amount of *mana* shared between each dimension. It's like … energy. When a person is born, they draw *mana* from the other side, and that energy becomes their soul. Then, when that person dies and goes to the other side, over time, they fade back into the fabric of our world, and the energy comes back to our side. This energy is found in all living things. In our plants. In our animals. In us."

"But …" Shiloh shakes her head. "There can't be a limited amount of energy. There are more people in the world now than there used to be. So where did that energy come from?"

Surprisingly, Miles is the one who answers her: "The logic checks out. If births in our world are like a tap, they increase the energy on our side. But then, since there are more people, more people are dying, and that would raise the energy on the other side over time." He glances at Ella. "Right?"

Ella freezes mid-reach for the hourglass, a smile growing on her mouth when she nods. "That is the reason for death. It is how the What Comes After brings energy back through."

"Does this have something to do with why ghosts fade away?" Francesca asks.

Ella nods. "Each dimension must operate in balance, so when that balance is tipped beyond what is normal …" She tips the hourglass over. "The other dimension will draw energy back." She tips it in the other direction.

I try to catch up with what she's already said. I don't get it, but Miles, as always, is quicker than me.

"You're saying the other side is killing people here to restore the balance?" he asks.

Ella's head snaps toward him. "People. Plants. Animals." She tips the hourglass over again. "Anything with energy."

"Your parrot?" I ask.

Shiloh glares at me, but I feel like I was stating the obvious. Ella draws absentminded spirals in the dust covering the table.

"But why doesn't the other side pull all its ghosts back across first, instead of taking *mana* from living people?" Miles turns to Francesca. "You said there aren't that many ghosts around, right?"

Francesca nods. "I hardly saw any."

"I would imagine the veil has already taken as many of its own souls back as it can." Ella rocks back and forth. "But the strongest ones have found ways to resist the pull, so the other side, as you call it, has resorted to stealing energy from the living. From us. They are watching us, you know."

I check with Francesca again to be super mega sure that there isn't a ghost in here right now, and she nods at me again. Nobody is watching us, you batty old broad. Nobody is here. But no one else seems as weirded out as me by how clearly this woman has gone crazy.

"Resist the pull?" Shiloh asks. "What do you mean?"

Ella's hands start arranging invisible objects in front of her. "The tide is strong ..."

"But they have to be resisting somehow," Shiloh says, like she's desperately trying to pull something sane from the crazy lady's nonsense.

"It is easy for the veil to take the souls from those whose bodies are already failing them. The elderly. The sick."

Shiloh pales. "Kids?"

"Or those who have died before." Francesca raises her eyes to the old woman's. "Is that correct?"

Ella slams both palms flat on the table, but says, so calmly, "Yes."

Well, that's great. I mean, it makes sense. If a person died already, their soul's connection to their body would have broken once before. So it would be easy to break again.

I glance at Miles. He meets my gaze.

"So what you're saying is that all the weak ghosts have already been forced through, and all we have to do is find a way to force the stubborn ones back?" Shiloh asks, a tremor in her voice.

Ella bows her head. "Yes."

"And what happens if we don't?"

"The veil will take what it needs until the balance has been restored," Ella says. "With or without our permission."

The conversation dies after that. Everyone gets that look on their face like they've been kicked in the teeth.

The old lady wants her monocle back. Like that's happening. We can't exactly hand over something that's been melted into abstract art somewhere in the remains of that burned house. Even though my memories of that night are pretty much Swiss cheese, I'd take a guess that was my fault. Like everything else.

Miles has those ghost glasses on him because he's the kind of nerd who actually plans ahead, but I'm not letting him hand them over. I have a feeling we'll need them.

So I reach into my pocket and give her the horseshoe magnet I've been carrying around like a binky.

"Use this to keep the ghosts away," I tell her, keeping my voice casual so I sound like I actually care. The old woman's nuts, but I wouldn't want to see her get eaten by a tractor. "Works better than salt or any of that sage crap."

She looks at me like I'm trying to sell her oceanfront property in Ohio, but she takes it anyway.

I bail before she changes her mind. We all scramble to get our boots on and head back into the snow like the world's most pathetic Arctic expedition. Miles picks up Francesca like she weighs nothing,

The wind's gotten worse. I try burying my face in my jacket collar, but surprise surprise, it does nothing.

"So that was promising, right?" Shiloh pipes up. "All we have to do is find a way to get all the stubborn ghosts to go through, and all of this will go back to normal."

She says it like it'll be easy. There's not much she can't do, but this is a tall order.

But I'd follow her off a cliff. I'd follow her into battle. I'd follow her to the ends of the earth.

"You got a plan, Scooby?" I ask.

She shakes her head. Turns to Francesca.

"Can you open a gate?" Shiloh asks. "Gather them all up in one place and force them all through?"

I turn to Francesca. Everyone does. She cranes her neck to look up at us, but she's chewing at her lip. I get a sinking feeling because I know that look. She knows something we don't.

So I say what no one else will. "Spit it out, Frankie."

"There is a tiny problem," she practically whispers. "I am no longer able to use my abilities."

11
Shiloh

My stomach drops. "What do you mean, you can't use your powers?"

Francesca's fingers twist in her lap, her rainbow mittens rubbing against her skirt. "I can no longer move anything with my mind. I can still see the dead, and I can hear them and communicate with them, but I cannot move anything or open up passages to the other side."

The wind whips around us, biting at my exposed skin and making my eyes water, but I barely feel it. "When did this start?"

"After I exploded Leonard. Immediately after."

"But ... why?"

She lifts one shoulder in a half-shrug, her ivory curls whipping around her face. The gesture makes her look small and even more vulnerable than I thought possible since she's literally in a wheelchair. Me piling on is going to do nothing to help her.

So I go over to her and lean down to wrap my arms around her shoulders. She stiffens against me. I know it's an awkward angle and an awkward hug, and I'm about to let go when she relaxes. Her scarf is soft against my cheek, smelling faintly of lavender and something else that's uniquely her.

"I'm sorry," I whisper. "What Leonard did to you wasn't fair."

She says nothing. I didn't even think it was possible for her to lose her powers. I want to say more, to somehow make this better, but what can I say when Francesca has lost such a big part of herself?

"I hate to be this person," Jonah says, bouncing on his toes and breathing onto the hand that isn't tucked away in the sling. "But can we please talk about this somewhere warm?"

Take another swing from your flask. That would warm you up.

I bite down hard on my tongue. I'm not in the mood for Jonah's whining, especially after what he pulled earlier, but if I'm honest, my own toes are going numb and the wind cuts through my jacket like it's made of tissue paper. There's no way I'll be able to think about anything in this wind, so I grit my teeth and manage a nod before we pile back into the car, the heater rattling to life with a smell of burning dust as we head to a pizza place on the edge of town.

The glass doors resist when I push them, squeaking loud enough to make me wince. Heat pours over me and clings to my skin like steam, carrying with it the smell of dough and melted cheese, and suddenly I'm starving.

The lighting in here is bad. The place is dimly lit by uneven yellow bulbs that flicker enough to make my eyes ache and cast weird dancing shadows on the checkered red and white plastic tablecloths. The windows are fogged so thick I can't see the street. Outside, snow is piled high against the glass.

We order by the slice and take a booth in the back, as far away from the cold glass as we can get. The cracked vinyl seat squeaks under me as I sit and rest my arms on the sticky tablecloth. Francesca stops her chair at the end of the table, and Jonah and Miles sit across from me. It's just us and an old guy in the corner in here, who's devouring a slice like it's the last pizza on earth. His gray hair sticks out in wild tufts. Cheese strings hang from his mouth. He doesn't look up.

I grab my slice, breathing in the steam curling up from it before taking a bite. The sauce burns my tongue, but I don't spit it out.

Francesca stares at her plate, looking at it like the pizza is going to eat her instead of the other way around.

"I am sorry," she says.

"None of this is your fault," I reply, swallowing a too-hot mouthful of crust and cheese. It burns all the way down. "You did nothing wrong."

Her thin lips press into a flat line. "I hope I can still be of assistance without my abilities."

"You can." I wipe the corner of my mouth with the side of my thumb. "There has to be a way to send the ghosts back without your powers."

But if there is, I'm coming up empty.

Silence stretches between us, broken only by the sounds of chewing, the low hum of the heater working overtime, and the occasional creak of the windows against the wind.

"Just to make sure I understand," I say finally. "There are too many ghosts on this side, so we need to send some back over?"

Miles nods. "Ella didn't say we had to send back *ghosts*, per se. She said we had to send *life force*."

A glob of sauce slips from the edge of my mouth and lands on the table with a wet splat. I wipe it up with my finger and eat it. God, Dad would have a cow if he could see me right now. "Your point?" I ask.

"Well, life force can be anything."

I pause, frowning. "You want to round up a bunch of people you don't like and, what, sacrifice them?" I poke at a melted stretch of cheese stretching between my plate and the slice. "Can I volunteer my dad?"

Miles shoots me a pointed glare. I guess not everyone can appreciate my sense of humor.

"What I'm *saying*," he presses, "is don't plants have life force, too?"

I blink. "You want to kill some flowers?"

"I was thinking more like starting a fire, but nothing will burn in this cold," Miles says. "But even then, I doubt there's much energy in a tree. I haven't seen many ghost forests floating around."

I sure wouldn't want to visit one of those.

"What else has life force other than plants, animals, and people?" I ask. I'm not killing any animals.

Jonah swallows a bite, grease shining on his lower lip. "Maybe there's life force in people that isn't, like, their actual soul."

My brow creases. "What are you talking about?"

"You know." He raises his eyebrows at me, keeping his face unreadable. "Life force."

Is he being serious right now?

I kick him under the table. He yelps, almost knocking over his Coke. Normally, I'd laugh. But right now, it just feels stupid.

I'm done with Jonah. He's not helping.

"What about the ghosts in the cemetery?" I ask Francesca. "Could we send them back?"

"I presume they all would have already been forced

through, as they are much weaker than the old souls." She pauses. "How do you think the stronger souls are resisting being drawn over?"

"No idea."

"They must be drawing additional energy from somewhere." She takes a sip of water, then stops, her face draining of color. "When I was on the other side, everything appeared dimmer. More faded and colorless than here. The grass was gray. Rather like the people. It was as if something was being drawn out of the world itself. Perhaps that is what Ms. Ruggles meant. Energy is being drawn from the other side as the number of people here grows. Me exploding Leonard must have demanded so much energy from the other side that it ripped open a passageway, and now the other side must redress that balance. Perhaps we should—"

She stops. Her eyes dart to something next to our table.

I hate it when she does that. "Who's there?"

Her hand lifts, reaching toward empty air. "Evangeline says she can feel a force pulling her. As though she is being tugged by a rope. She did not feel it in Columbus, but it got stronger the nearer she got to Bethany."

I've seen Francesca do this before—talking to ghosts I can't see—but it still messes with my head, even if I know they're there. I choose my words carefully. "Do you think Evangeline is strong enough to resist being drawn back over?"

Francesca goes still, listening to something only she can hear. Then her face folds in on itself.

"She does not know. She has never felt anything like this before."

Crap.

Even if I can't see Evangeline, I know how much she means to Francesca. Losing her would crush her.

"Maybe she should go back to Columbus," I offer. "She can wait there until this is over."

Francesca holds her bottom lip between her teeth, then shakes her head. "She wants to stay."

Another uncomfortable silence falls over us. Overhead lights cast harsh shadows on our faces, turning skin sallow and eyes sunken. Miles chews on his bottom lip. He's thinking. I can practically see the gears turning in his head as his analytical brain tries to figure out a solution to this problem. Jonah's on his second slice of pizza now, eating like it's the first thing he's eaten all day which, come to think of it, it probably is. I'm still mad at him, and the drinking scares me, but watching him like this hurts as much as any broken bone I've ever had. He tries so hard to put on a smile and make everyone laugh, but as soon as he thinks no one is looking, he lets the facade slip. But I'm looking. I'm looking all the time.

I nudge his knee under the table. "Hey."

He snaps his head up, blinks, then focuses on me. His smile is automatic, but it doesn't reach his eyes.

"You good?" he asks.

I nod and reach over to steal a piece of pepperoni from his slice. He doesn't need to ask if I'm good. I'm the one who's worried about him.

I'm trying to think of something to say to him when my phone vibrates hard against my hip.

I dig it out. Mom's name lights up the screen.

Oh God. Is she calling to talk about the pictures? Did she see that Facebook post? I consider not answering. I really don't want to be shamed for that right now.

But it could be about Max. Picturing him alone with Mom when he's sick makes my heart race, so I pick up.

"Hello?"

"Shiloh." Mom sounds winded. "You need to come home. Your brother. He's not drinking water."

A cough rips through the speaker. Blood drains from my head. I knew I shouldn't have left him. Mom can barely hold it together on a good day. What was I thinking?

"Is he awake?" I ask. "Did he throw up?"

"I ..." Her voice cracks. "I can't do this."

What does it mean she can't do this? All I asked her to do was to give him water and to call me if he got worse. That was it. She had one job.

"Did he get worse?" I ask, unable to stop the panic from getting in my voice. "Is he delirious? Did he pass out?"

"I don't know. Please come home." She hangs up.

I lower the phone, trying not to completely lose it and snap the stupid thing in half. *I don't know.* She doesn't *know* if he passed out?

I should never have left him. Max needs me. He only has me, and I left him with her. What kind of sister am I?

I raise my pleading eyes to Jonah. He understands what's happening without me having to say anything. I could hug him for how fast he reaches across the table to scrape together our plates, shoves the last of his crust in his mouth, and dumps all our garbage in the trash by the door.

He jerks his thumb at the door, mouth still full. "You guys coming?"

It takes forever to get Francesca in the car. Miles and Jonah try to move fast, but there's only so fast they can move. I keep my mouth shut and focus on how my fingers feel digging into my palms, trying not to show how bad I want to scream at them to *hurry up*, but Francesca is my friend. She's going as fast as she can.

But nothing matters when Max needs me.

The five-minute drive feels like an hour. I say nothing. Just wring my hands and watch the blur of snow outside the window. As soon as Miles pulls into my driveway, I yank the door open before the car stops and run up the driveway. My boot slips. For a second, I'm airborne, and then I slam down, my hands skidding across the asphalt. Pain shoots up both arms. I swear through clenched teeth, shove myself up, and keep going. The door handle is cold enough for me to feel it through my ski gloves.

I wrench it open and stumble into the house. "Mom?"

Nothing. I run down the hall to Max's room, my wet boots tracking in snow, but I don't stop.

His door is cracked open. A sliver of light spills into the hallway. I push it wider, wincing as the hinges scream, and step inside. The air is thick with the smell of sick kid. Max's lamp is on. The dim bulb throws warped shadows across the posters on his walls. Max is a small lump in the bed, tangled in sweaty sheets and propped up by pillows that have seen better days. He clutches the pink hospital puke container I brought home when I had my concussion.

I run over to him and crouch by the bed, pulling my glove off with my teeth and wiping away the glob of spit that's running down his chin. The smell of vomit hits me as it sloshes around in the container, sharp and sour enough to make my eyes water.

Max groans. I press a hand on his forehead. Hot.

I turn around to yell for Mom again, but find her already standing in the doorway.

"Why is it so cold in here?" I ask, my words turning to fog

in the air. Was she even sitting in here with him? God, I can't believe I left him alone with her.

"I turned the heat up."

"Turn it up more." I try to keep my voice even. She'll shut down if I push her too hard. She always does when anyone shows even a little frustration with her. Cold bites my nose, making it tingle and burn like I'm holding my face in a freezer. This kind of cold can't be good for Max. His immune system is already struggling. "Did you get him to drink?"

She wrings her hands together. "He vomited."

Crap. Max needs fluids or we'll end up in the ER, and who knows what else he'll pick up there. The bulb on the lamp flickers and goes out for a second, plunging us into darkness before sputtering back on.

Wait.

Icy fingers seem to wrap themselves around my throat. The cold seeps deeper into my bones. Something clicks in my brain.

This isn't a normal cold.

I know this feeling. I know it way too well. The prickly sensation that's crawling up my spine, the way the air feels thick and heavy, like I'm trying to breathe underwater. The kind of quiet that makes the hairs on my arms stand on end. Like something is waiting.

Something is in here.

I can barely form the words. "Mom, can I have a second alone?"

She stares at me for a long couple of seconds before turning around, yelping in surprise to find the others waiting behind her. Mom clutches a hand to her chest, shooting me an accusatory glare.

Francesca raises a hand, smiling like she's totally unaware that Mom is mad. "Hello, Mrs. Oleson. It is nice to see you."

"Uh, you too, Francesca."

Mom gives me one last glance before stepping out past the others and disappearing down the hallway.

I wave them in. Francesca rolls her chair in and immediately stops. Her eyes go so wide I can see white all around her irises. She is staring at something below the ceiling.

I've known her long enough that I don't want to know the answer to what I'm about to ask. My heart tries to punch through my ribs, and my palms are slick with sweat as I gently cover Max's ears.

"Francesca." I keep my voice low. "Is there a ghost in here?"

Francesca gives a small, jerky nod.

"Where is it?" My voice comes out hoarse. "Who is it?"

She keeps staring at the empty space above Max's bed, her mouth working silently like she's trying to form words but can't get them out.

But I need to know. "*Talk to me.*"

Miles produces a Ray-Bans case from his pocket with shaking hands, handing it to me. "Here."

Huh? I open the smooth case and find the ghost glasses folded inside.

He has got to be kidding me.

"You couldn't have mentioned you had these before?" I hiss at him.

"I carry them around with me," he says. "But I didn't think we'd need them if we had Francesca with us."

The brass frame is shiny enough to catch the weak light from the lamp, like it's been polished—which, if Miles has had anything to do with it, it has been.

I jam the glasses onto my face. The plastic pinches the bridge of my nose. Everything tilts and goes yellow like the room's been dipped in sickness. It takes a couple of seconds of blinking to get used to the way that the lenses warp the room and turn the air murky, like I'm seeing it through pond water. I focus on taking deep breaths as I look around. Max's face is a pale smudge on the bed. The sheets are twisted and damp with fever. Shadows ripple across the walls, stretched thin like they're trying to crawl out of the corners, and I see it.

I scream.

Stumbling backward, I crash into the bookcase behind me. Plastic dinosaurs rain down, clattering across the floor.

Jonah runs to me. His face looks longer than normal through the lenses, like I'm looking at him through a funhouse mirror. "What's wrong?"

I point up over his shoulder at the ghost, my hand shaking so bad I can barely keep it steady. The thing hovering over my baby brother is nothing like any ghost I've seen before. The man is old. White-haired and wrinkled. He hovers four feet above Max's bed, floating face-down with his eyes closed, and he's so tall that his feet spill over the end of the mattress. The ghost is so gaunt that it looks like all the blood was drained from his body before he died. He has sharp cheekbones and liver spots staining his exposed hands. His suit looks expensive. A misty tendril snakes out from between his teeth and buries itself in Max's chest, sinking straight through his skin like some kind of parasitic root. The tendril pulses. Almost in the rhythm of a heartbeat.

I grab Max's teddy bear and swing it like a weapon. The bear sails through the ghost. His eyes stay closed.

Crashing to my knees, I reach under the bed until I close my hand around a horseshoe magnet. I climb onto the bed, the mattress sinking under my weight, and plant one foot on either side of Max as I drive the magnet into the ghost's chest. Nothing happens.

To my left, Miles pulls a magnet from his own from his coat pocket. Of course he has one too. He's the eternal Boy Scout and always comes prepared. He creeps up on the other side of the bed and levels it at the man.

The ghost flickers.

The tendril recoils, slithering out of Max's chest and sliding between the man's teeth, vanishing into his mouth.

He rolls over midair and opens his eyes. I gasp. His thin lips curl into a smile. I teeter on the mattress. Cold cuts through my bones. I don't budge.

Now, what do you think you are doing?

The voice echoes inside my skull. The taste of copper floods my mouth. How am I hearing him right now? Not through my ears, that's for sure.

"Never mind what I'm doing," I snap, even as my voice shakes. I don't want to let whoever this asshole is see how scared I am. "What are *you* doing to him?

His smile widens. He floats closer until his face is inches from mine, so close I can see the ridges in his waxy skin. He runs his tongue over his bottom lip.

The young ones taste the sweetest.

He moves his mouth like he's slurping something up, and grins through it. Bile burns in my throat. Yelling through my teeth, I swing the magnet straight into his face. My hands scream in pain like I've plunged them into a bag of dry ice.

"Get *out!*"

His chest shakes in a laugh I can't hear before he turns and shoots up through the ceiling.

12

Shiloh

I grip the magnet so hard my knuckles burn. Oh my God.

Oh my God.

"What the hell was that?" Jonah asks.

The magnet shakes in my hands. Cold metal bites into my palm, but I can't let go. Those eyes. They were beyond mean. That ghost was powerful. I could feel the energy surging off him like some kind of force-field, vibrating through the air.

Max. It was feeding on Max. The tendril, that glowing ...

"What the hell did you see?" Jonah demands.

I can barely form the words. "It didn't work."

"What didn't work?"

"The *magnet.*"

The room sways around me. My balance shifts. I stumble on the mattress, tripping over Max's small feet to catch my balance, but he doesn't notice. He's not even looking up at me, standing over him with one foot on each side of him.

That ghost was ... inside Max? Feeding off him? What the *hell* was it doing?

Careful not to step on Max, I climb off the bed, my foot coming down hard on the floorboards. I lift the puke container from his hands, the sour stench clinging to my nose, and put it on the floor. At least I didn't spill it. His skin is clammy and drained of all color. I reach down to him. He's still running a fever, but he feels less hot. Or maybe it's because the ghost made it so cold in here that he's cooler too.

Black spots press into my vision. I'm about to completely lose it.

"Max, I'm going to be right back, okay?"

He manages a tiny nod. Those bruised hollows under his eyes look like thumbprints.

I bolt across the hall and crash into my room, gripping fistfuls of my hair. The strands twist between my fingers until my scalp burns, but it does nothing to stop the way my head is spinning. Every beat of my heart mixes with the footsteps of the others as they follow me. As soon as my door clicks closed, I whirl around to face them.

"It was a ghost," I say, the words tumbling over each other in a rush. "But it didn't look like a normal ghost."

Francesca dips her head. "I saw it as well."

"It was doing something to Max."

"What was it doing?" Miles asks, his eyes darting around the room. "Is it still here?"

"I don't know." I rip the glasses off my face and give them back to him. He jams them onto his nose but doesn't scream like a baby, so I don't think he sees anything. "It had this tendril coming out of its mouth and was reaching down, right into him like—" I mime the tendril with my arm, then feel dumb because I look like a zombie, so I drop it.

Miles's mouth falls open, glancing between Francesca

and me. He steps back and swallows hard, and Francesca's pale eyebrows knit together. I grip the neckline of my sweatshirt. I can't breathe. There is no air in here. Jonah goes to wrap an arm around me, but I push against his chest. I can't hug him right now, not when my heart is beating this hard, and what is hugging him going to do, anyway? He's not going to fix anything with a hug, and I don't want to get close enough to smell the alcohol that is still leaching out of his pores.

That's not fair. Or is it? I have no idea and don't have the capacity to think about that right now, so I wrap my arms around my stomach, trying to breathe because I know I'm supposed to. I felt like I'd seen the thing before somewhere. Not because I have, but because almost all of my nightmares are about ghosts coming to kill Max.

Jonah leans on the edge of my bed, making the mattress dip under his weight. I can feel how much he wants to come forward and hug me, and even knowing that makes it a little easier to get air in and out of my lungs.

"Tell us what you saw," he says, his voice gentle and low. "Leave nothing out."

I may be mad at him right now, but his voice is grounding me, so I try to hold on to it so that I can stay standing. Drawing in a shaky breath, I describe it as best I can. Francesca's eyes widen as she digests the information in a very Francesca way, all quiet and surprised, like she didn't see it for herself. Miles also takes this in a very Miles way.

"Ghosts are *feeding* on people?" he demands.

"I don't know what it was doing," I say, "but it sure looked like it."

"Oh my God, they're feeding on people," Miles says. "They're stealing their life force. That's how they're getting strong enough to resist crossing over. They're becoming so powerful that the other side isn't strong enough to pull them across."

The realization settles in the pit of my stomach like a stone. He's totally right. That's how ghosts are making themselves strong enough to stay. By feeding on people. That's why so many people are dying. I bet that's also why we couldn't see any ghosts on the street. They are all inside our houses or hospitals having a good old-fashioned feast. The image makes me want to scream. Or throw up.

"But why would any soul do that to another person?" Francesca asks, her fingers nervously tracing the armrests of her wheelchair.

"Maybe it isn't aware of what it's doing," Miles suggests.

Francesca and I shake our heads at the same time. We both heard him. He knew exactly what he was doing and wasn't sorry about it at all.

The young ones taste the sweetest.

Oh God. I *heard* him.

"He talked to me," I say, the words barely making it past my lips. "Tell me you guys heard him, too."

Miles and Jonah shake their heads. But Francesca nods. My beige walls press in toward me. I dig my fingers into my temples until it hurts, gritting my teeth so hard my jaw screams.

"I could hear his voice *inside* my head." The pressure behind my eyeballs builds. "I didn't think that was possible."

"F-feeding must make them extra powerful." Miles has that crazed look in his eyes he gets when his brain is moving too fast for his mouth to keep up. "These ghosts, they have to be awful people if they're willing to feed on kids to stay alive, but it makes sense if you think about it, right? They get this chance to be back on Earth instead of going to whatever bad place is waiting for them on the other side, because every time Francesca talks about it, she makes it sound like the most depressing afterlife ever, and it's not fair that everybody has to go to the same place no matter if you were bad or good—"

He stops talking and gulps for air. I haven't slowed down enough since all of this started happening to consider it before, but I imagine Miles thinks about it a lot, because he thinks about everything a lot. And what he's saying is true. Every person who dies has to spend the rest of eternity on the other side. That can't be all that's waiting for everyone ... can it?

Miles thinks about death more than I do. Probably because he has died himself, although come to think of it, everyone in this room has, except for me. I like to think about Dad or other people who I hate going to the other side when they die and being cold and miserable forever, but what about good people like Max?

Or Max himself? Kids haven't even had a chance to be bad.

I press my fist to my mouth and push the thought from my head. Max is *not* going to die. I won't let him.

But I know why Miles is scared. He doesn't look capable of putting it into words, so I give him a small smile before turning to Francesca.

"Have you ever seen any good places on the other side?" I ask. *Please say yes. Please give him something that will calm him down.*

"There was one beautiful place I got to see," Francesca says. "It was a huge plain with long grass in every direction, and there was an elephant."

An elephant field. Not exactly my idea of heaven, but hey, I'll take it.

I raise my eyebrows at Miles and slide down to sit with

my back against my door, the wood cold and solid against my spine. "An elephant field sounds nice. Maybe like Africa or somewhere."

He stares at me. I guess I can't blame him. If I wasn't distracting myself with trying to act strong for him, I'd lose it myself.

"Okay, so the elephant field might not be your ideal place to go," I say, rubbing my arms, "but it was for someone, and the fact that there was a nice place for that person means there are probably more nice places we don't know about for other people. But none of that matters right now because we need to get rid of that asshole who's been feeding on Max."

"But how can we fight ghosts if they're too strong for magnets?" Miles asks, his voice cracking.

"Wait, didn't that ghost fly away when you held out those magnets?" Jonah says, leaning against the wall beside me.

I shake my head, digging the toe of my boot into the carpet, trying to push down another wave of nausea rising up my throat. I forgot I was still wearing my outside boots. "It wasn't because of the magnets. Those things have been under Max's bed for months. If they actually repelled these ghosts, none of them could have gotten close enough to feed on him."

Jonah frowns. I feed my hands through the sleeves of my sweatshirt and lean my forehead onto my knees. Holy hell, this house is cold. Somehow, even my teeth ache.

"Hold on," Miles says. "Remember what Ella Ruggles said about the pressure from the other side? How it pulls things back like the tide?"

I lift my head, a twinge of pain shooting down my neck. "What are you getting at?"

He makes a yanking gesture with way more energy than I have right now. "The other side always takes the path of least resistance. It's already grabbed the weaker ghosts, but these powerful ones are fighting back harder than human souls would. If we could weaken them somehow, so they're weaker than normal souls, the other side might grab them before any living people. We might not even need to open a gate."

"But we already tried magnets," I remind him. "They did nothing."

"Those magnets didn't work," Miles says, "but these supercharged ghosts are still made of the same energy as normal ones, just more of it. So we need stronger magnets."

Could it be that simple? A floorboard creaks under me as I sit up straighter.

"Jonah." Miles snaps his fingers and points. "Do you still talk to Sid?"

"Sid?" I ask. "Who's Sid?"

Jonah shakes his head, his dark hair falling into his eyes. "I haven't heard from him for ages."

"But you used to."

"Sure, I used to, but—"

"Does he still work nights at Meadow Ridge?"

Jonah nods. Slowly. "What's he got to do with anything?"

Miles grins. "I have an idea for how we could end this."

13
Miles

I grip the handles of the shopping cart with sweaty palms. Clearing my throat, I approach the first uniformed employee I find, who happens to be standing by the doors because Walmart still does that thing where they keep employees at the door to greet customers even when it's a couple of minutes to close.

"Excuse me," I say, "but do you know where I can find a neodymium magnet?"

The girl blinks like she's half-asleep. I can't blame her. I'd be dozing off, too, if there wasn't enough adrenaline pumping through me to power a small city.

"A what?"

"A neodymium magnet?" Great, my voice is doing that squeaky thing it does when I'm nervous. I catch my reflection in the glass doors to remind myself yet again that I'm a full-blown adult now and not sixteen. I can do this. I clear my throat. "It said online you carry them. I looked on the website before coming."

"I don't know what you're talking about."

"Could you check to see if you have them in stock?" I ask. "Please, it's kind of urgent. In an end-of-the-world-as-we-know-it kind of way." I let out an awkward laugh that must make me sound unhinged.

The girl gives me a look like she's wondering why a grown man is having a meltdown over magnets. I would be wondering the same thing. She asks me how to spell it and looks them up on her tablet, and sure enough, they are in stock because the website was not wrong, and she is able to point me in the direction of the relevant aisle. Got to love the Internet.

I push the cart down aisle four, turning to look at Shiloh, who's walking next to me. The others decided to wait in the car, so it's just us. She … is it rude to say she's looking pretty rough? The only thing keeping her from looking like she's auditioning for a zombie movie is the flush on her face from the cold.

I try not to picture that photo of her on Facebook with the bruises. I tried, I really did, not to go back and look at that again after Jonah showed it to me in the car, but I'm not as strong as I wish I was. All I could think of when looking at them was that night she came to my house with those red stripes on her back … I had sex with her when her back looked like that and I had no idea. I was having one of the most euphoric moments of my life while she was lying on those welts. She must have been in so much pain. It doesn't matter that I had a good mattress.

I try to push the memory from my mind, but the tight feeling in my chest doesn't go away. I wonder if she's thinking about those photos, too. Probably not. She has Max to worry about. I was never good at reading her mind, but in case she is and because I know she doesn't like talking about her feelings, I offer something to distract her with:

"These magnets are supposed to be more powerful than regular magnets," I say, my voice carrying an authority I'm still not used to. "We can't use them to create electromagnets because they're permanent, but I'm hoping they'll be strong enough to impact those ghost monsters."

Shiloh nods, but she's not looking at me. I have a sneaking suspicion that my impromptu lecture on magnet properties went in one ear and out the other.

Her eyes travel over the other shoppers. "Do you think people are looking at me weird?"

Uh ... I follow her gaze to a middle-aged woman in the drinks aisle who is eyeing Shiloh like she's a wounded baby deer. I'm used to Shiloh being stared at. A lot of people have always known who she was because she's the sheriff's daughter, which makes her a quasi-public figure in this tiny town, but then she was also stared at because of the warrant that was out for her arrest, and then for the arrest itself and then for the whole 'careful or she'll skin you alive' rumor. But the way this woman is looking at her is not like she's scared of her.

I try hard not to look at her the same way. "Maybe she's staring because you're walking with me?"

"No one knows who you are. Unless they recognize you from when you were a cop."

"I still look older than you," I say. "Like, I should be worried about male pattern baldness older."

She snorts. "Your hairline's fine."

I run a hand over my hair. Shiloh gives me a small smile and then looks back at the ground as she walks, her boots making soft squeaking sounds on the floor. I should reach out. Do something to comfort her. But I don't know. Talking to her feels easy because we talk all the time on the phone, but seeing my body next to hers in this too-bright space, how tiny she is compared to me, and how she looks exactly the same as she did last summer when I started making excuses to go into Rite Aid just so I could see her face—I don't know. It has me overthinking everything.

I want to touch her shoulder. That is a normal comforting gesture for a friend to make.

I reach out to lay a hand on her shoulder but freeze when I see my giant hand with its long fingers stretching out and the veins running beneath my skin. I may have stopped going to the gym, by which I mean I have never actually been to the gym, but my hands still look strong enough to bend metal. They're big hands. Capable hands. How can they be mine?

The pressure in my body starts to rise like I'm breaking out in hives. My shirt suddenly feels like sandpaper against my skin. I become hyperaware of every inch of my body, like I'm wearing a suit that's both too big and too small at the same time.

I stop walking, my breath coming in short gasps that echo in my ears. Shiloh rests an arm on my shoulder.

"You okay?" she asks.

I give her a nod, but I can't find the words, which is a weird feeling because I usually have too many of them. The room spins like I'm trapped in a centrifuge, and I hang my head and try to focus on my feet pressing into the ground. What were those grounding techniques my old therapist taught me?

I'm standing on the linoleum floor. There are freezers on both sides of me, with blue signs declaring the low low prices unbeatable anywhere but here.

This body is *mine*.

It is mine. Even if it sometimes feels like I'm piloting a mech suit made of flesh.

I tighten my grip on the cold metal cart handle until my knuckles go white, wheeling it toward the aisle where the magnets are. Shiloh gives me a funny look but doesn't press me on it, which I appreciate because my skin feels like it's trying to crawl right off my body. The cart gets hard to push when one wheel gives up. God, why do these carts always have that one wheel that doesn't work and ruins the entire thing?

I point at the shelves of magnets, trying to keep my hand steady. "Get all the neodymium ones you can find."

Shiloh knits her eyebrows. "What are you going to do?"

I attempt a smile, but I bet it feels more like a grimace. "Get us some snacks."

Turning away, I try to press down the clammy feeling that's spreading through me as I head to the snack aisle. My fingers drum against my thigh as I scan the shelves. Focus on snacks. What would Shiloh like?

I grab a bag of Goldfish, and the crinkle of the package is unnaturally loud. She'll be happy with these. She used to bring them to school as her snack every day, and I swear it was one of the only times I saw her smile when she opened that bag.

I catch myself. What am I doing? Just because she's the only person in the world who talks to me right now doesn't mean I have any right to open that box, especially given the hundred reasons why that would not be okay.

Should I put the Goldfish back? I'm running through the millions of options I have when the hair on the back of my neck stands up. Hold on—is someone watching me?

I turn around to find a woman staring at me from at the

end of the aisle. The Goldfish bag slips from my fingers, hitting the floor with a hollow crinkle.

My mom stands with a shopping basket in the crook of her arm. She's wearing her favorite cable knit sweater, the pale green one with the big neckline that doesn't look unlike the one I'm wearing right now. Did I subconsciously pick this out because it reminded me of hers? She's ten feet away from me, and the smell of her lavender perfume hits me even from here, although maybe I'm imagining that because I'd know that smell anywhere. I haven't seen her in months. Not since I snuck into our house to slide magnets under her bed.

What is she doing here so late?

Maybe I should wave. She has to suspect that something is wrong with me. She looked like she knew who I was that day she caught me outside our house. She looked me in the eye and didn't scream or anything, like she knew there was nothing to be afraid of. Sure, if I ever told Shiloh about it, she'd tell me I'd lost my mind, but I didn't say anything to Shiloh for exactly that reason. My mom might not know how to explain it, but she knows something about me is familiar. Or maybe she recognizes me as the cop who told her that her son was dead. That's something she'd remember.

Wave. Do *something*.

I go to wave, my arm feeling like it weighs a thousand pounds, but Shiloh appears next to me before I can. She dumps a handful of magnets into the basket, picks up the Goldfish, and tosses them into the cart.

"Good call on the Goldfish." She goes back around and grabs the handles. "Ready to get out of here?"

There's a hollow clatter at the end of the aisle. I glance back over to see my mom stepping away from the plastic basket on the floor, her black braid flying behind her as she runs away from us. Her footsteps echo through the nearly empty store. My chest constricts like someone's wrapping barbed wire around my lungs. That's my mom. And she's running away from me. What does she think? That I'm some older guy who stole her son's girlfriend? That Shiloh forgot about her son quickly enough to have replaced him already?

Shiloh lets out a sharp breath. "Oh."

I go to run after her but stop, because what would I even say to her? Hey Mom, yes I am your dead son? Remember how that cop came to your house and told you that your son was dead? Well, actually, that was me, and I am still your dead son even though I don't look like him anymore, and strictly speaking, I'm not dead?

The thought makes me want to throw up. I don't think there's any way to come back from that.

I look back at Shiloh, whose lips are pursed. She knows. "Maybe she didn't see me."

God, I wish I could tell myself that. The overhead lights suddenly feel like they're drilling into my skull.

"Are you ever going to tell her?" Shiloh asks.

"I ... want to."

She nods. I know she gets it. We have talked about it at length, and she is well-versed in all the conflicting feelings that go on inside my head. Maybe this is a good thing. Maybe seeing me with Shiloh will give my mom further proof that I am who I say I am when one day I work up the courage to tell her. If that day ever comes. When. If.

A tinny voice comes over the intercom announcing that the store will close in five minutes. I stare at Shiloh for a long couple of seconds before I hang my head and manage a nod, wiping the cold sweat off my brow with the back of my hand as she wheels the cart to the checkout.

14

Shiloh

Some of the lights in the nursing home are still on, making the windows glow like orange eyes. Icicles dangle from the eaves. The paths and steps have been shoveled and covered with salt so the old folks can walk without a sudden outbreak of broken ankles and smashed hips. Cold wind tugs at the American flag out front and stings so much it makes my nose run. The four of us are standing in a line, looking at the glass doors. Well, Francesca is technically sitting, but it's the same deal.

I turn to Miles, working at a piece of Goldfish cracker that's stuck between my teeth with my tongue. "Tell me again why you think there will be ghosts in there?"

"So here's the deal," he says, the duffel bag on his shoulder jingling with magnets as he shifts his feet. "Old people and kids are dying way more than usual, and we know that ghosts are literally eating people's life force to survive, so they've got to be hanging around places where there's lots of vulnerable people."

I'm still confused. "But Ella Ruggles told us the other side was taking people's souls, and then we saw that ghost feeding on Max, so which is it? Are ghosts eating people, or is the other side stealing souls?"

"Both," Miles says. "The other side is pulling through as many ghosts as it can to restore the balance. The only ghosts left on this side are the super strong ones that can resist being pulled through, and ghosts get that strong by feeding on living people's energy. Some people are dying because their souls are naturally weak and the other side is dragging them across, killing them, but others ..." He swallows hard. "Well, they're ghost food."

Ghost food. Fantastic. After all this, Max is now ghost food. "Okay."

"Great," Miles says. "So, you guys ready?"

As I'll ever be. I give him a slight nod. He nods a couple of times too, then steps ahead of us and walks right through the sliding glass doors. I raise my eyebrows and exchange a look with Jonah, who hangs his head and snorts with laughter. I guess the two of us have rubbed off on Miles in more ways than one, but I don't know if that's a good thing.

Salt crunches under my boots with each step, and the gritty bits stick to my soles as I cross the asphalt. The sliding doors part with a soft hiss and I step inside. A sour smell slaps me. I immediately wrinkle my nose. The smell is like decomposing feet and ripe food mixed with vinegar and some kind of strong cleaning product. God, if the ghosts don't get me, this smell might. Jonah gags, but Francesca, like the perfect angel that she is, doesn't make a face.

The cold doesn't completely go away in here. It's not cold enough for us to see our breath, but with all the ghosts that are no doubt in here, they must be cranking the heat up to keep ahead of them. The walls have this faded floral wallpaper that's peeling at the corners and practically begging to be replaced. I resist the urge to cover my mouth and nose with my sleeve as I follow Miles up to the front counter.

There's a woman sitting behind it, slumped in her chair. Her hollow eyes are glued to her phone screen. I don't blame her. Anything would be more exciting than watching the paper peel from these depressing walls.

Miles clears his throat, and the woman looks up from her phone.

"Uh, good evening," he says. "I'm here to visit someone. Well, not someone specific, more like a general visitation."

The woman stares at him. Of course she does. What a completely idiotic thing to say.

"Visiting hours close at nine." She gestures toward the clock on the wall, its hands showing ten-thirty.

"Right," Miles stumbles on. "But you see, this is kind of a special circumstance. I mean, not special in an alarming way, just ... important." He looks at me like I could somehow bail him out of the hole he's digging himself into. "I'm not explaining this well, am I?"

I rub my eyes. So much for killing ghosts here. This woman is about to kick our sorry asses into Sunday.

The woman glares at him, her eyes moving to the duffel bag slung over his shoulder. "Who did you say you're here to see?"

Miles opens his mouth but, by some miracle, Jonah steps forward and rests his hand on the chipped surface of the counter. "Is Sid working tonight?"

I'm not exactly sure what I was expecting Sid to look like, especially since nobody would tell me anything about who he was or why we were coming to see him, but the man who walks out looks nothing like what I guessed. He stands before us like a wiry scarecrow, his arms and legs long and spindly, his face gaunt and his cheeks sunken. The jury's out on whether he's a meth addict in his twenties or a sixty-year-old sober guy. He's dressed in dark green scrubs that swamp his skinny frame. His shoulders curl, making him seem like he's trying to withdraw into himself.

Jonah flashes the guy a grin. "Siddy, old buddy, old pal. How've you been?"

Sid drops his hands into his pockets, the fabric of his scrubs rumpling as he shrugs his shoulders up to his ears. "Been doing the same old thing."

"Glad to hear it."

Jonah takes Sid's elbow and walks him away from the counter. I step after them, giving the woman behind the desk an awkward smile and stopping right behind Jonah's shoulder.

"Listen," Jonah says, keeping his voice just above a whisper. "I need to get in to see a patient."

"I'll bet you do." Sid shoves his hands deeper into his pockets. "New security rules prevent anyone from coming in after nine. I keep coming up short, so I'm better off following the rules, wouldn't you say?"

Jonah leans up and whispers something I can't hear in Sid's ear. The man nods. Jonah steps back, and Sid clasps his hands together like a kid trying to look responsible.

"M'kay." Sid raises his eyebrows at me. "Who's the patient?"

I have no idea what to say. Miles was the one who was supposed to have this part of the plan covered. But by some miracle, Miles tells Sid a name he recognizes. Sid brings the four of us around back, past the woman behind the counter who doesn't seem to care nearly enough to be the security person at this facility for senior citizens.

The smell gets worse the deeper into the building we go. It mixes with something sweet and clings to the roof of my mouth. The dirty blue carpet muffles our steps. Somewhere behind the walls, the overstressed heating system rattles, and shadows dance at the corners of my vision. I can't shake the feeling that we're being watched. I peer through some open doors and see pool tables and big communal TVs.

Jonah comes up next to me. There's a lopsided grin on his face as he looks over his shoulder.

"Do you think if we find a ghost, it'll ask us for an autograph?" he whispers. My shoes stick slightly to the floor with each step, probably from spilled juice or something else I don't want to think too hard about. "I mean, we're kind of local ghost-hunting legends at this point, being personally responsible for opening the gate that brought them here."

I know he's trying to get me to laugh, but this is not the time. Does he ever take anything seriously?

I keep my voice low so Sid doesn't hear us. "What did you tell Sid?"

Jonah's smile wanes. I hate that it makes me feel bad. "I told him I'd bring him something. You know, if he helped us."

Oh. That must be how Jonah knows him. From selling him drugs.

I don't know if it's because of him showing up half drunk, but the thought makes something knot in my stomach. "You told me you don't do that anymore."

"I don't." He looks at me funny. "But he doesn't know that."

I stare back at Sid, studying the sharp bones jutting out from his shoulder blades. He may not be a meth addict. Jonah told me he never sold hard drugs and I believe him, but who knows what else Sid gets up to in his free time? I don't like that he's leading us down an empty hallway in an unfamiliar building, and I especially don't like picturing him hanging out with Jonah alone.

"You used to hang out with this person?" I ask.

"I mean, 'hang out' is a loose term."

"I feel like I should call CPS on you."

He rolls his eyes, his easy smile doing things to my stomach. "My social worker will be pleased to finally meet you."

It takes me a second to wrap my mind around his words. Did—did he just say what I think he said?

"You talk to your social worker about me?"

Red climbs up onto his face. Gooey warmth spreads through my chest. He looks away, and I bite down on my bottom lip to keep myself from smiling.

Sid stops in front of a closed door and jerks his thumb at it. "This here is Old Martha. Far as I'm aware, she's asleep. Go in and wake her up if you need her. Won't bother her none."

He wiggles his eyebrows at Jonah and slinks off down the hallway. I might be going out on a limb here, but Sid doesn't seem qualified to take care of anybody, especially not old people. I wonder if he thinks Jonah is here to steal her OxyContin.

I gesture melodramatically at the door. "Well, Miles, do you want to lead the way to *Old Martha*, because apparently, that's a real person you know?"

"My great aunt Martha lives here," he says, and I feel like an idiot. "I used to come here and visit her sometimes."

I didn't know he used to come here. But I guess I hadn't known him long before this all started.

Miles drops the bag of magnets onto the floor with a soft thud that still sounds too loud. The rasp of the zipper makes me wince as he opens it, revealing all the neo-whatever magnets we bought at Walmart still in their packaging. Miles rips one out of the plastic and hands it to me. The cool metal slips into my palm with a reassuring weight, although if the ghosts in here are anything like the one in my house, I'm not sure how much I trust this thing to do anything against them. Miles hands one to Jonah. But when he tries giving one to Francesca, it veers off and snaps onto the metal arm of her wheelchair with a loud *bong*.

Francesca gasps. I hold my breath, straining to hear footsteps or voices approaching.

But no one comes. The only sound is someone's muffled TV down the hall.

Great job, Sid. These people are so safe.

Miles yanks the magnet off the chair. Francesca holds it between her knees in case it develops a mind of its own again while I fidget with mine, running my thumb over the smooth surface. The metal warms under my touch, but my palms are so sweaty that I'm scared I'll drop it.

"So," Miles says, placing a hand on both mine and Jonah's back like we're doing a team huddle. "Does everyone remember the plan?"

I nod. Miles only walked us through it, like, a hundred times in the car.

"You and Jonah take the glasses," Miles tells me. "I'll stick with Francesca. She can be my glasses."

I side-eye Jonah. He meets my gaze. He looks borderline excited about this plan, as though disturbing a bunch of sleeping old people is his idea of fun. I consider asking if I could go with Francesca instead since I'm not in the mood to talk to Jonah alone after what he pulled earlier, but asking to change the pairings would make the problem worse because then Jonah would know I'm still mad at him. I don't want to talk about anything right now. I want to focus on the mission.

Miles glances around at all of us. "Any questions?"

Nope. Jonah and Francesca shake their heads.

"Good," Miles says. "Good luck, and, well, let's go kill some ghosts."

Miles gives us a thumbs-up, then pulls open Old Martha's door and rolls Francesca's chair up to the threshold. She shakes her head. No ghost. So he wheels her down the hallway away from us.

I exhale through my nose and shove the ghost glasses onto my head. They catch in my hair, holding it back from my face.

I turn to Jonah. "Ready?"

He nods. We walk in the opposite direction from the others.

15

JONAh

This place smells like death. I don't just mean death as in it smells gross. I mean the smell moves something deep inside of me that makes me want to get the fuck out of here.

I side-eye Shiloh. "Did Miles say how many people died in this place?"

She shakes her head. Says nothing.

Yep. I messed that one up. I knew showing up half in the bag would be a problem, but you know what? I'm tired of her judging me so hard. She knows I drink sometimes. Just because I drink doesn't mean I'm her dad.

The thought hits me like a gut punch. Did I just—*fuck*. I wish I could take that thought away. Is that what this has come down to?

Shiloh stares ahead, chewing on her bottom lip as she surveys the hallway like she's expecting something to jump out of the shadows. God, she's so cute with her game face on.

So focused. No BS. I swear, it's all I can do not to pull her into the next sleeping senior citizen's room and kiss that concentration right off her face. But she's too focused on the job and still too mad at me to find that endearing. I guess I have the opposite problem and find her too endearing to focus on the job.

I got to fix this. I'm letting everything get all messed up.

I open my mouth to say something, but Shiloh steps ahead of me, pushing open a door with a creak of hinges. She puts on the glasses and peers into the shadows, shaking her head and handing the glasses to me. I already know there won't be a ghost, but I do a sweep, anyway. No ghost. Just some old guy doing his best impression of a corpse.

I wonder if it hurts. Dying.

It probably hurt like hell for Aunt Moe when she couldn't breathe, and where was I? Sitting on my ass with my headphones cranked up down the hall If I'd gotten up. Checked on her. Done literally anything—

Stop. Don't go there.

I close the door and turn to her to find Shiloh walking away. I hang my head for a second before charging forward to catch up with her.

"Hey." I touch her shoulder, but she shakes me off. "Can I talk to you for a second?"

"I don't want to talk."

But there's a tremor in her voice. I step around in front of her, blocking her path. Her blonde baby hairs stand up from the static electricity left behind by the beanie she had on.

I search her eyes, desperately trying to catch them. "Shiloh, I'm sorry."

She says nothing. I sigh. God, I'm such a mess. Can't even get a simple apology right.

"I'm sorry for punching that guy at school," I say, "and I'm sorry for showing up at Miles the way I did. I messed up."

Shiloh looks at me then. I swear it takes everything to keep my hands where they are.

"You know how I am with drinking."

Her words are a knife to the stomach. "Yeah. I do."

"My dad ... alcohol does things to people. It turns them into someone else." She digs the toe of her boot into the carpet. "I thought you were better than that."

There it is. The comparison I've been dreading. Her alcoholic dad and me. She does think we're the same. I have to blink up at the ceiling panel lights to stop myself from crying.

But I catch myself. No. That's dumb. Shiloh knows me better than any person in my life, and there's no way she thinks I'm the same as her pathetic excuse for a dad because I sometimes drink. Everybody drinks. They just don't all go home and beat their wives and children.

I know she's scared. She's got every right to be after what she's been through, and because I love her, I shouldn't be walking around like I have been acting like that means nothing.

"Okay," I say. "I will never drink again."

Shiloh narrows her eyes. Then scoffs. "Yeah, right."

"I'm serious."

"This isn't funny, Jonah."

"Am I laughing?" I raise my eyebrows. "I will never drink again in my entire life." I put up two fingers like I'm miming the Scouts' Honor, but then realize that probably looks sarcastic, so I put them down, because I'm not messing around. "I promise."

"What's going on with you?" she asks, and I let out a short sigh. Damn it. I shouldn't be surprised that I'm not getting off the hook this easy. "Why won't you talk to me about what you're going through?"

"Shiloh—"

"You're walling me out," she says. "I know you're going through something bad, but I could help if you let me. Do you still not trust me?"

"Of course I trust you."

"So what is it?" Her voice cracks. "Because you're pulling away from me, and I don't understand why."

All the hurt on her face makes me want to throw myself off a bridge because I put it there. Like throwing myself off a bridge will make her feel better, like she's not going to care if I did that. I've seen this look before. It's on her face every time she's talked about her mom in the past couple of months and every time she has ever talked about her dad. It's the look she gets when talking about someone she trusted letting her down.

I'm just another person who promised not to hurt her and did it, anyway. Story of her life. God, it's the story of mine. She's so far out of my league she might as well be in a different solar system, and it's only the damage that keeps her with me.

I know I got to do better, but I don't know how to put into words that sometimes in this new house, I think I hear Aunt Moe laugh down the hall, but it's the heat kicking on or branches scraping the window or some other stupid thing my brain invents to torture me with. Sometimes I think I hear Bessie step on a creaking board or make that satisfied grunt she lets out when she gets comfortable on the carpet. And yeah, maybe I drink to shut those sounds out, and also shut up the voice in my head that won't stop screaming *why didn't you do something? Why weren't you faster? Why are you such a failure?*

But I can't tell Shiloh any of that. I can't dump my crap on her when she's got enough of her own to deal with.

I reach for her face, holding her cheek for a second before dropping my hand. "I'm sorry. I'm messing everything up with us. I love you, I just ..."

God. I've talked to her about my crap before. I told her about the times I've hurt myself. Things I had never put into words. So why is this so hard?

"I'm having a hard time."

The creases disappear from her forehead. Before I know what she's doing, she wraps her arms around me.

"Stop." I try to move away. "I don't deserve—"

"Shut up." Her arms are strong around my waist, and she buries her nose deep into my shirt. "Just shut up."

I try to laugh it off, but the sound comes out as a choke. Her hands grip her wrists as she clings to me. Damn it. When did I become such a mess?

I wrap my free arm around her shoulders and crush her against me, pressing my face into her hair so no one, not even any ghosts that might be watching, can see me fighting back tears. She smells like shampoo and flowers from the hand cream she has been using ever since it got so cold that her knuckles started splitting.

"I got you," she says, her voice a breath into my neck. "I'm not going anywhere."

I close my eyes, feeling tears spill out onto my cheeks. That right there is the thing that terrifies me the most. That she stays. Even when I give her every reason to walk away like everyone else in my life ever did, she holds on tighter. I focus on her warmth against me. How solid and real she feels. I hold her tight enough to press the arm that's in a sling against my ribs, sending out warning signals of pain, but I don't care. I want to be better for her. I want to pull myself together. I want to be a man who deserves her, not some screwed-up kid who's trying to hang onto her. God, I love her so much it hurts.

Grab her throat.

My spine goes stiff. I stare at the floor over her shoulder as my heart pounds in my ears. Where the hell did that come from?

It's the foolery. It means nothing. Just leftover crap from months ago bouncing around in my brain.

"Jonah?" Shiloh leans back, searching my face like she could feel the change in my body. "What's wrong?"

I shrug my shoulders up to my ears. "I—uh, it's nothing. I'm just on edge."

She glances behind her. "Did you hear something?"

"No." I search for something normal to say, something that isn't that I just thought about grabbing her neck like some kind of escaped mental patient. "I'm, uh, surprised that Max's stupid gecko is still kicking, you know, what with all the pets and people that are dying."

It's such an insane change of subject. Shiloh stares at me for a second before the corner of her mouth tugs up.

"Don't call him stupid."

"Sorry, you're right," I say. "His name is Bill."

She snorts with laughter. I grin. Making her laugh calms the pounding in my chest. I'm okay. She's okay. I haven't lost it. I'm here joking around with my girl, looking for ghosts in God's waiting room.

A cough sounds from down the hallway. Shiloh's finger presses against my lips with enough force to silence whatever stupid thing I was about to say.

Game time.

I drop my arm from around her and run to the corner, peering around it for anything that could have made that sound. A young dude in scrubs heads our way. His sneakers are practically silent on the carpet.

I grab Shiloh's hand and we run through the closest door as quiet as possible.

The door closes behind us. Somehow, the room smells worse than the hallway. Talcum powder battles it out with that sickly sweet old person smell that was in Ella Ruggles's house, but wasn't nearly this strong. Big machines hum and beep.

A woman who has got to be a million years old lies in bed. Her skin is so paper-thin, I swear I can see every blue and red vein stretching across her skeletal hands. Her white curls are spread out around her head like a bleached chia pet. The sheets rustle with each shallow breath she takes.

Somewhere in the room, a faucet drips.

Shiloh hands me the glasses and points at the space above the bed.

Right. Ghost hunting. Since we're trapped in here playing hide and seek with security, we might as well check for squatters.

I jam the glasses onto my face, playing it cool like this is not completely insane.

And I almost shit my pants.

Some crazy ass fucking ghost is hovering over the bed, a weird long tongue-like thing stretching out of its mouth and piercing straight into the old woman's chest. I thought Shiloh was exaggerating about it being supercharged. I was wrong.

The ghost is a woman. Her creepy glow reminds me of those cheap glow sticks you buy at the dollar store. She looks around forty and is hanging face-down above the bed, rocking one of those angled Karen pixie cuts, and the end of her pointy nose is turned up like she's spent most of her life being offended by something. Her hands are grabby little claws complete with fresh-from-the-salon acrylics not unlike the ones Moe used to get on special occasions, and she's wrapped in a plain white cardigan set that screams outlet mall. Ten bucks says she was employee of the month for making the most people cry in some unimportant power-tripping job.

"Found one," I say. "Looks like middle management in the Haunting & Cruelty Department."

"Let me see." Shiloh takes a look through the glasses, and the blood drains out of her face. Man, if Shiloh's scared, you know it's bad. "Okay, so do you want to use the magnets, or should I?"

Right. The magnets. I don't mean to be a smart ass, but this ghost lady looks way too powerful for a magnet. She looks like she'll report me to her supervisor if I even try anything. Still. Miles swore these more powerful magnets would work, so here we go.

Keeping the lenses trained on our creepy friend, I dig my magnet out of my pocket. The old woman's out cold—I hope —and the ghost has its eyes closed too, which is a small mercy that I'm not going to question. Each pulse from the ghost sends goosebumps up my arms. I swear the temperature drops every time the cord pulses, but I don't know how that's possible, so it has got to be in my head.

"I'll do it," I say, taking the magnet from Shiloh. No chance am I letting her go any closer to that thing than she already is.

She steps back. I push the glasses deeper onto my face before creeping up behind the ghost's shoulder. The woman is all hunched over, looking like some kind of demented vulture with that energy tendril sucking life from the old lady. Shiloh goes to the other side of the bed with another magnet because of course she does. She's always got my back and couldn't hang back and watch me do this alone.

I mouth "On three?" because talking seems like a real stupid move right now. The steady beep of medical equipment feels deafening in the silence. Shiloh counts down with her fingers.

We both go in with our magnets like we actually know what we're doing. I keep my distance from Shiloh's magnet because all we need is a nice loud clang to wake up the whole damn building. I can't tell if it's working. The ghost keeps doing its thing, like we're not even here.

"How long is this supposed to take?" I whisper to Shiloh, my breath visible so close to the ghost.

She shrugs, her shoulder trembling. "Miles didn't say."

Of course he didn't say. Because this is a half-baked plan. Miles is usually good with his plans. I'm usually the one who comes up with the Hail Marys.

I edge the magnet into the ghost's chest and oh my God, it's like dunking my arm in a frozen lake. The ghost flickers, making the shadows dance across the walls like a twisted light show. Something in its face twitches. The heart monitor's beeping speeds up.

Come on, you creepy bastard.

The ghost gets paler. I go for the money shot—right where that gross tendril connects to its face. The tendril starts to wind back, writhing like a living thing. Holy shit. It's actually working.

The ghost's eyes snap open. She turns her head to look at me. I drive that magnet in deeper. The ghost dives into the old woman's chest and disappears.

Uh … Shiloh and I exchange looks across the bed. The

machines go haywire, for sure alerting someone that we're in here.

"Do you think it worked?" Shiloh hisses.

The old woman on the bed opens her eyes. Her head swivels toward me, and I gasp. Her eyes are all white. There's no color in them at all.

16

Shiloh

The machines keep going crazy. My stomach drops somewhere around my feet, and the sickly sweet smell in the air clings to my lungs.

"What the hell is going on?" I ask. "Is the ghost still there?"

Jonah stares at me from across the bed. The woman lets out a guttural groan.

"The ghost didn't leave," he hisses. "I think it went *inside* that woman."

"What?"

The old woman's body jerks upright, her pink satin nightgown hanging loose from her skeletal frame. She's tiny. Has to weigh ninety pounds soaking wet. She bares her toothless gums at us.

So much for Miles's plan.

Jonah sprints around the bed and grabs my hand, yanking

me through the door. We run down the hallway. Our feet pound against the blue carpet.

An ear-splitting scream pierces the air behind us. Metal crashes against metal. I whip my head around to see the door swing open so hard it smashes into the wall, taking a divot out of the plaster. This tiny old woman hurls herself into the hallway like she's been shot from a cannon. Her shoulder smashes into the opposite wall with a crunch that should mean broken bones, but she doesn't even flinch. Instead, she drops to all fours and scrambles toward us, her mouth wide open.

Run.

We need to *run.*

My legs pump harder, muscles screaming. Jonah's grip tightens on my hand as we skid around the corner, my arm flailing as I try not to slip.

Sid appears out of nowhere. We stumble to a stop just before colliding with him.

"Jonah?" Sid's drooping eyes widen as he takes us in. "What the hell, man? You said you were gonna talk to Martha." His whole body tenses. "What did you do?"

My heart slams against my ribs. I shoot a desperate look at Jonah. He says nothing. I glance over my shoulder. No sign of the old woman.

Sid squares his stance, folding his arms over his green scrubs like he's trying to look like he's in control. His mouth opens. A wrinkled hand appears behind his head. Before I can even yell a warning, a pair of surgical scissors plunges into his neck with a sound like a boot squelching out of mud.

I scream. Blood arcs from Sid's neck and starts pumping onto his scrubs and the white wall. He drops to his knees. Behind him stands a shirtless old man who has to be pushing ninety. The man's white hair is mussed from sleep. His skin droops from his bones like melted wax, and his gut sticks out over striped blue and white PJ pants. But it's his eyes that make my blood run cold. They're white and streaked with red veins. Like only the backs of his eyeballs are showing.

The man yanks the scissors free. Blood drips onto the floor in fat drops. "Lois came to tell me you kids were causing trouble in her room."

There's a scraping sound behind me. I turn. The old woman is creeping up toward us, her bony fingers trailing along the wall like spider legs. We're trapped between them.

"Now then, missy." The man steps closer, scissors dripping. "What's that you've got there in your hand?"

My fingers are sweating so bad I can barely hold on to it. "A m-magnet."

"I've lived long enough to know trouble when I see it." His voice goes hard. "What exactly were you planning to do with it?"

I tighten my grip on Jonah's hand. Something in me snaps. Maybe it's fear. Maybe it's adrenaline, but I'm not going to let this eyeless asshole intimidate me.

I glare right into those milky eyes. "I'm planning to send you straight back to hell."

The old man smiles, wide and terrible.

"Oh dear. We can't have that now, can we?"

He points the bloody scissors at me, snapping them open and shut. Behind us, the woman laughs.

I drop Jonah's hand and launch myself over Sid's crumpled body. My boots slip in the growing pool of blood. I slam my shoulder into the possessed grandpa, almost losing my balance but catching myself against the wall.

Jonah grabs my hand again. We run.

I pump my legs harder. The lighting panels blur overhead. The woman's nightgown rustles behind us, mixing with the old man's wheezy breaths, but I don't look back. My arms pinwheel like a cartoon character as I almost wipe out on the slick carpet.

Where is the exit?

Oh God.

I turn to Jonah, my hair whipping around my face as I run. "Miles and Francesca, we have to find—"

A door flies open ahead of us. Miles runs out like he's being chased, pushing Francesca's wheelchair at top speed. Francesca's face is bone white. I stumble to a stop in front of them.

"I take it that didn't go well for you either?" I manage between gasps.

Miles shakes his head. The old man rounds the corner behind us, moving way too fast for someone his age.

I exchange a look with Miles. We all barrel down the hallway together. God, where are the security guys when you actually need them?

Dead. Probably. Like Sid.

The glass doors appear. We're almost there. We just have to get through the lobby—

The old woman steps in front of the exit. Miles shoves Francesca's chair into an adjoining hallway before she can see us. I drag Jonah behind the front desk and drop into a crouch.

I press my back against the wall, trying to make myself as small as possible. I'm scared to breathe too loud, but my lungs are on fire from running.

What do we do? I mouth.

He shakes his head, wiping at the sweat dripping down his temple. I crawl to the edge of the desk and peer around to check for the old woman. Instead, I lock eyes with the receptionist. Blood oozes down her blue scrubs like paint. Her phone is lying screen-up on the desk in front of her, sprayed with blood as her last TikTok loops.

I clap a hand over my mouth. The woman's face swims in front of me as I scramble back behind the desk.

Oh my God oh my God oh my God.

Jonah peeks around the desk. His face goes white. Footsteps shuffle on the other side like someone is dragging their feet across the linoleum. I press my back against the desk drawer as if I could somehow melt through it. A security camera's red light blinks down at us.

I stare up at the thing for a couple of seconds. My stomach sinks as I realize what that means.

I turn to Jonah, leaning so close to him that my lips brush his ear. "I need to call 911."

Jonah whips his head toward me, shaking his head.

"They're going to think I did it." I point at the dead receptionist, the hole in her neck dripping blood into a growing pool on the carpet like a leaky faucet. "I can't go back to jail."

"You're not going to go back to jail." He grabs my upper arm. "There are security cameras everywhere. Nobody's going to think you had anything to do with this."

Yes. They are. I can hear the cop's voice now.

What were you doing there in the first place?

I eye the black phone perched on the desk like a lifeline. Screw it. I'm not risking it.

Carefully, I raise my head above the desk. The entrance looks clear. Empty chairs and magazines are scattered across end tables.

Miles bursts out from wherever he's been hiding like a bat out of hell, pushing Francesca's wheelchair so fast the wheels barely touch the ground. There's a huge smile on Francesca's face as she stretches her arms out at her sides and her white hair streams behind her as they fly toward the exit. The old woman appears from nowhere, launching herself at them with arms outstretched. Miles rams Francesca's chair over the lip of the sliding doors and Francesca white-knuckles the armrests to stop herself from falling out.

The glass doors open. They run through them. The old woman stops on the threshold and stands there, watching them run through the parking lot. Weird.

I point at the exit. "Jonah, go."

"No chance I'm leaving you."

And there's no chance I'm leaving without calling the police. I peek over the desk one more time. The old woman is still staring out the glass doors. Her back is turned to us. I don't know where the man is, but I bet he's around, or at least it won't be long until he appears. I stretch my arm up slowly, trying not to make any sudden movements or knock anything over, and lift the black phone off its cradle. A muted dial tone plays on the receiver. I bury the speaker in my chest in case the ghost has given the woman supersonic hearing. My hands shake so much that I have to punch in 911 twice before I get it right. The cord dangles behind the desk as I sink back down next to Jonah, my heart hammering so hard I'm scared she'll hear it. I press the receiver to my ear.

"911, what is your emergency?"

"Old people are trying to kill us," I whisper so quietly my voice is barely a breath. "At the nursing home."

"I'm sorry. I'm having trouble hearing you." The old man shuffles past us, holding the scissors. I hold my breath until I'm sure he hasn't seen us. "Can you say that again?"

Both of those assholes are going to hear us if I talk louder, but I have no choice. I glance at Jonah and mouth, *Ready?*

He nods. I take a deep breath and yell: "Old people are

going on a murder spree at the Meadow Ridge nursing home. They're trying to kill—"

I barely get the words out before the woman launches over the desk. The receiver clatters to the floor as she slams me against the wall, smashing my skull into the drywall. Her fingers dig into my arms like talons. Pain explodes through my bicep. I gape at the pen sticking out of my shoulder.

I rear back and slam my forehead into hers like I'm head-butting a soccer ball. Stars explode behind my eyes, but she stumbles backward, and I manage to plant one boot square in her bony chest and kick. She goes sliding across the floor, her pink nightgown billowing around her.

Grandpa pops out from behind a plant in the corner, moving way faster than someone who needs help wiping himself should be able to. I grab a rolling desk chair and chuck it at his legs. He goes down hard. His scissors go spinning across the floor.

Jonah. Where is Jonah?

I look for Jonah and find him frozen by the desk, staring at my arm. A tiny bloodstain on my sleeve spreads like some twisted inkblot test. Seriously? He's getting squeamish about a pen wound now?

Someone lays on the horn outside. I whip around to see Miles parked in front of the sliding doors, leaning through the window and waving at us to come out. I bolt for the doors, but Jonah stands there. His chest heaves. He's got this death grip on his temples. My stomach drops when I realize what's happening. Behind him, Granny is getting up off the floor, using the desk for support as she regains her balance. The old man's already got his scissors back, ready for round two.

"Jonah." I try to keep my voice steady even though my heart's doing backflips. "Can you open your eyes, please?"

He does. They lock onto me.

Oh God.

Jonah lurches toward me, reaching for my throat. I duck, my hair whipping around my face as I scramble behind the front desk, my boots squeaking against the linoleum.

The old man charges at me with his scissors. I throw myself sideways, but my boots hit a slick patch of the receptionist's blood and I catch myself on the wall. The metallic smell makes my stomach turn.

The car horn outside blares again. The old man takes another stab with his scissors. I try to dodge, but my ankle catches the stupid rolling chair. The floor slams into me like a brick wall, knocking every bit of air from my lungs before my head cracks against the floor.

Jonah is on me in seconds. His full weight crashes onto my chest, his long fingers wrapping around my throat like he's trying to crush a soda can one-handed. The old woman's face appears behind his shoulder, her toothless mouth stretched in utter delight. I claw at Jonah's hand, but it's like trying to pry off steel bands.

"Jonah," I gasp, but I can't hear the words. "Jonah, *please*."

But he doesn't waver. I grit my teeth.

I buck my hips up with everything I've got. Jonah has lost weight since his accident, and I manage to throw him off-balance enough to ram my knee into his groin. His yell echoes off the walls. I get my arms free and swing hard, my fist connecting with his jaw with a satisfying crack that shoots pain through my knuckles.

"Wake up!" I scream so loud my throat burns. "Get a grip!"

He blinks at me. I wind up and slap him across the face, hard enough that my palm stings. I grab his sling and yank it off his shoulder, twisting his bad arm. He lets out a gut-wrenching scream, but his eyes clear, like someone flipped on a light switch. I throw the sling aside.

"Get up!"

He blinks. I push up onto my feet and grip his good hand, yanking him to his feet. The old woman rushes at us. I pivot and kick her as hard as I can in the shin. Something snaps. Suddenly, the woman can't run anymore. Miles is screaming through the car window, his usually perfect hair wild around his face. I drag Jonah after me and run through the sliding glass doors. Miles reaches behind him to open the back door. I practically throw Jonah inside before diving in after him, slamming the door as Miles floors it.

17

Shiloh

The tires screech. My body lurches forward as Miles accelerates and slams us back into the seats. I grip the ceiling handle, my legs shaking as I try to steady myself in the moving car.

Jonah sits on the opposite side of the back seat, pressed against the door like he's trying to get as far from me as possible. His blue eyes are wide, blinking fast, like he's still trying to take in what happened.

"Oh my God," he says. "Did I …?"

I don't even try to stop my voice from shaking. "Yes." My pulse thrums in my ears. I can't seem to catch my breath. This can't be happening. Not again.

"Shiloh, I didn't—" He reaches across the seat for my hand, but I yank it away. "It was the foolery. And maybe the adrenaline rush."

Or maybe what you drank earlier.

I press myself against the door until the handle digs into

my shoulder. I swear you could fit two adults between us in the back seat.

He promised. He looked me in the eye and promised he wasn't having those thoughts anymore. When did that change?

Or was he lying this whole time?

"Please, just—I'm sorry." Jonah's voice cracks. "I'm so sorry."

I bite down hard on the inside of my cheek to stop myself from screaming. Francesca twists around to look at me, a deep crease forming between her eyebrows. She saw it all. She saw Jonah try to kill me. Passing streetlights flash across Jonah's face, lighting up the tears streaming down his cheeks. My skin crawls like there are bugs under it, and I grip my forearms like I'm trying to hold myself together.

Jonah gasps, raising his finger and pointing at me. "Shiloh, you're bleeding."

I follow his finger to my shoulder. There's a spot of blood on my sweatshirt. I unzip my hoodie with shaking hands, peeling back the fabric to reveal a small puncture wound about the size of my pinky nail.

Jonah swallows. "Did I do that?"

"That crazy old lady stabbed a pen in my arm." I probe the wound, wincing at the stinging pain. "*You* tried to choke me."

The words are like sandpaper in my throat. Jonah's face crumples. I can't look at him. I can't figure out if I want to cry or punch him in the face again, so I try to focus on the snowbanks stretching along each side of the road.

Miles slams on the brakes at a stop sign.

"I'm sorry to always be the person with the pragmatics," he says, "but why did those old people attack us?"

I know we need to talk about the ghosts. That is the most

pressing thing for us to be worried about right now, but when I try to process what happened, all I can think about is Jonah's hand around my neck, gripping me with strength I only remembered he had. He *promised* he didn't get those thoughts anymore. I was supposed to be able to trust him. Out of all the people in my life, he was the one I should have been able to trust the *most*, and he said the thoughts were gone. But they weren't gone. They were waiting to explode again like a bomb with a faulty timer. Like Dad's rage. Always simmering beneath the surface until it exploded onto the rest of us.

Why did he lie to me?

I swallow hard, pressing my fingernails into my palms until it hurts. "A … a bunch of old people tried to attack us," I say, my voice sounding like it's coming from somewhere far away.

Jonah's eyes burn into the side of my head. I keep staring at my hands, watching the tendons turn white from how tight I'm gripping them.

"They were possessed by ghosts," Jonah says. "I watched a ghost go inside the old lady."

Miles twists around in his seat to look at us square on. "Ghosts can't enter bodies at will. A person has to be dead for a ghost to possess it."

"I don't know what to tell you," Jonah snaps, "because I watched it fucking happen."

The ghost did possess that woman. These aren't normal ghosts. Nothing about this is normal. Including the boy I thought I could trust now pressed against the opposite side of the car, like he can't get far enough away from me.

"But why would the souls attack us?" Francesca asks.

"Because we were trying to send them back to the other

side?" Jonah asks. "One old guy killed Sid. He said the old woman came to him for help killing us."

Miles drags his fingers through his dark hair, making it stick up even more wildly than before. "So you're saying they figured out what we were trying to do, and now we made a bunch of new enemies who know we're trying to stop them and have every intention in the world of coming after us?"

I say nothing. My throat still burns where Jonah's hand was. Something metallic coats my tongue. I can't talk about this anymore.

I lean forward over the center console to look at Miles. "Can we go back to your apartment?"

When we get there, I fling the car door open and stomp through the ankle-deep snow to the door. Jonah trails behind me. He hovers three steps back, clearly wanting to be there to catch me if I fall but too scared to touch me. Good. He should be.

The apartment is cold, but not cold enough for my breath to fog.

"Miles," I yell, my voice hoarse. "Why is it so flipping cold in here?"

"You try paying the bills," he says from somewhere behind me. "It is flipping expensive to heat a flipping apartment."

Right. Working at a bookstore probably pays about as well as my old job at Rite Aid—which is to say, not much.

I kick off my boots and march into the kitchen. My arm throbs where that woman stabbed me with the pen, and even though every cell in my body is screaming to get away from

Jonah, I also can't bring myself to tell him to go away. I need to clean the wound. He's drilled that into my head enough times that it has actually stuck.

Standing at the sink, I yank off my sweatshirt and roll up my T-shirt sleeve, goosebumps popping up on my bare skin. I try to get my shoulder under the stream of water. Through my curtain of hair, I catch Jonah leaning on the counter next to me. His hands keep twitching forward then dropping back to his sides, like he wants to help but is stopping himself. I force myself not to look at them since, you know, they're the same ones that were wrapped around my throat twenty minutes ago.

We were supposed to be past this crap. Jonah *promised* me that we were past this.

Pink water sloshes around the metal basin as I rinse the cut. Jonah gets the first aid kit from above the fridge, setting it on the counter next to me with shaking hands, then puts a bar of soap down next to it. The cut stings as I work soap into the folds. Jonah makes this little hissing sound that feels like someone stabbing me in the chest.

Stop feeling bad for him.

But I do feel bad for him. He didn't mean to attack me. It was the foolery. He had no control over what he did.

But does that make it okay?

Did the alcohol make what my dad did okay?

I slam the soap down on the sink's rim and turn around to look at him, grabbing a paper towel and pressing it against the cut. Under the bright kitchen lights, Jonah's face is all sharp angles and shadows. The hand that was in the sling is making and unmaking a fist, like he's trying to get used to having it free again. The sling is still on the floor in the reception area of the nursing home. I guess nobody will be going back to get it. I look at the fists he's making, and he stops.

"You told me you didn't get the foolery thoughts anymore," I say. "Why did you lie?"

Jonah presses his lips into a line. I slam my hand on the faucet handle to turn off the water.

"I get them sometimes," he finally says. "But they're nothing. Just intrusive thoughts."

"I hate to break it to you, buddy, but that back there was more than an intrusive thought." I work my bottom lip between my teeth, biting hard to give myself something to focus on. "So, just to make sure I understand, we can be, like, hugging, and then you suddenly get the urge to smash my face into a wall?"

He flinches. From the living room, I hear Miles and Francesca moving around, but neither one of them has come close to the kitchen door. Smart.

I may not have been here for months, but this kitchen is so familiar. I've been here before. We've both been here before. Jonah and me. But last time felt a lot different from this.

"I never got the urge to act on anything. But in there ... I don't know what I was doing. I blacked out."

I grip the edge of the counter. "You knew you were having those thoughts, and you lied to me about it."

"I didn't mean to—"

"I don't care." I jab my finger at my neck where his hand had been. "How am I supposed to feel safe with you if you can do this?"

Jonah pushes away from the counter and steps back. I ball up the bloody wad of paper towel and throw it in the wet sink, yanking some fresh sheets to mop up the water I got everywhere. I don't want to trash Miles's apartment. It's not fair for me to come in here and make a mess.

Jonah's breathing is pained. I know he didn't mean to hurt me. I wish I could say that mattered. When he first got dosed with the foolery, I understood. He was drugged. I understood that the drug was taking a long time to work its way out of his system, but it was supposed to be gone by now. How am I supposed to trust him when he's fine one second and then flips for no reason?

"You need stitches." Jonah's voice comes out hoarse. "That cut is deep."

"It's fine."

"I can take you in the morning. We can—"

"Stop talking."

I turn away from him, gripping the sides of the sink and staring down at my warped reflection in the metal basin. I shouldn't turn my back in case he decides to lose it on me again, but Miles is in the other room and at least *he* won't let anything bad happen to me. Jonah's breath hitches. So does mine, because he only breathes like that when he's trying not to cry. I want to turn around. I want to pull him into me and say it's okay, that I get it. That I love him. That I *know* he'd never do anything to hurt me on purpose, but I can't.

Because that's what my mom would do.

The realization hits like a fist to the stomach. I slap a hand over my mouth because I suddenly know what that means.

No.

It was the foolery. The drug is still not out of his system.

But it should be by now, and how long can I keep saying that? It won't matter how much of the drug is still in his system if I end up in a body bag, or get good at doing at home first aid like Mom so I can avoid going to the ER every weekend, getting sympathetic looks from nurses until they're familiar enough with me to realize I should know better.

I turn back around. I can barely find my voice. "Jonah."

His face drains of color so fast it's like someone pulled a plug. He takes an unsteady step toward me before catching himself. Of course he knows what's coming. This boy can read my mind.

"No."

"Jonah, I—"

"*No.*"

"I don't know what to do."

"Not that." He grabs a fistful of his hair, leaving it standing up wild, then gestures at me with both hands. "I love you, okay? I know what happened was bad, but I swear, it's never going to happen again."

"How can you say that?" I rub my nose with the back of my hand, trying to hide how it's starting to run. "How do you *know* that?"

"Because I do. The foolery did that. Not me. You know I would never—"

"But you did."

"I didn't *mean* to."

"But you *did*." I take a deep breath that shudders through my whole body, blinking hard against the burning tears threatening to spill over. "You—"

"I'm sorry I lied," he cuts me off. "I shouldn't have done that, but things were going so good with you and me, and I was scared I was going to mess it up. Or scare you."

"God forbid you should scare me—"

"I'm not good at the whole boyfriend thing." His words tumble out so fast they trip over each other. "This whole thing is new to me. I had crappy examples. My dad wanted nothing to do with me, and my mom skipped town as soon as she could get rid of me, and my sister never talks to me, and

Moe died, and I mess up everything I touch. I didn't want to mess us up. We're too important. *You're* too important. God, Shiloh, if I thought there was even a chance of that happening again ... do you honestly think I would ever do something like that on purpose?"

I brace my hands on my hips and let out a shaky breath because I don't think that. Not for one second.

I grip my hands into fists to keep them from shaking. "Jonah."

"Do you understand how much I hate myself for that ugly thing that's inside of me?" he asks, voice splintering so hard I have to wrap my arms around my stomach and close my eyes because I can't do this. "I know I've been messing everything up. I know that, and I'm sorry, but you're the only thing in my life that has ever made me feel like maybe I could be more than what everyone else thought. You're the one person who ever believed in me, so please believe in me now. I'll get it under control. I'll tell you every time I get one of those thoughts. I can wear handcuffs. I don't care. But I will learn how to control it."

"How?" I ask. "By going to a foolery support group?"

"I'll start one," he says, without missing a beat. "With a bunch of ghosts Francesca can set me up with."

"Be serious."

"I am. I know I've been messing everything up between you and me, but I'm ready for this. You and me are supposed to be together. We've been through too much to let anyone else win. This will be a bad day we'll look back on in twenty years and be confused because we forgot it even happened. I can see that now. I could never see it before because I could never picture myself older than eighteen, but I see my whole life now, and I see it because of you."

I'm crying now. So hard.

"Please." Jonah reaches for my face, then steps away and forces his hand down at his side. "I know I've given you every reason to, but please, Shiloh. Please don't give up on me."

His face blurs through my tears until everything becomes a smear of color. I taste blood. I must have bitten my cheek, but I don't feel any pain because nothing hurts as much as his words. I never believed anyone could love me this much, not after all the things Dad told me growing up and all the things I told myself before I finally stopped listening to him. I try to say something, but all that comes out is a whimper. My body shudders as I try to hold back another sob, but it's too powerful and the sound that comes out is harsh and loud, like it's breaking things on its way out of my body. I cover my mouth with my hand to keep it in, then gasp for air, each hiccupping breath hitching so hard it hurts.

I have to say it. I have to get the words out. So I say them so quiet I can barely hear them.

"I told myself it would never be me."

I watch the words slam into him. His face crumples. All remaining color drains from it.

"But I'm not your dad," he says.

"I know." I press a shaking finger onto my chest. "But the feeling I have is the same."

Something in his eyes dies. His shoulders slump. He seems to fold in on himself.

I can barely see through the tears. "I'm sorry."

Some sound between a gasp and a sob escapes him. I clamp my hand over my mouth and bite down on the fleshy part of my thumb to make the pain stop. A sob rips through me so hard my legs give out. I slide down against the cabinets until I'm sitting on the floor. This isn't happening. I can't breathe. I can't do anything except press my face into my knees and try to muffle the sounds that are tearing out of my throat. What the hell am I doing?

Miles steps into the kitchen doorway. Our eyes meet, and he immediately turns around and walks out.

"Please," Jonah begs. I look up to see tears streaming down his cheeks. He wipes them away as soon as they come out. "You can't take that away from me. I could see myself with you. I can't see myself alone."

I bite down on my knuckles to try to stop another sob, but it tears through me, anyway. He has nobody. Every other person in his life has left him, and now I'm leaving him, too. Deep down, I know he believes that he's not worth anyone staying for. I tried so hard to unravel that in his head and convince him that he was worth something, but now I'm throwing it away.

The muscles in his throat work as he swallows, over and over, like he's choking on words that he can't get out. His hands tremble at his sides, fingers curling and uncurling like they're searching for something to hold on to. He slides down the wall until he's sitting on the floor across from me and presses the heels of his hands into his eyes. Every part of me screams to crawl over to him, to hug him, to take it back, but all I can do is wrap my arms around my stomach and try to press the bad feeling down harder. I made a promise to myself a long time ago. I swore I'd never let anyone hurt me again. Even if they were sorry after. Because they're always sorry after.

But this is different.

This is *Jonah*.

The boy who holds me through my nightmares and makes me laugh when everything else gets too much. The boy who runs his fingers over my scars like he loves them. The foolery made him do this. He got through it. He *stopped*.

After I punched him in the face.

I look at him across the kitchen and find him already staring at me. It's too much. I stand up and brush past him through the living room and into Miles's room, slamming the door behind me and crumpling onto the floor. I clamp my hands over my mouth as a scream rips through my throat.

18

FRANCESCA

I do not know how to look any of my friends in the eyes after Miles carries me up the stairs in his strong but gentle arms and places me on his couch. He goes back down and comes up a second time with my wheelchair and moves me into it.

He sinks into the worn brown armchair across from me, his dark curls sticking up in all directions like an untidy bird's nest. I cover my mouth with my trembling hand and clear the phlegm from my throat.

"May I please use the restroom?" I ask.

He springs to his feet, his socks nearly slipping on the soft carpet. "Do you need help?"

A small smile tugs at my mouth. "I have been relieving myself on my own for months without any help at all, Miles, so I believe I will manage."

Miles presses his lips together into a thin pink line and gives me a thumbs-up, his cheeks coloring a tiny bit. "Sounds good."

I go to push down on my wheels, but something makes me hesitate. Perhaps it was the earnest enthusiasm with which he offered to help me, but there is something I feel compelled to say to him.

"You are a good person," I say. "I am quite honored that I am able to call you my friend."

His eyebrows twitch, and he gives me a funny look. I do not suppose he would have been expecting me to say this.

"I don't know if you should be, but thanks."

I smile at him. He smiles at me.

With that no longer weighing on my chest, I push hard on my wheels, fighting against each lump in the long-piled carpet as I make my way to the bathroom. Shiloh stands at the sink in the kitchen, bending down to rinse her shoulder while Jonah reaches over the refrigerator to retrieve a first aid kit. Shiloh told me Jonah no longer felt the effects of the foolery. I had hoped that she was right—but hope, as I am learning, goes away quite easily.

The bathroom door clicks closed behind me. I do not actually need to use the restroom. I need a moment alone where I do not have to pretend that everything is all right.

Rolling closer to the sink, I look in the mirror. The girl staring back at me is hardly more than a soul herself, all pale and trembling, her face framed by white curls that appear to drain what little color remains in her skin like snow stealing the warmth from winter branches. The tiled walls press in around me. A tingling sensation spreads through my chest and down to the tips of my fingers.

What sort of souls *were* those?

In all my years of seeing the dead, I have never encountered anything like them. I shiver only thinking about them, about how wrong they felt. Not like the gentle souls I knew from the cemetery who only wanted someone to listen to their stories or play with them. The way these ones moved, like oil through those poor elderly people's bodies, forcing them into action as though the confines of bone and muscle did not concern them at all … they were so *angry*. They did not want to find somebody to talk to, or to make a new friend. They wanted to hurt us. Perhaps even to feed on our souls, although I cannot understand why. Souls were all once regular people. Regular people should not want to feed on other regular people. Well, I suppose some do, but they are certainly not people I would like to make the acquaintance of.

Souls should not be able to enter another person's body unless that person is dead. Not even Leonard could do that, which is why he had to kill the children before putting souls into their bodies.

I remember the old soul as she looked up at me after slipping into that poor elderly woman, her smile curving like she was offended by us disturbing her so late in the night.

You're going to be sorry you did that.

Thank goodness Miles was able to tie her to the bed with the cord of her robe before she could follow us out of the room. My fingers grip the arms of my wheelchair so tightly that my nails create half-moon shapes in the rubber. Each breath feels like I'm trying to inhale water through a straw. The room spins, shades of white and gray bleeding together like the most horribly boring watercolor painting of all time, and I press my pointer fingers into my temples. The only thing that could stop these strong souls is my abilities, as they are still made of energy that I could manipulate if I concentrated enough. But my abilities abandoned me as soon as my body became too weak to channel them. There is only one way I would be able to use them again.

I would have to die.

I am not ready to die. I have already given so much of my

strength to everybody else that I hardly have enough left to continue living. I do not want to give any more.

I glance around the small bathroom, my heart pounding so hard against my ribs that it drowns out everything else.

"Evangeline, are you there?"

She will know what to do. She will be able to tell me how I can overpower those mean souls. But the quiet feels wrong, and I do not want to even consider what this could mean.

"Evangeline?" I try again. "Please, if you hear me, will you come?"

No reply. She is usually good at hearing me when I call out to her, as she can hear things from much farther away than normal people can. Where is she?

The other side could not have taken her already. I saw her before we entered the nursing home, her pale glow like a guiding light in the shadows as she floated beside me up to the glass doors, but I did not see her afterward. What if something happened to her? What if those souls stole her energy as well?

No. They could not have done anything to her, because if she was hurt, or if the other side had pulled her across the veil away from here ...

I slam my palms down on the armrests of my wheelchair. I did not *ask* for any of this. I was not exactly happy, but I was perfectly content with Evangeline in Columbus, going to school and existing in a world of our own. I want to go back home where everything makes sense, and the dead are kind and gentle, and nothing hurts.

"Evangeline?"

The wall ripples. The tiles pulse and shift like there is something living behind them, pressing against the surface from the other side of the wall. The bathroom light goes out. In a couple of seconds, it comes back on.

Goosebumps prickle my arms. I hope desperately that it is Evangeline and not one of those terrible souls that might have followed us here from the old people's home. Please let it be her. But even as I think it, something feels wrong, like when you wake up and know it's going to be raining before you even open your curtains.

"Evangeline, is that you?"

A pale, glowing fog seeps through the wall and stops nearly a foot in front of my wheelchair. Over the course of a few seconds, it stretches and grows denser, ultimately taking on a human shape. The air catches in my throat.

Oh no.

It is Evangeline, but something is horribly wrong. Her usual glow has dimmed to hardly more than a flashlight under a blanket. Her edges blur and shift as though she cannot quite hold herself together, like a morning mist that is about to dissolve in sunlight. Her ringlets that usually bounce with such life now hang limp and translucent, barely visible under the harsh lights that would already make it harder for me to see her under normal circumstances.

"Oh." I reach out, trying to touch her, but my hands pass through her shoulders into empty cold air that makes my fingers tingle. "Evangeline. What is happening to you?"

"I'm having a hard time holding it back," she says, her voice drifting like a fading echo. "The other side … it feels so strong."

It must be pulling her through already. That is why she looks so faded. "We will leave now."

Evangeline's eyebrows leap up. "No."

"We will return to my house," I say, the words tumbling out quickly but not rising in volume. "You go ahead of me. Go back to the house and wait for me there. I will have Miles drive me right now."

"You would leave your friends to do this on their own?"

I cannot say I like the idea of doing that, but I am not willing to lose Evangeline. "I must stay with you."

She gives me a sad look. "Francesca, you know just as well as I do that Shiloh's brother won't live if you do that."

That is not my fault. Through the closed door, I can hear the soft creak of the armchair where Miles sits, probably fidgeting like he always does when he is worried.

"Real people have always been mean to me," I say.

The words come out much louder than I intended. My throat tightens, as though somebody has wrapped a scarf around it too tightly around my neck and is squeezing.

Evangeline floats closer, her form rippling like heat waves rising from a summer pavement. When she smiles, it makes my chest hurt, which is unusual because her smile usually makes me so happy.

"Francesca." Her voice is so gentle. It is as though I can feel her words on my skin. "I don't belong here... not anymore."

I lean forward in my chair. "Yes, you do."

"I don't," she says quietly, the words slipping out like a secret she has been holding for too long.

"But we have had this conversation before." I try to touch her hand, but her form ripples as it struggles to hold its shape. "It is true. You were not meant to return since you were already dead and Leonard had to break quite a few rules to find you again, but you belong here now."

With me.

The unspoken words stick in my throat like honey, but sour honey that makes me pucker my face.

She shakes her head. The last itty-bitty piece of warmth I had been holding onto in my chest crumbles away.

I cannot believe this. That she would even say such a thing.

"You cannot return to that awful place," I say.

"It is not awful," she says. "There are many places across the veil that you have not seen. I get to have every person I ever cared about in one place with me, and I get to feel peace. And how could peace ever be something awful?"

"But I am not there."

Her expression softens. "Francesca, don't be silly."

"I am not being silly."

"I've enjoyed our time together so much that I hadn't considered what you might be giving up because of me."

What does she mean by giving up?

"You have a life," she continues. "Real people who care about you. You need to live it."

"I do not want to be with real people. None of them have ever accepted me for who I am."

Evangeline glides closer. The temperature drops several degrees, making a shudder run through me. "The friends you have now do, and some of the other kids at your school, too. I truly believe they're kinder than you realize."

Her ghostly form flickers, her glow dimming as though she were a dying firefly. I gape at her words. She has been with me for long enough to see how people treat me, floating beside me through the hallways while other students whisper and point. How they look at me as if I am broken or strange or wrong. She knows better than anyone how unkind people are to me because I am different, and she would know better than to suggest that as a reason for her going away.

Does she not want to be around me anymore?

Could she have gotten bored with watching me go through life in my wheelchair doing the same thing day after day? Is that why she wants to go?

"I will come with you," I say. "To the other side."

Her eyes widen, the silvery irises catching what little light remains of her fading form. "You can't."

"Why not? I know it must have been rather boring following me around, and you have been so kind to do it, so now it is my turn to follow you." I try but fail again to take her hand. "I can go with you across the veil. You can see Maude again. Edmund as well. I would quite like to properly meet him. I need to die if I have any chance of using my abilities to send all the souls back, anyway, so I will do that, and then I can join you on the other side."

She pulls away from me. "That's not what I want."

"But I want to be with you." The words feel small in my mouth, like something a small child might say, but I cannot stop them. They are the truest thing I know.

Evangeline smiles again. The look in her eyes reminds me of the last rays of sunset.

"You have so much life ahead of you," she says. "You're going to grow old someday, and I won't. You really won't want me hanging around when you're all gray-haired and wrinkled."

"I am already wrinkly." I gesture to my pale, paper-thin skin stretched over too-visible bones.

She rolls her eyes. "I had my own life, and I experienced so many wonderful things before my life ended, but you have hardly experienced anything."

"I can live on the other side," I say. "I can live with you."

"That is not living," she says gently. "That is the opposite. I want you to go home, to this new place, and be with people who treat you kindly. But for that to happen ... I need to go."

My heart drops all the way to the floor, leaving an aching emptiness behind.

"Please." The word catches in my throat. "Please, do not leave me alone."

"You're only alone if you choose to be," she says. "When it's truly your time—when you're a hundred years old and far more wrinkled than you are now—then you can come find me. And I'll be absolutely thrilled to see you. But not a moment sooner, do you hear me?"

I grasp for her arm, my fingers finding nothing. "But when will that be?"

She presses her face so close to mine I swear I can feel her on my nose. "You will know when it is time."

Then she disappears into the air.

The cold goes away, replaced by the stale air of the small bathroom. The bathroom light flickers with an electric hum, but there is no reason for it to do so anymore besides a faulty bulb that Miles must replace.

I press my shaking hands against my face, feeling tears on my palms as I try to hold back the sob that is building in my throat. She could not have left me here. In this world of the living where nobody understands me, where everything is too bright and loud and ordinary. I told her no. I told her I did not want her to go. Why does nobody ever listen to anything I have to say?

More tears stream down my face. I press my hands hard against my mouth to keep the sounds from escaping because I do not want anybody coming in here to check on me. My chest heaves with hiccupping gasps as I try to draw air into my lungs, but it feels as if I am trying to breathe from underneath a blanket late at night and I pull the covers over my head to talk to Evangeline so that my voice does not wake up anybody else in the house, except this time there is no Evangeline. And there will not be. Not ever again.

A knock at the door makes me jump.

"Francesca?" Miles calls. "You all right in there?"

No. I am not all right. I do not believe I have ever been all right, or that I ever will be. Everybody has always acted as though something is wrong with me only because I could see beautiful things that they could not. My own brother and father could not bear to look at me, and until I became useful to Shiloh, she acted the same way as everybody else, crossing the road when she saw me and gripping Max's hand tighter as if I might jump out and gobble him up. Jonah paid me no attention at all. Even Miles used to turn up his nose when I walked past him. If Max had never gone missing, I do not believe Shiloh would have ever spoken to me.

The only people who were kind to me were the souls in the cemetery. They never minded that I was different.

And now the other side has taken them as well.

Miles knocks louder this time. "Francesca? Please let me know if you're okay."

Oh my goodness.

This is what I have been searching for all along, is it not? A way to truly belong?

I have existed in some kind of half-world my whole life, not quite here and not quite there, like a flower trying to grow through a crack in the sidewalk. But perhaps that was never where I was meant to bloom.

Perhaps I am supposed to be on the other side.

That is why I do not belong in this world. That is why I have always been able to see the other one. My heart pounds against my ribcage, but the sensation feels distant, as though my body already knows it is something that is keeping me here for a limited time. Perhaps after this, I can finally find peace among those who have always accepted me as I am.

Miles bangs hard. *"Francesca."*

"One minute." I force steadiness into my voice. "I am all right."

"Okay," Miles says after a pause that stretches like taffy. "Well, let me know if you need anything."

"Be careful, Miles, or I will think you were eager to join me in your bathroom."

His silence makes the corners of my mouth twitch upward despite everything. I can picture him on the other side of the door, his face turning the color of strawberry ice cream, his mouth opening and closing like a bewildered fish. His footsteps shuffle away across the carpet.

I curl my hand around the doorknob, staring at the empty space where my ring finger used to be. The stump looks a lot like a rosebud that never got to bloom.

Sighing, I push the door open. Miles sits hunched over his knees in his armchair like a concerned gargoyle, his hands twisting together in his lap while he studies the carpet as though it holds all of life's answers. The way his thoughts seem to tie themselves into knots is quite endearing. I imagine his brain literally turning into a pretzel, all golden-brown and twisted, and for a moment, a bubble of laughter rises in my chest. But then reality crashes back down like the opposite of a comforting blanket, burying any warmth I might have felt.

"Could you please get Shiloh and Jonah?" I ask. "I need to speak with all of you at once."

Miles's eyebrows draw together, but he nods and stands up. Jonah's low voice rumbles too quietly for me to hear what he is saying. He drags his feet all the way back to the living room and sits on the edge of the couch.

Shiloh emerges from Miles's bedroom, although I am not sure why she would be in there. Her nose is pink at the tip, as though she has been crying. She curls into herself on the opposite end of the couch from Jonah, her arms wrapped around her middle. I do not blame her for wanting to keep far away after what I saw Jonah do to her, but he looks even more beaten-down than she is, as though he can hardly keep his head lifted up.

I wheel myself to face them all, my fingers dancing along the hem of my sweater.

Shiloh leans forward on the worn couch cushion. "Are you okay?"

A sad smile tugs at my lips. The gesture feels hollow, like a porcelain doll moving without life behind its painted face, because I am not okay, and I don't think I ever will be, at least not in this world.

"I have been thinking about our problem," I say, my voice not much louder than a whisper. "To send the souls back across the veil requires my abilities, but I am too weak to channel them in this body."

"What are you saying?" Shiloh's voice carries a tremor of understanding that tells me she already knows.

I force myself to meet her eyes. The words feel like broken glass in my throat, but they are the truest thing I have ever said. "The only way that I will be able to use my abilities again is if I die, so I am going to need one of you to kill me."

PART 2
HALF iN LoVE WiTH EASEFUL dEATH

19

Francesca

The color drains from Shiloh's face, leaving her skin as pale as a soul's.

"No," she whispers, then her voice rises: "*No*. Absolutely not."

"Shiloh, I—"

"That is not happening," Shiloh says. "How could you even suggest something like that?"

"Everything bad that has happened is my fault." The words taste like pennies on my tongue. Saying them makes my chest feel hollow as if someone has reached inside and scooped out everything that made me real, leaving behind an empty body. "I opened the passageway, so everybody who is dead is dead because of what I did."

I do not actually believe that, because I had no way of knowing that any of this would happen or even that I could have been capable of doing such a thing, but I do believe I am the only one who can stop it, so dying is the best thing for me to do because then everybody will get what they want. Including me.

"You did it by accident," Shiloh snaps. "None of this is your fault."

I run my thumb over the stump where my finger used to be. "I do not know a way to reverse this without using my abilities."

"We'll think of something else."

"Perhaps we could if we had more time," I say, "but there is nothing else we can do that will save Max in time."

This affects Shiloh. I knew it would. There is a tiny change in her expression, but it is gone in a second.

"Why are you so calm about this?" she demands. "You're talking like your life means nothing."

Perhaps it does not. I certainly would be happier without it, and the life I could have after this one is over would be better. On the wall behind Shiloh's head, I notice something that I had not seen before. There is a large number of photographs and newspaper clippings connected by crisscrossing red strings. I lean forward, squinting to read the words. There was a two-headed baby cow born at the Thompson farm. Its misshapen face stares out from a grainy photograph. There were power outages that left whole streets dark. So many crops have withered in their fields like they have been touched by something evil.

But it is the obituaries that make my throat close up. They are all over the wall, forming a grim border around the edges of this tragic collage that Miles has obviously put together. Each face stares out at me with a serious expression or a gentle smile. I recognize some of them. There is Mrs. Richardson, who used to own the peculiarities shop, and who kept an entire collection of ceramic cats lined up in her shop windowsill. And Mr. Alva, a kind old man who was one of the few people to still wave at me, who always had on a different colored bow tie that he changed every single day. Their eyes follow me. All of them. I can hardly breathe, and I am grateful for my chair because it keeps me from crumpling to the floor.

"Can't you astral project from the bathtub like you did before?" Shiloh asks, her voice drawing my attention back to her face.

"I could," I say, "although the last time I did that, it nearly killed me, so I do not see the purpose." She opens her mouth to argue, but I lift my trembling hand to stop her. "I have already decided. Dying is the only way I can save everybody."

And be with Evangeline.

Shaking her head, Shiloh buries her face in her hands. I wish I could go over and lay a hand on her shoulder, but my hands are trembling so much that I do not trust them to guide my chair. She should not be upset about this. I never belonged here and quite frankly, it is a miracle I have been able to survive so long inside this body at all. There was no world in which I could have survived much longer than I already have, and even now it feels as though pieces of my body are already dying slowly, with death circling around me like a patient vulture. But I must die tonight if that is what gives us a chance of stopping more people from ending up on that wall.

"There has to be a loophole," Jonah jumps in. "Can you die in a way you can come back from?"

"I am not sure that I understand."

"You know," he says, although I do not. "Leonard used to bring himself back to life all the time. Could you do that, but come back in your own body? Or another one. One that works better, like Miles did." Jonah forces a grin.

I suppose I *could* come back inside of my own body. But if I did that, I could not go to Evangeline.

"It would be like what happened to me," Jonah says. "I was dead, but then I came back."

Shiloh gives him a sad look. "You coming back to life was a miracle. You want to risk Francesca's life for the possibility of another one?"

"There are different ways to die." Jonah does not look at her. "I knew this guy once who OD'd on oxy. His heart stopped and everything. But then the cops came in and shot some NARCAN up his nose and boom." He snaps his fingers. "The guy's back in the room."

"That's not how NARCAN works," Shiloh says. "You can't use NARCAN on someone who's already dead."

Jonah's face tightens. "Says who?"

"Uh, my dad." Shiloh tightens her arms around herself. "The cops all carry it."

"Can we use NARCAN and CPR?" Jonah pushes back. "You know, to keep the heart pumping?"

"Are you actually insane?" Shiloh's voice rises. "You want to kill Francesca and *hope* we can bring her back? *That's* your brilliant plan?"

Miles sinks deeper into his chair as though he can pretend he is not here. A chill trickles down my spine like a drop of freezing rain.

"What if it doesn't work?" Shiloh continues. "What if the CPR fails and you can't bring her back or—"

"At least it's a plan," Jonah snaps. "What's your brilliant solution? Let more people die? Let Max die?"

The blood drains from Shiloh's face. I resist the urge to cover my ears and bury my face in my lap.

"So we murder Francesca instead?" Shiloh asks. "That's so much better?"

"It's not murder if—"

"If what? If we wish hard enough that she comes back? That's *insane*."

Jonah throws his hands up. "At least I'm not shooting down every idea without offering anything better!"

"Please stop fighting," I tell them, and they both whip their heads around to me, seeming to realize how loud they had been yelling at each other. Shiloh's face reddens.

"Sorry," she says, glancing at Jonah, who is staring at his shoes. "But there has to be another way."

I clasp my hands together, looking at each of my friends' serious faces as they try to come up with an idea to do this differently, in a way that keeps me alive, but there is none. I have made up my mind. I know my abilities, I know the extent of them (at least as well as I can know such a thing), and I have interacted with the other side enough to know with certainty that this is my only chance of succeeding at this. Then afterward, once it is done, I can go find Evangeline and she can introduce me to all of her friends on the other side that I have heard so many stories about.

Miles sits up in his chair so quickly that I would be surprised if he did not pull a muscle in his back.

"That guy," he says. "What was his name?"

A couple of seconds go by before I process what he said. "Who?"

"Fiona's friend," he says. "The one who was h-housesitting, who L-Leonard kept ..." He pauses, then clears his throat. "The guy with the red hair who Leonard kept prisoner. Remember?"

He waves his hand over his head, although I am not sure why. All of us know what hair is.

But then I remember who he is talking about, and it is my turn to sit straighter in my chair. The memory of the house fire rushes back to me. I found the man tied up in the basement after Shiloh untied me. I suddenly realize where Miles is going with this, and I do not like it one bit.

"Fiona said he was researching something," Miles says. "That's why Leonard kept him prisoner instead of, you know, doing what he normally did to people. Whatever this guy knew had to be important enough for Leonard to keep him breathing, right?"

The man had orange hair. He was locked in that enormous cage, his face pale and his limbs weak as he gripped the bars. Evangeline picked the lock. She is so clever. I try extremely hard to remember what he called the topic he researched for a couple of seconds before the word rushes to me.

"Rebirth," I say. "He called it rebirth."

Miles points at me like that is what he had been thinking about. "Did he tell you what it was about?"

I shake my head, but Miles is correct about one thing. Whatever rebirth is, it was important enough to Leonard that he kept him alive instead of using him as a host body for another one of his friends, especially when all Leonard was trying to do at that time was bring his friends back from the other side.

Shiloh turns toward Jonah but does not look at him as she points at his phone. "Do you think Fiona would have his number?"

Jonah dials a number and puts his phone on speaker, holding it out between all of us. The ringing sounds impossibly loud in the quiet room. I raise my eyes to the clock mounted on the wall. The hands point accusingly at the late hour. Any normal person would be sleeping right now, although I am not sure I would consider Fiona a normal person.

The ringing stops. On the other end of the line, there is some muffled rustling.

"Jonah?" a hoarse woman's voice answers. "Jonah, if this isn't life or death, I swear to God, I'm going to drive over to that little hick town of yours and slap you in your pretty little face."

"It is," Jonah says. "Life or death, I mean. What's the name of that friend you had housesitting the Soothsayer's place?"

The line is silent. A loud scratching sound comes over the microphone and makes me want to cover my ears.

"Are you talking about Colin?"

"Yes," Jonah says. "Colin. We need to talk to Colin."

Fiona lets out a high-pitched yawn that sounds nearly operatic. "I'll text you his phone number, but don't call him unless it's an emergency. He's a deep sleeper, and he might not be as nice about being woken up in the middle of the night as I am."

Shiloh taps Jonah's shoulder with two gentle pokes. Her eyebrows go upward as though she is trying to tell him something without words. Understanding blooms across his face.

"Can you send me his address?" Jonah asks.

There is a prolonged pause. "Is everything okay?"

Jonah nods, even though she cannot see him. "It's fine."

"Colin is ... he's not wired like normal people," Fiona says. "Do you need Phil and me to come down there?"

"No," Jonah says, far too quickly for it to sound credible. "But will you keep your ringer on in case?"

Jonah ends the call before she can reply. He tries calling Colin, but I can tell from his frown when it goes to voicemail that we will not have any luck reaching Colin through the phone. The blue glow from his GPS map casts strange shadows across his face, making him look like one of the marble angels in the cemetery when the moon hits them just right.

"The guy lives in Utica. Half an hour away." Jonah looks up at me, and I can see the question on his lips before he asks it. "You want to go talk to him?"

My stomach does a funny flip-flop, like when you miss the last step going downstairs. I would prefer to keep this simple and have one of them kill me, but I suppose I had not thought about the methods yet. I do not want them to strangle me. That sounds unpleasant. Drowning in the bathtub would be even less good. We do not have poison, at least none that I can think of, and I do not particularly want a death that involves blood or stabbing. I could try astral projecting in the bathtub and hope I do not wake up. Judging by the look on Shiloh's face, I am quite aware that none of them will volunteer to kill me, or even hold my head underwater. This may be the only way I can get them to agree to let me go.

I suppose it should feel nice that none of them are happy to send me across the veil in order to save the town. Perhaps I should not have been so hard on them. They may have become my friends because of what I could do, but they care about me more than that now.

I sigh, and then nod. "Leonard chose to keep this man alive, which means he knows something quite important, I think, because he truly enjoyed killing people."

A glimmer of pain flashes across Jonah's face. But it is gone in a second.

"Okay." He stands up and claps Miles on the shoulder. "So, buddy, you driving, or should I?"

20

Shiloh

I double-check the apartment number on the buzzer panel, keeping my eyes fixed on the numbers so I don't have to look at Jonah. "You sure this is the place?"

"Apartment 3B." He purses his lips. "Yep."

Great. I tug on the drawstring of my hoodie as a gust of wind blows gritty bits of snow against the glass doors behind us, making them rattle. The apartment building is a dingy brick structure with a small vestibule that we are all standing in right now. The security light above the entrance shines on the dirty carpet.

I find the buzzer for apartment 3B, hyper-aware of Jonah standing behind me and how I'm turning my back on him. I shouldn't be so defensive. I know he won't do anything to me now. He lost it before because it was a period of high stress, but hey, I didn't think he'd lose it on me then either, so who am I to tell?

I jam my finger into Colin's buzzer. Longer than necessary.

No answer. I press it again and again because if he's as deep a sleeper as Fiona said, I need to make some noise, but still nothing. Jonah calls him again. The guy doesn't pick up, but it's ass-o'clock in the morning, so he has to be home.

I'm not in the business of breaking into people's houses anymore unless absolutely necessary since I'm not interested in getting pepper-sprayed in the face or, God forbid, arrested again, but I will if this guy doesn't answer his buzzer. I don't know how to break into an apartment building, but I'm sure I can figure something out.

I give it one more buzz, trying to ignore how Jonah winces when he rubs the back of his neck because he doesn't have his sling anymore.

A crackly voice comes through the speaker. "Hello? Who's there?"

Oh my God. I'd thank my lucky stars, but I'm not convinced I have any with all the crap that's happened to me. I press my mouth close to the intercom.

"Hi, Colin," I say. "My name is Shiloh, and I'm here with my three friends. Fiona gave us your address. Can you buzz us in?"

There's a long pause. I guess he has a right to be suspicious of random people at his door after what happened with Leonard.

"Do you know what time it is?" A long pause. "How do I know you are who you say you are?"

"Uh ..." I guess there's no way to prove anything to him, at least not through a buzzer like this. "My friends and I need to ask you about your research."

"My re—"

"We have a ghost problem," Jonah's voice cuts in as he leans toward the speaker over my shoulder. I steal a look at him. Our eyes meet. He steps away from me, and my stomach drops because that's not what I was telling him to do. "We need to figure out how to get rid of them without, you know, any more people dying, so can you let us in or what?"

"Fiona sent you? Because of ghosts?"

"Yes," I assure him. "Fiona sent us."

I hear a sigh. A couple of seconds go by before a buzzer sounds, releasing the front door lock, and I lead the group inside. We file into the building and head for the elevator, which creaks and rattles its way up to the third floor. The hallway is dimly lit with worn carpeting and a distinct smell of old cooking and cleaning products.

When we reach 3B, a short ginger-haired man is standing in the open doorway, wearing a green fleece bathrobe tied around his waist and a pair of Ugg slippers. He points a can of mace at my face. I've never been maced in the face before, and I'm pretty sure it would suck, but at least getting maced would distract me from the hollow feeling in my stomach and all the ways my brain keeps coming back to Jonah.

Colin eyes us before demanding that we show him proof of Fiona sending us here, so Jonah pulls up his call history, which calms him down enough to lower the mace. Miles pushes Francesca over the lip of the door and she lets out a yelp from the bounce. Colin's apartment is surprisingly warm. I guess being outside of Bethany means there's less ghost activity around here. I unzip my jacket, exposing my sweatshirt underneath.

Colin looks right and left down the hallway before closing the door behind us and sliding a bolt into place. "You want to know about my research?"

"Yes," I say.

"Why?"

I don't know how to answer that question because what if we're wrong about what he's researching, and I tell him what we need to use it for, and he gets freaked out and calls the police? What if the reason Leonard kept him alive is that, I don't know, he gives good back massages or something?

I figure honesty is the best way to go. "Because a ghost is eating my brother, and I have a feeling something you know could help us save his life."

Colin presses his lips together, but eventually, he offers me a jerky nod.

"I'm going to kill Fiona," he says. "Consider her a dead woman. Take off your shoes. I don't want all the dirt from outside in here."

He turns and scampers deeper into the apartment. The bathrobe is too long for him and flaps around his ankles. I stare after him, blinking because he said that with a completely straight face and usually I'd think anyone who says something like that is kidding, but he didn't sound like he was kidding.

I guess this is my cue to go after him, so I yank my boots off and then follow where he went. The floorboards are slippery under my socks. They are so shiny. I bet I could see the reflection of my legs in them if it looked. Colin flips on light switches as we move through his apartment, and I squint at walls that might've been cheerful yellow once upon a time but have since faded to the color of rancid butter, pockmarked with nail holes like he couldn't commit to hanging pictures in any location for too long. The hallway is so narrow my shoulders almost brush both walls. I'm surprised Miles can fit through it at all. He has to walk through at sort of an angle, being careful that the hubs of Francesca's wheelchair don't leave a line on the walls.

The place is freakishly clean, unlike my house, which is gathering cobwebs since I'm the one responsible for cleaning these days now that Mom can barely get out of bed. I peek into the laundry room, which looks more like a hospital operating room with cleaning supplies arranged in a metal rolling caddy, and then into what has to be Colin's bedroom with its unmade rumpled bed. A glass of water sits on his nightstand, perfectly centered on a coaster, while a white noise machine hums away like it's trying to drown out any busy thoughts. I'm glad it wasn't turned up higher or he never would have heard us. The whole place smells like lemon cleaning products and something else that doesn't belong in a house as clean as this one. I hate to say it, but maybe pee?

He stops in front of a door at the end of the hallway.

"Do not touch anything," he says. "I mean it. I don't want any of your greasy finger marks on anything."

I'm scared of what's going to be behind that door. He looks at each one of us for confirmation that we heard him, and then opens the door and flips on the light.

I gag and slap a hand over my nose. So this is where the pee smell comes from. I step inside, blinking as my eyes adjust to ... well, all of it. The room is barely bigger than my room at home, but Colin has transformed every inch into what I can only describe as a mad scientist's wet dream of a lab if that scientist had OCD and access to a label maker. Everything, and I mean everything, sits at perfect right angles, like someone went through the whole room with a ruler. Books line the shelves. Some textbooks, and others ancient and leather-bound. A mini-fridge hums in the corner, topped by a collection of orange pill bottles. The labels all face forward. There's a bare mattress on the floor. Which is weird because Colin's actual room is right across the hall. On a table next to it is a desktop computer and a boring white Coleman cooler.

Something squeaks behind me. I jump, whirling around to find a cage with four white mice staring at me with beady red eyes.

"This is where I conduct my research," Colin says through a yawn that seems to take over his whole face. "I apologize. You caught me at a completely unacceptable time to come to someone's home."

Francesca grips her wheelchair's armrests. "What precisely is it that you research?"

Colin's face lights up like he's been waiting for years for someone to talk to about it. He's suddenly super different from the mace-wielding guy from a couple of minutes ago.

"So after my first ghost encounter when I was six," he says, "which is a total horror story I'm not going to get into right now, I became fixated on what exactly a ghost is and how one comes to exist."

He reaches into the cage and plucks out one of the mice. The creature squirms as he carries it over to the plastic table in the middle of the room, its pink tail whipping back and forth.

"I found out that if you can trick your body into thinking you're dead, it will release your soul," Colin says, "but the real challenge was figuring out how to bring that soul back into its body once that connection is severed."

He opens the fridge. Cold air swirls into the room as he takes out a tray of vials. He returns to the table and grabs a pair of brass goggles that look like they belong in some mechanic's room, fastening them onto his head.

"As far as this side is concerned, if your heart stops, you're dead," Colin says, latex gloves making a sharp snapping sound as he pulls them over his thin fingers. He grabs a sterile needle package from a basket on the cooler. It crinkles as he peels it back, removes the needle and holds it up to the light. "Which explains why your soul can leave your body if you're in a coma, and why sometimes it does not come back even after you are resuscitated."

"But not everyone who falls into a coma has their heart stop," Miles says. "People go into comas for all different kinds of reasons."

"Sure," Colin admits, his brass goggles catching the light as he nods. "I'm using that as an example. But I know for a fact that when someone's heart stops, their soul disconnects, and in my research, I've found a way to do this in a controlled way. I call the process death walking. Catchy, isn't it?"

He's acting like he's talking to an audience. I wonder if he's practiced this, like some kind of magic show.

The needle punctures the rubber stopper of the vial. He pulls red liquid into it which looks thick and syrupy, almost like cough medicine but darker. The mouse's tiny claws scratch against Colin's palm as it struggles, its whiskers twitching. Francesca's fingers tremble as she peers through them. I catch the slight green tinge on her face. She shouldn't have to see this.

I step forward. "Is killing the mouse necessary?"

"You said you wanted to hear about my research, and you kids aren't going to trust a word that comes out of my mouth without seeing it done," Colin says, his voice taking on an almost sing-song quality. "I wouldn't trust me unless I saw it for myself either, but don't worry. The little guy will be fine." He smiles, revealing a row of even white teeth that look like they've been cleaned, scrubbed, and flossed to within an inch of their lives.

The mouse lets out a series of tiny squeaks. Colin's fingers pinch its loose skin. The needle slides in with a smoothness that makes me want to gag. The mouse's pink tail whips through the air as it struggles. Colin is humming a tune I don't recognize.

Miles steps up until he's standing right next to me, his shoulder brushing mine, and I breathe a little easier, feeling him there. "How long does this take?"

"I developed these drugs myself," Colin says, practically vibrating with excitement. Sweat beads on his forehead over the goggles, making his pale skin look waxy. "Each compound has been tested upwards of fifty times, and every single time they functioned as intended."

"On mice?" Miles asks.

Colin nods. "The speed of onset varies with body mass. My research with the mice provided extensive data on the correlation between the two variables, and based on those calculations, I expect the effects should manifest right about ... now."

The mouse seizes. Its ribcage convulses for a couple of seconds, paws twitching against Colin's latex-covered palm before it falls still, its whiskers drooping.

Colin holds up the mouse's limp body by the tail for us to see, the yellow lights casting a sickly pallor over its white fur.

I can barely find the words. "Is it dead?"

"Sure is," Colin says. "But it won't be for long."

What is that supposed to mean? Colin prepares a second syringe, drawing bright, almost neon-green liquid from another vial. The fluid glows like toxic waste in a cartoon I'd watch with Max. Colin looks like a supervillain from the same cartoon, his ginger hair sticking up and the goggles magnifying his eyes. He should be dressed in a white lab coat, rather than a bathrobe and slippers. I wince as the needle pierces the mouse's skin, and the liquid disappears inside its small body. The mouse lies there. Completely still.

Its tail hangs between Colin's fingers like a piece of pink string.

"Let me be absolutely clear about this process," Colin says, with not even a shred of empathy in his voice. "The red drug stops the heart, which allows the soul to disconnect, but then the second drug restarts the heart and allows it to maintain enough cardiac function to preserve the body. Not enough for consciousness, mind you. Just to sustain the body long enough to prevent tissue death while the soul is ... elsewhere. Because the body is in a vegetative state, it must be kept cold, as this will help slow the metabolic processes and prevent irreversible brain damage during the soul's excursion."

I wrap my arms around myself. Colin puts the mouse inside the cooler and opens the freezer with his foot, dumping a handful of ice over the poor animal's body. The cubes clatter against each other like bones, partially burying the mouse until only its tail sticks out. I'm sorry. I know he said it wasn't, but that mouse looks super dead to me.

Colin readjusts his goggles with trembling fingers, peering around the room with jerky movements that remind me of those wind-up toys that bounce off walls. "One of the ways humans differ from animal subjects is in their soul behavior patterns. Animal souls make an immediate dash for the other side. You have to be quick to catch them. But humans possess more agency in the matter."

His magnified eyes dart around the room. His head jerks left. Then up.

"There!" He points at a spot on the wall, then struggles for a couple of seconds to get the goggles off his face. "See?"

I do my best to squeeze the sweaty headset over my face, the elastic band catching in my hair. The leather padding leaves damp spots against my temples, and I try not to gag at the smell of body odor mixed with that chemical rubber smell that clogs my nose. The goggles are surprisingly heavy and warp the room, casting it in a dull sepia tone that's not unlike the lenses of the glasses we have. I wonder how many of these things are out there. He must have also taken this pair from the Soothsayer. He would have known her if he's friends with Fiona.

He extends a finger to the wall and shuffles over to where he's pointing. I creep after him, my sock-covered feet sliding on the polished floor, my hands hovering at my sides like a tightrope walker. One wrong step and I'll either face-plant the gleaming floor or, worse, fall on top of something important. God forbid I get finger marks on any of his things. Given how he nearly maced us at the door, I don't want to find out what happens when someone messes up his lab.

In the corner of my eye, I catch a flash of movement. I whip my head around to see a transparent mouse scurrying through the air. It runs above the floorboards, its tail streaming behind it like cigarette smoke caught in the wind.

Colin asks me where it is. I point at it, and he swoops down with surprising agility for someone in a bathrobe, trapping the spirit under a glass dome that looks like it belongs over a fancy dessert. The mouse throws itself against the barrier, its ghostly form rippling with each impact. Part of me is surprised that animals have souls, but then I remember that they did from the stories about Leonard's sideshow act. He killed animals and then reanimated them by putting their souls back.

Jonah asks to use the goggles. Our fingers brush when I hand them to him. I cross my arms tight across my chest and turn back to Colin, who's still bouncing on his toes like an excited puppy. At least someone in this room is having a good time.

"So," I say. "It looks to me like you just killed a mouse."

Colin holds up a finger and slides the glass dome across the floor until it's directly under the cooler, then draws blue liquid from another one of the vials.

"You need to make sure the soul is close to its body when you do this," Colin says. "The ghost has to be ready to go back—which, for animals, is easier than humans because they don't overthink things like we do."

Jonah hands me the goggles back, and I step closer to look at the limp creature buried in the ice cubes. Colin's hands move with practiced precision as he guides the needle into the mouse's body. Inside the glass dome, the transparent ghost-mouse flickers a couple of times and then vanishes. The real mouse's body jerks. Its pink feet kick out and a high-pitched squeak pierces the air. Its sides heave with rapid breaths as it tries to get out of the cooler. Colin sets it back into its cage with its mouse buddies. I press my face close to the bars to look for any signs that something is wrong with it. The mouse sniffs the air. Scratches behind its ear with a back foot. Grooms its face with its tiny paws.

Colin clears his throat behind me. "Does that answer your question?"

What a completely insane thing to say. "So the red drug stops the heart, the green drug keeps the body alive, and the blue drug brings the soul back?"

"Red stops the heart. Green gives it a restart, and blue keeps everything true. Simple."

I would hardly call this simple. "What's in those vials?"

"A combination of things," Colin says, his fingers tapping against the table. "I developed each drug myself. They all work as intended. None of this is exactly FDA-approved, of course, but can you imagine the possibilities?"

Sure, it works now, but how many tiny bodies did this

budget Dr. Frankenstein go through before getting it right? How many times did he watch those mice convulse and die for real? There has to be something seriously wrong with this guy for him to think it's okay to do this to another living thing. No normal person gets this thrilled about killing things, even if they do bring them back.

I suddenly want to get out of his apartment, to get as far away from the smell of pee and the sound of scratching from the mouse cage as I can.

Francesca removes her hands from her eyes. "Did you show this to Leonard?"

Colin smiles in a way that looks more like baring teeth. "I did it to him."

Francesca gapes at him. I do, too.

"You have done this to *people*?" she asks.

"Oh yes, quite a few, actually. All willing participants. Not Fiona, though. Still haven't managed to convince her. The procedure worked exactly as intended, but Leonard ... well, he could disconnect from his body just fine, but he wanted access to the other side and I couldn't help him with that part. You can trick your body into thinking you're dead in this world, but there's no tricking the other side. Only truly dead people can cross through those gates. He got pretty upset about that."

I can only imagine. A warm sensation rushes through my neck and spreads across my face, making my skin feel sticky with sweat under my hoodie. I rub the back of my neck, my fingers catching on the damp hair there, and turn around to look at Colin, giving him a close-lipped smile that feels more like a grimace.

"Can I have a second to talk to my friends alone?" I ask him.

Colin nods. I guess he's not going to let us stand in here

unsupervised in case we touch anything we're not supposed to or accidentally disorganize his system, so he ushers us out into the hallway and stays inside to clean up, humming the same tune as before through the closed door. The hallway lights are dimmer than his lab, cloaking all of our faces in half-shadows that make everyone look like badly drawn versions of themselves. I lean my back against the wall and cross my arms over my chest. Jonah leans on the wall across from me, searching my face. He knows something is up. Miles looks like he's going to throw up, his face taking on that greenish tinge I recognize. Only Francesca is looking at me like she knows where I'm about to go with this. She gives me a tiny nod, the wheels of her chair squeaking slightly as she adjusts her position.

I come right out and say it.

"This is the answer to our problem," I say. "Francesca can death-walk and send the ghosts back through. She won't be in her body, so she can use her powers."

Miles gapes at me. I swear it's like I told him I'm going to juggle live grenades or something, which come to think of it, probably isn't as risky as this plan. "Have you lost your mind?"

"Probably." I focus on moving air in and out of my lungs. "But what other choice do we have?"

"This is so risky." Miles strains to keep his voice down. "This is so beyond risky. And why Francesca? Colin says he's done it to other people. One of us could go. Someone stronger."

"Because I am the only one who has abilities," Francesca answers. "I can open a passage with my mind and send the souls back through it. None of you can do what I can." She says the words with an air of finality, and I know in my heart that she's right, but I wish to hell and back that she wasn't.

"Miles," I say, "I know it's risky, but the guy showed us that it works."

"Yes." Miles nods. "On *mice*."

"He's done it on people."

"Do you realize what that asshole just did?" Jonah cuts in. "That trick with the animals is exactly what Leonard used to do."

He stares only at me when he says it, like he wants me to hear his words.

"I'm not saying he's a good person—"

He shakes his head, pointing at the closed door. "Shiloh. That guy is the next Leonard."

No, he's not. "He's not mixing and matching souls."

"That guy is unstable," Jonah hisses. "He tortured that mouse like it was nothing. Do you think he's above mixing and matching bodies?"

"I think he's our best shot."

His eyes darken. "You want to shoot Francesca up with random drugs this guy cooked up doing illegal experiments in his spare bedroom, throw her body in a cooler, and what, hope she comes back?"

"Not just Francesca." I brace myself for his reaction. "I'm going with her."

21

Shiloh

"No," Jonah snaps, and I almost start crying again. "Not happening."

"She's not going alone," I say. "This will be dangerous, and she needs backup."

"So I'll go with her," he says. "It's not like I was planning to do much with my life, anyway."

It's my turn to gape at him. Less than two hours ago, he was trying to strangle me, and even with the foolery threatening to turn his brain into murder soup at any second, his first instinct is still to protect me. I wrap my arms around my stomach, trying to hold myself together because it suddenly feels like I might throw up.

"No."

"Are you actually insane?" Jonah hisses at me. "Do you think there's any possible way I'd let you do this?"

He can't let me do anything. It's my decision. And how exactly was he planning to stop me, anyway?

Oh God. I need to stop looking at him, because it's making me feel like some kind of monster. I end things with him, and then I volunteer to die right in front of him and ask him to help kill me? I know him well enough to see by his face that he's barely holding himself together as it is, and me doing this on top of everything else is too much. But I have to do this. I *have* to.

"I'm the one who asked you guys to help me save Max," I say, side-eyeing Miles, who's staring at me with no emotion on his face. "I was the one who asked you all to save him last time, so I'm not letting any of you go instead of me."

"Why do you have to go at all?" Jonah demands. His voice hits me like a physical thing. How can he still sound so protective after everything?

"To help Francesca."

"By doing what?" His voice gets louder. "You can't do anything as a ghost. Only Francesca has powers."

He's right, but still. "She's not going alone."

"This is a bad idea."

"Every plan we've ever made has been a bad idea!" I yell, and the humming coming from the lab stops. Red rushes into Jonah's face. I've never seen him this mad. Not even when the foolery had him. But I keep talking anyway. "Because that's what we do. We go all in on bad plans and hope we make it out alive. I dragged all of you into this, and now even people I don't know who had nothing to do with ghosts have lost everything, all because I wanted to save my brother." I pause, catching my breath. "I started this. I'm so sorry for everything I did. But now Francesca has offered to use her powers to send the ghosts back through. She can't be in her body to do that, and I, for one, am not interested in killing her, so this is our only option, and I'm not letting her do it on her own."

Jonah slams his palm against the wall and my heart jumps. "God damn it, Shiloh!"

"What would you rather I did?" I snap. "Make Francesca go alone? Have Miles go and leave me here with you so you can go all *Here's Johnny* on my ass?"

The second the words leave my mouth, I want to grab them back. The look on Jonah's face makes me want to throw up.

"Shiloh ..." His voice breaks on my name, and so does something inside me.

I blink away the tears that are pooling against my eyelids. Miles glances between us. He knows something is wrong. It's not like Jonah and I are being all that subtle about it, but Miles is both awkward and emotionally mature enough that there's no way he's going to ask.

I square my shoulders, shoving all the bad feelings down as hard as I can. I'm good at that. I've had practice.

"I need to do this," I tell Jonah. "So I'm going to do it."

"But—"

"Both of you stop arguing!"

I whip my head around to find Francesca glaring at us from where her chair is. Her hands are clamped over her ears so tight it almost looks like she wants to rip them off.

"Please stop talking about me as if I am not here," she adds.

Crap. She's right. This isn't a conversation I need to be having with Jonah. It's one I need to be having with her.

"I'm sorry," I say, and she lowers her hands. The sound of everyone breathing feels too loud in this cramped space.

Francesca rests her hands on her lap. She knows as well as I do that trying this is safer than dying, but I guess logically anything is safer than dying.

I understand why she's hesitating. She doesn't have to do this. It's a big ask, especially because it's for my brother, and she doesn't owe me anything given how many times she has saved all of our lives before, and this is another one on our long list of terrible plans. But if I had to make the choice, if I were in a position where I could trade her life for Max ... I don't even want to think about what I'd do in that position because I'm not.

I don't think I'm a good person. What I'm asking of her right now is not something a good person would ask—she'd never ask me to do this for her—but I do know one thing. I need to keep Max safe. That's my job. Protecting Max is all I've ever known how to do. It's who I am, and I need to hold on to that or else the world will get too scary and confusing and hard. I can live with being a bad friend. I can live with being a disappointing girlfriend, but I can't live in a world where I let Max die and didn't do everything in my power to stop that from happening, no matter what it took. And if that makes me bad ... well, that's all I know how to be.

I rest a hand on Francesca's shoulder, feeling how hard she's shaking. My throat feels like I've been gargling sandpaper as I force the words out:

"You don't have to do this," I say. "I'm not doing that thing where I pretend to be giving you a choice so that I can actually guilt you into it. I mean it. This is going to be dangerous, and if anything goes wrong ..." I swallow hard. "What do you want to do?"

Something unreadable flashes across her face, making the shadows under her eyes look deeper. "I would rather you killed me."

Well, that's not what I was expecting her to say. "*Why?*"

She focuses on the floorboards, but says nothing. I shake

my head, unable to wrap my mind around what she's saying. Is it because she's worried about me that she doesn't want me to come?

"I'm not killing you," I say. "I don't think any of us would, so that's off the table. I was the one who got you all into this mess, so I need to be the one to get us out of it."

Francesca's shoulders rise and fall with each careful breath. The hallway feels like it's closing in on us, barely wide enough for the four of us to stand without bumping elbows. Almost a minute goes by before she finally looks at me.

"All right," she says. "If Colin agrees to help us, I will go, and you can come with me."

Oh thank God, is my first reaction, because apparently I'm a horrible person. I hate the idea that I'm putting her in danger, but I equally hate knowing that Max is in danger. I wish that, for once, none of us would be in danger all the fucking time. Something burns behind my eyes, and I press my palms into them to wipe away the tears before they build.

"Thank you," I say. "Seriously."

She holds up a hand. Then nods.

"Wait," Miles says, speaking up for the first time in this whole conversation. "Wouldn't the other side … I mean, Ella Ruggles said the other side pulls the weak souls through. What if it pulls you through, too?"

Crap. I didn't think of that. Except wait, no—that's not what would happen.

"Colin said that Leonard tried to get to the other side when he was death walking, but he couldn't," I say. "No gate would open for him because he wasn't dead. Only real ghosts can go, and we won't be ghosts because our bodies will still be alive."

Miles grits his teeth so hard his jaw twitches. But he knows I'm right.

"See?" I say. "This is our only option. At least the only one we can do tonight, and we have to end this tonight, or—"

Max is going to die.

I might have scared that ghost off, but it'll come back, and Mom will sit there doing nothing. I get a horrifying realization. If that ghost goes inside of Max like the ghosts at the nursing home did, he will kill Mom like some real-life version of Chuckie. The ghost will be inside him, making him do it. I wonder if he'd be conscious of what he was doing. There's not enough therapy in the world to help him wrap his head around what would happen to him. I press my palm flat against the wall to steady myself, feeling the rough texture of the old paint under my fingers.

Jonah is grinding his teeth, deep creases stretching across his forehead. I know he hates this. I know exactly why, and I understand, and I also know he understands why I need to be the one to do this.

"You and Miles can help Colin manage all the drugs," I say.

Jonah says nothing. Miles makes a strangled sound.

"Where are you going to find a cooler big enough for a human body?" Miles almost squeaks.

Outside, through the grimy window at the end of the hall, a flurry of snow falls across the glass, probably blown off a tree or something and spiraling to the ground. I hope it's not snowing again. But something tells me cold will not be our problem.

"We'll figure something out," I say. "But that's what we're doing. It's settled. Girls versus boys."

I try to make it sound casual, like we're picking teams for dodgeball instead of planning what's basically temporary suicide, but my voice shakes enough to give me away. Before Jonah or Miles can say anything else, I barge back into Colin's lab. The pee smell hits my nose as I enter. I'm grateful Max never asked me for a guinea pig or hamster or any pet like that if this is how they smell.

Colin is still hunched over the mouse cage, and he actually flinches when the door opens like he forgot we were ten feet away in the hallway.

"You said you've done this to people before," I say, pointing at the cooler. "So what do I need to do to convince you to do it to me and my friend?"

Colin thinks it's a bad idea. He doesn't want anything to do with it, and he refuses to come with us to Bethany to manage the process himself. I was hoping he'd manage everything here, where he could keep control of everything under what he would define as laboratory conditions, but he says he'd have trouble keeping us cold on such short notice and our souls would have too far to travel to get all the way back to Bethany.

"You can only death-walk for a couple of hours before it becomes dangerous," he says. "Given what you're telling me, you don't want to waste any of that time traveling."

He agrees to give us the drugs for free because we're friends with Fiona. Miles types furiously on his phone as Colin rattles off instructions. As he measures out doses, he looks at me as if he's trying to figure out how much I weigh, and I suddenly realize that's exactly what he's doing. I try to press down the nausea that's rising up through me, the smell of animal pee and chemical disinfectant not helping the pizza in my stomach to settle.

The rickety plastic table wobbles as Colin counts different

vials and places them in the tiny cooler where the mouse was twitching around ten minutes ago. The glass containers clink against each other. Still, watching him do this is somehow less nauseating than picturing Max sitting up in his bed coughing so hard that he turns red in the face. Or rolling his eyes up until the whites show and going to look for Mom.

This is going to be fine. It *has* to be fine.

It worked on the mice. I watched one come back to life in Colin's hands. He's done it to people before. Hell, he even did it to Leonard, and that asshole came back.

Besides, Miles is good at remembering instructions. He got straight-As in science and even has experience in administering non-FDA-approved drugs.

"The order of drugs is critical." Colin taps each vial three times before placing them in the cooler. The glass makes tiny pinging sounds against the plastic. "Remember, red stops the heart, green gives it a restart, and blue keeps everything true."

Keeps everything true? What the hell does that even mean?

"Dosage is calculated based on body mass," Colin continues. "Too much overwhelms the system. Too little renders the procedure ineffective." He pauses to readjust the vials with latex-gloved hands until they're perfectly aligned, then adds, "I included an extra set in case of emergency, although I must emphasize how essential it is to get this right the first time."

Colin takes an antiseptic wipe to the vials of liquid, and I realize with a pang that even though he's using latex gloves, he's wiping his fingerprints from the glass and from everything he's giving us. It hits me that he doesn't want to do the procedure here because he might wind up with two dead girls to get rid of, and he doesn't want to do it anywhere else for pretty much the same reason. He wants to stay snug and warm and in control right where he is and wake up in the morning and go on with his life like none of this ever happened and like we didn't exist. I can't tell if he's a genius or pure evil, but he finishes wiping down the vials and ushers us from his apartment with a cooler full of drugs, tapping his slipper like he's irritated at the time it's taking us to put our shoes back on.

No one says a word on the car ride back to Bethany. The heater blasts warm air that blows the chemical air freshener smell right in my face and, not for the first time tonight, I want to gag. I wrap my arms around my stomach and drum my foot against the grimy floor mat, going over everything that happened in my head.

After fifteen minutes, Miles breaks the silence. "I'd just like it acknowledged that of all the crazy, half-baked things we've ever done or even considered doing, this is the most insane of all."

That is saying something, considering our track record.

He pinches the bridge of his nose, exhaling a long breath. "But if we're going to do this, we need to find a place for your bodies."

Yes. I slump back into the passenger seat. "What did Colin say the place had to have?"

"Well, it has to be super private, because we don't want anyone to stumble across Jonah and me hanging out with two seemingly dead bodies." He lets out a short sigh that sounds more like a wheeze. "Any interruptions and you could die. And because apparently, this whole thing isn't complicated enough, we need two human-sized coolers. Why are we even considering this?"

A bone-cold feeling spreads through my veins. I can't think of a single place like that.

But Jonah can. "I know a place."

Just from his tone, I can tell it's not a place I want to go.

22

Shiloh

Before any of us go anywhere, I need to grab some stuff from my house.

Miles stops in the driveway. "You sure you're going to be okay getting there alone?"

I nod. "Go get the electromagnet. It'll be faster if I meet you in town."

"You want me to come with you?" Jonah asks from the back seat, his voice carefully neutral.

He shouldn't be making that kind of offer, but I'd be lying if I said I didn't want him to come. Having him by my side has always made everything less scary. I want things to be less scary right now, but he can't come with me.

"I'm good."

I wave to Francesca, purposely not looking at Jonah as I zip my coat up to my chin and step out of the car. The wind howls in my ears, blowing stinging gusts of snow into my face, and I tuck my nose into my neckline as I trudge through the powder covering our front yard.

Unlocking the front door with trembling fingers, I push it open with my shoulder and quickly close it behind me, shutting out the wind. The familiar musty air of our house hits my nose. I may not be able to say exactly what it smells like, but it smells like home. Headlights flash against the window from the car as Miles backs out. I hope Mom's asleep. That way, I can get in and out without telling her where I've been. I feel bad not telling her anything because there's a good chance I won't see her again, but I have bigger things to worry about than filling her in when there's nothing she can do to help.

I peel off my jacket and kneel to untie my boots, the wet laces slipping through my frozen fingers. The wooden boards creak under my feet as I walk down the hallway. Of course they do. This house is old. I used to be grateful for it, because I always knew when Dad was coming, but now I wish the stupid things would shut up.

Max's door is open. I pause.

Will I wake him up if I peek my head inside?

I already know he's sick. Seeing him isn't going to tell me anything I don't already know, but there's this pull in my chest like a hook under my ribcage. I push the door open enough to see inside.

Oh God.

The chill cuts through my sweatshirt and raises goosebumps on my arms. It's cold enough in here to make my bones ache. Way too cold for a sick kid. I can picture the ghost hovering above Max. After we left, I'm sure it wasted no time in coming back. Max looks so small in his bed. His head lolls at an angle that makes my stomach flip. His chest rises and falls fast, like he's running from something in his dreams, but this isn't sleep. It's something else. Something worse.

Mom is sleeping in a chair by the door, covered in blankets. The ancient radiator clanks against the wall, but it's fighting a losing battle. I hold my breath and creep past her to Max, my socks silent on the floor.

He looks even worse up close. Sweat beads on his forehead. His breathing sounds wet and ragged, like there's something thick in his lungs, turning each inhale into a spluttering wheeze. I gently peel back the blanket and bite down on the inside of my cheek. The veiny gray rash has spread halfway up his arms, branching out like dead tree roots under his skin. His fingers twitch, making the bedsheets rustle softly, but I can't tell if it's because he's sleeping. I've nursed him through fevers before, but nothing like this. There are dark spots forming under his fingernails like bruises spreading under his skin.

I raise my eyes to the empty space above his bed. The hairs on my arms stand up. I swallow against the lump in my throat as I find Max's hand under the covers and wrap both of my own around it.

"Hey, buddy." I kneel on the ground next to him. "I'm sorry I left for longer than I said I would."

His hand feels so small in mine, burning yet somehow still cold. I press it to my chest. I hope he can feel me here.

"I'm not going to let you die. I'm going to protect you. Like I always have."

My thumb traces the rash. Something hot and all-consuming spreads through my chest. I'd trade places with him in a heartbeat if it meant that it would save him. I'd do anything. Give anything. Hell, I'd jam a carving knife into my throat this second if it meant the ghost would take me instead. The thought should scare me, but instead it fills me with a strange calm, because protecting Max is the only thing I've ever lived to do, and the only thing I have ever done well. I'm his shield against all the bad things in the world, and even when they get him, they can't hold on to him for long because I'm there to save him.

I don't care if death-walking kills me as long as it means he will continue being safe, but he needs me too much. That's what makes this so scary. I can't die, because I can't leave him with nobody but Mom, who can barely take care of herself, let alone be what he needs her to be.

I press a kiss to his forehead, the sickly sweet smell of fever clinging to his skin, then force myself to let go of his hand and stand up. I turn around and almost run right into Mom. She doesn't look happy.

"Where have you been?" Her voice is barely above a whisper, her breath sour with sleep. She's wearing the same pajamas she was wearing earlier. The same ones she has been wearing for days. Her hair falls in knotted clumps around her shoulders like straw. I try to move past her, but she's blocking the door, swaying like standing takes too much energy. "You've been gone for hours."

"I know." My chest tightens. "I'm sor—"

"Your brother ..." She hugs herself. "I thought about taking him to the emergency room, but I can't."

Of course she can't. She's too scared to leave the house. But as far as she's concerned, Max needs to go to the emergency room, and she can't get over herself for one second to do that one thing for her son?

I bite down on my tongue. I've been trying for months to get through to her, to get her out of bed, to at least keep her eating, but nothing reaches her. I used to get so mad at her. Yell and scream at her to leave Dad, to get out of bed, to stop crying, to stop doom-scrolling on her phone, to just wake up already, but she's not doing it on purpose. She can't help it. She's weak. She'll never be capable of protecting me, and she has spent so long without anybody to protect her that she doesn't even know how to protect herself. At least Dad is gone now, so I can do that for her. I may not like it, but it's no use getting mad at her for being exactly the person I know her to be.

So I force my voice to be as gentle as possible. "Don't worry, Mom. I'm handling it."

Her eyebrows pull together like she already forgot what we're talking about. "I think he needs electrolytes."

What he needs is for me to get rid of the ghost over his bed.

"How about you go sleep in your own bed, and I'll take over from here?"

"Your pictures. Cynthia Christensen sent them to me and I ..." She presses her hands to her face, shoulders curved inward like she's trying to make herself smaller. "I'm a terrible mother."

Oh God, I can't deal with this right now. Ashley's mom would have been all over that juicy piece of gossip. "You're not a bad mother."

"I am." She sniffles hard, wiping her nose with a trembling hand. "I'm scared, Shiloh. Is Max going to be all right?"

The pain in her voice makes my throat tight. I want to comfort her—I know how much she needs me to—but right now, the best thing she can do for Max is to stay out of the way.

"Max is going to be fine." I hold her shoulders and guide her toward the doorway. "If he's not better, I'll take him to the hospital in the morning, okay?"

A high-pitched whine emits from her throat. "I'm supposed to be the mother."

Well, I'm used to not having a mother, so I can handle myself without one.

"Go back to bed," I say. "I've got this."

She has barely taken two steps when a knock sounds on the door. I stop walking. So does she.

"Heidi?" Dad yells. "You in there?"

His voice is like a punch to the stomach. I can barely process it. This can't be real. I have to be hallucinating. I hear his voice in enough of my nightmares that my brain must be playing tricks on me. But one look at Mom's face tells me all I need to know.

No. Not *now*.

My knees tremble. Mom moves toward the door like she's in a trance. I grab her wrist. Too hard.

"What are you doing?" I hiss. "Don't open that."

My hand is trembling so bad that I can barely keep a grip on her wrist. Mom looks between me and the door, shifting her weight like she's actually considering letting him in. Is she serious right now?

"It's one o'clock in the morning," I manage through gritted teeth. "Why is he here at one o'clock in the morning?"

She won't meet my eyes. "He brought electrolytes."

The room tilts. I drop her wrist and my hand finds the wall, rough paint scraping against my palm.

"You *called* him?"

"He's your father. Your brother needs to stay hydrated, and I'm ... so afraid."

"Did you forget everything he did to you?" My voice sounds like it belongs to someone else. "Not just to you, but to *Max*?"

"He's not like that anymore," she says, and bile rises in my throat. It's not the first time Mom has said that to me. "He has done a course to manage his anger, and—"

"Is he sober?"

Mom grimaces. "He's not the same man he used to be."

Yes, he is. Oh my *God*.

I open my mouth, not even knowing where to begin because what the hell is she thinking?

Dad knocks again. Each rap sounds like he's about to break through the door. This is a cop's knock, the one they do before the door gets put in. The walls keep shrinking and the air feels too thick to breathe and he's right there, right outside, and Mom called him. She actually called him.

I open my mouth to tell her he is absolutely not coming inside our house when she runs past me and out of Max's room. The corners of my vision spot. How can it be that even after everything we've been through, things are the same as they always were and she still doesn't listen to me?

She's going to let him in. But I'm not letting him anywhere near Max.

I hear the door open. Wind howls through the gap, and heavy boots thud on the floorboards with a sound that is oh so familiar and puts the fear of life into me. Plastic bags crinkle.

"I bought everything on your list," Dad says, his voice sounding soft from down the hall. "I got Gatorade and the electrolyte stuff from the twenty-four-hour CVS in Mount Keenan. How's he doing?"

Mom mumbles something back, her voice small and mouse-like. My heart pounds so hard it feels like it's trying to break through my ribs. He's in our house. I'd just managed to convince myself that I'd never have to feel this trapped again, and now he's actually back in our house. Every cell in my body screams at me to run, but my feet won't move.

Footsteps approach. I step outside of Max's room and close the door, pressing my back against it.

Mom appears first. Dad follows her, his massive shoulders blocking the light from the window in the living room. My hands are shaking. I curl them into fists to hide it.

"Shiloh." Mom wipes her red-rimmed eyes, then gestures at Dad with a weak hand. "Your father would like to see Max."

I plant my feet wider, knees locked to stop them from buckling. I may not have gotten any taller since the last time I stood in front of him like this—he still has a few inches and a lot of width on me—but I'd also not killed anyone back then, and now I have. I've killed people bigger than him. Buried axes in their skulls and kicked them through banisters. Watched Leonard's brains slide down the wall of his trailer from when I shot him. So why does he still make me feel so small?

Dad is wearing gray sweatpants with a coffee stain above the knee and a Bethany Police zip-up sweatshirt that stretches tight across his shoulders, because it's the middle of the night, and he'd be psychotic if he was still wearing normal clothes in this weather. The bags under his eyes are puffy. Good. I hope he hasn't slept in days.

"Hey, Scooter-Girl." Dad gives me a nod. "I'm glad to see you."

I have to reach deep inside of me to find my voice. "Get out of my house."

I mean to sound strong, but my stupid voice trembles. Mom hisses my name. Dad's eyebrows lift. A deep laugh rolls out of him, and I catch a whiff of mint gum. I wonder if he's chewing it to mask the alcohol on his breath. He doesn't seem drunk. I don't smell any alcohol on him, and since my literal safety once relied on it I got pretty good at being able to tell.

"Your house?" He glances over his shoulder. "Last I checked, my name was still on the deed."

I say nothing. Dad sighs, running a hand over his buzzcut.

"I'm here because your brother is sick and your mother asked me to buy some things for him," he says.

Because she's a mess. Why the hell else would she do something like that?

He's taking advantage of her. He knows it. I know it. She doesn't, but she knows nothing about anything anymore. He has made sure of that, but then again, so have I. Gritting my teeth, I force my own guilt back. How hard would it be for me to get away if he tried anything right now?

Dad glances at Mom, who's hovering like a nervous ghost in her threadbare pajamas. "I didn't mean to barge in on you all like this," he says.

"Bullshit," I snap.

"*Shiloh.*" Mom puts her bony fingers on his forearm in a gesture of protection, looking even more fragile against his bulk. The gesture makes me want to hurl. "It's all right."

"I have it under control," I say, trying to stand taller.

Dad holds my eyes. I force my shoulders back so that I don't curl under his gaze. He may seem normal now, but I know how easy it is for this normal personality of his to disappear. He wasn't that bad most days, but it was the times when everything turned for no reason that made him scary. He usually changed when he was drinking, but it happened sometimes when he wasn't drinking too.

Has he seen the photos? I'd put money on it. I bet it's taking all he has to stop himself from ripping me a new one right now. I wonder if those photos will cost him his job. None of the cops seemed to care when the rumors were going around, but those people on Facebook seemed to care, and I doubt anyone will vote him back in after seeing proof like that. I wish Mom would understand that, instead of glaring at me with her red-rimmed eyes like she wants to slap me across the face.

Dad finally sighs and passes the plastic bag to Mom, the rustling sound unnaturally loud in the tense silence.

"Keep me updated," Dad tells Mom. "On Max."

Her thin brows wrinkle. "Ernest ..."

He holds up one calloused hand and turns back toward the front door, putting on his best hurt and defeated look. I sigh.

"Unbelievable," Mom hisses.

She drops the bag and chases after him, her bare feet padding on the wood. "Ernest, wait."

Did she seriously call *me* unbelievable? I walk to the end of the hallway and stand there watching Dad jam his massive feet back into his police-issue boots. Mom hovers near him like a nervous bird, her thin frame practically vibrating as she begs him to stay. He takes her by the shoulders—gently, for once—and whispers a few words to her, shaking his head sadly like a doctor giving a patient bad news, but I know it's an act. He steps out the door and says goodbye to Mom before heading back to his car.

I step up to the window to watch him go. His jacket stretches tight across his back, and his boots leave deep prints. Mom's shrill voice snaps at me from somewhere behind, dishing out the same old crap about how he's changed and how she needs him and blah blah blah, but I'm half-listening.

He acted calm. Too calm.

Did he not see the photos?

Before I even realize what I'm doing, I yank on my boots over my sweatpants and run after him. The wind burns my face. Snow crunches under my feet, getting into the tops of my boots and melting into my socks. I hunch against the cold wind that seems to be blowing right through my body.

"Dad!" I yell. "Stop."

He spins around, his eyebrows rising like he can't believe I'm following him out here.

Come on. You can do this.

No more hiding. No more fear.

"Did you see my photos?" I ask.

His mouth hangs open for a second before snapping shut, the muscle in his jaw working. "*You* posted those photos?"

"No," I say. "But I took them. Every single time you hurt me."

Dad's massive hands flex at his sides. My stomach turns. Those hands are like steel, calloused from years on the force. I know what those hands can do. I remember what they've done before.

"Are you proud of yourself?" he says. "Is airing our family's private business online is something to be proud of?"

"It is if it means you'll get fired."

He scoffs. "I won't get fired."

"I'm not so sure about that."

He says nothing. I step closer to him, snow crunching under my boots.

"I want to make something clear," I say, my words ringing out over the wind, steady and strong. I used to not let myself stare at him for too long so as not to give him a reason to pay attention to me, but I want him to pay attention to me now. I want him to hear what I'm saying. "You need to stay away from Mom. Stop sending flowers. Stop coming to the house. It's creepy and obnoxious, and we don't want anything to do with you."

He looks up at something over my head and runs a hand down his jaw. Even without alcohol on his breath, he's still intimidating as hell, taking up too much space in the snowy yard.

"Shiloh, your mother called me."

"That changes nothing." My hair whips around my face. My hoodie offers little protection against the bitter cold, but the adrenaline coursing through my veins keeps me warm enough. "I didn't post those photos today. I haven't said anything about them online, but I can, and if you ever come here again, I will."

Dad stares at me for a couple of seconds, his face unreadable in the shadows cast by a nearby streetlamp.

"Are you threatening me?" His voice drops, taking on that dangerous tone that used to make me want to disappear into the walls. Once, it would have terrified me, but not anymore. I exhale a long breath, a cloud forming in front of my mouth.

"I'll talk to everyone," I say. "Go on the stand. X-rays of my arm will prove it was broken like it looked in the picture. And ..." I steel myself, my wiry muscles tensing like they're ready to move. "I'll tell them about the Fun Palace."

Dad pales, the color draining from his weathered face until his skin looks close to white. The words hang between us, and a powerful tremble runs through my body, my teeth chattering despite my best efforts to keep them still. Dad never spoke again about what happened that day. He never did anything similar to me again—unless you count telling me to strip naked so he could beat me with his belt—but that didn't stop the nightmares from coming, and it didn't stop me from lying in bed every night feeling my skin crawl like I needed to peel it off. The beatings I could take, because his hands were angry, but the Fun Palace was something else. The Fun Palace wasn't anger. It was *desire*, and that was so much worse. I tried everything I could to forget about it, or convince myself I made it up, but nothing worked because it did happen. He knows that as well as I do. It's clear as day on his face, in the way his shoulders hunch forward like he's been punched.

"Shiloh." His voice comes out hoarse, almost strangled. "You don't know what you're talking—"

"I do," I say. "And so do you. We both know exactly what I'm talking about."

He says nothing. I step closer to him, the wind catching my hoodie and making it billow. He still dwarfs me in size, but for once, he seems small. Like the monster of my childhood has been reduced to this pathetic, desperate man in his stained sweatpants and police-issue zip-up.

And I love it.

"I'll tell everyone." I talk loud enough that he can hear me over the howling wind. "You will be ruined."

His hands clench into meaty fists at his sides. "You ungrateful bitch."

"Yeah? And what exactly do I have to be grateful for?"

I ready myself, not sure what he'll do next, but he flings open the car door and gets inside. The engine roars to life. I brace against the wind, wrapping my arms around myself as he drives away. I can't help but feel glad that my back is turned to the house because I know Mom is watching me and I don't want her to see how big my smile is as his taillights disappear into the whirling snow.

23

Shiloh

When I get back inside, Mom is waiting in the living room. Her thin arms are crossed, making her pajama top bunch up at the elbows. The small light on the fridge behind her catches in her messy hair.

"What the hell is wrong with you?" she hisses. "Your father was trying to help me and your brother."

I kick off my snow-covered boots harder than necessary, watching them topple onto the mat. "He wasn't trying to help. He's trying to get you back."

"He's changed." Tears track down her hollow cheeks. "He misses us."

"No, he misses controlling us." I yank off my wet socks and ball them up, my cold fingers fumbling with the damp fabric. "And you're letting him."

"I need him, Shiloh. Max is sick, and I can't—"

Oh, Max is sick? Really? Like I didn't already *know that.*

"You don't need him," I snap. "You need to go to bed and let me handle this."

"Stop trying to be the parent!" She jams a finger into her ribcage. "I am the mother here!"

"Then start acting like it!"

Mom's shoulders slump. She presses her palms against her face. Her blonde hair falls forward like a curtain, and something inside of me shrivels up. Crap. I shouldn't have said that. I should have known better. Yelling at Mom only makes her shut down thanks to all the things Dad did to her, and it's not fair for me to lose it with her.

"Mom." I step closer. "I'm sorry. I know you're scared about Max, but Dad is only going to make things worse."

She whimpers, wiping her nose with the back of her hand. "At least he brought electrolytes."

I should have done that. I was too busy trying to figure out a way to keep him alive. The irony is not lost on me.

"I know." I wrap my arms around her shoulders, feeling her crumple and melt in my arms, burying her nose in my shoulder. She feels so small against me, like a bird with hollow bones that would snap if I held her too hard, like her hold on gravity is beginning to drift like it did when she was

...

Dead.

Another thing that was my fault.

I don't actually remember the last time I hugged her, but I know she needs this more than I do. I should try to remember to do it more, especially after what I've put her through.

"Mom, the best thing you can do right now is go sleep in your own bed. I'll keep an eye on Max."

"But—"

"Please. Can you do this for me? Do you have anything that will help you sleep?"

She looks up at me for a couple of seconds, then goes to the bathroom to take a bottle of Ambien from the cabinet above the sink.

"Will you wake me if anything changes?" she asks.

I nod, even though I have no intention of doing that. She shuffles down the dark hall to her room. I follow a few steps behind to make sure she actually goes inside. Only when her door closes do I let myself breathe normal again.

Good.

I grab the CVS bag Dad brought and throw it on my unmade bed, the plastic crinkling as I dig through it to find a handful of Pedialyte packets and a bottle of yellow Gatorade. I roll my eyes. Max won't drink yellow Gatorade because he says it tastes like pee. How he knows what pee tastes like, I don't know, but I do know he'd never get close to that stuff. I mix one of the packets of Pedialyte powder into a glass of water and wake Max with a gentle poke on his arm, coaxing him to take a couple of sips before he pushes my hand away. Good enough.

I don't want to leave him alone, but Mom is more helpful asleep than she is awake, speed-dialing Dad. I push back his hair and press a kiss on his forehead.

I ease Mom's door open. Her breath catches in a slight snore.

I grab the extra magnets I came here for in the first place, shoving them deep into my backpack and heading for the door. I'm going to be late meeting the others. Max needs me, and I've already wasted too much time dealing with Dad. So I put on some dry socks, my boots and coat, thread my arms through the straps of my backpack, and head outside.

A gust of fresh snow blows into my face like needles. I tug my hood deeper over my head, trying to shield my already numb ears. I don't know when it started snowing again.

Probably when I was inside my house, but there's already a new dusting over everything, starting to fill in every tire track and even Dad's boot prints from when he stormed off a few minutes ago.

Stop thinking about Dad. He doesn't matter right now.

I can't believe what I said to him.

My boot slips on a patch of ice. I windmill my arms, stumbling to catch my balance on the asphalt. Oh my God, I'm so sick of this stupid snow, but it will be over once all the ghosts go back through the gate. Well, it will still be cold, because it's winter, and there will still be snow, just less of it.

I grip the fraying nylon straps of my backpack through my ski gloves. The whole town looks dead. Not a single porch light glows through the darkness. Not one TV is on in any window. I guess this town's median age has a bedtime and the only people up at this hour are the thirty-somethings living at home and playing video games in the basement. Dense storm clouds cover the sky like a blanket, but the blue-white gleam bouncing off the fresh powder gives me enough light to see where I'm going. The silence is suffocating. There are no cars, no voices ... nothing but the high whistle of the wind whipping through bare branches that cast spindly shadows on the snow.

I stop to look up at one particularly gnarly oak tree, its branches jerking up and down like something invisible is bouncing on it. A high-pitched giggle cuts through the silence, echoing down the empty street.

I duck my head and pick up my pace. I don't like walking alone anywhere in Bethany now. I should have said yes when Jonah offered to go with me because even though it would've been uncomfortable, and he probably would've tried to kill Dad when he showed up, at least right now, I wouldn't be walking alone. I only needed to pick up the magnets so they could've waited in the car while I went in and got them, but I wanted to see Max and check on Mom, and Miles had to grab some things from his apartment, so it made more sense to split up.

Something moves in the corner of my eye. Footprints appear in the powder right next to me, like some invisible person is matching my stride. The prints are huge. Way bigger than mine and pressed deep, like they belong to someone heavy. Someone like Dad. My heart pounds hard as I force myself to keep moving, letting out a shaky breath when the footsteps finally stop.

I'm almost at the end of my street when a light flips on in this house on the corner. Through the window, I catch sight of a person.

I stop.

It's usually hard to see inside people's houses, but the light from the window and the darkness outside make it easy. The man looks about fifty, with patchy gray hair and white stubble. He's wearing nothing but a pair of flannel pajama pants that hang loose on his skinny frame, leaving his sunken chest and prominent ribs exposed in the glow of the house. His skin has that rough, crumpled look of someone who has smoked too many cigarettes or spent too much time in the sun, and he's just ... standing there, staring at his wall like it's the most interesting thing he's ever seen.

I shouldn't be staring, but the guy's not moving in a way that does not look normal. He twitches his head. Shrugs his shoulders. Raises both arms above his head, then kicks each leg out one at a time like he's watching a workout video that's running somewhere out of my sight. The wind tears the breath from me as I watch him lumber over to his coffee table and grab a vase filled with dead flowers. His head twitches to the side again. Like he's trying to get a bug out of his ear.

He smashes the vase onto the floor. I jump back with a gasp.

His head snaps toward me. He extends a long finger at me as he focuses on me with pure white eyes.

Oh hell no.

I turn to walk away, trying to look casual so as not to attract more attention, but I make it a few steps before a door slams. I glance over my shoulder. The man is striding down his icy driveway and onto the road. He has thrown on a coat that flaps open, exposing his naked chest, because I guess he didn't bother to put on a shirt. Whatever is driving him doesn't need one.

He points at me. "You're one of those kids they said to watch out for. The ones from the care home. I'm supposed to kill you."

I turn and run as hard as I can. The sound of his heavy footsteps crunching through the snow tells me he's coming after me.

The road is like a sheet of ice under my boots. Each step threatens to send me sprawling. My heart thrums in my ears and I windmill my arms like an idiot, barely staying upright as I skid around the corner and onto the main road.

I sprint down the sidewalk past the dark houses. Christmas lights hang there useless and unlit against the gutters, offering no help or hope.

The man is gaining on me. Each of his strides covers too much ground, eating up the distance between us. The Rite Aid sign looms ahead, that stupid dot above the second i flickering from the faulty bulb. I'd give anything to see another person right now, but the streets are dead except for swirling snow.

I get as far as the sign when a hand clamps onto my jacket. The man throws me down. I hit the concrete so hard my teeth rattle. He crashes down on top of me, his meaty hands going for my neck.

I scramble to get up, but my boots might as well be greased. His weathered face looms less than a foot above me, so close I can see each red vein stretching across his flipped eyeballs. His hot breath reeks of stale tobacco. My hoodie bunches up around my throat as he grips it. Oh God. I can't breathe. He barely gets his hands around my throat before I drive my knee up into him. He grunts. I do it again, harder, and he makes a strangled sound. That move is becoming my signature. I climb to my feet and kick him hard in the face, sending him back onto the pavement with a sickening thud. I jump on his ankle for good measure. There's a crunch like stepping on packed snow, but wetter.

The man screeches. I turn and run even harder. I need to lose him. I can't kill him. He's an old guy possessed by a ghost. When the ghost leaves, he'll go back to being an old guy, and the cops will have a field day with that one. Just call me Shiloh Oleson, the senior citizen slayer.

I glance over my shoulder to see him getting up, dragging his bent ankle behind him. He can't run after me. Not with his ankle looking up like that. But I don't know if those ghosts feel pain the way normal people do. Oh God, what if they don't? What if I just made him angry? What if he keeps running, the stump of his foot leaving a bloody trail across the snow?

Why the hell is he chasing me, anyway? I don't know this guy. Or the ghost that has taken him over. At least I don't think I do. He said I was one of those kids to watch out for. Does that mean the ghosts from the old folks' home have spread the word? Are they all hunting us now?

I run as hard as I can down the road into the main part of town, praying a patch of black ice doesn't take me down.

There's enough powder on the road that I can't hide. He could follow my footsteps. My feet pound the asphalt. Black spots dance at the edges of my vision.

"Help!" I scream. "Someone, please, help me!"

Salt and sand crunch under my boots. My lungs are on fire, each desperate breath getting harder and hurting more. He doesn't slow down. He keeps running on that broken ankle like he feels nothing.

"Why are you doing this?" I yell back at him, my lungs screaming for me to stop. "Who are you?"

His labored breathing gets closer, a rasping sound that turns my bones cold. Above the wind I hear the uneven rhythm of footsteps getting closer, the thud of his boot alternating with the sickening click of what sounds like bone on asphalt. I can't outrun him forever. I'm going to slip on the ice and then he'll be on top of me in a second.

Somewhere to my left, an engine roars. I look behind me just in time to see a car shoot out from a side street and slam into the man with a sickening crunch.

24

Shiloh

The man flies onto the hood. I gasp as the sedan lurches forward with a screech of tires, shoving the man over the car. His head hits the asphalt with a crack. I stare at him, waiting for him to move, but he doesn't.

Miles stops against the curb in a spray of dirty snow. The passenger door flies open and Jonah bolts out, running to me.

"What the hell was that?" Jonah's eyes sweep over me. "Are you okay?"

"He ..." I point over my shoulder with an unsteady finger and gasp for air, my legs trembling and numb from running. "He chased me here."

"Who?" Jonah reaches for me and I don't even stop him. His hands grip my forearms to steady me. "Was he possessed?"

"No, Jonah, he wasn't possessed. He was just a neighbor who was having a bad night." I give him a look. *"Of course he was possessed."*

My heart is still racing, hammering against my ribs so hard it hurts, but I'm not sure if it's from running or from the way Jonah is looking at me, like he wants to walk over there and smash that man's face in with his boot. The possessed man hasn't moved, but that doesn't mean he's dead. Nothing seems to stay dead around here anymore.

"They're after us," I say, pointing at the man with a trembling finger. "He knew who I was. He knew what we did at the nursing home."

Jonah's grip tightens on my elbows. "They're organizing against us? All of them?"

I nod. "He said he was told to watch out for the kids from the nursing home and to kill us if he saw us."

"But how does he know that? Was he there?"

"One soul must have acted as a messenger," Francesca says. I step away from Jonah and turn around to see her behind us, rolling her chair closer over the snow. The wheels leave thin tracks behind, like parallel lines drawn with a ruler. "They must have gone to warn the others about what we're doing."

"So, what? They're like an angry ghost mob?" Jonah asks. "Like, burn the witch?"

"Sounds like it," Miles says. "We need to get inside now before more of them find us, and figure out where we are setting all this up."

Yes. They'll kill us if they catch us. Like that guy tried to kill me.

Above our heads, a wooden sign creaks in the wind. The red paint is scuffed and peeling like a bad sunburn, with darker patches where years of rain have eaten through. One of the chains holding it up has snapped, making the sign hang crooked, but the gold name is still easy to read:

I'm glad for the cold, because it means the smell of stale beer and deep fryer grease has not made its way outside like it usually does. The red bricks are crusty with salt stains. The windows are cloudy and plastered with faded NFL team logos and beer signs that are yellow at the edges. Through the grimy windows, I can make out barstools flipped onto the counter, their chrome legs catching what little light filters in from outside. A neon CLOSED sign flickers weakly, its red glow creating small pools of light on the snow-covered sidewalk as it tells everyone to shove off until tomorrow. It hasn't been that long since it closed. I know this because sometimes Dad would come home smelling like whiskey and onion rings well after eleven.

I jerk my thumb at the pub, glancing at Jonah because coming here was his super awesome idea. "You got a plan for how to get in there?"

He gives me a small smile. "We're going in the same way you and I got in last time."

I don't want to think about last time. I'm going to cry if I let myself remember the careful way he washed my torn-up knuckles in that tiny bathroom, but because it's relevant, I try to remember the name of the cook who let us in. "By asking Paulie?"

"Sure." Jonah nods. "By asking Paulie."

I don't have to be a genius to know that we're not going to be asking Paulie, especially not with a body lying in the road outside. Miles and Jonah pick up the body and drag it into the alley behind the dumpster. It may be the middle of the night, but there's always at least one cop on patrol overnight who should be making rounds if he's not too busy mopping up blood at the nursing home. The snow is falling steadily now and has already almost erased the signs that something happened here.

I grab a couple of bags from the back of the car and follow Jonah into the narrow alley around the side of the pub. Snow has been piled along the brick walls and against the blue dumpster, but unlike last time I was here, I don't see a single rat. I guess rats get cold, too.

Jonah goes up to the red door and takes out a lanyard of keys, the metal jingling as he filters through them. He fits one into the lock. It makes a loud scraping sound and the door opens.

I gape at him. "You have a key to Duncan's?"

"Don't act so surprised." His voice is lighter than it should be, given everything that happened between us. "You don't know everything about me."

"How do you have a key?"

"I copied Paulie's."

I don't try to hide my surprise. Jonah called Paulie an old friend of his, but I don't care how close Jonah and Paulie were to each other. Jonah is still a kid. I'm learning a lot tonight about Jonah and his borderline inappropriate friendships with random adults.

"Does Paulie know you copied his key?" I ask, keeping my voice steady despite the cold making my teeth chatter.

The cocky grin spreading across Jonah's face tells me that Paulie most certainly doesn't.

"I got it for emergencies."

"What kind of emergency other than the one we're in right now would require you to get your own key?"

Jonah pushes open the heavy door, glancing back at the others. "You guys coming?"

There are a hundred more questions I want to ask, but

I'm more than happy to get out of the cold so I climb the concrete steps, their edges worn smooth from years of use and stained with rust-colored patches where the salt has eaten through. Behind us, Miles turns Francesca's wheelchair backward and drags her up the stairs. I kick the packed snow off my boots before stepping into the back entrance of the bar.

The warmth hits me like a wall. So does that gut-punch smell. Burnt oil. Stale beer. Industrial cleaner. Goosebumps break over my skin as I remember that same smell clinging to Dad's clothes when he came home late, barely able to stand straight, scotch on his breath and rage in his eyes. I can feel him all over me in here.

Jonah closes the door with a clang that echoes through the kitchen, then locks it from the inside. When he flips on the lights, I squint against the glare reflecting off every surface of the industrial kitchen. Everything is made of stainless steel. The walls are lined with ovens and deep fryers. A massive prep table takes up most of the floor space. Pots and pans hang from a rack. A mop leans against one wall, its stringy head trailing into a bucket of murky water that should've been dumped hours ago.

I drop my bag on the prep table. Miles adds his stuff next to mine.

He tilts his head up toward the ceiling, craning his neck around like he's looking for something. "Us coming in here didn't trigger some kind of alarm, did it?"

Jonah settles against the counter. "It never has for me. I used to come here to crash sometimes."

"When?" I ask, still not being able to picture it. "*Why?*"

Jonah shrugs his good shoulder. I guess he doesn't want to talk about it.

"No alarm sounded when Jonah opened the door,"

Francesca says. "Which leads me to believe we will be all right."

Miles still looks concerned. But Miles is always concerned, so that's not saying much.

"Are you sure this place has the coolers we need?" Miles asks.

Jonah pushes off from the counter and goes up to a gleaming metal door at the back of the kitchen, leaning on the plastic handle. Cold air rushes out as the heavy door swings open with a whoosh.

I peer over Jonah's shoulder to see wilting heads of broccoli and long tubes of ground beef on the metal shelves. The air has a sharp metallic smell of rust and raw meat. A dingy thermometer mounted on the wall reads 35 degrees in faded red numbers. Jonah turns to face us, leaning against the door frame on his good shoulder with his good hand in his pocket like the cold doesn't affect him at all.

"Walk in fridge, baby." He grins. "Perfect for all your corpse-chilling needs."

What a gross way to put it. Even though he's trying to act casual, there's tension in his shoulders. Classic Jonah. Shoving down his feelings until his eyes give him away. His gaze meets mine for a second before he looks at the ground.

"You have to keep this open," he says, slapping the door. "It doesn't open from the inside."

This is all starting to feel too real. I can't keep looking at the tubes of meat or I'm going to lose it, so I walk back into the kitchen. The others trail after me. Francesca sits completely still in her chair. Miles is full-on hyperventilating, his fingers white-knuckled on the edge of the counter.

"Miles," I snap, making him jump. "I need you to get it together."

He shakes his head, his wide eyes darting around the

kitchen like he's looking for a way to escape. "What if you guys die? What if you die and can't come back and we have to get rid of your bodies or we will go to jail or your parents have to identify you in a restaurant freezer and—"

"Miles."

"I'm about to *kill* you."

"Temporarily," I say, even though the word feels weird in my mouth. I don't know why I'm the one comforting *him*. "And we'll come back, because you're going to follow the instructions, and if I know one thing about you, it's that you're good at following instructions." I point at his phone, sitting in the front pocket of his pants. "Can you read them out loud?"

Miles stares at his phone screen but says nothing. Great. Francesca and I are going to die because Miles is too busy having a panic attack to read the damn instructions, and the foolery will make Jonah too thrilled at seeing my dead body that he won't be able to give me the life-saving drug at all.

I grip the edge of the prep counter, trying to figure out how the hell I'm supposed to handle this. After a couple seconds, Jonah plucks the phone out of Miles's hands and clears his throat.

"Okay," he says. "First thing on this list is we got to keep your bodies cold."

I stare at him. Can I trust my life to Jonah if Miles freezes up? What if Jonah decides he wants me dead after all and chooses not to give me the green drug, and Miles is too busy breathing into a bag to notice?

I can almost see what he's thinking. His lips flatten into a line like he can read my thoughts too.

"I can do this," he says. "Shiloh, I promise."

Okay. I trust him. I probably shouldn't after everything that happened tonight, but I do because I know how much he loves me. In his right mind, he could blindfold me and walk me down a tightrope and I'd step every place he told me to.

So it feels as natural as breathing when I say, "Okay. What's next?"

He reaches into the open cooler and pulls out a cluster of drug vials all taped together with an aggressive amount of Scotch tape. "I give you the red one."

His voice catches on "red." He knows as well as I do that the red drug is the one that will kill us. Part of me wants to make some kind of joke that I'd be dead now anyway if he'd succeeded in killing me four months ago, but I can't bring myself to say that, given the amount of pain in his eyes. With him looking at me like this, it feels like it's just the two of us in the room.

I try hard to remember how to breathe. "How much?"

"You get two ccs." Jonah checks the phone. "Francesca gets one."

"Does it say anything about what to do if it doesn't work?"

"Nope."

Fantastic. "Fine. Then what?"

"The green one." He pulls out a cluster of green vials. "This one jumpstarts your heart, and you get bigger doses. Two ccs for Francesca. Three for you."

Some part of my mind wants to make a joke along the lines of him calling me fat, but it's not funny and feels wrong for this moment.

"How long do we have until we have to go back into our bodies again?" I remember Colin told us, but he told us a lot of things and I already forgot.

"It says here two hours."

That's it? I hope it'll be enough. I can't tell if it will or not.

It's not as if I've practiced this before. What if I don't know how to move?

"So what happens when we come and tell you we want to be brought back?" I say. "What do you do then?"

"Give you the blue one." Jonah takes out two more vials. "Same dose as the green stuff. Three for you. Two for Francesca. All the drugs go to go into the muscle. He recommends the shoulder so you don't have to take off your pants."

The situation has to be serious if Jonah was able to say that with a straight face.

"Are you sure you can handle this? I trust you, but I also know how you are with needles. You might have to give us the shots if Officer Panic Attack over there is still busy hyperventilating."

Jonah pales, and I immediately hate myself for bringing it up. I know why he hates needles. He has told me some memories of what it was like growing up with his mom, just casually as they came up in conversation. Stepping on a plastic cap when he was ten and screaming, thinking it was a needle and was going to make him high. Watching his mom shoot up by flashlight in their tent. Finding a used needle in his sleeping bag. He has a good reason to hate needles, but this is a life-or-death moment, so I can't be scared of hurting his feelings.

"I'm not going to mess this up," he says. "I don't like them, but I know how to use them."

I hate that he does. I hate his mom for putting him in a position where he learned that, and it makes me want to take a trip to Florida to introduce the woman to my fist, but I nod. His eyes stay on mine. Those stupidly beautiful blue eyes. I want to hug him. Even though things are all kinds of wrong between us right now and I can still feel the phantom pressure of his hands around my throat, he's still Jonah, my Jonah, and I don't want to go through this alone.

But I pinch the bridge of my nose and ask Francesca to help Miles get himself together because she's better at the warm-and-fuzzies than I am and I have no sympathy for him since Francesca and I are the ones doing the scary thing, not him.

I lay everything out on the floor of the fridge, the concrete seeping through the damp knees of my pants. In a minute or so, Francesca joins me, her face scrunching up as she pushes the heavy wheels over the lip in the door. She doesn't ask for help. I don't want to embarrass her by helping her anyway, so I force myself to stay put as she comes inside. I close the door but leave it cracked. I don't know how much air gets in here, but dying of oxygen deprivation before we can even take the drugs would be a pretty special kind of stupid.

I turn around to face Francesca who, despite everything, gives me a shy smile.

"Will you help me get out of the chair?"

I nod. She loops her arm around my shoulders. I slip one arm under her knees and the other behind her back. She's so light it scares me. The chair rolls backward as I carry her to the back of the fridge.

I go to put her down but hesitate. "The floor's going to be freezing."

"Is that not the point?"

True. I guess both of us are going to get cold one way or another.

I lower her onto the ground, making sure her head doesn't bump the metal shelving. I ball up my jacket and slip under her head. She opens her mouth to protest.

"I can't wear it anyway," I say.

She takes off her hat and jacket because even though it's

cold without them on, as she said, we have to be cold. She gives me her jacket to use as a pillow. I lie on my shoulder and look at her. She smiles back at me.

"This is perhaps the most peculiar sleepover I have ever been to," she says, and I burst out laughing.

"What, you've never had a sleepover in a walk-in fridge before?" I joke. "Because I have."

She giggles. Her small hand finds mine in the cold, our fingers intertwining.

"You have been a good friend." She tightens her grip. "I had never called anybody my friend until I met you."

I drop her hand. Prop myself up on my elbow.

"Nope," I say. "We're not doing this."

She holds my stare. "This is our only chance to do this."

"Stop talking like you're going to die. It's freaking me out."

"But—"

"This is going to work." I'm not as fast to accept my death as she apparently is.

She gives me a small nod. It's quiet for a couple of seconds.

"Shiloh?"

I slump back down onto my arm, wincing at the freezing concrete pressing into my sleeve. "Yeah?"

"Do you think it's possible to stay sad forever?"

I open my mouth to reply, but the words don't come because I … don't know what to say. Goosebumps ripple across my arms, the cold cutting through my skin and settling deep in my bones.

"Yes," I say, thinking of Dad and the way he fell apart after Uncle Jim died. I spent so much time being scared of him that I rarely stopped to think about how sad he was. That sadness changed him forever, but being sad isn't an excuse for the way he hurt us. "I've had bad things happen to me but I'm not always sad, and I hope I won't be sad for the rest of my life. I think I'll find a way to carry the sadness. I might need to carry it for the rest of my life, and that'll be hard, but I can do it if I get a good grip on it."

The second the words leave my mouth, I know I lied. That may be true for some things. Dad should have been able to cope with losing Uncle Jim without destroying himself and everyone around him, but if I let myself think about this night ending and having to say goodbye to Jonah ... nothing will get me through that. I'll be sad for the rest of my life.

I shove the feelings back down where they belong. I can't let myself feel any of those things right now, because if I let myself feel even a fraction of what's pooling in the bottom of my ribcage ... Francesca needs me right now. I try to think of something to say that I know is not a lie.

"I know this is scary and the odds are stacked against us," I say, "but I've spent my whole life fighting a battle I could never win and if it's taught me anything, it's that you can never quit. The only thing you can do when you can't fight anymore is keep fighting."

Francesca presses her lips together. I don't think that landed the way I wanted it to. My life story's not exactly inspirational.

So I try a more optimistic approach. "It's only a death sentence if it kills us." I smile so she knows this is supposed to be a joke. "So we can't let it kill us."

The door creaks open and Miles and Jonah come in carrying a first aid kit between them like lifting a box half the size of a microwave is a two-person job. Francesca's hand slips from mine as Miles sets the kit by my feet, giving me the most awkward close-lipped smile I've ever seen in my life.

Oh boy. Here we go.

Jonah crouches next to me and drags the first-aid kit closer. His careful fingers tremble as he peels back the Velcro on the first aid kit, the ripping sound way too loud for how quiet it is in here. He presses a cotton ball to the Betadine bottle, brown liquid soaking through the white fibers, and holds out the cotton ball like he's asking me to take it.

I clench my chattering teeth until my jaw aches. "Can you do it?"

He pinches the cotton ball. A drop of brown liquid drips onto the concrete. "You sure?"

I nod. He's going to have to get closer to me if he's going to stick those needles in my arm. His hand pauses above my shoulder, hovering there like he forgot how his arms work. I roll up the sleeve of my black firefighters T-shirt. The goosebumps spreading across my exposed shoulder make my flesh look like chicken skin. He presses the cotton ball to it. God, it's like being touched by an ice cube. I flinch.

He jerks his hand back. He really is worried about hurting me. "You okay?"

"Yeah," I say. "It's cold, but I'm fine."

He keeps going. The brown liquid spreads across my shoulder in expanding circles, pebbling my skin with goosebumps. I focus on Jonah's face instead of his hands, because watching him work on my arm is making my stomach do weird flips. I want to lean into him so bad. I know it would be wrong and I need to hold strong because I was the one who told him I had to end things and he's the one who attacked me, but I'm so scared and I need him.

I do what he usually does when emotions get too real. "Dang, you're getting my whole shoulder there. That's going to be one big needle."

He shoves the cotton ball into a plastic bag with more

force than necessary. The Betadine is drying on my skin now, making it feel tight and weirdly cold.

Our eyes meet. He swallows.

"Please don't do this." His voice is barely a whisper. "For me."

I wrap my hand over his, feeling the calluses on his palm. He draws in a sharp breath. His eyes lock onto where I'm touching him, studying our hands like they hold some kind of answer.

"You'll stay with me?" I ask. "The whole time?"

"Always." He pauses. "Just don't do anything stupid."

I grin up at him because he knows as well as I do that this whole plan is maximum-level stupid. He swears under his breath and turns to disinfect Francesca's shoulder. I watch Miles standing across the room by the open door. He's squinting at the instructions on his phone like they're written in hieroglyphics.

"You good there, bud?" I ask.

He ignores me as he tears open the sterile packaging, the crinkly plastic echoing in the small space. He screws the needle onto the syringe. The red liquid looks almost beautiful as he draws it up, like cherry Kool-Aid or melted Swedish Fish. The needle quivers between his fingers while he measures out 2 ccs, tapping the side to get the air bubbles out.

He kneels next to my shoulder, which is stained orange-brown from the Betadine and covered in goosebumps. I turn my head toward Francesca, finding her pale face in the industrial lighting. She gives me a wobbly smile, reaching for my hand with fingers that feel like icicles. I grip back. Both of our palms are slick. I count the rust-spotted metal tracks holding up the shelving units on the ceiling.

"Are you ready?" Miles's voice cracks on the question.

Nope. Not even close. But I nod anyway, because what else am I supposed to do?

I glimpse the needle hovering right above my skin and find Jonah across the room. I don't need to say anything. He knows. He gives me a nod.

It worked on the mouse. I watched it work. The mouse was fine.

But what if something happened to it neurologically, something I couldn't see because it was a mouse?

I should've asked Colin more questions about the mouse.

I can hear how hard Miles is struggling to breathe. I reach up and wrap my free arm around him, my muscles straining as I lift my upper body off the floor. He catches my weight.

"Shiloh, what—"

"You can do this," I say, low enough that only he can hear me. "I love you."

His chest rises and falls with a shuddering breath. I let go and lower myself back down. The concrete feels even colder than before as my fingers find Francesca's again. I raise my eyebrows at Miles, trying to look braver than I feel. Miles blinks hard. Tears pool at the corners of his eyes.

Before my brain can process anything else, he stabs the needle into my arm.

There's a pinch as the needle breaks skin. I hiss a breath in through my teeth.

Miles pushes the plunger. Pressure builds as the red liquid leaves the syringe. The cold floor under me seems to leach any remaining warmth from my body. I wait for something to happen. My fingers dig into Francesca's sweaty hand. Miles drops the needle into a trash bag with a hollow plastic clatter, leaning back onto his heels.

"Update?" he asks me. "What are you feeling?"

I focus my attention inward, but I can't feel anything

except for how cold I am. I forgot to ask how much this would hurt. How did I forget to ask how much it would hurt?

"There will be a delayed response." Miles wipes his forehead with his sleeve. "The mouse didn't seem to be feeling anything until it did."

Fantastic. Miles draws a syringe of the green liquid. His hands shake as he double-checks his phone for dosages, flicking the air bubbles out with his nail.

"Jonah," Miles calls over his shoulder. "Can you keep her talking?"

Jonah comes over to sit next to me. He smiles, but the corners of his eyes crease.

"You know what I never told you?" He rolls the beads on his hemp necklace. "That Goldfish are a shit snack."

A laugh bubbles out of me. "Seriously? That's what you need to tell me right now?"

"Seems as good a time as any to bring it up. They taste like cardboard dipped in fake cheese dust, and it's weird to me that you think they're better than Cheese-Its."

I force the words out through my chattering teeth, trying to ignore how my whole body is shaking. "But Goldfish are the snack that smiles back." My words come out slurred like I'm talking through ice cubes.

"Yeah, and that's creepy as hell. Why should I want my snacks to smile at me before I eat them?"

Cold crashes through me like I've been dunked in a lake. I try to answer him, but my tongue feels heavy and useless in my mouth.

"Ch-Cheese-Its," I force out through numb lips, "suck."

A crushing weight slams into my sternum. The pressure radiates outward in agonizing waves, my ribs creaking under the strain like they're being squeezed in a giant's fist. I gasp for air, but it's like trying to breathe at the bottom of a pool.

Jonah leans forward, his face swimming and blurring like I'm seeing him through frosted glass. His hemp necklace swings back and forth, the multicolored beads blending together in a smear of rainbow. "Shiloh?"

I can't move my tongue. Oh my God, what the hell was I thinking? What if this is it? What if the red drug is the only one that works? The pressure in my chest crushes me, squeezing tighter and tighter until—

I die.

PART 3
The body dropt not down

25
JONAh

Shiloh stops.

Her hand goes slack in Francesca's. Her head lolls to the side and her hair spills onto her face.

No no no no no.

"Shiloh?" My voice breaks. "Shiloh, can you hear me?"

She doesn't move. Doesn't breathe. Just flops over like a doll. The thin air suddenly feels thick enough to choke on.

I shove my trembling fingers under her jaw, checking for a pulse, but there's nothing. Everything around me slows to a crawl. What the fuck? What the everloving *fuck*? I *told* her not to do this. She should never have done this.

"Does she have a pulse?" Miles asks from somewhere behind me. "Did her heart stop?"

I swallow hard against the bile rising in my throat, acid burning the back of my mouth. I try her wrist, pressing harder now until I feel bone because maybe I missed it. Maybe her pulse is there and I'm too stupid to find it.

"Jonah," Miles says again. "Do you feel a pulse?"

I barely manage to croak out a "no" before a thought enters my head and knocks the wind out of me:

Good. The bitch is finally dead.

Oh my God. *No.*

Enough.

I'm done with this.

That's my girl right there. My. Girl. I told her I got her.

What the hell am I doing?

I give my head a hard shake and the world crashes back around me. The biting cold seeping through my jeans where I'm kneeling. Miles yelling. Shiloh lying on the ground, her usually fierce brown eyes staring up at the ceiling, empty and vacant, and her skin already taking on this grayish tone that makes my stomach roll. I dig my fingertips into the ground so hard they burn. I mess everything up between us by acting like an asshole, but I'm not going to mess this up. I'm sure as hell not going to let her die.

"Give me the green one," I snap at Miles, stretching my hand back over my shoulder and not taking my eyes off Shiloh. "Now."

"Are you sure you can—"

"I said *now.*"

Miles gives me the syringe. I jam the thing between my teeth, tasting the sterile plastic and trying not to think about what I'm about to do as I climb over Shiloh. I pour some Betadine onto her other shoulder. My nose twitches at the smell. The amber liquid leaves trails down her pale skin and pools on the floor. As much as I hate to accept it, I know my shit about this. She's going to get three injections tonight, and I can't jam multiple needles into the same place unless I want to turn her muscle into hamburger meat.

I hold the syringe up to make sure there's no air in it and

line the needle up against her skin. Leave it to that creepy backyard mouse scientist to make the lifesaving drug look toxic. He should've put a skull and crossbones on the bottle for more effect.

I slide the needle in, forcing myself not to look away even though my stomach roils. Don't think about the needle. Think about her. I push the plunger down slow so the pressure doesn't build up, then yank out the needle and toss it aside, hearing it clatter across the floor. I lean back on my heels and give her a couple of seconds before feeling for her pulse.

Nothing. The silence in the fridge is deafening.

Come on.

I count twenty of the longest seconds of my life before checking for her pulse again. It's there. Slow and sluggish, but there.

Thank fuck.

I collapse onto her, pressing my forehead onto her stomach like I've done a million times before and closing my eyes so hard tears press out of them. That … was the most stressful minute of my entire life. Whose crazy idea was this?

I lift my head enough to glare at the girl under me. She is one crazy rat bastard, but this was just crazy enough to work. Her eyes don't look dead anymore. They look like they're focused on something out there I can't see. I go to close them for her so they don't dry out, but then I realize what I'm doing and what it looks like and stop myself. If she wakes up with dry eyes, we can deal with that. I'll go buy her eye drops in the morning.

I flex my fingers to get them under control because my body feels like it's vibrating apart, pins and needles shooting through my hands. Francesca looks ready to crap her pants, seeing everything that just went down. I point to Shiloh and raise a thumb, knowing how dumbass I look. I can't force

Francesca to do this. It has to be her choice, but imagining Shiloh doing this scary thing alone makes me want to plunge the red needle into my own leg.

Francesca curls a finger toward herself like she's beckoning me to come closer to her. I do. Her breath is warm against my ear when she leans up to whisper. Her voice is tiny. I can barely hear it over the hum of the fridge.

"I had always looked forward to dying," she whispers, "but I wish I could have known how it felt when it became my turn."

Oh man, do I know that feeling. I'm embarrassed to admit how much of my life I've spent waiting to die. I was so sure dying would make all my bad crap go away and everyone around me would be relieved at not having to deal with me anymore, but I was wrong. I did die. I know that feeling, and all I could think about when I could hear Shiloh's voice pulling away was how much I didn't want to go. I knew in that moment that all the reasons that made me wish I could die while I was still growing up were not worth letting go for, but it was too late to do anything to stop it.

I never heard Francesca admit that before. I wouldn't have pegged her as being like me in that way, but I guess it makes sense when all the people you love are dead. She wants to be like them. She wants to be *with* them.

"There's a reason all these asshole ghosts want to stay," I tell her. "Nothing beats being alive."

"But there must be a good place on the other side where I can go," she says.

I catch a glimpse of Miles standing on the other side of her. He shifts his weight from one foot to the other and holds that skinny needle in one hand like it might bite him. I keep my eyes on Francesca, watching her fingers play with the hem of her sleeve. I feel like I need to tell her that she's not dying so she's not going to the other side at all, but I get the feeling that's not going to do much. One look into her eyes tells me she doesn't want to come back. She may have already been planning on not coming back, so I got to be careful what I say.

"Aunt Moe told me something once," I say. "I didn't get it then, but that's pretty typical for me. She said the beginning of your life is like starting a road trip at night. You can only see a few feet ahead of you, just what's in the headlights, so it feels like you're going nowhere, like everything's slow and the same because you can only see the road and you have no clue where you're headed. But she said if you just keep driving, eventually it'll be morning and you'll see how far you've come, where you are, and that now you're somewhere worth going." I usually hate remembering Moe, but for some reason, this memory doesn't make me want to feel sad. "She said my job was to stay on the road, even if I couldn't see where I'm going yet. I did a crap job. I took every wrong turn, maybe even got off the road completely. I got to hope there's still time for me to find my way back, but you're different, Franks. You're still on the road. You're going somewhere good. Things will get better for you. I swear. You just … got to keep driving."

Oh God, did I say that out loud? Since when did I ever go around sharing deep thoughts about life like some after-school special?

Francesca's eyes fill with tears. Great. Now I made her cry. This is exactly why I don't talk about crap like that.

"How do you stay on the road?" she asks.

"By making decisions that are as good as you can," I say, "and by not giving up on driving."

She flings her arms around me and yanks me down toward her in a hug. Her grip is surprisingly strong for someone so small, and I'm so surprised by the gesture that I have no clue what to do.

"You are going somewhere good as well," she whispers in my ear.

I used to hope so, but now with Shiloh ... I messed that up so bad I don't know if I can ever walk it back. I turn my eyes to the ceiling. If I let myself think about that, there's no way I don't cry, so I wriggle out of her hug and force my face into an encouraging smile.

"So what do you say?" I ask. "You going to be a badass and save the world?"

She gives me a tiny nod. Miles comes up next to me with the needle, and I uncap the Betadine as she pulls down the neckline of her shirt far enough to expose her shoulder.

"Please hurry," she says. "Shiloh will be getting worried."

I quickly pour some Betadine on her shoulder. She screws up her eyes, and Miles stabs her.

26

FRANCESCA

I float upward as if carried by a gentle wind. I have not been a soul for quite a while, and I had forgotten the way the air seems to pass through me like silk. My limbs no longer feel heavy and unresponsive. I am free, floating several feet above my body, which looks rather small and fragile lying there on the cold floor.

Perhaps it is because I have spent so much time on the other side, but this in-between state feels much more comfortable than being alive. I wiggle my fingers in front of my face and then gasp when I realize something else and turn my attention toward my toes. I try to wiggle them as well.

They *move*.

I soar a few inches higher, extending my legs and kicking them through the air as though I were swimming. A laugh bubbles up inside me. I point my toes, then flex them, and then point them again. I will never be a ballet dancer, but I do not care. I swish my legs back and forth like a mermaid's tail.

They leave trails of silvery light in their wake. Any doubt that this is what I was supposed to do goes away.

I am exactly where I am supposed to be.

I spot Shiloh hovering near Jonah, her form casting no shadow against the metal shelves. I have never seen Shiloh as a soul before, and I am glad of it, but she appears the same. Her blonde hair is now as white as mine and floats around her face like wisps of fog. Even her ordinary clothes have transformed into something gossamer and delicate as they ripple around her. She reminds me of rainbows or the way sunbeams look when they pierce stained glass windows, substantial and made of nothing at the same time.

I have always thought of Shiloh as being strong, but her soul appears a much more delicate thing. She looks more childlike than the version of her that has been hardened by her life.

She watches Jonah, hovering a breath away from his shoulder. She must have heard what he said to me, about no longer being on the road. I can imagine the pain she must be feeling after Jonah lost his mind, and I know it is not his fault, but I also know that it will not be easy for Shiloh to forgive him. I am not sure when I discovered that people are so complicated. I wish that I never had.

She raises her eyes to mine. Her eyebrows leap up as she soars up to meet me.

"Hey." Her voice echoes a tiny bit. "How do you feel?"

Quite a bit better than I have for a long time, actually, but Shiloh would not like to hear that. "All right."

"Me too."

I peer down below us to see Jonah and Miles crouched over our bodies, watching our faces as if they are waiting for them to move.

Shiloh rolls her eyes. "Those two can be such idiots. Do

they think they're going to suddenly develop the power to see ghosts because they want to?"

She drops toward them, windmilling her arms so as to not move too quickly, and stops right in front of Jonah's face. His eyes stare right through her. She attempts to touch a piece of broccoli on the shelf, but her fingers pass through its deep green florets, leaving the faintest disturbance in the air like a gust of air conditioning.

She glances over Jonah's shoulder at me. "You can move things around like a normal ghost, right?"

Smiling, I join Shiloh and give the broccoli a gentle nudge. It quivers.

Miles snaps his head up, his straight hair bouncing with the sudden movement. "Did you see that?"

Jonah appears to remember the soul glasses and pulls them out of his pocket, wiping the lenses on his shirt before sliding them on. I glide around to the back of him so as not to scare him by how close I am to his face. He turns around. I give him a tiny wave. Shiloh crosses her arms over her chest.

"Finally," she says, even though he cannot hear her. "I was starting to think you'd just sit here staring at our bodies all night."

A smile tugs at my lips. Shiloh has a rather peculiar way of showing her love for Jonah. I believe it comes out as frustration when she is afraid.

His eyes meet mine through the lenses, their blue now tinted brown by the glass. A peculiar sensation floods through me, similar to butterflies dancing in a stomach I no longer possess.

"They're here." Jonah waves his hand to get the attention of Miles, who is still staring at the broccoli.

Jonah hands them to Miles, fumbling to get them off his face. Miles gasps.

"Oh my God," Miles says, and Jonah laughs as though he is relieved that at least the first step of the plan has worked. Miles passes the glasses back to him and looks like he is breathing a tiny bit easier now. "Are you guys okay?"

Both of us nod.

"Did you get your powers back?" Jonah asks me.

I suppose there is one way to find out. My attention drops to my hands. A tingling sensation rushes into the tips of my fingers.

I hold my palm out to Shiloh. "I am sorry about this."

"What are you—"

I thrust my hand forward. Shiloh flies into the shelves, dissipating into a puff of fog before slowly regaining her shape. I pump my arms above my head.

Yes.

I direct a gentle push of energy toward an empty saucepan hanging overhead. It sways with a soft scraping sound, the metal catching the overhead light and glinting off the rough ceiling.

I give Jonah a thumbs-up with both of my hands. "I suppose I did."

Jonah smiles, as though he understands, but taps on his ear. "I can't hear you."

Oh. That is true. We will need to find a way to communicate if this endeavor is going to be successful.

Perhaps Shiloh will know how. "Do you have any ideas about how we can communicate with them?" I ask her.

She presses her lips into a line. I suppose this would have been a good thing to have figured out before beginning.

"Well, Miles knows sign language, but I don't, and unless you do ...?" She raises her eyebrows, and I shake my head. "We should've brought a Ouija board."

Miles scratches his temple, deep creases appearing on his

forehead for a second before they disappear. His hair bounces as he stands up so quickly he nearly hits his head on the saucepan. He rushes back into the kitchen. After exchanging a look with Shiloh, I follow him.

I pass through the heavy door like I have done many times before. The sensation is similar to moving through cool jelly. Shiloh slips through the gap in the open door because I suppose she is not ready to try going through objects yet. Miles is already in the kitchen. He rummages through drawers, the sound of metal utensils clattering against each other filling the quiet as he mutters to himself. He grabs a stack of ordering pads, their pages slightly yellow and dog-eared, and a blue ballpoint pen from a ceramic cup near the phone. He scribbles the letter A on the first sheet before ripping it off with a sharp tear. Then B. He shoves each sheet into the gap on the fume hood so they hang up, the papers fluttering slightly in the draft from the ventilation system. Understanding of what he is doing settles in the pit of my stomach.

Shiloh grins. "He's making us a Ouija board."

I cannot say I have ever played with a Ouija board (partly because I did not have any friends to play with me and partly because I knew it would be silly since none of the souls I had known as a child could touch objects in the real world), but I am rather excited to use this one. Miles tosses Jonah a paper ordering pad and the two of them get to work, with Jonah moving backward from Z. They hang up each letter and shuffle things around so that they can fit the entire alphabet all the way around the rim.

Shiloh flies over to the order pads, first to the letter "B," then to "I." Jonah follows her around the edge of the counter until he laughs.

"That's Miles," he tells her, and her grin stretches. "I'm the comic relief."

She spells out something else.

U R N O T F U N N Y

Jonah's smile grows. It is a strange thing to be smiling about, but I suppose he is glad enough that she is all right and able to communicate with him to find anything she says quite funny.

Shiloh turns to me, her smile waning. "What do we need to say to them?"

I hold a finger to my chin as I plan my words before waving to capture Jonah's attention and gliding up closer to the order slips. The papers flutter softly in the draft. I make sure that I pause at each letter to ensure Jonah understands me. The soft scratching of Jonah's pen against paper is the only sound in the quiet kitchen as he follows me. It feels peculiar communicating this way and the process is rather time-consuming, but eventually, I finish spelling out my sentence and Jonah reads the words he took note of out loud.

"We. Will. Return. To. Farm." He pauses, glancing up at me. "Do you mean the Monroe farm? You're going back to the gate you opened?"

I nod. Shiloh turns to me and asks, "Why?"

I open my mouth to respond to her but pause because I may as well explain it to everybody at once. I try to get my meaning across in as few letters as possible.

B A R R I E R T H I N

"Is the barrier thin because you opened a portal there before?" Shiloh asks, her voice echoing slightly in the space between what Ms. Ruggles would have described as the layers of cling wrap.

"That is what I am hoping," I say.

Jonah's fingers drum against the metal counter, the hollow tapping echoing through the quiet kitchen like raindrops on a tin roof. "Want us to come with?"

Shiloh shrugs and looks at me, but I shake my head. They would have to drive there. I do not even know if the road out to the farm has been plowed, and a car out there at this time of night would draw attention to our presence. Besides, they need to safeguard our bodies.

N O

Jonah and Miles exchange a glance.

N O T S A F E

I point to the closed door of the refrigerator and then to my body and Shiloh's. If something happens to Jonah or Miles, neither of us will ever wake up again.

Miles nods. Jonah's deep frown tells me he does not like it, but he does not say anything to the contrary.

"Okay, well, go do your thing," Jonah says. "We'll be here when you're done."

Shiloh drifts toward the window and reaches her hand out for me. "You coming?"

I grip her hand. Her fingers feel cool against mine, as though I am holding onto an ice cube and just as solid. I guide her through the glass, and we leave our bodies and anchors to this world behind.

27

Francesca

I am not entirely sure what I was expecting death walking to feel like, but as it turns out, it is quite similar to being a soul.

I pass through the window, closing my eyes as the particles in my body separate and come back together like some being from another world breathing. The glass passes through me like cool silk. Opening my eyes to the alley, I blink a number of times before I can make out the falling flakes of snow eddying through my body and carried by the wind. Shiloh releases my hand, and we both glide into the middle of the road. The town feels as though it is sleeping. Some shutters are closed like eyelids that are vertical instead of horizontal. The fresh layer of snow is untouched save for the occasional paw print of a wandering cat, which must be rather cold. Miles's car appears innocent enough, parked outside Duncan's with its own new dusting of snow on it. Everything looks the same as it did when we walked into the restaurant thirty minutes ago, as quiet and still as it was when we were bracing ourselves against the flakes blowing sideways on the wind. I am grateful that I can no longer feel it.

The soul of a little boy jumps up and down on the awning of the bakery, as if he is attempting to shake the snow off the top. The fabric ripples with each silent impact, yet his ghostly feet make no sound as they land. He giggles. The sound echoes, hollow and distant like wind through an empty tunnel.

I raise my hand in a gentle wave and call out, "Hello."

He notices me. Before I can say anything else, he drops through the wall of the building and disappears.

I lower my hand. "I did not mean to frighten him."

"He's probably scared, anyway." Shiloh drifts closer so she is hovering right beside me. "I doubt he understands why he's here any more than we do."

She is right. Many of the souls that came over, especially the children, would have no idea why they suddenly reappeared here. Some of them would have responded to this by becoming angry and wanting to do anything to stay, but others would be scared, waiting for the other side to bring them across. I wonder how this soul is managing to resist the pull. He did not look evil. Could he also be feeding on other souls?

Shiloh glides out in front of me. "Come on, let's go send that sucker back."

I am not sure I agree with her referring to the boy in such a way. "You do not know that he is bad."

"Yes, I do," Shiloh says. "I don't care if he's nice and not feeding on anyone else's soul. He's not supposed to be here. People are dying because ghosts like him are here."

"How unfair it is to blame somebody for their own existence."

"I'm not blaming anyone for anything. We just need to send them back where they belong, especially the ones who've gone full soul-eater." She points ahead of us, her arm leaving a subtle trail of mist. "So, the farm's this way, right?"

I glide over the road, reaching down to brush my fingertips across the asphalt. The surface is bright with new snow. Occasional icy puddles reflect our glowing forms. I must say, it is quite a lot easier moving around in the middle of the winter when you are not encumbered by the cold. Or bound to a wheelchair.

Shiloh flies out ahead of me and points. "That's the farm up there."

I nod. It is difficult to see anything in the swirling snow, but even though Shiloh and I are quite a lot dimmer than I have been in the past when projecting, enough light comes from our figures that I am able to see the blackened nubs of corn underneath piles of snow. The stalks peek through the white blanket like charred fingers reaching for the sky. The stalks must have been sheared. Perhaps to remove the reminder of the decay.

Shiloh touches a nub, but her fingers pass right through the stalk. "All this died because of the ghosts coming through, didn't it?"

That is the only explanation that makes sense. The corn is simply another thing that died because of my actions.

"I feel so bad for the Monroes, losing their crop like this," Shiloh says. "They must've lost so much money."

And Talulah.

I try to swallow the lump inside of my throat. I am not sure why I feel as though I have a lump inside my throat because I am made of nothing, so my throat does not technically exist, but I do.

In the distance, the old barn looms at the edge of the field, its jagged outline appearing and disappearing through the whirling snow and cutting into the leaden sky like a broken black tooth. The closer we get to it, the clearer it becomes that the barn has seen better days. At least I hope it has, because the days it is seeing now do not seem pleasant.

I did not spend much time looking at the barn after the explosion because I was busy being carted away in an ambulance, but the barn is somehow still standing and at least half of the roof is intact. Large pieces of the walls are missing. Some rotting wooden boards stick out of the snow like splintered bones. Ribbons of yellow caution tape flutter in the breeze, half-buried in the snow mounds. I would have thought that the tape would have been taken down long ago because I suspect whatever investigation the police led into what happened here that night has concluded, but I do not know much about the police or how they conduct investigations. A quiet thrumming comes from inside.

"Well," I say. "I suppose we should go in there."

Shiloh drops her eyes to my hands, and I notice how tightly I am wringing my fingers together.

"Don't be scared," she says. "What's the worst that could happen to us, anyway?"

I know she is attempting to poke fun at the fact that we are already dead, but we are only temporarily dead, and there are still many things that could go wrong. Besides, there are far worse fates than being dead.

She floats backward toward the barn. "I laugh in the face of danger. Ha ha ha ha!"

That is precisely the sort of attitude that has gotten her into trouble in the past, but I follow her anyway.

As we approach the building, I remember something. "Did that police officer ask Miles any more questions about what happened with the souls?"

"Lindsey?" Shiloh shakes her head. "I think she's trying to pretend none of this ever happened."

I suppose Lindsey having that reaction would make sense. I cannot imagine anybody would be keen on learning that the way they see the world is not the way that it actually is.

Once we reach the barn, I drift out in front of Shiloh through an opening in the wall. It does not take my eyes any time at all to adjust to the change in the light as I pass out of the snow and into a much deeper darkness. Old rafters creak in the wind, and flakes of snow fall through the gaps in the ceiling. A rusted pitchfork with missing tines is propped against one wall. In the corner are the skeletal remains of what must have once been a tractor. The hole I had opened in the center of the floor is no longer there, but I can see the edges of where it once was. The warped floorboards form a large ring, as though a rough and imperfect circle had been burned into the wood, and the boards in the middle of the ring are warped but sealed, save for ethereal tendrils that writhe upward like serpents seeking warmth.

The humming grows louder. Or perhaps it is not a humming, but a deep rumbling that vibrates through me like the purr of some massive sleeping cat.

Could the other side be making that noise?

I force myself closer to the opening. A tingling feeling spreads through my arms like static electricity seeking ground.

"Help me search for the membrane," I tell Shiloh.

Shiloh hangs back, her form casting wavering shadows on the dark floor. "The membrane?"

I quickly remind her that it is possible to see small patches of the other side in our world, and that the barrier can be visible to keen eyes in quite well-hidden places. I flatten onto my stomach and attempt to wrap my hands around a warped board, but I cannot make contact long enough to pull on it.

Interesting. I should be able to pry that open. Perhaps I am not quite as strong in this form as when I am on the other side.

I run my fingers around the rim of the enormous hole, which is nearly the size of the parachute we used to play with at school. The wood feels charged with static electricity under my touch, making my fingers buzz as I search for any places, no matter how small, that could mark the barrier between this world and the other side. The sensation reminds me of touching a television screen after it has been turned off. That subtle vibration that makes the tiny hairs on my arms stand up. I work my way methodically around the circumference of the hole, pressing my palms flat against each section of the wood.

After what feels like ages of searching, I notice something peculiar about one of the tendrils of energy reaching up into the barn. While the others wave and writhe like ribbons in the wind, this one appears more substantial. I follow it down to its source until my nose nearly touches the floor. At the base is a small hole about the size of a quarter.

I smile.

I swipe my hand hard across the snow, blowing it into the air with the force of the impact and revealing the hole. The edges of the hole pulse as I press my face up against it and peer through. Sure enough, I can see the other side through it. Usually, the colorless dimension mirrors this world in a rather unusual fashion, often in a way that makes gooseflesh rise on my arms, but in this case, the barn on the other side still appears to be standing.

"Is that the other side through there?" Shiloh asks. She bends down to look more closely, and her arm passes through my shoulder like a cold draft, making me tremble.

I nod and press my fingers against the squishy membrane, watching it ripple like gelatin beneath my touch. It stretches around my fingers but does not break. I pinch two bits and pull them apart. The strange substance glows where my fingers make contact, but the membrane springs back with a twang.

"So, how are you going to do it?" Shiloh asks. "You know, open the gate?"

Something dark and heavy stirs inside of me. I stare at the tiny opening.

"I suppose I will have to do it with my mind, but I am not exactly sure how. I have only done it once before."

"I bet it'll be easier this time," she says. "You're not messing around with powers you don't understand anymore."

Perhaps. I have tried to rip through the membrane before, and I was unable to do so, but I did that when I was on the other side. Will it be different from this side?

I can do this. I am capable of doing this. I opened this one, after all, and that one was quite big.

But look at the damage I caused.

Closing my eyes, I rub my hands over the smooth coolness of my arms as I try to calm myself. There will be no damage this time. I must not be afraid of this.

I stretch into a standing position, doing my best to root my feet against the barn floor and focus until I feel something beneath them. The wooden boards creak under me, although

I am fairly certain I am not the one making the sound because I have no weight. The wind whistles through the gaps in the timber. I bend and hold my hands over the opening. The other side is right there. I can feel it against my palms, as though I am touching the surface of a calm pond. It is thrumming … churning … gurgling. Like an empty stomach.

It wants those souls back. It is hungry. I simply need to help it take them.

I imagine reaching my hand through the membrane, channeling the familiar tingle from my core and down through my arms. I focus the energy into the tips of each of my fingers and press the concentrated force against the membrane. A rubbery tension pushes back against me. I persist, imagining my power as countless microscopic hands all working in unison to pry apart the barrier between worlds.

The membrane ripples like a stone has been dropped onto it, sending small waves across its surface that shimmer with an otherworldly phosphorescence.

I raise my hand. The barrier wobbles. The atmosphere shifts, becoming thick and heavy, as though the air itself has transformed into syrup. I pull my hand up higher.

A tiny hole rips open with a sizzling crackle that reminds me of bacon in a hot pan. The opening spreads like paper held against a flame.

I laugh, a rough sound coming out of me that echoes strangely in the charged air. Concentrating hard, I peel back the edges of the hole, which feels like stretching apart warm taffy. Until there is a loud crack.

The hole rips open.

The sound reverberates through me like a thunderclap. Wind roars into the depths, whipping around me with such force that the barn's remaining walls groan. The gale pulls wisps of energy from me like threads from an unraveling sweater, but it does not drag me toward it.

I whirl my head around to look at Shiloh, hovering mere feet behind me. Colin said that nobody can cross to the other side while death walking, which explains why we seem immune to the attraction of the hole, but everything else flies toward the opening at a frightening speed. The front of the tractor whips past us. The pitchfork hurtles right through Shiloh and into the gaping maw. Snow whips through the barn like microscopic bullets, collecting with all of the debris in a glowing blue ring around the vortex where this world cannot pass through. The wind screams in my ears, an otherworldly howl that drowns out all sound like the wail of a thousand lost souls compressed into a single terrible note.

I catch a flash of light as a silvery form flashes through the barn and passes through the hole so quickly that I cannot make out anything besides its scream.

Is that—was that a soul?

Another flash streaks past. Then another. They move too quickly to look like souls, spiraling through the air like leaves caught in an angry gale, but in one, I glimpse a nose. The shape of a hand. Some scream. I can hardly believe my eyes.

"Is it working?" Shiloh shouts over the roar. "Because it looks like it is!"

I ... I believe it could be. I train my eyes on the gap in the wall of the barn, waiting for more souls to come through, but none do. The roar of the wind grows impossibly loud as more debris gathers around the opening.

Until it stops.

Silence slams down around us. All of the floating debris crashes onto the ground in one big pile. I rub my fingers into my ears, but the sound did not come through them, so it does nothing to quell the ache.

I raise my eyes to Shiloh, who is staring at me with a smile stretching across her face.

"Was that it?" she asks. "Did we get them all?"

I would like to say yes, but the words are like glue because I very much doubt that it could have been that easy.

Nearly a minute of silence goes by. The humming of the other side rings in my head like tinnitus. I find the spot on the ground where the opening was a few seconds ago. There is nothing marring the membrane. The place where the opening had burned across it has sealed up.

Shiloh eventually clears her throat. "Should we go back and tell the boys what happened?"

I nod very slowly, unable to shake the feeling that something does not feel right. The other side had seemed so eager to reclaim those souls, yet not many had gone through. This passageway was quite far away from town. Would it have been strong enough to pull all of those feeding ghosts away when not even a magnet inside of their chests could dissuade them?

A scraping sound draws my attention toward the barn entrance. I whirl around and see an elderly gentleman shuffling through the gap in the weathered wall. His heavy coat hangs around his skeletal frame, dusted with snow that has not melted against the fabric. There is something most unsettling about the way he moves. His limbs jerk and twitch in a manner that reminds me of the puppets I once saw at a traveling carnival, where the puppeteer was quite inexperienced and made the dolls dance in most unnatural ways. His head tilts at an impossible angle, and I notice with growing horror that his eyes have gone completely white, like pearls set into his weathered face.

He looks directly at me. I notice his attention with a jolt.

Oh no.

"He can see us," Shiloh hisses. "Francesca, why can the scary man see us?"

I cannot reach the words. The man's head cocks to the side, his thin white hair hanging in stringy clumps around his face. I am too surprised to say anything. The man runs toward us at full speed, his muddy coat billowing out behind him like dark wings as his arms stretch toward us.

28

Francesca

I drag Shiloh upward, coming to a stop below what remains of the roof boards. The man's gnarled fingers claw through the space where we had been floating a second before.

"What the hell?" Shiloh hisses. "Who is that?"

I do not know, but I have no desire to make his acquaintance. The possessed man lets out a yell, stomping his feet and kicking at a pile of snow with the toe of his boot like an upset child.

"Hello, sir," I call down to him, as it seems impolite to not at least attempt civility. "How are you doing this evening?"

Shiloh stares at me open-mouthed, as though I have sprouted a second head made entirely of butterflies.

The man's ragged breaths form little clouds in the air. His coat flaps open as he paces beneath us, reminding me rather uncomfortably of a hyena I watched on television once circling underneath a tree where a leopard was eating a gazelle. I am not entirely certain what he could do to us if he caught us. Could he drain our energy as well?

Could he be one of the Monroes? Talulah's grandfather perhaps, or an uncle I had not known about? Goodness, how much loss must this family bear?

I do not believe the man plans on talking to us, and I do not think that anything we say would dissuade him from wanting to harm us, so I wave at Shiloh to follow me and we slip out of the barn through the hole in the roof. We come to a stop on the other side of the road among a group of dense trees that stretch their skeletal limbs toward the night sky, bending in the wind and creating a moving lattice of black against the dark gray. The snow has collected in the crooks of branches like little pillows where birds might rest. The white blanket on the ground muffles all sound as though the entire forest is wrapped in cotton. Well, except for the heavy breathing coming from Shiloh, which is a peculiar habit of souls I have noticed, since none of them actually have to breathe and technically cannot because they no longer have lungs. So many souls mimic the behavior of the living. Old habits are like singular socks after you have lost one of the pair. It feels wrong to throw them away simply because they are no longer useful.

"Do you think he will follow us?" I ask, keeping my voice low because I do not know how safely sound travels in this form. None of the possessed souls appear to be having any trouble finding us, which is rather inconvenient.

Shiloh peers back through the trees. "I don't know. But I've had it up to here with those creepy assholes and their weird eyes."

The eyes are not the thing that disturbs me the most, although they do remind me rather uncomfortably of marbles, and marbles do not belong inside a person's head. I can imagine Richie putting one in his empty eye socket to upset me.

I glide higher into the branches of a pine tree. Its needles still hold their green color beneath caps of white that remind me of powdered sugar on pastries.

"Our approach was wrong." I peer down at Shiloh, who is rising after me. "The portal was not strong enough to pull through the souls that have taken bodies. There must be more out there than the ones we have seen."

"Yeah," Shiloh says. "Word sure travels fast around here."

I wrap my arms around my stomach as the wind blows snow through the trees. Those souls are conscious. They know what they have to do in order to stay here, and they know we are doing something to stop them. If they are not above consuming other people's bodies to stay on this side, they will not be above killing us just for getting in their way.

"Screw them," Shiloh says. My eyebrows leap up at her words. "Seriously. Screw them. Who do they think they are?"

They probably believe that they are superior to everybody else. These are not good people, but Shiloh knows this already, so I believe she is looking for me to offer some cathartic agreement, or perhaps she would like me to make some sort of joke. I am not good at making jokes unless they happen by accident, which they often do.

"I do not believe that will help," I say, watching snowflakes drift through me. "There are quite a lot of them and it would take a great deal of time."

Shiloh's smile grows, but her eyes remain serious. She turns her face down at the ground some twenty feet below us, not flinching at the flurry of snow that comes blowing off a tree. "So, how do you plan to get them all through?"

"I do not have a plan. The souls inhabiting the living are

tethered to this side through their hosts. The bodies act as anchors that prevent them from being pulled through."

Shiloh scrunches up her face. "What if we made the gate, like, huge?"

I consider this. "While that could work, I am concerned about the force it would generate, considering how many objects were drawn into our modest opening."

"Who cares if that old barn gets destroyed?" Shiloh shrugs. "It's not like anyone's using it."

That is true, although … a peculiar thought floats through my mind like a soap bubble. "What if, instead of enlarging the opening, we were to bring every possessed person closer to it? The pull would be much stronger at close range, similar to the way a vacuum cleaner works better when it is right up against the carpet."

"You mean lure them all here?" Shiloh turns in the direction of the barn. "How? It's not like we can put up flyers for a Come Get Banished to the Other Side party."

I cannot help but smile. "Perhaps we could offer something they find irresistible?"

Shiloh nods slowly. She understands exactly what I am saying. "Us."

I nod, although my stomach feels rather like it is attempting to tie itself into a bow. "Perhaps we could traverse the town and collect them, rather like gathering butterflies, except in this case, we would encourage them to chase us back here."

Shiloh grins. "And once we get all those creeps to the barn—"

"I will open the gate."

I wrap my arms around myself, feeling peculiarly cold for someone who is incorporeal. The plan sounds logical when I put it into words, but I cannot shake the feeling that I am overlooking something important or that there is some clear reason why it would not work that I am simply not seeing.

Perhaps Miles will be able to tell me. He is rather good at noticing things other people do not.

"I would like to consult the others," I say.

"Yeah, Miles would lose it if we tried anything without running it by him first."

I cannot help but notice the singular omission in her statement. "I imagine Jonah would be quite concerned as well."

"Yeah, sure. Both of them."

She averts her eyes in a manner that causes me to tilt my head, because that is a rather unusual reaction for her to have at the sound of Jonah's name. I suppose the incident at the nursing home has cast a shadow over things, although I simply do not understand the big problem. Jonah's actions were like those of a sleepwalker. One cannot blame a person for what they do in their sleep. I have never seen anyone love another person quite like Jonah loves Shiloh. Well, except perhaps how Shiloh loves Max, but that love is different because the way I see it, loving her brother when she must protect him from the terrible things that keep happening to him is rather like being forced to learn an instrument she does not want to play. The love she has for Jonah reminds me of choosing a favorite color. People do not choose a favorite color because they must, but because something inside them simply knows it is right. But I suppose the trouble with sleepwalkers is that you must sleep next to them.

Before I can inquire deeper about her feelings, she turns and glides over the treetops with the casual grace of someone who has forgotten that heights are supposed to be frightening. I increase my speed and follow her.

29

JONAh

I jam a chair under the door. My hands won't stop shaking, but I manage to wedge it in there tight. Like that'll make a difference when those assholes come for us.

Or for Shiloh.

Got to keep moving. Got to keep talking.

"Got the kitchen done," I call to Miles, who's somewhere in the dining room. "You good over there?"

Miles pokes his head in from the hallway, wearing that expression he gets when he's about to tell me I did something wrong. I wonder what it'll be this time.

"Did you put magnets under all the windows?" he asks.

"And doors," I say. "The big one's in the fridge."

With Shiloh. Shiloh, who told me we're done. Shiloh, who died right in front of me—

"That's not a good idea," Miles says, and I sigh. I knew it. "The cold will stop the electromagnet from working, not to mention reduce its battery life. Besides, most refrigerators have metal walls which could interfere with or weaken the magnetic—"

"*Okay.*" I really don't need a physics lecture right now. We already talked about it. All the magnets stay around us, but when it's time for Shiloh and Francesca to come back, we take the things away in case they repel them. "But it's the most powerful one we have and we need it to protect us all from ghosts, so where do you want it?"

Miles opens his mouth, then closes it. I try not to think about the electromagnet in the fridge, sitting between Shiloh's feet. I for sure don't want to think about Shiloh lying on the ground surrounded by bunches of broccoli like she's not the most important thing in the world. Picturing her gives me a feeling like heartburn, or like someone lit a match and dropped it into my stomach. Did someone suck all the oxygen out of here?

"You good?" Miles asks in a tone that makes me want to punch something, but I've tried to punch too many things already today.

I am good. I'm peachy, except for the fact that there's no air in here and I can't fucking *breathe*. I grip the neckline of my T-shirt, glad for the stab of pain that shoots up my bad arm at the movement. Miles notices. Of course he does. The guy's a walking anxiety detector.

He scrunches his forehead. "You want to talk about it?"

Nope. I'm done talking. What I want is for Shiloh to stay alive long enough for me to tell her how sorry I am. I lied right to her face about the foolery and did the worst possible thing to her again just when she started to trust me. Shiloh's strong. She's always been strong, and honestly, I'd be pissed if she didn't want to end things after what I did.

She deserves better than not knowing what's going on in my head, but you know what? So do I. I'm used to not being able to control the crap my head throws at me. I thought it was my brain being useless at being a brain because that's how I was born. Chalk it up to all the booze my mom drank or the drugs she took while carrying me, breaking every cardinal rule of pregnancy and sucking at being a mom even before I was born. Could learning to control the foolery be as simple as learning to control my own thoughts? Can I even do that?

I twist one of the beads on my necklace, focusing on how smooth it feels between my fingers. I don't know much, but I do know what I told Francesca back there was right. I forgot all about that road trip lecture Moe gave me. Probably because I was fourteen and so high only dogs could hear me at the time, but I was never going anywhere good, and back then I was pretty sure I'd never make it past eighteen, but I can see that life now. I may have messed things up with Shiloh, but it's not too late to turn things around. It can't be. I'm not expecting her to give me another chance now, but maybe … I don't know. Maybe if I could show her that I can pull myself together, over time I can put my money where my mouth is and prove I can be a man for her. Maybe not the kind of man she deserves, but at least a man who's going to try with everything he's got.

I just have to make it through tonight. More importantly, I got to get *her* through tonight.

I give Miles a firm nod.

He opens his mouth like he wants to say something else when something slams against the window over the sink. My head snaps toward the kitchen so fast a twinge of pain shoots down my neck.

The glass isn't cracked, but that hit was hard enough to be close. Someone wants our attention. Or some *thing*.

Miles knits his brows. "Maybe it was a bird?"

"In the middle of the night?"

He gives me a look like *I don't know.* I guess owls are nocturnal, aren't they?

I force my legs to move. Every ounce of common sense I have left screams to run the other way, but since when did I ever listen to common sense? I grab a knife from the block and climb onto the counter, pressing my face up against the glass.

Something shifts across the pane. I jerk my face away as lines form in the frost like invisible fingers drawing in steam. The lines thicken. Shift. Form into something that makes my blood run cold. A perfect handprint pressed against the glass.

"Oh shi—"

The window explodes.

I throw myself off the counter and onto Miles as the glass rains down. I try to tackle him, but the guy's built like a linebacker compared to me and I barely move him. The ghost glasses. Where the hell are the ghost glasses?

I dig them out of my pocket and jam them onto my face. I close one eye and run the other over the prep table ... the alphabet written out on order pads ... pots ... pans ...

This ghost of a middle-aged woman floats above the knife block like a cooking show host from hell. She's a tiny thing, barely five feet tall and skinny as hell. Her hair is curled. Her floral apron shows decades-old splatters that look a hell of a lot like blood, and half her face is caved in like somebody went to town on her with a rolling pin. Maybe her husband because dinner was late. Her manicured fingers wrap around a meat cleaver. Something tells me I'm not the first guy she's tried to hack apart since she crossed over from the other side.

I can barely find my voice. "*Get down!*"

The cleaver whistles past my ear as I hit the deck. It clangs into the wall exactly where my head had been.

I raise my head. The ghost charges at us. Her mouth stretches into a silent scream that seems louder than any actual sound.

I roll away, biting back every curse word I know as broken glass digs into my palm and my bad arm lights up with white-hot pain as my weight falls on it. A blast of cold flies past my shoulder. I yank a cast iron pan down from the counter and swing it at her. It passes through her leg and cracks a floor tile because apparently I forgot how ghosts work in the five seconds since I put on these stupid glasses.

Shiloh.

I need to get this thing away from Shiloh.

"The dining room!" I scream. "Get to the dining room!"

Miles takes off down the hallway, his boots slamming against the floorboards. I lurch after him, flipping the lights off to make it easier to see the ghost and almost tripping over my own feet in the scramble.

"What the hell is her problem?" I hiss, pushing hard to catch up.

Miles makes a choked sound. Right. Stupid question.

The air's charged with something I can't see. A metal stool slides off the bar. Before I can leap out of the way, the stool's leg swings sideways like a bat, slamming into my shin. Pain flares through the bone. I yell through clenched teeth and hop back, ripping off the glasses because I can't see in those stupid things.

A scraping noise. Another stool drags itself across the scuffed floor toward Miles, moving like it's got a mind of its own.

"Look out!"

The stool flies at him. He barely dodges it and it smashes into the bar with a crunch.

Miles vaults over the wreckage to get to me. "Where is it coming from?"

I shove the glasses at him. He's better off with these things than I am, and the second he gets them on, his eyes go huge, pupils locking onto something right behind me.

He points. "Behind you!"

I hit the floor hard. The wood is warm and sticky under my hands, years of polish mixed with god-knows-what clinging to my palms. There's probably some blood in there from the broken window too but now is not the time to check that out. I crawl toward the bar, fingers scrabbling against the rough underside of a toppled stool until they close around the horseshoe magnet I tucked there earlier. I wave it in the air like an idiot.

Wait.

The electromagnet.

I need the big one. The one that might actually do something against this bitch.

"Miles!"

"What?"

"Cover me."

"*What?*"

God, I sound like an action hero in a dumb war movie, but there's no time to cringe at myself. I drop the magnet and run for the kitchen, dodging flying cups and bowls like I'm in some twisted game of dodge plate. A glass whizzes past my ear and explodes against the wall, shards spraying my shoulder. The bar stools lie overturned on the floor. I can barely see enough to stop myself from tripping over my feet, but I keep moving.

I crash through the kitchen and hit the fridge in a half-skid, barely catching myself on the handle and yanking it open. There it is. Between Shiloh's feet. I grab it, my fingers brushing against Shiloh's limp leg. She looks so peaceful. Like she's taking a nap.

Focus.

I sprint back to the bar. The second I skid through the doorway, I stop dead. Miles is pinned to the wall, his feet dangling three feet above the ground.

I slam the electromagnet at his feet and flip it on. Miles screams. He crashes to the floor in a boneless heap.

I scramble over the broken glass and yank the glasses off his face, the frames still warm from his skin as I jam them onto my nose. I scan the room, the lenses making everything look like a creepy old photograph, but there's nothing in here now. Miles doubles over on his hands and knees, his shoulders heaving as he retches onto the ground.

All I can do is stare at him. "What was that?"

He spits bile, the acrid smell making me wince. "That *thing*." His body shudders. "Is it gone?"

One more look through the glasses. "Looks like it." I yank the damn things off my face. "What was it doing to you?"

"Feeding on me." Miles wipes his mouth on his sleeve. "At least it sure felt like it."

Jesus Christ. That woman didn't even say a word, just went straight in for the kill. Why are all these creepy fuckers trying to murder us all the time? Can't they ever give us a break?

A loud thud echoes from the kitchen. My brain goes blank. Miles and I exchange a glance.

I bolt down the hallway, almost losing the glasses as I skid around the corner. The kitchen's empty. No undead murder-mom in sight. Another crash.

It's coming from the fridge. The fridge where Shiloh is.

Oh god.

I practically teleport across the kitchen. My foot skids for half a second on something—soup? Sauce? *Blood*? But I catch myself on the counter and keep moving.

There they are. Shiloh and Francesca. Lying on the floor, holding hands. The fridge hums.

I drop to my knees and press two fingers against Shiloh's neck. Cold. Way too cold. But her pulse is there. Francesca is the same. Alive. Barely.

But something feels off. More than unconscious-people-in-a-fridge off. The hair on the back of my neck stands up. I turn, scanning the kitchen through these stupid ghost glasses, and that's when I see it. The cooler. Knocked over on its side. Blue liquid seeps out of it, forming a puddle on the concrete.

30

JONAH

I crash to my knees next to the broken glass, hovering my hands over the blue puddle. I try to scoop up the spilled liquid, hissing as shards of broken glass slice into my palms. The stuff is everywhere, mixing with dirt and God knows what else on this nasty floor.

"No no no." Blood mingles with the blue drug as I shove my hands through the mess. "Come on, you piece of shit, work with me."

A strangled sound comes from behind me. Miles stands in the open doorway, pressing his fist against his mouth like he's going to puke. I can't let him jam up on me. Not right now.

"Grab one of those syringes," I snap.

He rips open the sterile package with trembling fingers. A cold knot forms in my stomach, but I push it down. This isn't about me or my issues with needles. I cup the blue liquid in my bloody palms, but the stuff seeps between my fingers and drips onto the concrete. Miles dips the quivering needle into the mess. He draws it up slow, and I watch the dirty blue drug climb the plastic barrel. He presses the tip of the needle onto the floor, but all he drags in is air.

He holds up the syringe. It's half full. Tops. That's barely enough juice for one person, let alone two. And that's assuming we're cool with injecting floor crud directly into someone's bloodstream, which is not happening.

Oh my God.

I sit back on my heels, breathing hard as I stare at the syringe. "That wouldn't happen to be our only supply of the lifesaving drug capable of bringing Shiloh and Francesca back into their bodies, would it?"

Miles doesn't answer. He doesn't have to. Colin gave us backups, which we stored in the same place as the original doses. How dumb are we?

"I'm no doctor," I keep going, "and I've watched people shoot up some seriously questionable shit in my time, but even the most desperate guy wouldn't shoot up a dose that's more floor dirt than drug."

Miles nods, looking sick. "I know."

"What the *hell* are we going to do?"

He bends over, bracing his blue-stained hands onto the grimy floor and shaking his head. "I don't know."

"We can't give them this."

"I *know*."

We are so monumentally screwed. I've seen enough to know that the world doesn't cut anyone a break, but this is a whole new level of cosmic middle finger. I lift one of the vials off the floor. The tape around the outside holds some of the glass together in a sad kind of way, but there's still some there in the bottom of the container. I tilt the thing. Blue liquid pools at the bottom, caught in the curve of glass held together by tape.

"Miles. Give me two fresh needles."

He fumbles with the packaging, the crinkle of plastic unnaturally loud in the tense silence. He passes me a syringe, and I try to still my hands as I line up the first needle with what's left in the vial. I draw up the blue drug, watching the measurement marks on the side of the syringe like my life depends on it. Like Shiloh and Francesca's lives depend on it. Because they do. The needle scrapes against the glass as I try to get every last drop. The first syringe fills to exactly two ccs. That's enough for Francesca. I pass it back to Miles, who balances it on the metal shelf.

"Come on," I mutter through clenched teeth, positioning the second needle. "A little more."

Miles adjusts his grip on the vial, angling it so the remaining liquid pools where I can reach it. The second syringe fills slower. 2.5 CCs. Then all I drag in is air.

I lay the second syringe next to the first one. Shiloh doesn't have enough. Colin said she needed three.

Who the hell did this?

Probably that ghost. But how could the bitch have known what these were?

Miles grips handfuls of his hair like he's trying to pull his head off. "Why did I keep it on such a high shelf?"

One shot for each of them. It should be enough, but if something goes wrong or if something happens to the needles ... I leave smears of blue on my phone screen as I dial Colin's number. It goes to voicemail. Useless motherfucker.

"Colin, it's Jonah. The blue drug got smashed. We need more. Call me back."

I hang up and immediately call again, my fingers leaving sticky blue smudges on the screen. Voicemail. I curl my hand into a fist, feeling my nails bite into my palm.

"Listen, you creepy mouse-killing bastard, they're going

to die if we don't get more of that drug. So pick up your goddamn *phone*."

My voice cracks on the last word, echoing off the walls of this glorified meat locker. I press his number again, pacing the fridge as Miles watches me.

"Colin, I swear to God, if you don't call me back, I'm going to drive over there and wring your fucking neck."

I try him one more time. Nothing but that automated voice telling me to leave a message. The clock on my phone shows 2:47 AM. Why is he such a heavy sleeper? Did he turn up the white noise to block us out?

I run my hand through my hair, feeling it stick up from the dried blood and drug residue. Come on. *Think*. They each get one dose. We still have enough for Francesca and almost enough for Shiloh. We could divide it evenly. Miles could do the math. As long as we don't screw it up, they should be fine. Or we'll kill them both.

There's a knock on the door. I whip my head around.

"Police!" a deep voice barks from outside. "Who's in there?"

Jesus Christ. Perfect timing. Miles hisses in a breath that sounds more like a wheeze. I hold my breath, the cold air burning my lungs.

"Jonah, what do we do?" Miles hisses. "What do we *do*?"

I want to say run, but running would mean leaving Shiloh and Francesca in this fridge. But the cops can't find us here with two unconscious bodies and enough medical supplies to stock a black-market clinic.

Another knock. I press my face into the gap in the door to peer out through the gap.

"I know you're in there." A flashlight beam scans over the kitchen, glinting off the shards of glass and the meat cleaver still on the ground. I turned off the lights in the fight with the ghost, so at least they're not still on. "Come out!"

I swear under my breath. God, those assholes at Bethany PD know how to pick their moment.

Miles has his patented deer-in-headlights look, his face so pale that he looks about as dead as the girls do. I know he's debating what to do, his brain running through the same things I am and then some, given how fast he thinks, but I got to get that cop away from here.

I step away from Miles and jab a finger at Shiloh. "Stay right here. If things go south, get her out of here."

His mouth drops open. "You're not going to—"

I sure am. I step out of the fridge, pulling the door behind me until it clicks. Miles tries the handle, but that's the one good thing about this door not opening from the inside. Miles is smart enough not to press the panic button with the cops here.

My bad arm screams in protest as I raise my hands high over my head. "Don't shoot."

As if on command, the cop kicks open the door. The chair I jammed in there cracks and tips onto its side. So much for that defense.

The cop trains his flashlight on me, the harsh beam burning into my retinas like a laser. I curse and turn my head, the spots dancing in my vision making me dizzy.

"Do you mind?" I snap.

There's a pause. "Weatherby." The voice is heavy with recognition and sounds a little weary.

Of course he recognizes me. He and every other cop in this stupid town. I really wasn't that bad a kid. All I did was sell some drugs before all of this happened. People around here are starved for entertainment.

But I can't let him see it get to me. Through the glare, I

can't see his face, so I address him in general terms. "You mind flipping on the lights so I can see which of my old pals I have the pleasure of speaking to?"

The cop flips on the light. Oh dear lord, that's bright. I want to use my hands to shield my eyes, but I don't dare move them. I've been around enough cops to know what I can get away with and when, and this guy is pissed.

Oh. I know him. He's one of the old crusty detectives with a buzzcut and a permanent scowl etched into his grizzled face that makes me doubt he has smiled much in the past twenty years. One of the ones who threw Shiloh in jail.

His name comes to me.

"Finnegan." I grin. "Good to see you, man."

He doesn't correct me, so I assume I'm right. "What the hell are you doing here?"

"Well, Detective, I didn't break in if that's what you're thinking." The lie sounds stupid as I'm saying it, but I just got to keep talking until I can come up with a plan. "I was passing by when I saw the door open, and I thought maybe someone else broke in, so I came to check. I was going to call you if I saw something suspicious. Pinky promise." I wag the little fingers of both hands, which are still raised because you never know.

"At 2 AM? Try again."

"Okay, look. I'm sorry. I was here earlier, and I forgot my phone, so I swung by to grab it."

His gaze moves away from me. I side-eye the open bags of magnets and other crap open on the tables, their contents scattered like evidence of a kindergarten explosion, and the alphabet order cards strung up above them swaying slightly in the building's ancient heating system. Finnegan looks like he has no clue what to make of it all, but he knows I didn't come in here because I forgot my phone. I hope to hell he doesn't go through and see the mess we've all made of the bar.

"You realize this is breaking and entering. That it's a serious offense?"

"Sure." I grin. "I tried to call it Finnegan, but it would only answer to serious offense."

"Can it, kid," Finnegan grumbles. "That your car out front?"

I open my mouth to say yes, but pause, since no, it's technically not. It belongs to Miles, but I don't want any cops showing up here and recognizing it, or they might come looking for him. Finnegan turns his eyes down to talk into his radio. I try to ignore the burning in my bum shoulder that hasn't moved at this angle since my last physical therapy session. I bet my physical therapist would be proud of me for that if she weren't such a hard ass. I'm painfully aware of the closed door behind me. Miles isn't making a sound, though I swear I can hear him breathing from here. I need to get this cop out of here so he can get the girls to his car.

Finnegan holsters his gun and takes out a pair of handcuffs, making a twirling motion with his finger that makes the metal catch the overhead light. "You know the drill."

Do I run? Lead him far enough away from Miles that he can hit the panic button and get the door unlocked? I don't love the idea of running on icy sidewalks away from a guy with a gun. He has no reason to shoot me, but I guess he could probably come up with one after I was dead.

I turn around. Finnegan comes toward me, the handcuffs jingling as he walks. I got no choice. I have to run.

I sprint around the prep counter to the dining room, my heart hammering against my ribs. Finnegan yells after me. I trip over the full mop bucket, hopping on one leg to catch my balance and praying I don't slip because my balance is not what it used to be. But Finnegan stays standing in the doorway. His flashlight's on the ground. He opens his mouth. Blood pours through his teeth. He crashes to his knees and tips forward onto his face with a thud, revealing an old man standing behind him holding a long icicle gleaming crimson. The same man Miles hit with his car and dragged behind the dumpster.

The man runs his tongue along his broken front teeth and steps inside.

31

Miles

I press my ear against the fridge door, my heart literally trying to punch its way out through my ribcage.

Deep breaths. Take deep breaths.

But taking deep breaths is not helping me right now because there's not enough air in here. I don't trust that a fridge has enough ventilation for three people to survive for long. There's also a real chance that Jonah will be arrested and leave us behind in here to suffocate.

He said the door doesn't open from the inside. Surely there has to be a way I can open it in an emergency.

I strain to hear the voices outside. I recognize Jonah's from the tone, all high pitched and way too casual for the gravity of the situation. The police officer sounds gruff. It's a man. That much is clear. So it's not Lindsey, which is good because she would have recognized my car out front and Jonah would not have been able to talk his way out of the situation. The voice is too low to be Chief Schnebly's, but maybe it's Officer

Crumpler's? Or Officer Buzzcut's, whose name I never learned but I'm pretty sure starts with an N?

The magnets. The magnets are out on the counter. The officer has to suspect there are more people in here than Jonah, especially since the place has been more or less ransacked after our run-in with that ghost.

Stop. Panicking.

Jonah can handle this. He's good at mouthing off to cops. Although come to think of it, that's exactly what might get us all arrested.

I'm glad I at least closed Shiloh and Francesca's eyes because otherwise they'd *really* look like dead bodies. The cold is seeping through my pea coat into my bones. Is it getting harder to breathe in here? Jonah wouldn't have locked me in if I could die so quickly, would he?

There's a low laugh outside. I press my ear harder to the door and practically beg it to let me hear what's happening, but I hear nothing. Seconds pass. Something hard slams against the door.

I stumble back, glancing around for anything I could use to defend myself, even though my only option is a head of broccoli. The handle turns. Jonah sticks his head inside.

"We're getting out of here." He throws a key fob at me. I catch it, then almost drop it because of course I would drop our escape option. "Bring the girls to the car. I'm going to distract him. Okay?"

My stomach does a flip. "Distract who? The officer?"

Jonah's face drains of color, and he takes off running. I force my trembling legs forward and peek through the gap.

It's the man. The one I hit with my car. The one who should be dead, but is not dead because he's standing right there holding a bloodied icicle and moving way too fast for someone who got mashed by a freaking car.

His white eyes snap to me. I stumble back behind the door like that could make him forget he saw me.

"Hey, asshole!" Jonah yells. "Over here!"

Footsteps pound away from the kitchen. When I risk another look, the kitchen is empty.

Okay. Got to go. *Right now.*

Getting out of here feels like a bad plan, but so does barricading ourselves in a walk-in fridge. I run over to Francesca and grip under her arms. Her head lolls against my shoulder as I gather her up and try not to think about how much she feels like a doll.

Keep it together. Can you please keep it together for, like, five minutes?

I jog toward the door, pressing Francesca's head against my chest like maybe if I hold her tight enough, she'll be okay. Glass smashes in the bar room. I don't stop. Stopping means death and we can't die, even though it feels like I might drop dead from sheer panic because my legs feel like they're made of Jell-O and my lungs can't seem to get enough air.

I'm almost at the open door when my feet skid to a stop. A body lies face-down in an expanding pool of blood. The beige uniform sends an unexpected pang of relief through me, which makes me feel like a terrible person because what kind of person gets relieved at someone's death? But I'm relieved that it's not Lindsey. Or Schnebly. Or any of the surprisingly decent guys at the police station. This is one of Shiloh's dad's officers, which is not to say he wasn't decent, but it's also not to say that he was, and—

Breathe.

I try to step over him without slipping in his blood. More glass breaks from the dining room. Got to move got to move got to move.

I run down the alley, taking a bunch of mini steps on the

ice so I don't slip. I shift Francesca onto one arm and dig the key fob out of my pocket. My giant thumb slips twice before finding the unlock button.

The car chirps. I yank open the back door and lift Francesca into the seat with arms that feel like overcooked spaghetti. Her body curls over itself, her head slumping forward against the upholstery. She's so limp. I have to fight the urge to check her pulse again. There's no time.

One down. One to go.

I stumble back into the pub. My foot catches on the dead officer's leg and I nearly face-plant. Stupid giant feet.

I catch my balance on the prep counter and rush to Shiloh, hoisting her bony body onto my shoulder. I kick the door open maybe harder than necessary, my eyes darting around the kitchen for that possessed man, but he's not in here. Jonah won't be able to hold that guy for long. Not with his barely healed arm.

I hurry down the icy steps, holding onto Shiloh tighter as I skid on the asphalt of the main road. Every gasp burns in my lungs. I reach the sidewalk.

My foot skids out from under me. My stomach lurches. I twist my body hard to get under Shiloh, wrenching her on top of me so I can break her fall. She lands on my chest, cracking her forehead on the concrete over my shoulder.

No.

I push her up, her neck bending down at a painful angle, and lay her flat on her back, scrambling onto my knees to check her forehead. Blood trickles down from her hairline.

The edges of my vision blur. Colin said that any trauma to the body could prevent the soul from returning. What if I've killed her? What if she can't come back because I couldn't keep her safe for five minutes?

In the car. I have to get her in the car.

I force myself onto my feet, cradling Shiloh's head as I half-carry and half-drag her the rest of the way.

"I'm sorry." I lay her across the back seat next to Francesca, resting her head on the flat part of the seat to minimize any more damage. Jonah's going to kill me if Shiloh survives this. When. *When* she survives this.

Someone yells from inside. I want nothing more than to jump in the driver's seat and peel out of here, but I need to get the drugs. And *Jonah*. I'm about to sprint back inside when something catches my eye from down the road.

My whole body goes rigid.

Someone is walking down the street toward me. They're twenty, maybe thirty feet away, and the figure looks too small to be male. She's taking big steps like she's remembering how to walk, and she's dragging a long pole beside her that makes this awful scraping sound against the road that makes me want to press my fingers into my ears.

I can't move. But I have to move, because I don't want to wait for whoever that is to reach me, so I blip the car locked and run as hard as I can back into the pub. I leap over the dead body and rush over to the needles. The two blue syringes are still sitting on the shelf. My hands shake as I find a Zip-Loc bag, almost dropping it twice before I manage to get it open.

"Come on, for the love of God." I place the two needles into the bag, trying not to stab myself as I shove them into my coat pocket. If I drop these, we're done. Game over. No pressure or anything.

"JONAH!" I snatch both coats off the floor because Shiloh and Francesca will need them when they wake up. "WE NEED TO GO!"

In seconds, Jonah staggers through the doorway, clutching

his bad arm. His black hair is glued to his forehead with sweat. He grins at me. Blood stains his teeth.

"Ready?" he says, smiling like an absolute psychopath who thinks this is all totally normal.

Obviously. I grab the rest of the sterile needles. Both of us sprint for the door.

A woman steps into the doorway. She looks sixty-something, with a long gray braid trailing down her back and those backward eyeballs all of these scary people have. There's a metal garden rake in one of her hands that she's using like a walking stick.

I recognize her with a jolt of horror. "Is that—"

"Ethel from the bakery," Jonah confirms. "Or whatever's left of her."

"She looks m-mad."

"Do you think Shiloh stopped buying dinosaur cookies from her?" Jonah tries to joke, but this is not a time to joke because my heart feels like it's going to explode right out of my chest.

Ethel's smile is wrong. Like someone who's never seen a real smile trying to copy one.

"I heard some yelling over here and thought I'd c-come h-help," she says. "You look like sweet k-kids. I'm sure if you gave this up, we c-could forget any of this ever happened, couldn't we, Ian?"

The man drags himself out of the bar room and stops behind us, wiping his bloody mouth with the back of his hand. He shrugs.

"But they won't leave it alone," he lisps through broken teeth. "Will they?"

I glance around the kitchen, my brain firing in fifty directions at once as I try to calculate escape routes while cataloging every horrible way this could end. Suspects will typically block all exits, reducing escape options and giving them a tactical advantage in confined spaces. I need to maintain situational awareness. Identify any improvised weapons and tactical advantages. Remember my training, and—hold on. Where did that even come from? It wasn't me. It must have been from some cop training that Randall Zweering once did. Apparently, all of his knowledge becomes mine in times of high stress.

But that could actually help me right now. I know he's not actually living inside my brain because I spend every waking second of every day trying not to think about him, but like it or not, he's part of me now. His thoughts are my thoughts. His habits and learned behaviors and instincts can be mine, too.

Come on Zweering.

Do your thing.

Ethel is blocking the alley, which leaves ... what, as our exit? The dining room? The man is blocking our path. I breathe out a long sigh, trying to calm my head as best as I can under these circumstances. Please. Tell me what to do.

I breathe in deeply, feeling my mind shift as my thoughts organize themselves with uncanny precision. The cast-iron pans hanging above the prep station are heavy. They could deliver blunt force trauma if I can reach them. The knife block sits on the far counter ... too exposed, reaching that would require crossing into their attack range. I turn my head up to the sprinkler system. Foam-based. For kitchen fires. Would create immediate disorientation, reduce visibility, compromise footing ... I'm twelve feet from the main exit. Eight seconds at full sprint, factoring in the slick floor. The man is favoring his right side. Ethel's posture suggests full mobility but those white eyes mean she might not track quick lateral movement effectively. The thoughts aren't mine, not really, but they flow through me with cold clarity. For a second I'm not terrified Miles. I'm seeing everything through Zweering's eyes, his mind automatically breaking down the chaos into actionable intelligence.

But I still can't stop the anxious words from spilling out. "P-please don't do this," I beg, hating how small my voice comes out. "Y-You're not supposed to b-be here."

"Who says?" Ethel steps forward, crushing the dead officer's wrist under her foot with a crunch of bone that makes me screw up my face. "Do *you* say?"

I've been around enough school administrators to know that this woman is not hearing anything I'm saying. My heart races so fast that I think I might actually die right here. Are there more of them? Do they know about Shiloh and Francesca unconscious in the unlocked car outside?

Jonah raises his eyebrows at me. He's asking if I'm ready to run for it, but I can't move. My legs literally will not move.

The man grabs a meat tenderizer from a hook above the counter. My stomach does a gymnastics routine.

Something clicks into place in my brain. I scan the wall and spot the red control panel.

Go.

I dash across the kitchen, my body moving with a certainty that isn't my own. My finger pushes a button I somehow know is right. The alarm blares.

Foam erupts from the ceiling.

I press my hands over my ears, turning my body to shield myself as a mass of cold and slimy bubbles pours down on me. An overly sweet chemical smell fills the air. The foam turns the kitchen into a mess of white and pink as it mixes with blood.

In the corner of my eye, Ethel raises the rake. She swings it at me but stumbles. Her feet slip out from under her and she falls hard on the ground. The foam scatters and sloshes around me. It's everywhere. It's suffocating. What if we slip and fall, and they catch us?

Jonah vaults over the prep table like some kind of action hero. He launches himself toward the door and punches Ethel in the face.

I steady myself against the wall and waddle as fast as I can, the foam slipping under my boots. I tip-toe over the police officer's body, trying not to think about what I'm stepping over as I stumble out the door and into the alley.

Jonah's already running. I sprint after him, the wind cutting through my wet clothes. He yells at me to drive. I unlock the car and start it like I have a hundred times before. My breathing evens out as the engine roars. I've never been so grateful for anything in my entire life.

Our two possessed friends stumble out of the alley, wiping fire-suppressant foam off themselves and flinging it onto the snow. I'm hyperventilating now, but who wouldn't be when faced with murderous possessed people?

Zweering wouldn't be. He wouldn't panic. He'd assess. He'd act. I surrender to the muscle memory that lives inside this body. The panic recedes behind a wall of tactical focus.

Jonah slaps the dashboard. "Go!"

I hit the gas with measured pressure to maintain traction on the icy surface. The tires grip instead of slide, and the car pulls away with controlled speed. This isn't me. This is ten years of driving experience that I never had and yet somehow, it also is me now.

On the road, I check to see if those possessed people are following us and—oh no. Ethel stands in the middle of the road, waving her hands in the air and pointing at our car as she flings the foam off herself. I count five ... six ... seven ...

The blood rushes from my face. "Where are they all coming from?"

Seven—no, nine—*twelve* more possessed people move toward us at varying speeds. Some running. Some walking. A little girl no older than six steps forward. She's holding what looks like a butcher knife, dragging it behind her through the snow and leaving a thin scarlet line in its wake. I gulp.

"I'm really not trying to be a smart ass," Jonah hisses. "But I think they're here to kill us."

32

JONAh

Miles floors it. He stops trying to be a good driver and yanks on the wheel so hard we're sliding sideways on the ice like we're in Tokyo Drift.

There's a thump from the backseat. I turn around in my seat to see Francesca tipped over onto Shiloh, who's lying flat across the seats. Crushing her.

I rip off my seatbelt and reach across the center console, ignoring Miles screaming at me to sit back down because the whole goddamn car is basically sliding sideways. I try to shift Francesca's dead weight off Shiloh so they are lying parallel to each other, but then I see something that makes my heart stop dead. Red streams down Shiloh's forehead, matting her hair together. Blood. There's blood on her head.

"Stop the car!" The voice ripping from my throat doesn't even sound human. "Stop the car *right now!*"

Miles swerves onto a side street, tires struggling for purchase on the ice. "We can't stop! They're right behind—"

"I don't give a shit if Satan himself and his entire demon army are chasing us. STOP THE FUCKING CAR!"

He hits the brakes. The car stutters on the ice and I'm out before it's stopped, ripping the back door open and sending a stab of pain through my arm as I get in next to Shiloh. She's bleeding. She's bleeding a lot. I cradle her face, tilting it toward the weak light. Where's all the blood coming from? Her skin is cold. Morgue cold. Dead cold.

"What happened?" I snap. "What the hell happened to her?"

"I slipped on the ice," Miles says, and I want to punch his teeth in. "I tried to break her fall."

"You dropped her?" The words burn like acid in my mouth. "You fucking *dropped* her? Colin said no trauma. His instructions specifically *said*—"

"I know! I'm sorry, I—"

Two palms slap against my window and I let out a strangled yell. A young guy is there, his freaky white eyes boring into me through the window. He grabs the door handle. I jam down hard on the lock. His thin hair tosses in the wind as he pounds the glass. Miles squeals like a kid and floors it again, throwing me back against the seat. I curl myself around Shiloh, trying to shield her from every bump as we tear through the streets like we're in some twisted demolition derby.

"*Careful.*" I cup one hand around the back of her head. "You've got two unconscious people back here, not crash test dummies."

"I'm trying to get away!"

Yes, he is. Because we're in a car chase like in the movies. Except all the ice makes this a low-speed car chase, which means the *pedestrians* are winning.

I press my fingers to Shiloh's neck, counting the beats.

Her pulse is weak. So weak I can barely feel it. She's so fragile in my arms. One wrong move will break her, if it hasn't already. I brush her hair back, and the sight of blood matting those pale strands makes me want to throw up or kill someone. Probably Miles. I need to clean this up. Get it bandaged.

Or let her bleed out.

I barely register the thought. It's not mine.

I find my voice. "You got a first aid kit in here?"

Miles nods. I ease Shiloh across my lap and grope under the seat, almost sobbing when my fingers hit nylon. I know he didn't mean to drop her. He wouldn't do anything to hurt her on purpose. He cares about her, too.

I almost rip the alcohol wipe in half trying to open it. The cut isn't that big, maybe an inch long, but head wounds bleed like murder scenes and who knows what kind of damage is under it. I clean around the cut as gentle as I can, watching her face and praying for even a flinch. Nothing. The bleeding mostly stopped. It looks like a bruise is spreading across her forehead. What if her brain is swelling? What if she's got a concussion? Colin said trauma could wreck everything. It could turn this whole resurrection thing into permanent lights out.

I press my forehead close to hers, lowering my voice so only she can hear me.

"Please," I beg whatever sick cosmic force is running this show. "Just this once. Just let me keep her."

Because if she doesn't make it ...

"They need to stay cold," Miles says from up front, like that's helpful right now when Shiloh's bleeding in my arms.

"Can we open a window?" The suggestion leaves my mouth before my brain catches up. Stupid. So stupid. Those ghosts would be lining up to climb in.

"Opening the window won't get the car cold enough," he says. "We need to find another place."

I try to remember what that creepy mouse-killer said about temperature control, but all my brain can produce is white noise and rage. I need to stop holding Shiloh because my body heat will warm her, but it takes everything I have to push her away and hold her in place as Miles slides the car around corners.

He keeps darting these twitchy looks between the windshield and the dashboard temperature reading, like the numbers might magically change if he stares hard enough. "It's cold outside."

"You know what else is outside? All those possessed people who are actively trying to murder us."

Miles's breath comes in tiny gasps that make me feel like an asshole. "Do you have a better idea?"

I hang my head, desperately trying to think of something, but I don't have any more keys to restaurants with walk-in fridges or restaurants with coolers or gas stations with ice we could steal or literally anything else that would be helpful. "You got a place in mind?"

"Yes." His face does this thing that makes my stomach drop through the floor. "Unfortunately."

When he tells me, I unleash every curse word I know and then make up some new ones because apparently, the universe hasn't kicked me in the teeth enough times today.

But he's right that it's the easiest place to defend ourselves from, so I tell him fine. The drive there takes seven minutes, but those seven minutes feel like getting my teeth pulled without anesthesia. Not that I've ever done that. I had a buddy once who pulled his molar out with a pair of pliers. I'd have thought he was full of shit telling me that story if I hadn't been there when he did it.

My arm throbs in time with my pulse, the pain getting sharper now that the adrenaline's wearing off. Every bump in the road sends fresh waves of agony shooting from my barely healed break all the way up to my shoulder. That possessed bastard did a number on me back at the pub. The doctor prescribed me Percocet after I first had my surgery, but I chose not to take it—given, you know, everything about me— but I could go for one right now. I fish the small bottle of Tylenol out of my pocket and tip two pills onto my palm, jerking my head back to dry-swallow them. I took some a couple of hours ago. It hasn't been six hours yet, but this is a special circumstance, and I don't know how I'm going to make it through the rest of the night without some help.

Maybe I should pull my arm off, like my buddy did with his molar. That would give Miles a good story to tell.

I crane my head around to look through the rear window, half-expecting those white-eyed freaks to be running down the road following us, but they're not. At least they're not close enough for us to see. We must've outrun them. For now.

The grain processing plant finally emerges from the falling snow as we go under Route 13's overpass. I got to say, those three massive grain bins looming against the sky look way more sinister than they have any right to, like alien temples where those little green guys sacrificed virgins or something. The rust streaks running down the corrugated metal walls look way too much like dried blood. The place is still operational, but no one will be there at this time of night. Plus, it has high places and train cars and other things we can hide in without burying Shiloh and Francesca in the snow. I've passed these grain bins a million times. They were just ... there. The place where farmers stored their corn before sending it off to get ground into whatever the hell they grind corn into. But now? Well, they look impressive enough from here, but if we're going to have to climb up there on an icy ladder with two bodies slung across our shoulders, it won't be long until they look a whole lot taller.

Miles drives onto the gravel road. I grit my teeth and hold Shiloh in place as the car bounces over every goddamn rock. Jesus, it feels like someone's jabbing red-hot needles into my bones. Miles is driving like a grandma, like he's finally worried about jostling Shiloh and Francesca now that we're out of reach of the creeps, which I got to say is better than his audition for *Mad Max*.

The chain-link fence stretches across our path with this massive padlock that might as well have TURN BACK NOW DUMBASS written on it in neon letters. Miles hits the brakes so gently it takes five whole seconds for the car to stop.

"Security in this place is not what it should be," I say, trying to sound casual even though my heart's jackhammering against my ribs and my arm feels like it's being crushed in a vise. The fact that this dump barely has decent locks is a gift right now, but I'm not about to admit that out loud.

Miles is frozen behind the wheel, his knuckles white where they're wrapped around it. He looks like he's about to pass out or puke. Or both. He finally gets out of the car and grabs a pair of bolt cutters from the trunk because it is so stereotypical for Miles to have a pair of bolt cutters in his trunk. I wonder if he kept them from his old cop car. Do the cops let you keep any of that stuff? He had to surrender his gun, but do they make you surrender bolt cutters?

He probably got used to having so many random tools in his car that he went out and bought a pair for himself. That sounds more like Miles. He doesn't like breaking rules.

He stumbles out into the yellow beam of the headlights, his hands shaking so bad I'm amazed he can keep hold of the things. The lock snaps with a crack that echoes way too loud over the wind, and the chains slither down with a rattle.

He jogs back into the car and places the bolt cutters on the passenger seat. I want to tell him to breathe, that we got this, but I struggle to find the words. I got to be a better friend to him. I've been dropping the ball on that one.

Miles drives through the gate. I crane my neck up at the grain bins towering over the car. This whole place is straight out of a horror movie. The three bins are connected by a maze of rickety metal catwalks that screech and groan in the wind. Conveyor belts and loading arms jut out at right angles. Train tracks run straight under them, but there's no train here. Only three hopper cars under the loading arms. A motion sensor catches us and suddenly everything's bathed in harsh white light from the overhead floodlights. Great. Now every white-eyed bastard in Bethany knows exactly where to find us. We're going to have to barricade ourselves somewhere before they get here.

The walkways between the grain bins look about as stable as wet toilet paper, quivering in the wind like they're ready to send anyone dumb enough to climb up there plummeting fifty feet to the snow and gravel. One wrong step and you'd be painting the ground. Not that I'm planning on testing that theory.

Miles parks next to the train cars, his hands shaking so bad on the wheel I'm worried he's going to crash into one of them. I haven't been a good friend to him, and I got a lot of other things to make up for, so now is as good a time as any to start.

"Hey." I lean forward over the center console. "You're doing good."

Miles leans over the steering wheel and nods. "Thanks."

"Coming here was a good idea. Better than anything my

dumbass brain could've come up with." I swallow. "I'm sorry. For being such a dick to you lately. You've always had my back, even when I didn't deserve it."

He nods again, still staring up at the rusted metal train cars. "Someone has to keep you from getting yourself killed."

I reach over and squeeze his shoulder. I try to put everything I can't say into that gesture, all the thank yous and sorrys and I-don't-deserve-you-as-a-friends that would make us both uncomfortable if I said them out loud. He wipes his nose with the back of his hand, and for a second, he looks exactly like that scared kid I met in elementary school. The one who used to follow all the rules until I convinced him that breaking a few wouldn't kill him, although I guess it kind of did in the end. God, what did I ever do to deserve a friend like Miles?

"We're going to get through this," I tell him, meaning every word. Because if anyone can figure this mess out, it's Miles. It's always been Miles. "Okay?"

He nods. Pats my hand which is still on his shoulder, and I slump back into the seat. He clears his throat and points at the train cars sitting dead still on the tracks.

"I want to hide Shiloh and Francesca in there," he says. "So we can barricade them in there until they come back."

This is why he's the genius.

"You think they're full of corn?" I ask, because stuffing unconscious bodies into a car full of corn sounds like a recipe for suffocation.

Miles shrugs and steps out of the car, his boots breaking through the crusty snow with crunches that echo across the empty lot. I lay Shiloh's head down as gentle as I can and follow him, sizing up the rusty metal ladders bolted to the sides of each car. They're coated in about an inch of ice.

Miles snaps off a foot-long icicle and waves it at the nearest ladder. "You want to go first, or should I?"

Like there's any way in hell I'm letting him climb that death trap first.

I grab the icy metal rungs and haul myself up, biting back a curse as pain rips through my arm. Two steps up, I slip off and come crashing back to the ground, letting the curses rip. Miles looks at me, then gets one of his ideas. He gets the bolt cutters and hits the ladder with them. The metal booms and vibrates, but the ice on the lower rungs cracks, leaving bare metal, corroded to provide extra grip.

I swear I could take his face in my hands and kiss him right now. I take the bolt cutters from him and chip the ice off the rungs as I climb the rest of the way. It takes me fifteen feet straight up the side of the hopper car, and my fingers are already going numb with cold when I get to the top. One slip and I'm roadkill, but at least the ice is gone.

The train car is surprisingly wide. There's this big rectangular hatch in the middle—probably where they pour all the corn in before shipping it wherever the hell corn goes. I suddenly realize that for someone who grew up surrounded by corn and potato fields, I know nothing about farming. I yank back a rusted bolt. Miles climbs up as I get it open, both of us wincing as the car groans like it might collapse under us. I swear the wind is strong enough to make this god-knows-how-heavy thing shudder.

I peer down through the open hatch. The inside of this metal coffin is an empty cavity stretching maybe fifteen feet deep, with nothing but old corn dust coating the floor and walls that are rusted to hell. Another ladder runs down the inner wall. Apparently, one wasn't enough fun. At least this one has no ice on it.

Miles crouches next to me at the edge of the hatch. The

poor guy is shaking so hard that his teeth clack together. If he faints up here, I swear to God ...

Hiding the girls in this train car is actually kind of genius in a completely insane way. Which figures, since it's Miles. I may not like it, but it's better than anything my scrambled brain could have come up with. So I force a smile.

"Cool," I say. "Want to go get them?"

33

Shiloh

I soar through the window into Duncan's, scrunching my eyes shut as I pass through the solid glass. The feeling of doing that is beyond weird. Like I chugged too much sparkling water and my entire body is fizzing with bubbles. I'm glad it's over when I emerge on the other side, blinking and immediately coming to a stop.

What the hell?

The kitchen is a mess. Pink foam coats every surface like someone dumped a vat of Pepto-Bismol from the ceiling. It's dripping down the walls and pooling on the floor. There are broken dishes everywhere. Pots and pans on the floor. A meat tenderizer lies in a puddle of foam near the entrance to the hallway. The fridge door stands open. I glide closer to it, peering inside. Our bodies are no longer there.

"Perhaps something happened to the fridge, and they had to relocate our bodies?" Francesca suggests. "To keep them cold?"

Or someone found them. That would be my guess, based on all the wreckage.

Oh God, what if they got hurt? The foam is pink. It's not supposed to be pink. It would only be pink if it was mixed with—

No.

I look back toward the kitchen, going to brace my hand on my forehead but feeling it pass right through my skull, which is the exact opposite of comforting, when I glimpse something that makes my vision tunnel. There's a body lying face-down by the door. The body of a man wearing an all-too-familiar beige uniform.

Dad?

I stare at the man, unable to move. It can't be Dad. I just saw him, and he wasn't wearing his uniform—unless he went back to his apartment and changed. Did he come out looking for me? Did Mom wake up, find I wasn't home and call him again, telling him she was worried because she didn't know where I was? Did he get killed by one of those possessed people while he was looking for me?

I can feel Francesca staring at me as I press myself onto my stomach and peer at him, feeling a confusing wave of emotions crash over me as I see his face. Oh, thank God. It's not Dad. The close-cropped gray hair, the weathered face pressed against the tile, vacant eyes staring at nothing.

It's Finnegan. Just Finnegan.

But it's still *Finnegan.*

Finnegan was a grade-A asshole who had way too much fun throwing me in jail and spent his entire career sucking up to Dad, but seeing him dead feels wrong. A dark pool of blood has spread out from under him, mixing with the pink foam into something that looks disturbingly like strawberry milk. His wrist is bent at an unnatural angle, like someone stepped on it. He's lying in the doorway, so there's every chance someone did. I know I don't have to be sad about Finnegan dying, but I'm not glad about it either. Nobody deserves to die like this. Of course, people who don't deserve it die all the time, while plenty who do deserve it keep on living.

Static bursts from the radio clipped to Finnegan's chest. I jump at the sudden noise.

"Finnegan, please respond. What's your status?"

The radio hisses with dead air. My stomach drops as I realize what this means.

"Finnegan, do you copy?" A pause. "Finnegan, please respond."

I hover closer to the body, watching Finnegan's blood continue to trickle into the pink foam. He's been stabbed in the back. I don't know what could've made the wound, but it's bleeding a lot, soaking the beige fabric and streaming down his sides. He's been in my house. He's said hi to Mom. Shared a drink with Dad. Dad let him sit on the La-Z-Boy the morning after Max went missing. I've known him all my life, whether I liked him or not.

The radio crackles again. "Dispatch to all available units. Need immediate officer safety check at Duncan's Pub. Any units in the area, please respond."

"Copy that," a male voice cuts in. "Babin en route, ETA 3 minutes."

The name hits me like a punch to the stomach. Babin is one of Dad's guys and practically joined at the hip with Finnegan. He's the good cop to Finnegan's bad cop. Now he's going to be the one to discover Finnegan dead? I spent a lot of time being mad at those guys, but they were just doing their jobs.

If Babin is coming here … I may be invisible right now,

but Miles and Jonah are not. Finnegan hasn't been dead for long, so Miles and Jonah couldn't have gone far.

We need to warn them. They need to *hide*.

I turn to Francesca, shaking my hands out hard at my sides because if I don't move, I'm going to lose my mind. "Where do you think they went?"

Closing my eyes, I force myself through the wall again and go outside, flying up to the building's roof to scan the streets below. Miles's car is not parked out front, which means they got away, thank God, but where would they go? The blizzard is not letting me see much, but I'm one hundred percent sure that the place they went would have been Miles's idea. I'd bet money he was the one to come up with the solution to the problem. He's annoyingly logical under pressure.

I try to think about it the way he would. They would need to find somewhere cold, obviously, but also somewhere secure. They would also need to be able to access it, and it's not like Jonah has a key to every restaurant in Bethany. There's a pig farm on the edge of town that I'm pretty sure processes its own meat, but the Coleman family owns it and lives on the property, so getting caught would be a risk. Hell, the frozen food section at Walmart could work, although it's jammed with security cameras and all the way in Mount Keenan. Picturing my body being stuffed against the freezer glass between frozen pizzas and TV dinners makes me want to gag.

A police car whips around the corner, sliding to a stop in the new snow in front of the pub. Babin gets out and draws his gun, walking around to the alley with his knees bent like he remembers all of his training. His uniform buttons are under some serious strain, and his breathing is ragged from even this small amount of exercise.

I scan the horizon. On the other side of Route 13, a light comes on. I'd guess that it's coming from over at the grain processing plant. Some of the kids at school used to break into that place and drink there, even climbing the bins. On a clear night when it's not dumping snow, I bet you could have seen the edge of the world from up there.

Hold on a second.

The obvious hits me. "Oh, you've got to be kidding me."

"What is it?" Francesca asks next to me. "Is everything all right?"

I jab my finger toward the light. "Ten bucks says that's where they took us."

"Is it safe there?"

"God no." I laugh. "Jonah has been to parties there, but he doesn't like heights, so it was probably Miles who came up with the idea. Or maybe the lights turned on because a deer walked through the motion sensor, but there's one way to find out."

I tip forward toward the road, trying not to think about how fast the ground rushes up toward me. Being a soul is weird. I don't feel cold anymore, which is something I'm grateful for, but I can sense the frigid air passing through me and it's not what I'd call comfortable. Francesca rushes after me. She's way better at moving around than I am. I guess she's had more practice.

Lights are on in some of the houses now. The snow on the ground makes it light enough to see where we're going. It also makes it easy to see all the people walking around on the sidewalks or in the middle of the road who are up way past their bedtimes.

Mr. Peterson, my neighbor, walks alone in the middle of the street. I gape at him. That man broke his hip last week. How is he walking around right now?

An old lady steps out of a nearby house, wearing a fleece bathrobe that doesn't look warm enough for this weather. She closes her front door behind her and waves at Mr. Peterson, tying her bathrobe closed and tiptoeing gingerly down the stairs. Her white hair is pinned up in curlers. She hurries to Mr. Peterson, whispering something into his ear that makes them both grin way too wide. The woman looks up as if to search the sky. Her white eyeballs train on me. I don't like anything about that, so I shoot away from them, glancing over my shoulder to make sure Francesca is following me.

But there are more of them. Up ahead, old lady Jenkins hobbles out of the shadows, leaning on her cane with every step. A girl runs out from behind a parked car and everything inside me stops. I recognize her. She's in Max's class. I saw her this morning. She's the one who coughed into her elbow as she ran into the building. She's a first grader and is wearing *My Little Pony* pajamas that are now soaked with snow. Her brown hair is knotted from sleep, and her face is blank, which makes my stomach churn. She beelines for a man and a woman lurking under a nearby tree. I recognize them as Mark and Nicole Yoo, high school friends of my parents who used to come to our Fourth of July parties when I was a kid. Nicole has her black hair in a messy bun on top of her head. Mark looks like he threw on the first warm things he could find in his closet, including a hunter's orange skullcap and a pair of snow pants. Nicole points up at us. Mark and the girl snap their heads up.

I surge forward, staying low enough to see the people on the snow-packed roads but high enough to avoid any reaching hands. One glance over my shoulder shows me that the little girl is chasing after us. I knew these ghosts were organizing, but I didn't expect there to be so many of them.

This portal Francesca opens is going to have to be a freaking black hole.

I fly over the Route 13 bridge and rush toward the processing plant. The floodlights grow brighter as we get closer. A harsh laugh escapes me when I see Miles's car parked by the train yard. I knew it.

Miles and Jonah are crouched on top of one of the hopper cars. I could cry for how glad I am that they still have both arms and legs. They're carrying something. The world around me comes to a stop when I realize what it is.

Francesca points. "Shiloh, is that ... you?"

I can only stare as Jonah drops down a steel ladder and Miles lowers my body inside the hopper car. Something dark stains my forehead. Is that ... *blood*? Seriously? What the hell happened while we were gone?

Jonah climbs a couple of rungs up the ladder, reaching to grab my hips. He takes my weight on his bad arm. I wince. So does he. Miles grips my shoulders from above. My T-shirt snags on a bolt. I lurch out of Miles's hands.

Jonah catches me. "*Careful*. Jesus Christ, you already dropped her once."

Hold on. He *what*?

"I'm sorry," Miles says. "My hands are cold."

Jonah rolls his eyes. A car crawls down Route 13, completely unaware that we're here. Completely unaware anything at all is wrong in Bethany. I envy whoever's in there. Jonah wraps his arms around my waist and steps down another rung. Miles lifts my arms, wrapping them around Jonah's neck like I'm one of those stuffed sloths you buy at the zoo. Jonah pauses to readjust his grip. I know I don't technically have a heart when I'm like this, but some pressure spreads through my chest where my heart should be. I drop next to him. He steps down one more rung.

"I got you." He presses his face against the side of my head. "Don't worry, Scooby, I won't drop you."

Him calling me "Scooby" makes me want to cry. I reach for him, but my fingers pass through his arm. I wish I could tell him I'm okay. He doesn't need to be so careful with me. But of course he's being careful with me. That's what Jonah does.

Unless he's wrapping his hands around my throat.

You know what? No. I'm done with this. I love him so much it physically hurts, like someone reached inside and is digging their nails into my heart.

But he still put his hands on me.

How the hell am I supposed to make sense of that? How can the boy who's handling my unconscious body like this and the one who tried to kill me be the same person? It's not the same as Dad. Jonah getting drugged wasn't his fault. What am I supposed to do with any of this?

I can't cry right now, but I also can't bring myself to move away from Jonah because I'm close enough to see the tears clinging to his lashes and close enough that if I were solid, I could reach out and wrap my arms around him and rest my chin on his shoulder like I used to when I went to sleep. He's talking to me. He may not know I'm listening, but some part of him still wants me to hear him. So I listen.

When he reaches the bottom, Jonah presses me against his chest and I swear I can feel his hands even from where I am. Miles comes down and balls up my coat, resting it on the floor next to Francesca's body. Her hands are folded over her stomach like a corpse at a funeral. At least there's no blood on her head. Jonah lays my body on the jacket, brushing his fingers against the blood clumping my hair. The dimness of the train car makes the creases on his face look more pronounced. I swear he looks older.

"You sure Mouse Man said nothing about what to do in case of injury?" Jonah asks Miles.

"Yes."

Jonah digs out his phone, dialing a number and pressing it to his ear. I can hear the quiet rings. Someone must pick up because Jonah's whole body jolts.

"It's about time," he snaps. "Listen up, you creepy asshole. We have a problem. Shiloh hit her head when we were moving her. She was bleeding and—" He cuts off, listening. "Yeah, we cleaned it and bandaged it, but—what? How bad is—hold on."

He puts the call on speaker. Colin's voice fills the train car. He sounds like a cartoon mouse.

"—any damage to the physical body impacts its capacity for soul retention. The longer the soul stays separated, the higher the probability of adverse outcomes, such as permanent brain damage, brain death, or even complete rejection."

"So, what are we supposed to do?" Jonah yells into the phone.

"Bring her back," Colin says. "Immediately."

"Done."

No. They can't bring me back now.

"Jonah," Miles says, his voice low, like he's being careful with his words. "If we bring Shiloh back now, Francesca will have to finish this alone. Do you think she can handle that?"

Of course she can handle it, but that's not the point. I need to do this with her. I promised.

Francesca stares at me. I shake my head.

"I'm not going."

"Shiloh ..."

"What if something goes wrong?"

"You will die."

"I don't care."

Francesca gives me a look like she knows I'm lying, then offers me a small smile. "I promise I will be all right. You did not do very much to help me at the barn, so this is something I am perfectly capable of doing alone."

I bite down on my bottom lip, but the sensation is a far-away pressure. I don't want to leave her. Not after everything she's been through because of me, and not when she's doing this to help Max. But the idea of brain damage is not all that appealing to me, and the thought of being stuck as a ghost forever, watching Max get better but not being able to be there to stop Mom from taking Dad back without me there to protect him … that's not happening. Francesca's right. She doesn't need me. All I did was create problems for her. She's the one who fixed them.

Francesca gives me one of her gentle smiles that somehow makes me feel worse. "Go on."

I want to drive my fist into the wall. *Damn it.*

Miles, why did you have to drop me?

This is happening so fast, but I still have time to do one more thing. I surge forward and wrap my arms around Francesca. I don't know what I was expecting to feel since we're both basically made of nothing, but somehow, my arms stop around her shoulders like she's solid. Maybe it's because we're both made of the same kind of nothing, or because of some weird ghost physics I don't understand, but as soon as we make contact, it's like thousands of static sparks zap my skin and I can hold her. She doesn't feel warm or soft. She feels sharp and tingly as we occupy the same space, like our particles are reacting to each other's and our energy is becoming one.

I need to let go, but I can't bring myself to do it. In the

end, her arms drop from around me first, and I have to fight back a sob.

"Thank you," I say. "For everything, okay?"

She stares at me for an extended second. I get a twinge in my gut, like there's something she's not telling me, but then she gives me a firm nod.

"I know."

She manages a smile. Jonah curses under his breath and sets his phone on the floor. Colin's voice echoes off the metal walls.

"The blue compound must be administered into the muscle," Colin says. "It can be any muscle, but I recommend the shoulder because it is the easiest to access."

Miles hands Jonah a Ziploc bag with two needles in it. Only two doses? What happened to the rest of the drug? Jonah sets a needle down on my chest before rolling up my T-shirt sleeve.

"I need to disinfect this." He points at Miles. "Can you get the first aid kit?"

Miles climbs up the ladder out of the hopper car. Jonah grabs the phone and holds it up to his mouth.

"The vials got smashed," he says. "I got two and a half ccs."

Colin hums. "That may not be enough, but you can try. You need to locate the soul. The soul must be in proximity to the body for the connection to re-establish itself."

"I need to find the soul, too?" He braces his hand over his eyes, curling until his knuckles turn white. "What the *hell*, man? What if she's not here?"

I am here. I try to grab his arm.

"Jonah," I say. "Go get the glasses."

Jonah yanks at his hair like he's trying to pull the answers straight out of his brain.

"The *glasses*," I practically scream. "Put on the stupid glasses!"

Either he's developed mind-reading abilities or we think alike, because his hand suddenly shoots into his pocket. He gets the glasses on with all the grace of someone trying to catch a baseball with their face.

His eyes meet mine. The breath rushes out of him in a gasp.

"Shiloh."

He says my name like a sob. I can't help the big smile from spreading over my mouth. He sits back on his heels, looking down at my body and then up at me like he's trying to figure out if I'm here. I raise my hand in the most pathetic wave known to man.

"I'm sorry," he says. "You hit your head. Colin said ..." He wipes his nose with the back of his hand. "I know everything is messed up, and I'm so sorry I made a mess out of everything, but Shiloh, please, I can't lose you."

I hold on to his words like I'm grabbing hold of his hand. I know I'm not supposed to, and I know it's a bad idea, but all of this is so confusing and right now, staying away from him seems like the bad thing to do. I reach for his arm, my vision blurring as my face screws up around a sob. His hand passes through mine like he's trying to grab hold of me. His fingers are red and numb from the cold. Anything could go wrong here, so while he's wearing the glasses, I point to myself, make a heart shape with my hands over my chest and point at him. He smiles a smile I swear makes something warm in my chest, even in this form.

"Uh, hello?" Colin asks from the phone. "Is anyone there?"

I give Jonah a nod. He clears his throat and gives Colin an update. Miles clomps back down with the first aid kit, dropping it on the floor and grabbing the alcohol to disinfect my shoulder. Jonah tells Miles I'm here. Miles starts staring around even though he'll never see me without the glasses, which Jonah needs right now.

I glide backward away from Jonah, feeling a shudder course through me. Holy crap, looking at my own body is messing with my head. My skin has turned a terrifying shade of gray. My lips are almost purple. The floodlights from outside cast harsh shadows across my face, making the hollows under my eyes look more skull-like. My black Bethany Fire T-shirt is all bunched up, showing off a strip of stomach that's covered in goosebumps. The dried blood on my forehead looks almost black against my cold-bleached skin, stark under the hasty bandage job. I swear if I didn't know better, I'd say this body looks like it's been pulled right out of a morgue freezer.

My stomach does a flip as Jonah positions the needle against my skin, his jaw so tight with determination that I'm worried he might crack a tooth.

"Okay, Scoob," he says. "Jump in."

The needle goes in. Jonah pushes the plunger and sits back on his heels. All three of us stare at my body like it's going to do a backflip or something. I don't think I've paid this much attention to myself in my entire life.

Is something supposed to happen? Or am I supposed to try to go into my body on my own?

I guess I have to do this myself. Jonah told me once that when he died and the paramedics were trying to bring him back, he had to line up his arms and legs with his body's, so I position myself above my body and try to sink down on top of it like I'm putting on a morbid costume. I line up each limb. Arms with arms. Legs with legs. God, I understand now what Miles is talking about when he calls his body a meat suit. That's exactly what this feels like, like I'm trying to squeeze back into an empty shell.

I hold still, waiting for something to happen. Nothing does.

Until the edges of my vision go dark and, just as quickly as I came out, I go back in.

PART 4
REAdY to die

34

Shiloh

"Shiloh?" The voice sounds like it's coming through a layer of glass. "Can you hear me?"

The pain hits like a bomb going off inside my skull. Everything is too bright. Too sharp. I scream, but I can't hear my own voice because every nerve ending lights up like my head has been split open by an axe. So much pressure builds in my head that I swear my brain is going to burst out through my ears. Every single cell screams to life at once, but it's wrong.

Air. I need *air*.

I try to gasp, but my lungs feel like they're frozen. My arms reach out to hold on to *something*. Hands grip my shoulders. I curl onto my side, retching and gasping.

"Easy."

Jonah. It's Jonah's voice. He's talking to me. His hand brushes my hair back. I flinch. His fingertips feel like sandpaper against my scalp.

"You're okay."

I'm okay.

Jonah's here.

I try to focus on his face, but it's a blurry mess. Something churns in my stomach. I try to puke. Nothing comes.

"C-cold," I force out through chattering teeth. The word feels wrong, like my tongue is too big and doesn't fit in my mouth. Something soft lands on my shoulders. I clutch the coat with numb fingers, gripping hard to stop my body from shivering. Every movement sends fresh waves of pain through my muscles. It feels like someone's taking a cheese grater to them under my skin.

Jonah is crouched next to me. His hands hover over my arms like he's ready to catch me if I tip over. His eyes dart between my face and something above my head. He's still wearing the glasses, so it's probably Francesca. Some logical part of my brain knows I shouldn't reach for him, but right now, everything hurts too much for me to think straight, like someone's stabbing an ice pick into every inch of exposed skin over and over again.

"Can ..." The words come out slurred. My tongue feels thick and clumsy in my mouth. I swallow hard, tasting copper, and try again. "Can you hug me?"

"Jesus, Shiloh, of course I can hug you."

Jonah slides down next to me, stretching one leg on either side of my body and holding me against his chest. I lean onto him as tremors rack through me, each one feeling like my muscles are being torn apart and stitched back together wrong. One of his hands rubs slow circles on my back through the coat.

"I got you." His voice is steady. "Just breathe."

I try to match my breathing to his. Every inhale feels like I'm swallowing glass, but slowly, so slowly, the tremors that are wracking my body start to get smaller. My head still feels like someone is beating on it with a hammer, but it's better than the white-hot poker feeling from before. My muscles gradually start to unlock as sensation creeps back into my hands and feet, and holy hell, I wish it wouldn't because everything hurts like a mother as my circulation comes back. I stay curled against Jonah, letting his warmth and presence ground me while my brain tries to knit itself back together.

Miles holds a finger in front of my face. I groan and try to bat his hand away, but my coordination is so bad I might as well be trying to catch flies while blindfolded. He waves his finger back and forth like he's trying to hypnotize a cat.

"Shiloh," he says. "You have a head injury and possible neurological damage, so I need you to listen to me and do as I say. Follow my finger."

I try. The finger splits into two fuzzy images. Concentrating makes my head feel like it's being crushed in a vise.

"Your pupils are equal but sluggish," Miles says. "Any nausea? Dizziness? On a scale of one to ten, rate your—"

"Yes to both." I want to go to sleep and maybe die. "And nine."

Miles prods at the bandage on my forehead, making me hiss with pain. "You probably have a concussion."

"Probably?" Jonah's arms tighten around me. "She definitely has a concussion, and you want to know why? Because you fucking dropped her."

"How many times do I have to tell you it was *slippery*?"

"I'm tired," I mumble, which doesn't even begin to cover the bone-deep exhaustion that's threatening to drag me under.

Jonah runs careful fingers through the ends of my hair, and each touch sends electricity down my spine. Some tiny voice in my head whispers that I'm in dangerous territory and it's not good for me to let him touch me like this, but right now I don't care. His touch is the only thing that feels normal. "Miles, she has to eat something. You got anything in the car?"

"I might have a protein bar."

"Can you get it?"

He's back in a couple of minutes. Jonah unwraps a bar that smells like peanut butter, but when I take a bite out of it, it crumbles like I'm eating Styrofoam.

I open my mouth while I chew. "This is disgusting."

"Eat as much as you can," Jonah urges. "You'll feel better."

"I'm not trying to be alarmist or anything," Miles says, "but we do have an army of possessed people coming after us that could be arriving here any second, so we need to decide what we're going to do about that."

"The possessed people," I croak, "are all over town."

"We know," Jonah says. "They found us at Duncan's."

"I saw a dozen." My stomach churns like I'm going to be sick, and I put the bar on the ground. No way am I eating any more of that. "Probably more."

"That's ... not good," Miles says, winning the award for Most Obvious Statement Ever. "Do you think they know we're here?"

"They were headed in this direction." A thought comes to me like a sucker punch. Oh my God. "Francesca. She opened a portal at the farm, but it wasn't big enough. We need a bigger one."

Miles draws his eyebrows together. I'm probably making about as much sense as a drunk penguin, so I force myself to explain what went down at the barn, each word feeling like I'm lifting weights with my tongue.

"So we need to lure all the possessed people here," I finish, my mouth starting to cooperate with my brain. I need to get myself together because we haven't accomplished anything yet except for giving me the biggest headache of my life, which is saying something because I've had some serious concussions in the past six months that I'm still waiting to catch up with me. It's a miracle I remember how to say my own name. "When they get here, Francesca will open the gate."

"You're not luring anyone anywhere right now," Jonah says. "You can barely sit up."

"I can." My fingers dig into the cold metal as I push myself away from him. The world tilts. My stomach lurches, but like hell am I going to let him see that. "See?"

Jonah frowns. I look up at Miles, trying to ignore how the simple movement makes my head feel like it's splitting open.

"I can go," I say.

Miles's forehead creases. Jonah's jaw works as he stares at me. I know that look. That's his I'm-about-to-say-something-I-know-you-won't-like look.

"Stay here," Jonah says. "Miles and I will round up the possessed creeps and bring them back."

I open my mouth to protest, but my head throbs like it's reminding me he's right.

"I don't like it either," Jonah says, "but you'll be safer in here than with us."

There's a war going on behind his blue eyes. I hate this. They're all putting everything on the line for me and I'm sitting here doing nothing. Jonah's arms loosen around me, and the loss of his warmth makes me wrap the jacket tighter around my body. He helps me lean back against the wall of the grain car, making sure I'm steady before he lets go completely.

"Call us if anything happens." He presses my phone into my hand. "We'll come right back."

"How are you going to lure them?"

Jonah stares at me for a second but says nothing. I can only imagine what kind of plan he's going to come up with.

I watch as they climb the ladder and keep the manhole cover open, leaving enough space for air and a beam of light to come in. Snow dances in the beam. It's almost pretty.

"We'll be back soon," Miles says through the gap. "With company."

"Be careful."

Miles's face disappears. Jonah takes his place.

"You stay right there," he says. "I mean it. Don't come out for anyone."

I nod. He looks like there's something else he wants to say, but Miles yells his name and he presses his lips together and disappears.

I hear them climb down the outside ladder, making the entire grain car shudder until they hop down. I lean my head against the wall, pulling the hood of my jacket deeper onto my head. I can't believe I'm stuck here while they go play hero. I need to get strong enough so I can help hold off those possessed assholes when they get back. I force myself to take another bite of the protein bar. God, what I wouldn't give for a burger right now. Or better yet, to be out there with them. Each swallow feels like pushing sand down my throat, but I keep eating anyway because passing out won't help anyone.

I wish I had something so I could see Francesca. I'm sure she's close, probably even in here with me. I press my knees together, trying to conserve whatever body heat I have left. I don't think death-walking gave me frostbite. Or brain damage. That I know of. My brain can't be in good shape after all of this. I hear the car drive away, leaving me alone with nothing but the wind whistling through the hatch above me. Something scratches against the outside of the car. Probably a gust of wind, or some snow falling down.

Closing my eyes, I try to focus on staying awake despite every cell in my body begging for sleep. The boys will be back soon. I need to get better. Get my strength back.

I take another bite of the protein bar, then another, mechanically chewing and swallowing. My throat still feels raw, but at least I can swallow without wanting to throw up now. I finish the bar, crumpling the wrapper in my fist and shoving it into my pocket. The sugar helps. Some strength returns to my limbs, though moving still feels like trying to swim through concrete. I clench and unclench my hands, feeling the sensation creep back into them. The bone-deep cold that had turned my hands into useless chunks of ice is finally fading, replaced by an irritating pins-and-needles sensation that makes me want to shake them out until they work again. But at least I can feel them.

The sound of tires crunching on gravel makes me freeze. I strain to hear, staying still against the metal wall.

A car door opens and then closes. Did the boys forget something? How long has it been since they left?

"Francesca?" I whisper. "Who's here?"

I know she's here. The air shifts in the car. The snow in the beam from the floodlights swishes, but I can't hear anything, and there's no way we can communicate.

Outside, footsteps crunch in the snow. It's only one person. I can hear each footfall.

Who the hell is here? Is it one of the possessed people already?

I press myself harder against the wall, wishing I could melt into the metal. I'm in no position to run. Hell, I can barely stand. But there's nowhere to hide in here. If someone were to look down …

My eyes lift to the manhole cover. It won't help me. Those covers are designed to be sealed from the outside with heavy clamps. But maybe I can slide the thing back into place. At least then, if someone looks up here, they won't immediately see that the cover's been moved and know someone's inside. It's not much of a plan, but it's better than sitting here waiting to be found.

Bracing my hand against the wall, I stand up as slowly as I can. Black spots flood my vision. I focus on each step and swallow the bile that rises in my throat.

I reach for the metal rungs welded to the car's interior wall. Gripping the first rung sends shooting pains up my arms. This is going to suck. I test the bottom rung before putting my weight on it. Then the next one. I move so slowly that every creak blends into the howl of the wind outside until I'm maybe eight feet in the air. I grit my teeth and keep climbing.

I grip the top rung and reach through the round port above me, but there's nothing to grab. Just smooth metal and exterior clamps that I can't reach. I push against the manhole cover to slide it back into place, but my fingers slip on the smooth surface. The cover scrapes against the metal. *Come on.* It moves centimeter by centimeter. My arms burn with the effort.

And then a face appears in the opening.

35

Shiloh

I scream. My foot slips off the rung and I lurch sideways, my fingers scrabbling against the smooth wall.

Callused hands clamp around my wrist. Pain flares through my shoulder as my weight falls on it, and my legs kick at the ladder trying to get purchase.

"For Christ's sake." His voice is tight. "Stop thrashing around before you kill yourself."

My toe finds the ladder. I try to pry his hand off, but his fingers might as well be steel bands. I dangle suspended between his arm and the floor. I know he's stopping me from falling, but all I can hear screaming inside my head is *he's touching me.*

Of all the people, all the ghosts who could've found me in a confined space in the middle of the night on my own with nowhere to run to, it had to be him. How the hell did he know I was here?

"Let go," I say, but my voice comes out like a gasp.

"I've been driving all over this goddamn town looking for you, and this is what I find?" His grip tightens until the bones in my wrist grind together. "Breaking into private property in the middle of the night in a goddamn blizzard? What the hell, Shiloh?"

I try with all my strength to wrench my arm free, but my muscles are weak, and my head has started to pound again. Dad's other hand appears through the manhole. He hauls me through it like I weigh nothing, practically throwing me onto the curved metal surface of the car's roof. My knees fold under me like paper straws. The howling gale hurls snow into my face so hard I tear up, and I rub my eyes to stop the world from spinning as I try to catch up to what is happening. What is he doing here? How did he find me?

Breathe.

Assess him.

He's talking normally, not slurring his words, which means he's sober. That shouldn't surprise me since it's three in the morning, but he doesn't need alcohol to be dangerous. His hands are clenched at his sides. His knuckles are white. His jaw is locked. His bloodshot eyes are sharp with that dangerous look that makes him more monster than father. Like the Minotaur from Max's mythology book. The smell of mint and cigarettes clings to him, but there's something else under it. Barely concealed rage. He's not a cop finding somebody trespassing at night. He's in that dangerous space between cop and dad, where rules don't apply and consequences don't matter. When he's in cop mode, he's predictable. When he's in dad mode, he's a gun with a hair trigger.

I try to swallow the lump that's rising in my throat,

scanning the frozen field that stretches away from the processing plant in all directions, but there's nothing out there but a gravel road and empty white space. The sky is filled with snow. I was all big talk at home earlier, but I could've run into the house and he wouldn't have done anything in front of Mom. But now?

The ladder behind him is my escape, but I wouldn't make it three rungs before he caught me. He's got me. He has to know it.

I roll my shoulders back and lift my chin because I'll die before I let him see I'm scared.

"What the hell is this?" Dad's words are ripped away by the wind. "Are you out of your goddamn mind?"

"What are you doing here?"

"Your mother called me," he says, and I let out a sharp breath. Of course she did. "She woke up, and you were gone. I've been driving all over this town looking for you while Scott Finnegan is lying dead in my favorite bar. He's *dead*, Shiloh. I've known him all my goddamn life, and he was a good officer and a friend, and you're out here ... what? Robbing a train?"

I wonder if Mom even fell asleep before she realized I was gone. Part of me wants to be mad at her for that, but I can't because trying to find me in the middle of the night is actually a good parenting move, and who else is she going to call? Mom thinks she's protecting me by calling Dad, but I don't know how to get it through to her that I haven't been safe alone with him since I was twelve.

Oh God. Francesca. She's still down there in the train car. Did Dad see her? I lean forward, drawing his attention away from the manhole and up to my face.

"Shiloh." Dad's voice drops to that dangerous register that makes my insides knot. "What are you doing here?"

I run through all the different options in my head, trying to figure out how I should play this. I need to get him to leave, but he's sure as hell not leaving if I tell him why I'm here. I search the road. There's no sign of the possessed people. I need to get Dad out of here before they come. I've seen what those ghosts do to people who get in their way. I might hate him and not want him anywhere close to my family, but I don't want to see him get ripped apart right in front of me by a possessed lunatic, either.

Could I jump from the roof of the car? Are the snowdrifts thick enough to cushion my fall? Would I even be able to run?

I beg my foggy brain to wake up because all that it comes up with is: "How did you find me?"

"Justin Hudson's a buddy of mine," Dad says, and my eyebrows pull together. "He owns this place, so when his cameras picked up two boys carrying what looked like the body of a girl through his plant, he called me. I had to check, because your mother called and this feels like one of those nights when anything could happen. So I left my dead officer lying where he fell and came here in case it was my own goddamn daughter these perverts were carrying for Christ only knows what reason, and here you are."

So this Justin guy can afford cameras, but the grain bins look like they're one gust of wind away from falling down?

I glance around until I find a security camera mounted on a pole near one of the floodlights. It's aimed right at us. Blinking like a mechanical eye. Something clicks in my brain. "Was it that security camera up there?"

Dad follows my finger, and something like realization moves behind his eyes.

I shift my position, angling my body to face the camera more directly. His anger is still barely under control, but I think of Detective Finnegan lying dead and any dad watching two people carrying his daughter's body to somewhere secluded and sheltered, and a part of me almost feels sorry for him.

Dad peers over the edge of the train car. "Who else is here with you?"

"No one."

"Don't you dare lie to my face. Those tire tracks aren't mine, and Justin saw two other people on the cameras carrying you in here. Who are they and what did they want to do to you?"

Quick. Think.

But nothing I come up with sounds even remotely convincing, so I raise my chin. "I'm alone."

Dad's eyes narrow. The muscle in his jaw jumps.

"You know, Shiloh, I've about had it with your attitude. I've been driving all over town looking for you, and you still want to treat me like I'm the bad guy?"

If the shoe fits. But I bite my tongue.

"I did the stupid classes." His voice rises with each word. "I've stayed sober. Sure, I've made mistakes, but I hate to break it to you, so have you, and I'm done with you acting like you run things in our family."

"We're not a family."

The words hang in the air. Something shifts in his expression. It doesn't take me long to realize what he's thinking.

We're alone out here. Miles away from town with one security camera as our only witness. He could drag me off the ladder and kill me right now out of camera shot, and no one would know. I'd be gone. The only thing standing between him and coming home, between him and Mom, would be wiped off the earth.

I took her down from the train car—the camera shows that—but she ran off into the snow. Must've frozen to death. God knows I tried.

He could get away with it, too. Trying to save his daughter from two potential rapists.

His eyes flick to the empty landscape, then back to me.

I get onto my feet, shooting my arms out at my sides as the wind threatens to blow me over. Dad stands too.

"Here's how this is going to go." Dad's voice is dangerously quiet. "You're going to climb down from here and get in the car, and I'm going to bring you home."

I find the strength from somewhere to jump over the manhole and put at least five feet between us. The smart thing to do would be to say yes, but if I get in a car with him, I might as well be agreeing to him killing me somewhere else. "I'm not going anywhere with you."

"Do you think this is a negotiation?" he snaps. "I'm not a goddamn killer, Shiloh—"

"I have to stay here."

He steps over the manhole, not even glancing down to see Francesca in there. I step back again. His shadow stretches across the metal roof and swallows mine. The metal under my boots seems to vibrate with his anger. I can feel it building, that dangerous energy gathering around him that used to make me want to disappear into the walls.

"I need you to hear me when I say that I can't deal with this right now," Dad says. "This night has been a shit show. First, I got a call that the nursing home turned into a goddamn war zone. Bodies in the halls. Blood everywhere. An old man stabbing an aide with scissors."

Bile rises in my throat. I did call 911 when I was there, and naturally he'd find out about that because he's the sheriff ... wait, that was before he came to our house? Does he know I was there? Did he hear my voice on the 911 recording?

He presses on. "Then someone called in a break-in at Duncan's, and when I got there, I found Scott dead on the floor. I've got guys putting out fires all over town. People acting like they're out of their minds. Wandering the streets. And now I find my daughter out here. You say you love your brother, so why can't you even stay by his side while he's sick?"

His words hit like a slap. My hands ball into fists. How dare he say that to me?

I take another step back, feeling the edge of the train car behind my heel. Focus. Dad is trying to bait me.

Some of his words sink in. Hold on.

"You saw the people wandering in the road?" I ask. "In town?"

He blinks at me. "Yes."

"What are you doing with them?"

"Got every unit out there rounding them up one at a time," Dad says. "Going to take them to the middle school gym. I have no clue what's going on. Looks like some kind of mass hysteria, maybe."

The middle school gym. They're going to try to gather all the possessed people together in one place.

Oh god no.

"Dad." Something hot tries to claw its way up my throat. "You need to get all your guys out of there right now."

He steps closer. I can't back up any further without falling. "What did you say to me?"

"You have no idea what you're dealing with," I say. "Those people are dangerous. More of your guys are going to die."

"What the hell do you know about this?" He grabs my face, his fingers pinching the soft part of my cheek as he tilts my head to the side. "Are you involved in this somehow? Is that what you're doing out here?"

I shake my head as much as he'll let me. He presses his mouth into a line and shoves my face away.

"I'm done with this." He grabs my arm hard enough to leave marks. "I need to get you home."

I try to pull away. "Dad, please—"

"*Enough.*" He yanks me forward, away from the ledge hard enough for me to trip over my feet. "You threatened me at the house, and now you're making me chase you all over town while you're out here … what, doing drugs? Is that what this is? Or something else with those two boys?"

"I'm not—"

Static bursts from Dad's radio. My body jerks at the sound. Dad's free hand moves to the radio like he's scared I'll try to run the second he reaches for it. He's not wrong.

"Sheriff, we've got a sit …" The voice cuts in and out. "Some of the …" More static. "Requesting …"

Dad shakes the radio like that's going to fix the reception. "Damn it." He yanks on my arm. "Come on."

I throw my body to the ground, but he drags me across the metal. My boots slip on the ladder as he forces me down ahead of him, one hand steady on my collar like I'm some runaway dog he caught. Every step sends fresh jolts of pain through my still recovering body. As soon as my feet hit snow, he jumps down and drags me away from the train car. My knees wobble with each stumbling step. I feel like I'm moving underwater. Every time my boots catch in the deep snow, it feels like my joints might tear apart, but Dad yanks me harder, like I'm nothing but dead weight.

Dad raises the radio. "Kyle, you there? What's your status?"

Babin. He's talking to Babin.

"Sir, we've got a problem." Babin's voice is tight. "The second we try to take these people anywhere, they lose it."

Dad's knuckles whiten. "What's happening?"

"We were going up to them one-by-one, just talking to them, and it was working, but then—I had Larry Hall. I walked up and tried to talk to him. Wanted to see if he was all right. He stared through me, but he wasn't aggressive until I told him he had to come with me. Then, Jesus, the man went feral. He was on me in a second. Teeth first. I barely got him off, and then he ran away laughing."

Dad opens his mouth to say something when a burst of frantic shouting drowns him out. No.

"Kyle?" Dad barks. "You there?"

Some male shouting. Then a scream.

Dad's face drains of color. "Kyle, *are you okay?*"

The radio cuts to static.

In the distance, faint pops echo across the fields. I whip my head around.

No.

No no no—

Dad tries to get through again, gripping the radio so hard I swear it's going to break. I gasp for air, my chest heaving, but none can get into my lungs. Those cops—how many are there? Those possessed people will kill them for being in the way. Like they did with Sid. Or that woman behind the desk at the nursing home. I don't care how well-trained the cops are. Those possessed people are stronger.

Babin believed I was guilty, but he was nicer than Finnegan. He once let me sit in his cruiser when I was eight. He always brought his golden retriever Bosco to our Fourth of July picnic. He shouldn't be there. He's going to die.

So is Dad if he goes back there.

"Dad, please," I say, but it's like my voice doesn't even reach him. "You need to leave me here and go home."

He shoves his radio into his pocket. "I got to go help them is what I have to do—"

"*No.*" My voice breaks. "Please. I know you've never listened to me about anything, but I need you to listen to me now. Those people are dangerous. They're going to kill you."

He whirls on me. "What the hell are you talking about?"

"They're *possessed,*" I plead. "By ghosts. I know it sounds crazy, but it's true. They're coming here, and they'll kill anyone who gets in their way."

"Ghosts?" His lips curl. "Have you lost your mind?"

"No, I swear, you—"

"What kind of drugs are you on?"

"I'm not on drugs!" I'm crying now. "You're going to die if you go there! You heard it yourself!"

Dad yanks me onto my feet. I cry out in pain. "We need to go."

"*No.*"

But Dad drags me across the snow. I dig my heels in, kicking with everything I have, but he's too strong.

"I'm taking you home."

"Dad, please!"

But he's not listening anymore.

"You're hurting me." I gasp, but he doesn't loosen his grip. And those words never stopped him before.

He yanks open the back door of his patrol car. My breathing comes fast. "Get in."

I can't leave. Not with Francesca's body still in there unprotected, or with Jonah and Miles coming back. I will not leave them to do this alone.

"You think you're in charge here?" Dad snaps from over my shoulder, and it takes everything in me to keep my feet on the ground. "You've got this … *delusion* that you run things around here, but let me be real clear about something. If I say get in the car, you're getting in the goddamn car. If I want to see my son, I will see my son. If I want to see my wife, I will see my wife, and if I want to move back into my house, I will move back into my own house." He leans in close enough that his breath is hot on my ear. The edges of my vision blur. "So help me God, Shiloh, get in the goddamn car."

He shoves me forward. I catch myself on the door frame.

My vision tunnels. Blood rushes in my ears.

Something inside me snaps.

Suddenly I'm twelve again, tumbling down the wooden stairs to the basement and cradling my arm after the bone snapped. Then I'm fourteen, watching the door handle turn when it should be locked. I'm sixteen, flinching at the sound of ice clinking in a glass and the creak of the springs in his La-Z-Boy recliner. I am every silent scream. Every swallowed plea. I'm not going to roll over and die for him. That is not how this ends.

Something courses through me. Call it adrenaline. Call it hatred, because I hate him more than I've ever hated anyone, but whatever it is, it makes me strong.

I spin around, ripping my arm free with a guttural scream that tears from somewhere deep inside of me. I drive my knee up between his legs with enough force that I hope something ruptures. His breath whooshes out as he doubles over.

It's not enough. I want to destroy him.

I swing my fists at his face. I scream through the pain as I try to cave in every feature I inherited. His nose. His cheekbones. His jaw. I want to erase them. I want to break every one of his bones until there's nothing left of the monster who lives in the shadows of every room and makes me check that the doors are locked twice before going to bed. My arms are not like wet spaghetti now. I suddenly feel like I can flip a car.

He catches my wrist, his nose curling in disgust. Good. Let him see what he created.

"What the hell do you think you're doing?" he hisses.

Screaming through gritted teeth, I drive my boot into his shin and sprint away through the deep snow.

36

Shiloh

I stumble across the train tracks. Lose him. I need to lose him. The metal rails catch my boots, but I manage to stay on my feet even with the world tilting at the edges of my vision.

"Shiloh!"

Dad's boots crunch behind me. In this empty place, there's nowhere to hide. Dad can outrun me. He's done it hundreds of times before, and if he catches me, he'll drag me back to that patrol car. Or worse.

I glance around, searching for somewhere, anywhere, I can go where he can't reach me. Something creaks overhead. I look up. The massive grain bins loom above me, blurred by the snow stinging my eyes.

Could I … no.

Am I strong enough to get up there?

Dad is getting closer. Before I can talk myself out of it, I run as hard as I can to the far side of the closest bin and grab hold of the ladder. The ladder reaches straight up the side of the grain bin and disappears into the snow. The pounding of my heart drowns out everything but Dad's approaching footsteps. Climb. I need to climb. Either I die down here or I die up there, so I'll take my chances with the ladder.

The metal bites into my palms as I haul myself up, gritting my teeth through the pain, but somehow I climb until I'm ten feet in the air. The ground falls away under me with terrifying speed.

"You've got to be shitting me." The metallic clang of Dad's hands slamming against the ladder reverberates up through my hands. "*Shiloh!*"

I glance down at him. He stands at the bottom of the ladder, snarling up at me like some kind of animal. Blood has smeared across his lips and chin. Probably from where I hit him. He lunges for the ladder. The metal shudders under his weight.

Oh God oh God oh God.

Go.

I pull my body up another rung. Each step sends a stab of pain through my muscles. The rungs are so cold they feel hot but I can't slow down. Can't stop. Can't catch my breath.

The rung under my right foot rattles. I cry out as the section of the ladder lurches away from the metal wall. For a second I'm falling, clinging onto the ladder with everything I have, but then the ladder jerks to a stop, still hanging on by what feels like a single bolt. I close my eyes. Press my forehead against the rung before dragging myself up with everything I have.

I can barely hear anything over the howl of the wind and my desperate gasping. Dad closes the gap rung by rung. I'm so high up. The height makes my chest constrict and my fingertips tingle with pins and needles. I reach the first platform. The grated surface bites through my sweatpants where I land on my knees, and the metal vibrates under as I scramble across to the next ladder and leap for the rungs.

A hand closes around my ankle.

Dad yanks so hard my knee stretches. I bring my free leg up and drive my boot heel into his face with every ounce of strength I possess.

He yells and staggers back. How did he get past the loose section? Fate or God or something must have helped him, but that's impossible. I've seen what's on the other side. There are no trumpets. No blinding white light. Just the same depressing world. A world I don't want to go to right now.

I haul myself up onto the next rung, then the next, climbing so fast my arms feel ready to tear from their sockets.

I don't stop until I reach the top and haul myself over the edge onto my hands and knees. The wind slashes at my exposed skin. I drag myself onto my feet on the narrow steel catwalk connecting all three grain bins like a skeletal artery. The metal under me is covered in sand and salt, and crunches with each unsteady step. A gust rocks me sideways. I grab the waist-high railing, the metal so cold it feels like it's fusing to my skin, and try not to look down because if I do, I'm going to puke. Do I run across the catwalk and climb down? I need to run long enough for Miles and Jonah to get back.

Metal creaks behind me. I spin around to find Dad dragging himself onto the walkway. I stagger backward, my knee throbbing where Dad grabbed it.

Dad stands still. His shoulders heave with every ragged breath. There's new blood on his forehead where I kicked him. The wind howls between us, whipping his jacket against his chest.

His eyes aren't angry anymore. They're vacant in a way I've seen only a handful of times in my life, and never when he's sober. His nostrils flare. His body angles forward. This isn't Sheriff Oleson. This isn't even Dad. This is the monster that lives inside of him. The one I met that day when he told me to take my clothes off and chased me through the house with his belt. The one who has always, deep down, wanted me gone.

He's going to kill me. He's actually going to kill me.

I step back, wiping my tears away so fast I can pretend they weren't there. "Why do you hate me so much?"

I have to scream over the howling wind. Dad doesn't react. But the words and the tears pour out of me.

"Why couldn't you ever be a normal dad?" I yell. He steps toward me like he didn't hear me, which makes me clench my fists. "What did I ever do to you? Huh? Why did you have to make my entire life *hell*?"

I can barely get the words out over how hard I'm crying. I take another step backward, my boot slipping on the metal. My muscles coil as I prepare to run, but there's nowhere to go but across this narrow bridge. His shoulders shift slightly forward. I know that posture. My body recognizes the threat before my mind does, every nerve ending firing in warning.

He lunges at me. I turn to run.

His hand clamps around my jacket, yanking me backward with such force that my head cracks against the railing. I collapse on the platform as the world spins in a nauseating kaleidoscope of stars and shadows.

My cheek presses hard onto the gritty metal. Dad looms over me, chest heaving as he wipes blood from his forehead with the back of his hand. With a frustrated scream, he brings his foot down toward my ribs. I roll away. The platform booms as his boot connects where I'd been a second before.

I push myself up on quivering arms and try to run. I make it two steps before he shoves me from behind.

Something warm and sticky trickles down my cheek as the cut below my hairline opens up again.

I frantically scan for something I can use to defend myself, but he's on me in seconds, flipping me onto my back and straddling me. His fist connects with my jaw. Pain explodes through my head. He grabs my shoulders, slamming me back down until my head cracks on the metal and the air flies from my lungs. His hands close around my neck. They dig into my skin with bruising force as I thrash under him, legs kicking against his weight.

"You ruined ..." He squeezes harder, eyes gleaming with something beyond rage. "My life."

Through my sobs, Dad's face distorts, his flaring nostrils widening, the muscles in his neck bulging. Half bull, half child-eater. Eyes that have decided I won't leave this place alive. He gives my neck a shake. I blink against the tears streaming into my hair.

"You are nothing." Veins pulse at his temples. Blue ropes under his reddened skin. "You have always been *nothing*."

I ... can't ... the corners of my vision curl in. The pressure in my head subsides. I struggle for air, strength bleeding from my limbs as Dad's face swims above me. This warm feeling spreads up from the tips of my fingers through my chest and up my neck. I ... want ... sleep. I picture Max lying in his bed at home. He's sleeping already. He has the softest pillowcase. I imagine the cold metal turning into cotton and hear Max's small breaths right in my ear—

No.

Sheriff Oleson prefers his victims weak, but I'm not weak. I'm too big for him to push around anymore.

I am my father's daughter. Stronger than my mother ever had to be. I am Max's protector. I am my own protector. The only thing I can do when I can't fight anymore is keep fighting.

With strength coming from somewhere deep inside me, I let out a strangled scream and buck my hips up with everything I have. His grip loosens enough for me to gulp in a precious half-breath. I wedge my hands between his arms and push up, creating enough space to kick both of my legs into his chest.

He tips backward. I scramble to my feet, gulping down frigid air and throwing myself across the catwalk. I reach the far edge and spin around. Dad is charging like a bull, arms pumping at his sides, closing the gap with every second, but my hands are already fumbling for the ladder. Dad lunges for me. His fingers graze my jacket as I drop down past the first rung.

I climb down faster than I climbed up. Each step sends a stab of pain up my legs, but the pain feels like it's happening to someone else. I am bigger than it is. I have to be. Blood spatters the rungs as I spit. Dad's boots appear above me, stepping down at my hands with terrifying speed. I reach the first platform and scramble across it to the next ladder.

Dad jumps and lands between me and escape. The platform booms under his weight. He reaches for me. I stagger away, my lower back hitting the railing. His momentum carries him forward. I step sideways. He teeters against the railing, arms windmilling as he tries to catch his balance. Screaming through gritted teeth, I shove him.

He falls.

37

Shiloh

His scream splits the air, bouncing against the grain bin wall as he plummets through the darkness.

I collapse against the railing, peering down through tear-blurred vision to where Dad lies motionless in the snow.

Oh my God.

Oh my God, what have I done?

I need to go down there. I need to go see if he's okay.

Or make sure he's dead.

I force my body down the ladder. Each rung shakes under my grip, or maybe that's my hands. Is this real? Did I—did I push my own father off a grain bin?

By the time I reach the ground, my body is shaking so hard I can barely take any steps. His body tipped backward. He fell. Tumbled back right onto the snow. Because I pushed him.

I killed him. I killed my own dad.

But I didn't mean to. I just wanted him to stop. To get away from me. He was trying to hurt me. He was going to—

But I pushed him. I pushed him, and I watched him fall, and I didn't look away.

I step closer to him, circling wide around the grain bin to where he fell. He lies there. Unnaturally still. Blood trickles from his temple, staining the snow under his head scarlet. We're behind the grain bin. It protects us enough from the wind to make everything way too quiet.

I did this. I watched him fall.

And I was glad.

"Dad?" The word tastes wrong, like I'm speaking a language I forgot. "Dad, can you hear me?"

Nothing. A sob gurgles up from my throat, my bruised windpipe burning with every shallow gasp.

"I …" I clear my throat between strangled breaths. "I didn't mean …"

But at that moment, with his hands around my throat, I wanted him gone. Wanted him to stop. Forever.

So I pushed him.

I sink to my knees. With trembling fingers, I press my fingers to his skin. His neck is hot to the touch. I fumble to find the right place, pressing harder than I mean to, shifting my fingers over the stubble at his jawline. My own pulse hammers so loud in my ears that I can barely focus on anything else. What if I can't find it because there's nothing to find? What if he's actually dead?

Then I feel it.

I press harder to make sure I'm not imagining it, counting the beats in my head like they taught us in health class. His pulse is strong and regular, like nothing happened at all. Like he didn't fall twenty-five feet from halfway up a grain bin. Like I didn't push him. I look harder at where he fell. In the shelter of the grain bin, a big snowdrift has formed, big enough to cushion the fall of even someone Dad's size.

I don't know what to feel. He's alive. I'm not a murderer. I didn't kill my own father, no matter how much I hate him.

But he's alive.

That means he's going to wake up. And when he does ...

A low groan escapes his lips. His eyelids flutter and I scramble backward, my heart thundering against my ribs. He's waking up. In minutes, he'll be conscious, and when he is, he'll laugh at whatever God he prays to and come for me again.

I run to his car. Please be unlocked. My frozen fingers fumble with the door handle. It gives way with a click.

I rummage around the floor, the glove box—where would he keep them? I yank open the center console. Jackpot.

I grab the metal handcuffs and his department-issued taser. The battery indicator shows it's fully charged. I run back, my breath coming in white clouds, and round the corner of the grain bin.

The spot where Dad was lying is empty. The depression in the snow is stained with blood.

I spin around, eyes darting across the empty landscape. Boot prints lead from the place he fell, leading to the other side of the grain bin. I clutch the taser.

The wind dies down like the world is holding its breath. The handcuffs jangle in my pocket. I try to quiet my breathing. The footprints weave drunkenly. Sometimes drag.

I round the corner of the grain bin. The footprints in the snow stop like he disappeared.

Something scrapes in the shadows to my right. I spin around, taser raised, but there's nothing there. Shadows pool between the bins.

"Dad?" I call out, hating how my voice trembles. "Where are you?"

Silence answers me. Complete and utter silence.

"I know you hate me, but you don't have to do this." I take another step forward, squinting through the pounding in my temples. "You can let me go."

A soft exhale from behind me is the only warning I get. I spin, but too late. Something heavy slams into my side. The taser flies from my grip. Dad's weight crushes me, his knees pinning my arms.

His hands go straight for my throat, fingers digging into flesh that's already bruised from minutes ago.

"You tried to kill me," he snarls. "My own daughter."

I thrash under him, but I can't break his grip. My vision tunnels the way it did up on the grain bin.

"I should have ... done this ... years ago," he pants.

My right arm is trapped under his knee, but my left can reach into my pocket. Where is it? Where's the taser?

Dad's face swims above me, his features blurring. His teeth are bared in a grimace. He grunts like an animal.

My fingers close around something solid in the snow. One of the handcuffs. I swing it as hard as I can. It connects with Dad's temple. He howls, his grip loosening enough for a desperate breath. I swing again, the metal edge gouging a line down his cheek. A curl of flesh comes away from Dad's face like a piece of potato peel. One hand leaves my throat to clutch at his face. My knee connects with his kidney. He grunts and lets go, holding his face as he stands and staggers a few feet back in the snow.

"You evil bitch." Blood drips from his temple and into his eye.

My hand frantically searches the snow beside me. Come on.

My fingers close around the taser.

As Dad starts to run toward me, I aim the taser at him and pull the trigger. His body goes rigid, every muscle locking as electricity courses through him. He topples sideways into the snow.

I scramble back, gulping down air through my bruised throat. The taser's trigger is still depressed under my finger.

One ... two ... three...

Dad's limbs twitch in the snow.

Four ... five.

I release the trigger. Dad goes limp, his chest heaving with shallow breaths.

I push myself onto my knees and grab his wrists. His skin is clammy, and I drag his heavy arms behind his back, the position awkward with him lying on his side. I struggle to line up the mechanism, my fingers numb and clumsy from the cold and all the adrenaline. The first cuff clicks into place around his right wrist. I yank his left arm back, ignoring his groan as I secure it. The metal teeth ratchet closed with a series of small clicks. I check them twice to make sure they're tight enough.

"Shiloh," he slurs. When he can't move his arms, confusion crosses his face. Then realization. "What the hell do you think you're doing?"

I turn and go back to his car, rummaging through the trunk until I find a coil of rope and a roll of heavy-duty silver duct tape. When I get back to where Dad lies, he's thrashing around like a fish on a dock, spitting curses that would make a prison guard blush. I use the rope to tie his legs together as he tries to kick me. I focus on the mechanical things. Wrap the rope. Pull it tight. Secure the knot. That way, I don't have to think about anything else. I tear off a strip of tape, the sound cutting through the night like a gunshot.

"You really are something," he snarls. *My own daughter.*"

"And in the Fun Palace, you were my own father. And I was twelve. So shut up."

I slap the tape over his mouth. His eyes burn above the silver strip. I add another piece for good measure, pressing down the corners with my trembling fingers. Angry grunts press against the tape.

I back away and sink into the snow a few feet from him, far enough away that he can't reach me if he gets loose but close enough to make sure he doesn't. Cold seeps through my sweatpants and burns my skin. My throat throbs with each heartbeat. I can barely draw air into my lungs, and everything hurts so bad that I whimper with each breath. It's about time he ended up in handcuffs. Maybe I belong in them, too, but at least I'll be someplace far away from him.

My own fucking daughter.

I am his own fucking daughter. I'm more like him than I was ever able to admit before this moment. Did I enjoy that? Did I enjoy those fleeting few minutes when I thought he was dead?

I may be strong like him, but we're not the same. I'd never lay a hand on someone weaker than me. But I guess I'm not weaker than him anymore.

Salt stings my lip. I wipe the tears away, but more come until I'm sobbing so hard I can barely breathe. Each gasp rips through my throat and pounding head. I try to muffle the sounds, pressing my sleeve against my mouth like I've done a thousand times before when I had to keep quiet so Max wouldn't hear me, but what's the point? I don't need to hide anything anymore.

I almost died. My own father almost killed me.

And I almost killed him.

I don't even know what scares me more.

I sob so hard it comes out like a howl. The wind howls right back.

I don't know how long I sit there crying. Ten minutes? Twenty? Dad's struggles quiet down to occasional shifts and grunts. My sobs taper into pathetic hiccupping sniffles.

I can't shake this weird feeling that I'm not alone. Like someone's watching me. Not Dad—he's right over there trying to murder me with his eyes—but something else. Someone.

"Francesca?"

No answer, obviously, but I swear I can feel her here.

I sit there with Dad until headlights sweep across the grain bins. I lift my head, lifting my hand to shield my eyes from the glare. A car engine grows louder, tires crunching on fresh snow before coming to a stop.

Car doors slam. Someone screams my name. Not someone.

Jonah.

I try to stand, to go to him, but my legs might as well be made of jelly. He runs over and drops to his knees next to me, and his entire body goes rigid when he sees my face and neck. When his gaze shifts to Dad lying bound behind me in the snow, something primal flashes across his face. His jaw tightens so hard I can see the muscle jumping beneath his skin, and his eyes darken with a rage I've never seen before. Not even under the control of the foolery.

"Oh my God, Shiloh."

Another rough sob rips out of me. He reaches toward my neck, but he hesitates. "Did he do this to you?" The question comes out deadly quiet.

I try to nod, but it makes everything hurt worse. Jonah's whole body coils like a spring about to snap. He's breathing hard through his nose, eyes darting between me and Dad with a look that scares me.

"I'll kill him," he hisses, already rising. "I swear to God, I'll—"

"Jonah." My voice is this pathetic rasp that barely makes it above a whisper.

He pauses for a second, but only a second, before he drops back to my side, cupping my face with so much gentleness that it makes fresh tears spill down my cheeks.

"Can you breathe okay?" His eyes scan every inch of my face like he's cataloging each bruise.

I nod, even though I don't know if I can or not. My lungs burn like they're not getting enough air, but I'm gulping in as much as I can. Something cracks open inside my chest. I can't hold myself up anymore, so I reach for him, and he catches me with a broken sound.

His arms lock around me. I cry harder. His breathing is loud and hot against my ear, and his lips press hard against the top of my head as he knits his hands into my jacket.

"He's going to pay for this," he whispers into my hair. "I swear on my life."

Dad has gone quiet. I turn to check that he's not planning something, but he's just looking at me in Jonah's arms, seething so hard he looks like he wants to flip a table.

Miles reaches us. I don't look up at him, but I can see his boots in the snow and hear him panting.

Jonah pulls back just enough to look at me again, his thumb wiping away my tears.

"Shiloh." His voice drops to something dangerous, something I've never heard from him before. "What do you want us to do with him?"

Dad makes a muffled grunt through the tape, jerking against his restraints. But he can't get to us. Jonah's question hangs in the air. I can see it in his eyes. Not just what he wants to do to Dad, but what he's capable of doing. For me.

Jonah starts to stand. I grip his wrist and shake my head.

"Just …" My voice is this pathetic rasp that barely makes it above a whisper. "Did you find them all?"

Jonah and Miles look at each other. Dad goes still on the ground, and I notice suddenly he's staring at Miles like he's seen a ghost, and I realize he knew Randall Zweering. Seeing him here, with Jonah and with me, must not be computing in his head. But that's not my problem right now.

"We need to find someplace to hide," Miles says. "They saw us in the car, and they're not far behind."

I wipe my eyes, wincing as the stab of pain flares through my tender nose. "All of them?"

Jonah nods. "I guess so, yeah. The cops were trying to round them up, and they weren't having that at all."

"Are the cops dead?"

Miles gulps, then rubs his neck. "I saw one man down, but it was nobody I knew. He was, uh, one of your dad's guys."

Oh no. Babin. Could it be Babin? He can't be dead too.

We need to stop this. Before anyone else gets hurt.

I can't see the possessed people coming, but that doesn't mean they're not on their way. Miles and Jonah help me to my feet, each one keeping hold of one of my arms as I sway between them like a drunk person, my legs still feeling like they're made of overcooked spaghetti.

"What do you want to do with him?" Miles asks, jerking his chin toward Dad.

I force myself to look at the man who raised me. Snow has already started dusting his shoulders, and little flakes are catching in his eyebrows. There's something I've never seen on his face before. Something almost like fear. For the first time in my life, I can see Max in his face.

"Could you put him in the back of his car?" I ask, turning to Miles and leaning almost all my weight on Jonah. "Please?"

They both stare at me like I've lost my mind.

"After what he did to you?" Jonah's voice is tight with anger. "Are you kidding?"

"I know, but I can't..." I try to swallow the words. "They'll kill him."

Jonah doesn't waste a second. "So?"

"You've seen what those people can do," I say. "Nobody deserves a death like that."

Miles nods. Jonah looks like he wants to light the entire processing plant on fire, but I know Miles gets it. He squats to grab hold of Dad's legs and drags him through the snow, shoving him into the back of his own patrol car and slamming the door.

"I guess he'll be safer in there than out here, at least," Miles says as he rejoins us. "And he can't go anywhere."

I nod. I don't know how I feel. Nothing about this feels good. I wrap my arm around Jonah's waist and let him take most of my weight. Miles holds me on the other side. Every step is a battle against the pain shooting through my body, but their arms around me keep me standing.

"How many are coming?" I rasp.

"Forty. Maybe more." Miles glances over his shoulder. "We left the scene in a hurry, hoping they'd follow us, but they stopped at the town limits like they were planning something."

"Planning what?"

Jonah's grip on me tightens. "No clue."

"Are we going to have to fight them?" I ask.

Miles shrugs. Jonah presses his mouth into a line, which gives me a queasy feeling in the pit of my stomach. We can't fight forty people. I can barely stand, and even if I could, Jonah and I could barely handle two of those assholes at the nursing home, let alone forty of the supercharged bastards.

I think of the blank-faced little girl in the *My Little Pony* pajamas. How many children are in that crowd? How many old people? How do we fight the ghosts without hurting the bodies they are in? I guess we do what we have to do. I was too busy trying not to die for it to bother me back at the old folks' home.

I scan the dark shadows between the grain bins, searching for any sign of Francesca, but there are none. I'm sure she's close. That she has some kind of plan. But no matter where she is, I have to find her so I can tell her they're coming because in a couple of minutes, she'll have to open that gate.

Or this will be the hill we die on.

38

Francesca

I hover above the road, my spectral form casting no shadow as the snow flies through me. From up here, everything looks like it belongs in a snow globe, except this one is real, and it is not a very nice snow globe.

I nearly forgot how to move at all when Shiloh climbed on top of that grain bin. I tried to scream, do anything I could to help her, but my voice could not reach her evil father. I have never watched someone fall from so up high before. The way his body tumbled reminded me of the doll Richie once threw from the upstairs window of our old house. I thought he was dead. I thought Shiloh had killed her own father.

As I watch Jonah and Miles carry Shiloh into the main processing building to hide, I allow myself to think that perhaps she really will be all right, but that feeling dies as quickly as it came.

Because something terrible is coming.

I can see them in the distance, where the road bends around the edge of town. Some have limbs that swing too stiffly. Others move with jerky steps like those wind-up toys nice old Mrs. McGillicuddy used to keep in her classroom when my father used to bring me to talk to her about how I could see spirits. The possessed people appear as a strange procession, their bodies black cutouts against the landscape. I cannot see their faces from here, but I know their eyes would reflect the light like polished silver coins dropped into wishing wells that grant curses instead of wishes. There must be dozens of them. More than dozens. Perhaps forty souls wrapped in stolen flesh moving along the road.

I drop closer, soaring until I trail a good ten feet behind the stragglers so that none of them see me. Most of them do not speak to one another, but mutter to themselves as though they are practicing words, tasting sounds, or re-learning the mechanics of tongues and teeth and lips.

"This body is slow," whispers a boy, flexing fingers that do not belong to him. "But warm."

"I don't know if I like this," mumbles a small girl wearing pajamas dusted with snow. "But I don't want to go back there."

I do not like to admit that I understand what she is feeling. The other side is empty and gray and lonely. But that doesn't make this right.

At least Evangeline will be waiting for me when I go there.

Even thinking about her brings a small smile to my face. I have been so preoccupied with opening the gate that I have not had time to miss her, but all I need to do is open the gate, and then I will be done. I can go and find her. I do hope she will not be angry with me for coming sooner than she wanted.

An elderly man in striped pajamas pauses, his breath making clouds that disappear on the wind. He turns to the black-haired woman beside him.

"You know, I spent eighty-three years in this world the first time," he says. "Wasted most of them, so I'm not letting any kid take my second chance. I'll break every bone in their bodies before I let that happen."

He flexes his arthritic fingers. A sick feeling comes over me. He does not get to have a second chance at the expense of somebody else's first. These souls have taken what isn't theirs, and they must go back and accept their death. Leonard tried to bring back all of the people he cared about and give them second chances. He had been a good friend to Evangeline when they were children. Or so she told me, although she did not much like talking about him after what she knew Leonard had done to me. Evangeline did not deserve to be killed at her father's insistence on such a cruel performance. Natalie Dorado did not deserve to have cancer strip her from the earth when she was barely eleven, and Poppy Rooney did not deserve to be murdered by Leonard before she could find out if life would one day get better for her.

They were all children. They should have lived entire lives, but nobody dies because they deserve to. They die because it is the order of things. They die because they die, because of the cruel nature of the world, or because other people want them gone. The world has an order to it. Leonard attempted to change that order, and I did too, but like it was not Leonard's choice to choose who lives and who dies, it is also not mine.

My friends are preparing to fight. I must open a gate before they have to die as well.

I soar through the air, moving faster than any physical

form could manage. The grain bins cut a jagged shape against the sky. I dive toward the nearest, passing through the wall as easily as stepping through a curtain of mist.

I am not sure if there is a membrane inside here, but I do not have long to find one, so I must look everywhere. Millions of dried corn kernels form a golden hill in the bin. Tiny flecks of dust dance in the air, spinning where my glow touches them.

I hover above the corn, trailing my ethereal fingers through the surface. Every kernel shivers as I pass through it.

"Where are you?" I whisper. "I know you're here somewhere."

There must be an opening some place close. The other side is hungry enough that the membranes should not be difficult to find.

A memory bubbles up from deep within me, of my mother holding my hand and walking past a different cornfield years ago. The humid air had been thick with the scent of growing things and the promise of rain.

"These fields have seen more than you ever have, and more than you ever will," she had said to me, holding a finger to her lips. "If you're really quiet, you might be able to hear them whisper."

I had thought she meant that the corn was talking to her, like in those fairy tales where plants have secrets, but she must have been teaching me to listen for the other side. My mother may not have been able to see souls or know how to explain the things she sensed, but I know she heard the whispers, too.

I drift lower into the corn. The rustling surrounds me like tiny waves on a golden sea.

Listen.

Feel.

The world falls away as I concentrate, stretching my awareness outward. There should be a vibration, a hum, a peculiar resistance that marks where this world and the other side touch. Every membrane has a signature. Similar to the subtle difference between two identical musical notes played on different instruments. I spiral deeper into the bin, pushing through layers of corn. The light cannot reach down here, but my own luminescence casts everything in a soft blue glow.

Nothing.

Uh oh. What if there is no membrane here after all?

That cannot be. The other side is always pressing against ours, seeking entry points like water searching for cracks in a dam. There will be one here.

I push myself up and out of the bin, floating through the storm to the next one. This one is nearly empty, a thin layer of yellow dust coating the floor like golden snow. I scan the metal walls, the curved ceiling, and the concrete floor, searching for that telltale shimmer or subtle distortion, but there is nothing but the sound of the wind buffeting the empty dome.

I pass through the door of the third bin and find it half-filled with corn. Something feels different here. The air seems to vibrate with a subtle energy, but I cannot see anything along the walls, so I dive into the corn, allowing it to envelop me as I close my eyes. I push through the kernels like I am swimming in some sort of strange dry liquid until I reach the floor. I feel it rather than see it. Something resists me. I stretch my awareness outward as if I am unfurling a paper fan, letting my consciousness brush against each edge of the metal bin.

I open one eye. The kernels nearest to my face have taken

on a subtle glow. Pressed on the concrete floor, a tiny spot of membrane is pulsing. I smile.

The membrane barely gives under my touch. It is small, but the energy is immense, as though I am having to drain a swimming pool with a drinking straw. How can I open something that will be large and powerful enough to pull dozens of souls through?

A low rumbling sound comes through from the other side. Perhaps I can make it grow.

But I will need to tear it wide once I open it, and I cannot open it until all of the souls have arrived, so I push myself up and out of the bin. The possessed people have reached the fence now. One woman in the front climbs up the chain links. The others behind her appear to realize the gate is open and push through it.

I have not been inside the main building, but I assume it is some sort of processing shed. I slip through the wall to find Jonah, Miles, and Shiloh gathering what they can to defend themselves. A catwalk runs below the ceiling, and quite a lot of equipment fills the space. There is a grain sorter with a cracked canvas belt, a separator, and an auger system that does not appear to have been turned on in quite a while. A rusted ladder leads to the metal catwalk, which in turn leads to a partial loft where boxes and empty sacks are stacked in the corner.

Miles pushes a heavy table across the concrete floor, jamming it under the doorknob. Jonah takes a pry bar out of a bucket in the corner. His eyes flick toward Shiloh, who is leaning against a work bench.

"You should find somewhere to hide," he says. "You look like you went ten rounds with a semi."

Shiloh pushes off from the bench and picks up a rusty

pipe, her small hands looking fragile wrapped around the metal. "You think we can take them all?"

"No chance," Miles answers. "But hopefully we won't have to. And if we do, they'll have to come up that ladder one at a time."

They walk to the ladder and start to climb to relative safety. I want to tell them I'm here. I want to tell them I've found a membrane and I have a plan, but my voice cannot bridge the gap between our states of being.

I pass through the wall again, soaring high to get a better view. I must choose the exact moment. Too early and it will not be strong enough. Too late, and my friends will be in danger. The possessed people are closer now, muttering and lurching like they are growing excited. Some carry weapons. Kitchen knives. Garden tools. There is a baseball bat in the hands of Mrs. Winters, who works at the library and, to my knowledge, has not played a sport since she was a girl. Ethel, the kind lady who sells cookies at the bakery and who called an ambulance for me after I'd spent the night in her dumpster what seems like a lifetime ago, leads the group. She turns to address the others.

"Check every building," she commands. "Find them."

Uh oh. I cannot be out here. They can see me.

I soar to the top of the grain bin, flattening onto my stomach to watch them approach. Below, the townspeople advance with unnatural coordination. I count them silently. Thirty-seven … thirty-eight …

Ethel marches in front, wearing a nightgown and snow boots. She tilts her head like a predatory bird. I remember she smelled nice, like perfume and sugar.

She walks right up to the police car. The emergency lights flash, painting the snow in alternating red and blue. She peers through the back window. Her breath fogs the glass.

"We've got one in here," she calls out. "Not one of the kids."

Something in me twists at the sight of Sheriff Oleson handcuffed in the back seat. Even from my hiding place, I can see him thrashing against his restraints. Shiloh must have left him in here. I think that must have been a hard thing for her to do, knowing what was coming, but she could not free him, so she locked him where she thought he would be safest.

A man presses his palm against the window. The sheriff falls still.

"Get him out," the man says. He tries the door handle, but the car is locked. He searches until he finds a large rock and smashes the window. The glass cracks. He strikes again. The glass shatters inward, tiny fragments sparkling like red and blue diamond dust in the police lights.

Sheriff Oleson kicks at the broken window. Ethel reaches through the opening. Blood runs down her arm where the glass has cut her, but she doesn't seem to notice. How strange that a soul borrowing a body would care so little for its condition.

A man opens the back door. Sheriff Oleson's boots connect with his chest. The man stumbles but doesn't fall. Ethel laughs and grabs the sheriff's ankles. Two more people join her and drag him from the car.

I hover my hand over my mouth. Sheriff Oleson tumbles into the snow, his wrists still handcuffed behind his back.

"What do we do with him?" Ethel asks, her borrowed face tilted toward the man.

"I'll handle him." The man crouches down beside Sheriff Oleson's head. "Remember me, Sheriff? Mike Chambers. You got me for clipping that clerk at the Gas-N-Go. Ring any bells?"

Sheriff Oleson blanches. He struggles against the handcuffs.

"Lonnie, what the hell are you talking about?" he snaps. "You're not Chambers."

The man grabs the skin beneath his own chin, pinching it between thumb and forefinger. He punctures his chin with his fingernail and peels a strip of skin up to his bottom lip. I cry out in alarm and cover my eyes with my hands, peeking open my fingers to still look.

"I sure am," he says, his voice lilting with unnatural pleasure like he did not even feel the pain. "Just borrowing this face for a while. Surely you recognize an old friend, don't you?"

The sheriff glances between all of the faces surrounding him. "Lonnie, what's going on?"

The man licks up the blood running down his chin. Sheriff Oleson tries to scramble backward, his boots slipping as he pushes with his legs, but the people close in around him.

"Please." All traces of the intimidating lawman have vanished. "Please don't do this."

I should look away, return to the membrane, but I cannot tear my eyes away.

The man circles Sheriff Oleson, examining him like an interesting insect. He kicks snow into the sheriff's face. Sheriff Oleson spits blood onto the white. The man draws back his fist. Sheriff Oleson curls in on himself. But as the blow is about to fall, a young woman in a pair of pink snow pants waves to get the man's attention.

"We've got them!" she yells. "They're hiding in the main building."

The possessed man pauses, fist still raised. He looks between the cowering sheriff and the processing plant.

"The door's blocked," the young woman adds. "Come and help us get in."

The man growls but steps away from Sheriff Oleson, kicking more snow into his face.

"Lucky day, Sheriff," he spits. "But don't worry, I'll be back to finish our reunion." He turns toward the other possessed people. "Everyone to the main building! We need to get those goddamn kids!"

The group moves together toward the processing building. Sheriff Oleson lies trembling in the snow for a few seconds, then wriggles underneath the patrol car. He presses his face against the snow as though he is trying to make himself as small as possible as more possessed people walk past, their boots crunching inches from his head.

"Surround the building," whoever is inside Ethel calls. "Watch the exits. Anyone tries to run, take them down, but remember—we want them conscious."

My stomach knots. Why? Conscious for what?

Some test windows. Others gather at the main door. Their stolen bodies press against it, wood creaking under their collective strength as they form a circle around the building. A man at the center raises his hand.

No more waiting. They are all close enough.

I rush back to the grain bin, passing through metal and corn until I reach the membrane once more.

"Please," I whisper at it, as though it is a small creature or a tiny friend. "I need you to open. They're coming."

The membrane stretches under my touch as though it were waiting for me. On the other side of the wall, I hear people shuffle past on their way to the processing shed.

I press my palms against the membrane and try to push my consciousness through it, imagining my entire being as a current flowing between worlds. The membrane bends with a soft sigh. I reach deep inside myself for that feeling that allowed me to tear a hole in the fabric of reality at the barn. I must not be afraid of this power anymore. I must embrace it.

For my friends.

For all of those people whose bodies have been stolen.

For myself.

I concentrate every particle of my being into my fingertips. The membrane thins like a soap bubble that is about to pop.

"Open," I whisper urgently. "Please."

The membrane quivers. Crashes and shouts echo from the processing plant. I try to keep my focus and press harder. The membrane shimmers, the color shifting from pearlescent to a deeper iridescence, like oil on water.

But then the energy simply dissipates and spreads into the surrounding corn kernels, which glow for a moment before returning to normal. The membrane contracts. Now it is even smaller than before.

"I don't understand." I press my palms against the spot once more. "Why won't you open?"

I gather every ounce of strength I possess. The pressure mounts until it feels like it might tear me apart.

"OPEN!"

I push all of the power onto the membrane. There is a slight lurching sensation beneath my palms. I open my eyes, but all I see is the unblemished surface. I opened it before. I should be able to do it again. Why isn't it working?

What if I can't do this? What if my ability only works when I do not try to control it? What if my friends die because I cannot open this gateway when I promised them I could?

I throw myself against the membrane again and again, growing weaker with each attempt until my fingers turn to wisps that I can no longer see. I rise above the corn, knotting my hands through my hair as I stare down at the gleaming mound of kernels. The membrane is down there. It is still down there, as impassable as the wall between life and death should be, but never has been for me. I realize what this means, but I do not want to accept it because it cannot be true at all, because if it were true, it would mean …

It would mean that I cannot open it.

39

Miles

Someone throws themself against the door. The table I shoved under the handle rattles.

"They're going to get in," I hear myself say, clutching a fire extinguisher to my chest like it's going to save me from anything. "There's too many of them."

"Shut up," Jonah snaps. "No one's getting in."

Another body hits the door. From where we're hiding behind some wooden pallets on the upper catwalk, I can't actually see the table under the door, but I can hear it breaking apart piece by piece, which is somehow much worse.

I gulp down a breath, running my tongue over the roof of my mouth because it's so dry.

"Fran—" Shiloh winces from the pain of speaking, and so much heat rushes into my head that I temporarily forget about the forty possessed people who are trying to break down the door. She swallows, screwing her face up and pushing through the pain to force out her words: "Francesca better hurry up."

Yes. Francesca *had* better hurry up. If she doesn't open that gate in the next thirty seconds, those people are going to come in here, and that would be a huge problem because I don't know how the three of us can fight forty people. Even if we manage to take down one or two, there are dozens more waiting, and it's not like they're monsters. Well, the ghosts are, but the bodies belong to regular people, which means if we actually fight back, we would be assaulting a bunch of normal people, including old people and children.

Like the old man I ran down outside Duncan's. But I can't handle that particular reminder right now.

I chose a fire extinguisher because I figured I could spray it in their eyes, and at least that would be non-lethal, but it's suddenly looking a lot less effective than the pry bar Jonah chose or even Shiloh's pipe. God, I can see the obituary now. *Randall Zweering, 26, died because he was too moral to hit someone with a pipe.*

I'm totally going to die.

I'm not ready to die yet—or am I? I sometimes think I am, especially when I'm up late and can't sleep because my mattress is too soft and my body feels like a giant uncomfortable meat suit I don't fit in properly, but being ready to die feels different from not believing I deserve to be alive, because I don't want to die yet. I'm as unprepared as I was for the first time. I guess no one usually gets to practice— except me, apparently—but there are so many things I haven't done. Like telling my mom who I am. Or actually learning how to use the weights in the gym. I've always wanted to go to England and see the lakes where Wordsworth and Coleridge wrote their poems.

That's it. If I live through this, I'm telling my mom who I am.

What if—oh God—what if one of those possessed people *is* my mom?

I hug my knees to my chest and try to keep breathing. *In for three seconds … hold for five seconds … out for seven seconds … like Dr. Chen taught me, but my lungs feel like they're filling with concrete instead of air.* Shiloh lays a hand on my knee. I raise my eyes to the ceiling so that I don't cry, which is exactly what my body wants to do right now because we're about to die. We're absolutely about to die.

I can hear muffled voices on the other side of the door. I press my back against the wood, closing my eyes so hard that my temples throb and little white spots dance behind my eyelids.

One of the legs on the table snaps. The door swings open so hard it smashes against the far wall, the sound like a gunshot that makes every muscle in my body contract at once.

No one screams. No one charges in, which is—wait, why aren't they rushing in?

I peer around the wood at the door, my pulse hammering so hard in my throat I'm choking on it, but there's only snow swirling in the doorway.

What are they doing? Are they waiting for something? I can hear them breathing. A shadow shifts on the snow. I know they're all there. Standing still.

Oh God. They're toying with us.

Ethel from the bakery steps inside, dusting snow off her shoulders. She lifts her nose and starts literally sniffing the air like some kind of predator. The woman who used to give me free cookies when I'd stop by the bakery is now sniffing the air like she is trying to smell me.

I press myself flat against the wood, trying to make my six-foot-something frame small, which is basically impossible. I take in tiny sips of air that don't even come close to satisfying my lungs.

"I kn-know you're in here." Her grandmotherly tone has turned sharp and mean. I wonder if she's stuttering because whoever Ethel used to be is fighting in there somewhere. "I'm here to k-kill you. My friends have this p-place surrounded, and none of us intend to let you leave with your bodies intact."

Her boots drag across the concrete floor. Pause. Scrape. Pause. I press myself harder against the wood, hoping the pressure might somehow stop my heart from exploding. I realize that compared to Jonah and Shiloh, I'm the adult here. I'm the muscle. It's me who's supposed to protect everybody with my size and my strength. It doesn't matter that inside this meat puppet is a kid whose idea of a fight is to outsmart someone. That's not going to work here. But neither is wishing I had a brown paper bag to breathe into.

"B-but before that happens," she continues, "I w-wanted you to meet someone special. A d-dear f-friend of mine has finally been able to join us. Why don't you come say hello?"

The meaning behind her words takes a second to hit me. This must be part of how she's playing with us, which means that whoever it is—oh God, is it someone we know?

I peer around the edge of the boxes. A small figure steps into the building.

I can only glimpse fragments of him. The red coat that's zipped up to his chin. The tiny pajamas. Blue with those cartoon T-rexes wearing sunglasses on them.

Oh God. Oh God no.

I feel cold looking at him—but that's not right, because

my face is burning, my chest is on fire, and I'm pretty sure I'm about to throw up. He's only lit by the floodlights outside, but it's enough to reflect off his backward eyes, and those gray veins crawling up his neck and into his cheeks like toxic roots.

My lungs compress like all the air got vacuumed out of them. Shiloh raises her eyebrows like she's asking me who it is, and my brain short-circuits because I am absolutely not telling her. She leans forward, shifting her weight to peek around the pallets. I clamp my palm over her mouth and yank her against my chest. Her body goes rigid.

"I'm sorry," I hiss into her ear. "I'm so sorry, Shiloh, but you can't look."

She goes still, like something in my voice registered. Her pulse hammers where my wrist presses against her neck.

"I thought it would be poetic," Ethel says. I peer around the corner to find her running her fingers through Max's hair. "Having the girl's brother find you ... having him kill you."

Shiloh goes still. The thing wearing Max's body straightens.

"What luck." The voice coming from Max sounds wrong. It's still small and high-pitched, but drawn-out, like the speaker is enjoying every syllable. "When I took this child, I had no idea what he would prove to be to you, and what fun he would bring me."

I want to throw up. Like actually vomit right here on this catwalk, but that would mean vomiting on Shiloh.

"I must express my condolences." Max's lips curl into a smile that looks so wrong on his face. "His soul was particularly delicious."

The words hang in the air. Max's soul was particularly delicious. Past tense.

Shiloh stops breathing. I can feel the exact moment when she processes what those words mean.

But … no, that can't be right. Those old people were still alive at the nursing home when the ghosts slipped into their bodies, but … wait, did they come back after they were possessed? I wish I could remember, and it wasn't like we could have stayed to find out.

Shiloh's fingernails dig into my arm so hard they break skin. I look past her at Jonah, who has gone super pale.

"Young souls have this sweetness to them," Max's tiny voice continues. "Like a fine citrus with a hint of sugar." The thing controlling him smacks his lips together like he's recalling a pleasant meal.

I tighten my grip on Shiloh, pressing her against me as tears stream down her face and soak into my palm.

"Did you hear that?" The ghost cups a hand behind Max's ear. "Was it a little mouse trying so hard not to squeak?"

He turns, the whites of his eyes scanning upward. I jump back behind the wood. Shiloh thrashes against me for a second, but I tighten my grip.

"Wouldn't that be a fitting end for this little girl?" Ethel sneers. "To be killed by her own brother?"

I feel sick. Completely, utterly sick, like my insides are being liquefied and my brain is short-circuiting all at once. I press Shiloh harder against me, feeling her shuddering breaths against my palm. If they have Max, what did they do to Shiloh's mom? Is she here in this crowd somewhere? Only ghosts that are feeding on people can possess them, and she wasn't sick, so nobody could have possessed her, but if she got in the way of him leaving the house like all the orderlies got in the way at the nursing home …

"Find her," Ethel says. "Use the boy to find his sister."

"With pleasure," Max says. "I do so love a good hunt."

Run. We need to run. This building is small, and if Max finds us, there's no chance any of us will be able to use our weapons. Shiloh would roll over and die rather than lay a hand on him.

I will not jam up. I will not panic. I close my eyes and force myself to take breaths that actually fill my lungs.

We've … we've got the high ground, which will buy us maybe a minute. I hope Francesca is opening that gate right this second because if she does, all of this will end, but I can't bank on it. I may have stopped going to the gym, but I'm still the strongest of all of us. Ethel said the place is surrounded, but there has to be some way we can get out of here. I scan the walls until my eyes land on something I hadn't seen in my urgent attempt to barricade ourselves in here.

A window.

The back wall has a small window. Barely the size of two microwaves stacked on top of each other, but big enough for Jonah and Shiloh to get through. There's maybe thirty feet of catwalk to get there, then a one-story drop to the ground where the snow could cushion our landing. If it's not big enough for me, at least I can buy them some time.

Those people won't expect us to jump. But we have to go before all the others have time to swarm under the window, ready to catch us.

I lean across Shiloh over to Jonah, pointing at the window and raising my eyebrows. Jonah curses under his breath, but he doesn't say no. He knows as well as I do that staying here is not an option.

I keep my hand firm on Shiloh's mouth. She's limp in my arms. I hope she knows that the only way she has any chance of saving Max is by staying alive, but will she be strong enough to leave him here and jump?

Where is Francesca?

"Shiloh," I hiss, as loud as I dare. "I'm going to take my hand off your mouth, but you need to be quiet and follow me, okay?"

The smallest nod. I let go of her mouth, and she wipes it with the back of her hand. I grab the fire extinguisher and motion to Jonah. We can't crawl to the window. It will make too much noise. We'll have to run as fast as we can and just hope we get through it before anyone catches up with us.

I count down with my fingers. Three … two …

The ladder creaks. Like someone is climbing up.

I spring to my feet and sprint for the window, my footsteps thundering across the metal catwalk.

"THERE!"

I crash against the wall, my fingers fumbling with the rusty window latch. But it doesn't budge.

I twist over my shoulder. "It's jammed!"

Jonah slams his pry bar against the lock. It bends but holds. He tries to get it open with his fingers. There's no *time*.

I swing the base of the fire extinguisher against the glass. The window spiderwebs. I swing again and the pane explodes outward. I punch out the jagged pieces as best I can, trying not to pay attention to the horde of footsteps rushing into the building. I force my head through into the howling wind and peer down at the fifteen-foot drop. There's snow at the bottom, but it's hard to tell how much. A white-eyed woman's head appears at the top of the ladder. There's no time to overthink. I just have to do it.

Taking a quick breath, I pick up Shiloh and help her through the window, legs first. She's limp, and looks pretty much resigned to anything now. I hold her hands and lower her as far as I can before dropping her into the snow. She grunts from the impact, but I hear nothing break.

She crawls to one side as Jonah jumps out the window after her, not waiting for any help from me.

I glance over my shoulder. The white-eyed woman is running for me. On the ground, Max and Ethel seem caught in indecision before running out through the main doors around the back of the shed to where Shiloh and Jonah are now doing their best to wade out of the snowbank. Jonah yells for his pry bar. I toss it down to him.

I force my shoulders through the window, panicking for a second that I'll be stuck there watching while my friends get killed, but I wriggle harder until my chest and then my waist are through. I grab the ledge below the window and somersault as my legs come free. The world spins for a fleeting second as I fall, but then the snow hits me in the back, knocking my breath out of my lungs. There has to be three or four feet of snow built up in the shelter of the building.

Two possessed people lumber around the corner toward us. I pull myself free from the drift, stumbling into shin-deep snow where the wind blows harder. Three more figures stagger around the other side. I scramble toward Shiloh through the snow as Jonah wraps a protective arm around her.

A hand clamps onto my shoulder. I swing my fist around and connect with a woman's jaw, immediately wincing because I feel uncomfortable hitting a woman. She doesn't release me. Those white eyes narrow at me as her other hand pulls back.

"I don't want to hurt you," I wheeze, elbowing her in the sternum. But she doesn't flinch.

Something inside me clicks into place. Not panic. Not fear. Something cold and clinical and absolutely not Miles.

Training.

I drive my thumb into the pressure point below her ear,

exactly where the carotid artery branches. Her grip loosens enough for me to find my feet on the snow. I shove her back. She stumbles.

I run, throwing a punch that connects with a teenage boy's face. His legs fly from under him as pain flares up through my knuckles. I pivot, driving my fist into a random man's stomach like I knew exactly where he was, and grab Shiloh's hand.

Jonah and I practically drag Shiloh forward. She fights hard to stand, but her body will not cooperate and the toes of her boots skid on the ground every other step. I don't know what her dad did to her. I don't want to know.

I run as hard as I can. Screaming voices and pounding footsteps gain on us with every step.

"Where are we going?" Jonah yells at me. "What's your plan?"

My plan? My plan was that Francesca would have opened the gate by now and sent all of these people through it. *That* was my plan.

Shiloh lifts her limp head up at the massive grain bin. "Climb."

Absolutely not. "Are you insane? You want to climb all the way up there?"

"They can't … all follow." She winces as her feet tangle under her. "The ladder … is narrow."

"You've been up there?" Jonah asks.

She nods. I don't even want to think about what she was doing up there, or whether she was up there with her dad, but as much as I hate the idea of climbing, my legs are pumping too hard for me to come up with a better idea. So we run toward the grain bin.

Shiloh reaches the ladder first, grabbing the freezing metal rungs with both hands and hauling herself up with a pained scream that makes me want to cry. I yell at Jonah to go after her and he does, steadying her with a hand on her back to keep her from tipping backward. I go to follow them when Ethel rounds the corner, her white eyes reflecting the moonlight as she hurls herself at me. I drive my elbow into her stomach. She barely reacts. What the hell? I hit a senior citizen hard enough to drop her, and she's unfazed? What do I have to do? Kill them?

I step backward as she advances, her nightgown billowing in the wind.

"Get away from me!" I yell.

She bares her bloodstained teeth. I strike her sternum with more force. Her hands claw at my arms. I shove at her, but she's like a brick wall in a nightgown.

More people lurch toward me from around the grain bin. My elbow catches a bald guy in the temple. He drops. But two more replace him.

I should be climbing the ladder. I *need* to be climbing the ladder.

Shiloh and Jonah are already ten feet up. If I don't move now, I'm dead.

A bony hand grabs my wrist. I yank free. Another catches my collar. My boot lashes out, smashing into someone's shin with a loud crack, but they barely stumble. I throw a punch. Another. I surrender to muscle memory. This body is trained. It *knows* how to fight. But it's like hitting sandbags that keep moving. A weight slams into my back. I lurch forward, barely catching myself before I fall. A guy with sunken cheeks clambers onto me. Nope. Nope, nope. I throw him off, but more hands latch onto my arms. My back slams against the ladder.

Yes. *Yes.* Climb. *Now.*

I grab the rungs. A hand snatches my ankle. I kick, my

boot colliding with a forehead, then haul myself up. I'm inside a cop's body. I should not be this exhausted, but oh my god, my arms are shaking. I never should have stopped going to the gym.

Jonah reaches down. "Miles! Come on!"

Fingers grab my boot. I glance down to see a man with a bushy orange beard hanging on to my ankle as I climb. I stomp down hard on his fingers. He falls.

Shiloh and Jonah move agonizingly slow, but I'm far enough behind them that it doesn't slow me down.

I grip a rung that *moves*.

The ladder pulls a foot away from the curved wall of the grain bin. Every one of my muscles seizes up. The rung beneath my foot rolls.

Oh God. Carefully, so carefully, I ease onto the next rung. The ladder is loose, but it's still holding on. I step onto the next loose rung, holding my breath as I haul myself up.

A hand wraps around my ankle.

No.

I kick. My boot collides with a face, but the hand doesn't let go.

Ethel's lips curl back in a grin as blood stains her teeth. She digs her fingers into my leg, then reaches up and grips the back of my jacket, climbing me like *I'm* the ladder.

The bolt groans. I barely get a second before it rips free from its mooring with a sound that punches through my chest.

I scream. My hands claw at the rungs as a whole section of the ladder peels away from the wall. I tip backward. Shiloh looks down, and for a second, the world stops. I've seen that look before. I saw it when Leonard had that gun against my side, except that time she was frozen. Now, her mouth opens in a scream and her face is a mask of unbridled terror.

The ground rushes up too fast, and I hit the ground before I'm ready. My vision explodes into white-hot pain. My ribs feel wrong. My ears ring. Everything hurts.

I blink up into the stormy sky. Shapes loom over me. I see the gleam of teeth. White eyes staring down at me.

My vision goes away all at once.

40

Shiloh

Miles is lying on the ground with pieces of the ladder scattered around him. I'm standing next to Jonah on the first platform now, and the snow is falling too thick for me to see much else.

"MILES!" I scream. "MILES, GET UP!"

He doesn't move.

The possessed people rush toward him. A man I don't recognize with a thick orange beard reaches him first. He grabs Miles's shoulder and flips him onto his back. Miles's head lolls.

I can't breathe. Can't think. My vision narrows to that single point below where Miles lies on the snow, and it's everything I can do to keep a hold of the railing as I scream his name again and again.

A boy I recognize from school drops to his knees beside Miles. There's something long in his hand. Something that glints in the overhead light.

"NO!" I scream so hard I taste blood. "GET AWAY FROM HIM!"

The boy lifts a long, rusted nail, the kind that looks like it's been pried out of something ancient. He presses the tip against Miles's cheek. Miles's lips part in a ragged breath. The boy presses down until he draws blood. Miles's body arches in agony, but the wind carries the sound away.

I'm sobbing so hard. Jonah grabs my wrist, trying to drag me to the ladder, but it's like they all forgot we're up here. A woman with brittle yellow hair crouches at Miles's feet. She peels off one of his boots, then the sock beneath. She's saying something, but the wind won't let me hear her. She takes the nail from the boy's hand and slams the point under his toenail.

Miles finally screams.

They *laugh*.

The woman yanks the nail out, and blood wells up instantly. Miles buries his hands in the snow like he wants to move away, but his body won't let him.

Orange Beard tilts his head up at me like he just remembered I was there. He raises his voice to scream over the wind.

"You wanna watch, sweetheart?" he calls. "Or you wanna come down and join the fun?"

I don't even think. I slide under the railing and jump.

But Jonah grips the back of my jacket and yanks me back against him. "We got to keep climbing."

"But *Miles*—"

Jonah's arms lock around my waist, pushing me toward the second ladder. "Go."

I push against Jonah's hands, trying to force my way back down to Miles, but Jonah is stronger than me. Especially now.

His fingers dig into my sides as he pushes me past him and upward, one rung at a time.

I turn to look down. The woman with the nail reaches for Miles's other foot. Miles barely struggles. He can't move.

I scream for him. Jonah pushes up on my body, and I grip the rungs. My body moves mechanically, hands reaching for the next rung like I'm one of those possessed people now. Like something else is controlling me.

Up we go. Rung after rung. The top of the grain bin seems so far away, but my body keeps climbing anyway because that's what bodies do. They try to survive.

Jonah keeps pushing me upward, his hands on my boots whenever I hesitate.

"Come on," he says. "We're almost there."

I don't want to be almost there. I want to be with Miles. I want to grab a broken piece of the ladder and drive it straight into Orange Beard's throat. I want to tear that woman away from Miles and make her *feel* what he's feeling. I want to throw myself between them and let them take *me* instead.

I reach the top and haul myself over the edge, my arms trembling with exhaustion as I collapse onto the narrow bridge. Jonah climbs after me. The walkway is barely two feet wide, and the flimsy railing wobbles when I grip it like it did the first time I was up here. The wind up here cuts like a knife, stealing my breath and freezing the tears on my cheeks. I crawl to the edge of the platform, my body moving on autopilot as I peer down.

A crowd has amassed around Miles. Two of the bigger men have hauled him upright and are gripping his arms so tight his shoulders strain. He sags between them, his head lolling forward. Orange Beard steps in front of him, tilting his head like a fisherman admiring his catch. He says something. I don't need to hear what. A wiry man steps forward, rolling up his sleeves like he's preparing for a job. He slams his fist into Miles's stomach.

Miles jerks, but the men hold him up. Another takes a turn. Like they're making a game of it.

I choke on a sob. Some of the possessed people get tired of playing with Miles and start looking around. One of them snaps their head up to look at me. Another breaks away from the crowd surrounding Miles and stalks around to the other side of the grain bin. The ladder is broken on this side now, so they must be coming up the other side.

"What do we do?" I rasp, wiping my eyes. "Jonah, what do we do?"

He stares down at Miles with an empty expression, like he's watching this happen on TV instead of right in front of us. *No*. This is not how this ends.

I grab the railing with both hands and shake it as hard as I can, the rattling sound echoing across the empty fields.

"FRANCESCA!" Her name rips through my throat. "WHERE ARE YOU?"

Some of the possessed people around Miles look up at me. I don't care.

"FRANCESCA!" I'm screaming so hard something gives way in my throat, a sharp tearing sensation that floods my mouth with the taste of copper. "OPEN THE GATE! NOW! PLEASE!"

I collapse against the railing, the metal digging into my bruised ribs. Then it hits me.

"The glasses," I rasp, spinning around to look at Jonah. "I need the glasses."

Jonah blinks, like he's coming out of a trance. "What?"

"The ghost glasses." I pat my pockets, knowing they're not there. "Do you have them?"

Jonah pulls out the battered frames. I shove them onto my

face. The world shifts, and I try to see through the distortion of the cracked lens.

Francesca hovers a few feet away from us, her spectral form fluttering like a candle flame in the wind. She's sobbing, her mouth moving in what looks like a desperate plea, but I can't hear a word.

"Oh thank God," I say. "Francesca, you need to open the gate right now."

Francesca points toward the grain bin under us, then makes a pushing motion with her hands like she's trying to force something open. Then she shakes her head. Understanding settles in the pit of my stomach.

"Why can't you open it? You did it before!"

Francesca shouts something. I can tell by the way her mouth stretches wide, but it's like watching TV with the sound off. I point at my ear.

"I can't *hear* you."

She looks around frantically, then places her finger against the frost covering the rounded roof of the grain bin and starts to write.

CANTOPEN

"Why not?" I'm crying so hard I can barely get the words out. "You have to!"

She writes more.

TOOSTRONG

"What?" I shake my head. "No. There has to be a way. Miles is going to die, you have to—"

At the other end of the catwalk, an elderly man who looks like he should be using a walker instead of climbing a grain bin pulls himself up onto the bridge, wiping his palms off on the front of his pants. He raises his hand in a sluggish wave and starts walking toward us.

Below us, Miles has stopped fighting, but the possessed people haven't lost interest in him yet. He must still be conscious. Still alive. Still able to feel pain.

My heart jackhammers against my ribs like it's trying to punch its way out. The platform seems to tilt beneath me. I grab the railing to stay upright.

There has to be a way to open it. *Think.*

Francesca writes more.

D Y I N G.

My stomach lurches like missing a step in the dark. "Who's dying? Miles?"

She shakes her head and spells out another word.

G A T E.

The word means nothing. *Gate.* What about the gate? Is the gate dying?

Francesca's finger stabs down, pointing at the hopper car below us. Then at herself.

"*You're* dying?"

Another sharp shake of her head, but there's hesitation this time. Like she's second-guessing herself.

I don't understand. *I don't understand.*

My thoughts are slamming against each other, tripping over themselves, breaking apart before I can hold on to them. I try to put the pieces together. Everything I've learned about ghosts. About the other side.

The gate opened before. For Francesca. At the barn.

395

Ella Ruggles said the other side would be hungry. She said it wouldn't take much. Just a crack. Enough to let the other side get its fingers in, then it would take over and pull the souls back where they belong. The only thing it needs is some help to poke through.

Oh.

Oh.

Something Colin said. His voice echoes through my skull.

You can trick your body into thinking you're dead, but there's no tricking the other side. Only truly dead people can cross through those gates.

The Monroe farm. Francesca opened the gate, but we didn't get dragged through because we weren't dead. You can't cross to the other side unless—

Unless you're dead.

Death opens the gate. The other side is bringing across all the energy it can. If a brand-new soul appeared that was too weak to resist, the other side would drag it across before it even had the chance to settle. That's easy energy. And as soon as the small hole appeared, Francesca could rip it wide open. Wide enough to swallow them all.

My heartbeat is everywhere. My temples. My throat. My fingertips. It's so obvious now. So simple.

Someone has to die.

Before those people can kill Miles, because if I have anything to do with it, it's not going to be him.

I breathe in deep. My body is shaking, but inside, at the center of me, there's stillness. I'm the one who started this. I dragged everybody into this mess because I wanted to find Max. To save Max. It was all for Max. Everything I've ever done has been for Max.

I couldn't save Miles last time. But I can save him now.

Francesca's shaking her head, her ghostly form flickering. But it doesn't matter. She's already too late.

Because I know.

I've already decided.

I turn to the edge of the platform. Fifty feet. High enough. The fall will do it. A clean break between this world and the next.

My fingers curl around the railing. The metal bites deep into my skin, but I barely feel it. I barely feel anything.

Francesca darts in front of me, her mouth forming frantic words. I take off the ghost glasses and place them on the ground.

Jonah's focus is still on the possessed man ambling toward us, taking his time, safe in the knowledge that we have nowhere left to run. But they can't see what I can see. They don't know the door I can open, the one way out of this.

Jonah isn't watching me. Good.

I take a breath, focusing on how the icy air feels sliding down my throat, and go to my happy place.

Max.

His tiny fingers wrapped around mine when he was a baby. His gap-toothed grin the morning after he had his first visit from the Tooth Fairy. The way he always looked at me made me feel like I was his whole world. One day I hope he'll know what I did. I hope he'll know that this was for him, that everything I've ever done was for him. I hope he doesn't stay sad for too long. He's going to wake up after this. He has to. This is the only chance he has. The only chance any of us has.

I glance over my shoulder at Jonah. He steps forward to put himself between me and the grandpa sauntering down the catwalk. Still protecting me. Even now.

My hands grip the railing. I try to squeeze the fear out

through my fingertips, try to turn it into something else, but I can't. I'm so scared. I've never been this scared.

The wind claws at me, shoving at my back like it's trying to do the job for me. My body knows what I'm about to do, even as my brain fights to process it. My breath won't come. My knees want to buckle, but I can't let them. I swing one leg over the railing. The air catches under me like a living thing. The cold seeps deep into my bones. Into my blood. I search the crowd below for a crop of blond hair, a red coat, or anything I recognize. It only takes me seconds to find him. He's standing on the edge of the group gathered around Miles, but instead of looking at Miles, he's staring right up at me and smiling. He probably thinks I'm doing this because I'm too scared of being ripped apart by the possessed people.

I stare out at the surrounding fields. The sky is so huge up here. The snow stretches away like an endless sheet of white. I could almost believe this world was peaceful.

"Shiloh?" Jonah's voice sounds so far away. "What are you doing?"

I don't turn around. If I see his face, I'll lose my nerve.

"I love you," I say. "Make sure my dad doesn't get Max, okay?"

"What?" A sharp inhale. "Shiloh, *no.*"

I jump off with everything I have left. Jonah's scream rips away in the wind.

The wind roars in my ears. The ground rushes up. So fast. Too fast. I close my eyes.

41

Francesca

Shiloh tumbles through the air, her arms and legs flailing like she has forgotten that people cannot swim through the sky. I am screaming, but nobody can hear me. I rush alongside her as she falls, my fingers passing uselessly through her mortal form as her eyes split wide with terror.

I am still screaming her name when she hits the ground.

Her body lands so hard it displaces the snow. There is a sound like when I step on autumn leaves, the sound of bones and things inside her breaking all at once. Her body lies twisted. One arm folds under her. Blood pools underneath her hair, spreading across the snow like red watercolors bleeding into a piece of blotting paper. Her chest rises and falls once, a faint, fluttering breath that almost looks like a mistake, then goes still.

What did she do that for? She cannot die. She ... has to protect Max. She has to make sure her father does not come back to her family. She has too many people who need her.

I was the one who was supposed to die.

I did not want to stay here. I had already decided that I was not going to return to my body after this. That is what I had gone up to tell her. D Y I N G. I was going to go down there, back to the grain car, and hold my nose shut until my body stopped breathing.

I never meant … I did not say …

It was supposed to be me.

I was only trying to say goodbye.

My passing would have been a gentle release. If somebody had to cross through that gate to open the passageway, it should have been the one who has been lingering too long at the threshold, not the one who could least afford to leave this world. I am the ghost. *I* am the one who doesn't belong.

I hover beside Shiloh, my form trembling with sobs that make no sound. My hands flutter over her as I try to figure out what to do, or how I can help. The air grows heavy like it does before a thunderstorm.

Some of the nearest possessed people turn toward us, their veiny eyeballs reflecting the moonlight in a way that makes them glow like twin pearls. One of them—a woman with iron-gray hair escaping from beneath a woolen hat like frightened snakes—takes a step toward us. Her face hangs slack, like she has forgotten how to wear it properly, and dark gray veins trail up her neck into her jawline like the roots of a poisonous plant seeking soil. Behind her, a man whose skin seems pulled too tight across his cheekbones tilts his head.

My eyes go back to Shiloh in time for a shimmer to appear above her body. At first it is merely a disturbance in the air, like heat rising from a summer pavement, but then a long sliver of soul rises from her chest. Her soul unfolds from her body like a butterfly from a chrysalis, glowing with a soft white light. She blinks down at her body. I have seen this moment before with other spirits, but never before has a soul looked less confused.

Shiloh meets my gaze, her eyes wide with surprise and something else. Recognition perhaps. Or understanding.

A pinprick of light appears on the ground beside her body's head, as tiny as a firefly trapped under ice. I feel it immediately. The other side rumbles.

She reaches her hand out to me. I curl my fingers around hers, our forms glowing bright white as they connect. She manages a small smile.

"Get them all, okay?"

She hardly has time to get the words out before the pinprick expands into a circle of light and traps her legs. Her fingers fly out of mine. The circle grows wider and Shiloh's form stretches toward it, elongating in a way that would be impossible for flesh to do. So quickly that I nearly miss it, the other side yanks her soul through the opening.

I shake my head to force the tears from my eyes and watch them disappear into the air as they fall off me. I will not lose this opportunity.

I plunge my hands into the hole in the membrane. The material stretches like taffy under my fingers. I grab hold of the edges of the membrane with my mind, opening my arms as wide as I can.

The world implodes.

Wind roars through from the other side, whipping around me as I stay exactly in place. It does not try to claim me. I cannot cross because I am not dead.

"Come!" I scream into the wind. "Take them back!"

Power surges through me. Each particle of my being vibrates at frequencies I never knew existed. I am everywhere and nowhere, stretched across the membrane between worlds like a living bridge. The hole beneath my hands grows hungrier, its edges pulsing with an iridescent light that casts strange shadows across the snow, but I am not afraid. I am not only a girl who speaks to ghosts. I am a bridge between worlds. I am balance. Simply because I can choose who lives and who dies does not mean I have to. The other side will do it for me.

And it will do it now.

"I am Francesca Russo," I declare through gritted teeth. "And I command you to *OPEN!*"

The hole responds with a sound like the earth itself splitting open. The opening widens until it is large enough to swallow a car. So much wind screams up from the depths, carrying whispers and moans and half-formed words from the countless souls on the other side from which the energy is made. Something tugs deep within my core as if something is trying to pull my essence in multiple directions at once, but instead of fighting it, I surrender to it because I have this feeling deep inside of me that there is nothing to be afraid of. My spectral form shimmers and expands, growing brighter until I am nothing more than radiance with consciousness, my edges blurring into the light that surrounds me.

A soul tears free from the gray-haired woman nearest to Shiloh's body. One moment, she is standing. The next, her head snaps backward. Her mouth stretches impossibly wide and from it emerges a writhing, luminous shape. The soul rips free from her throat, arms reaching out and clawing at the air as it tries to go back, but it elongates as the other side claims it, then disappears with a final wail.

The old woman's body collapses into the snow. I try to see if her chest is moving, but I cannot tell from all the way over here.

She is only the beginning. All around us, the possessed

people begin to convulse. Their backs arch, their limbs jerking and twitching as the souls possessing them fight to stay inside. From their gaping mouths emerge writhing forms. The souls claw at the air, at their hosts, at anything they can reach, but they are no match for the gate. The force drags them screaming through the hole. Some look human. Others are barely recognizable as once-human shapes, their faces twisted by the speed at which they are moving. The air fills with the sound of screaming that makes every part of me want to cover my ears, but I do not need to.

I catch a small scream from over my shoulder and turn, my stomach lurching at the sight of Max. He is on his side and convulsing in the snow as a particularly large soul tears itself free from his small frame. The soul of a gaunt and wrinkled man claws at Max's face, his fingernails leaving deep scratch marks across the boy's cheek. I want to rush to Max, to shield him from any more harm like Shiloh would have done, but I cannot move from my position.

The soul wrenches free and shoots through the hole to the other side. Max goes still. My heart squeezes like someone has wrapped an invisible hand around it, but I cannot go to Max right now. I must hold open the gate.

I watch the bodies drop one by one as souls wrench from them and surge through the opening. One old man notices what I am doing and charges toward me, but as soon as he gets close, the other side claims his soul and the body tips forward into the snow.

I can barely process it. I can hardly think. This is working, this is good, this is—

Something shifts in the periphery of my vision. I recognize the figure and immediately turn to look.

My stomach lurches.

No.

Miles is standing ten feet away from me in the snow. For a moment, my mind refuses to accept what I am seeing as if my brain is trying to protect me, but there is no protecting me from this.

I had not seen what those people did to him. I had been too busy, too preoccupied trying to get Shiloh's attention on the grain car, but the damage is undeniable. His pea coat is hanging open and has deep stains soaking through the fabric. His hair is stiff with blood and matted to his forehead and temples, and his face—goodness, his face is almost unrecognizable, a mess of split skin and swollen flesh, one eye nearly swollen shut and with a jagged gash running from his cheekbone to his jaw. He is missing a shoe. His bare foot presses against the snow, and his toes are streaked crimson.

The gray-haired woman and the orange-haired man lie beside him, their souls already ripped away, their bodies nothing more than empty husks, but Miles is alive. He is on his hands and knees, his arms trembling under his own weight, his back arching as his spine goes taut like he's being yanked from the inside.

Something is not right. His soul is slipping. Why is he writhing?

With sudden, terrible clarity, I understand.

A soul is being pulled from Miles as well.

His own.

The gate does not care who belongs and who does not. Not when it is this close. The gate is claiming him like all the others.

"No," I breathe. "NO!"

Miles turns his face up to the sky, screaming and clawing at his chest like he is trying to rid himself of pain. Pale light seeps from his eyes, his mouth, and his skin. His back bows. His breath rasps like he is drowning in air.

I try to move toward him, but the gate anchors me in place. He is too close to the edge. His soul is slipping free.

No.

Miles is not like the others. He has earned his place here. This body is his now. I gave it to him.

I thrust my hands at the gate. "CLOSE!"

For a moment, the force lessens. The edges of the opening begin to contract like a flower closing for the night.

Miles screams.

I pour every ounce of my will into closing the opening, imagining the membrane healing like skin over a wound. My mind wraps around the edges of the tear. I press as hard as I can.

The gate quivers. Its edges waver, contracting then expanding again.

Miles tears free. His soul rises to hover above his body, his eyebrows leaping up almost as though he is afraid. He looks like Miles now, not the police officer whose body he was occupying. I see him suddenly as I saw him not long after I first met him, when he sat on the steps of my trailer waiting for me after he died the first time: warm skin, impossibly thin, and all ungainly angles and uncontrollable hair. Those wire-framed glasses that were always slipping down his nose now sit where they need to be, perfectly positioned as if they are truly part of him rather than an object he wore. His curly hair drifts in gentle waves around his head.

Our eyes lock across the impossible distance, and oh, the terrible understanding that floods his gaze. He looks so frightened, yet somehow at peace, as though some part of him always knew this moment would come, that his borrowed time was just that: borrowed.

But it does not *have* to be.

The hole drags him toward it. His hands swipe in the air,

reaching toward his body. I gather every particle of my being, focusing my will into a single point like my mother showed me I could do with sunlight through a magnifying glass.

"Please," I whisper, no longer commanding but begging. "Please, you have to *close*."

The hole is merely the size of a soccer ball now. I am almost there. Miles and I exchange a glance. I scream as I pull the edges together. He slips through the mouth the instant before the gate closes.

42

FrANCeSCA

I stare at the place where the hole just was, which is now only an enormous pile of snow and dirt gathered around us. Every particle of me emits a hum. Tiny threads of my form peel away. It is not painful, precisely, but it feels profoundly empty, as if I am becoming less with each passing second.

Shiloh. Gone.

Miles. Gone.

Gone?

They cannot be gone. There must be a way to fix this … this … *problem* I created. I have reached those on the other side before. It is what I do. It is who I *am*.

I try to reach for them now, but my thoughts skip like flat stones across a calm lake and I … I cannot … I cannot feel them. My edges are peeling away faster now. I could perhaps go back into my body, but then what? What good would that do? Could I reach through and grab them? Bring them back the way I did with all of Leonard's friends? I have done it before. I know I have, but not like this, not when my body feels like it has been fed through an old washing machine and is barely holding itself together. I could not even get out of the grain car without help. That kind of effort would finish me completely. Does that even matter?

I was already planning to join the ghosts permanently, so maybe I could bring Shiloh and Miles back and then slip through and rejoin Evangeline. Yes. *Yes*, that makes a peculiar sort of sense. My final act of kindness. My last offering. Some sort of trade. But *no*, that would not work either because I would need to stay in my body long enough to guide them back to theirs, and I may not survive crossing over and returning them to their bodies.

The gate.

I could reopen the gate between the worlds.

I could try to rip the membrane again, make a doorway big enough for Miles and Shiloh to return to the world of solid things, and then close it again.

But no, that is madness as well. All of the other mean spirits would come through when they came back, and then we would be right back where we started. The souls would be stronger this time. I cannot unleash such horror upon the world again, not even to save the people I love.

I cannot do what he did.

I will *not* be Leonard.

The world is all topsy-turvy and spinning like a carnival ride that has broken free from its moorings. The air feels thick as molasses around my arms and legs, and the dirt still whispers with electricity from where the hole was open, but is now gone.

I press a hand onto my stomach to try to quell the nauseated feeling that is rising through me as I take in all of the fallen bodies scattered across the snow. There are so many, spread like a child's collection of dolls thrown from the sky. Did I … did the gate? I thought I was saving them by sending the ghosts back across, but what if the ghosts killed them as they left?

I approach the nearest body—a man lying face down in the snow. His arm twists underneath him at an awkward angle. His finger twitches.

I freeze, hardly daring to hope. Did I imagine that?

A woman curls her fingers. Behind her, a girl's leg jerks. Someone is crying. Perhaps a child.

I cover my mouth with both of my hands. Oh, thank goodness.

Most of them are still, but now that I am looking, I see the slow, steady rise and fall of their chests beneath torn clothing. Their faces have changed. They are no longer angry. They are slack. As if they're merely sleeping. But the ground tells a different story. It remembers. It holds the splattered blood, the streaks of dirt, and the various discarded weapons that have fallen out of everybody's hands.

Ethel is nearby, and I notice for the first time that her coat is buttoned wrong. The man with the bright orange hair is sprawled on his back with his eyes open. These were … people. People with homes. With lives and families who loved them. They had been ordinary before something terrible took them and now they can be ordinary again, as long as they can recover from this. I have spent so long believing the people in this town hated me for who I am— *knowing* they did—so I am surprised when an unexpected warmth unfurls in my chest. With shelter and medical attention, they will all be safe now. Because of the girl who claimed she could talk to spirits.

And because of Shiloh.

She lies near me. The crimson stain beneath her head has

stopped spreading and has frozen in the bitter cold. Her brown eyes are open, staring up at a sky she can no longer see. Or maybe she sees something else. Perhaps she is looking at Jonah, who is still standing on top of the grain bin.

Oh no.

Jonah.

I had completely forgotten about him in the rush to open the passageway. My attention snaps upward to the towering structure, where a small figure stands on the edge of the highest platform.

I soar upward as fast as I can. Jonah stands frozen mere feet from where Shiloh jumped. His mouth opens and closes, but no sound emerges. He stares right through my face at Shiloh's body on the ground far below.

Something about the trembling of Jonah's shoulders turns the world around me dim. Evangeline told me that everyone has their time, and if there is anything I have learned from the souls, it is that endings are not really endings at all. They are doorways into something else, but nothing about this feels like a doorway. Or if it is a doorway, Jonah cannot go through it because he is still alive.

I was supposed to be gone. I had *decided* that I would be finished with all of this. No more feeling like I do not belong no matter where I go. No more seeing things that no one else can see. Only peace, like the perfect stillness of the cemetery at dawn, surrounded by people like me. But Jonah is standing up here all by himself. His fingers wrap around the railing, as if it is the only thing keeping him tethered to this world, and I *know*, the way I sometimes know things, that if I do not stop him, he will let go.

A feeling like hot honey trickles down my throat. I do not want this responsibility sitting on my shoulders. It is heavy and uncomfortable. Shiloh was supposed to be up there with him, smiling and whole and so terribly alive, not me. I want to scream until my voice breaks, until the stars themselves shudder, but before I can, a thought slides into my head.

Bodies can survive without souls. Mine did. I remember being on the other side, hearing the machines going *beep beep beep* from so far away.

So why not Shiloh and Miles?

I could do it. I could keep their bodies here, tethered to life the same way I am still tethered, and hold them in this world until their souls find their way back. But I would need to get them help, and to do that I need to go back inside of my body.

I tilt my face up toward the gray sky, feeling the snow fall through me. Is it my imagination, or is the power of the wind falling? Is the snow becoming lighter? I shake my head a tiny bit because, oh my goodness, Evangeline would be laughing herself silly right now if she could see the position I am in. She would grin in that way that makes her eyes crinkle at the corners and say, "Told you so." She told me I would know when my time was about to end. Even though I do not want to go back or feel the exhaustion settled deep in my bones, this is not my time.

But if I am going to do this, I must hurry.

I put my hand to the frosty surface of the grain bin where the wind has scoured the snow away, waiting for the wind to cease before writing, where Jonah is sure to see:

I W I L L B R I N G T H E M B A C K

W A K E M E U P

He looks at the letters that are appearing as if by magic and a look comes into his eyes. He glances around as if trying to find me, then grabs the ghost glasses from the floor and begins to make his way down the ladder.

I wonder if I can bring myself into my body without the use of the blue drug. It may not work, as death-walking is a process that is different from the usual order of things, but I did return to my body once before, in the hospital. I swoop down through the top of the train car. Goodness, my body looks so cold and weak in there, curled like a comma on the floor of the grain car. Is this all that has become of me? A failing collection of bones and tissue and faltering organs?

I banish the negative thoughts. This is the one body I have, so it will have to do.

I flip onto my back, closing my eyes and imagining making myself fit as though I am trying to squeeze into clothes that have grown too small. The body resists as though I am trying to push together two magnets with matching poles, but I am not taking no for an answer.

I push harder. My spectral fingers reach for the real ones that lie curled on the metal floor, and—

Cold.

So much cold courses through me that it feels as if I have been dropped into a frozen pond. My blood feels like slush. The back of my throat tastes like metal, but the cold only lingers for a moment before a strange warmth tingles underneath my skin. I lean my head back, inhaling deeply as the warmth spreads, knitting together tiny fissures I never knew existed, soothing inflamed tissues and coaxing reluctant blood vessels to expand. I lie absolutely still as the warmth settles into my bones, not entirely erasing their brittleness but reinforcing them with enough strength to bear weight. Enough to sustain me. Enough that I do not need to leave.

Enough to stay.

I wiggle my fingers, which respond with sleepy

obedience, but my legs do not respond at all. I suppose that is all right. I have grown accustomed to the chair, after all, but it does mean I will need help to climb out of here.

I am not sure how many seconds pass before a shadow passes over the open hatch.

"Francesca?" Jonah's voice breaks, as if he cannot comprehend what he is seeing. "How did you—"

"I did not require drugs to bring myself back," I say, trying for a smile that feels wobbly on my face. "You must help me climb out of here. I have an idea of how we can save Shiloh and Miles."

He disappears from the opening, his boots reemerging after a couple of seconds as he almost runs down the metal ladder. Pulling my arms around his neck, he lifts me into a piggyback ride. My legs dangle uselessly in the air as he climbs up one ladder and down the other, jumping onto the snow and running to Shiloh.

He puts me down on the snow beside her. I look right into her empty eyes as I urge Jonah to call 911. He stammers through the call, and I nearly cry with relief when the woman on the other end of the phone assures him that help is on the way.

In order to have any chance of preserving their bodies, we must keep their blood pumping, and I try my best to explain this to Jonah through my chattering teeth. He immediately begins compressions. I peer over him at Miles, who is lying in the snow ten feet away. I cannot do anything to help him because I cannot crouch over him without the use of my legs, but Jonah cannot keep two hearts beating at the same time.

I will not make him choose. I may not be able to move enough to do compressions, but there are others around me who can.

Some of the formerly possessed people are stirring in the

snow, their normal eyes blinking as they seem to wonder where they are. I do not wish to cause them more distress, but I am desperate enough not to care at the moment.

"Is anybody a doctor here?" I yell out at the mass of confused faces.

One old man looks at me for a couple of seconds before shaking his head. A young woman twenty feet away raises her hand. She climbs onto unsteady feet and staggers toward us through the trampled snow, her dark hair hanging in damp tangles around a face that is still pale with confusion.

"Hey." She gets on her knees beside me. "I'm a nursing student. Do you know what happened here?"

I blink at her, trying to ignore how odd it is that I had seen her face all white-eyed clamoring toward the ladder minutes ago, but there is no time to tell her everything I would need to in order to explain what has happened here. I shake my head and point at Miles. "Can you help him?"

She tilts Miles's head back with practiced ease, pinching his nose and breathing into his mouth twice before looking over her shoulder at Jonah to tell him exactly what he should be doing. I sit deeper in the snow, bracing my body against the wind as I release a long sigh, as if trying to tell my body that everything is going well.

Until a shadow falls across Shiloh's body. I lift my head and suddenly remember all of the things that are still not going well.

Sheriff Oleson stands over us, staring down at Shiloh. One handcuff is still dangling from his wrist, but his other hand is free. Shiloh must not have tightened them enough.

"What happened?" he demands. "What the hell did you do to my daughter?"

Jonah ignores him and continues compressions. Sheriff Oleson steps closer. Jonah positions his body as if to shield

Shiloh. Sheriff Oleson does not waste a second. He drops to his knees and slams his shoulder against Jonah's, sending him flying nearly a foot. I yell at him to stop and push myself forward, but my uncooperative legs betray me and I tumble over Shiloh's feet.

Sheriff Oleson begins compressions himself. Jonah turns his eyes back on the sheriff. I understand what he is going to do only a moment before his body goes tense.

But before he can launch himself upward, a burly figure steps toward us and grabs Sheriff Oleson by the collar, yanking him backward with surprising strength.

"The hell are you doing?" the sheriff demands, smacking the hand away.

It is the man with the orange beard. Jonah's eyes widen with recognition, as though he also realizes this is the same man who was trying to tear Miles apart minutes ago. The bearded man does not appear to remember anything about what happened. I wonder if any of them do. I surely hope not.

"I think you'd better step away from the kids," he says.

A tiny smile tugs at the corner of my mouth. I glance at Jonah, who is gripping his shoulder and staring at both men as if he would like to rip off both of their heads.

"Are you kidding me right now?" Sheriff Oleson's hand twitches at his hip. "I'm her father, and—"

"I've seen what kind of father you are, and I'm not going to say it again. Step away from the girl."

I am not sure what he is speaking about, but Jonah clearly is because he whips his head up to stare at the man with the orange beard as though he cannot believe what he said. Sheriff Oleson raises his voice, but his focus is on the orange-bearded man now and not on us, so I find Jonah's eyes and point at Shiloh and he resumes compressions. In the distance, a siren rings out into the night. I stop paying attention to what Sheriff Oleson is doing and turn to look at Shiloh. Another older woman has gotten to her feet now and has put herself between Shiloh and her father. Jonah's injured arm trembles with each compression, and he counts under his breath. Some time passes before the orange-bearded man kneels beside him.

"Hey, kid," he says. "Let me take over."

Jonah shakes his head. "I can't ... she needs—"

"I've got her," the man says. "I promise."

Jonah lets out this dry sound and falls backward, surrendering Shiloh to the bearded man. My chest tightens, watching him curl forward and wrap his arms around himself as though he is attempting to stop sobs from escaping.

I dig my hands into the snow, feeling the cold burn into my palms as I drag myself a couple of feet to the side, leaving little trenches in the snow like the tracks of a wounded animal. When I try to wrap my arms around him, he holds me away, bracing his hand on his forehead like he is trying to hold his thoughts inside.

"She jumped." He gasps, staring at her body, not at me. "She just—I couldn't—"

"I know." The words taste like ash in my mouth. I try to hug him again and this time, he allows me to fold myself around his shaking ribcage. "But there was nothing you could do."

He is crying so hard he can hardly get the words out. "She left me."

I know she did, but not the way he thinks, and not because she wanted to. My tears come without sound, tiny warm droplets landing on his shoulder.

"She saved us," I tell him. "All of us."

But I do not believe he cares, and I continue to hold on to him until the ambulance arrives. There is one ambulance at first for upwards of fifty people, but more help is coming, and the early arrivals call for help. I can see emergency vehicles peel off Route 13 and down the gravel road, their sirens cutting through the night as they line up along the perimeter of the field.

Every person is triaged with remarkable efficiency. The most serious cases are taken away first while those with more minor injuries huddle underneath silver blankets. Some simply stare at their hands as if they don't quite recognize them. Others weep quietly, unable to explain why they're standing in snow-covered fields in their nightclothes when they should be home in their beds.

On the other side of the train cars, a paramedic wraps a blanket around Max and carries him to an ambulance. Sheriff Oleson doesn't notice. He is still looking down at Shiloh with an expression that is quite unreadable. He is too busy hating his daughter to notice that his son is here at all.

More paramedics load Shiloh and Miles into separate ambulances, continuing CPR as the doors slam closed and the vehicles whip away, and I utter a small prayer that they are able to convince their hearts to resume beating because nothing about this plan will work if both of their bodies stay dead. I am not sure who I am praying to. I do not believe anybody can hear my thoughts when I am here, but there are many things I still do not know, so perhaps I am wrong.

Jonah fights the paramedics who try to attend to him, insisting he is fine because he wants to go with Shiloh, but he is not fine at all. Eventually, a stern-faced EMT manages to ease him onto an ambulance bumper, cleaning the gash on his forehead and cutting away his sleeve to reveal swollen skin mottled with bruises covering his upper arm.

I find myself propped against the bumper of another ambulance, a blanket draped over my shoulders by a harried paramedic who promises to return. My legs are still refusing to cooperate, but that is nothing new, and a strange vitality hums beneath my skin. The gate is closed. Balance has been restored. But the empty feeling in the pit of my stomach will not go away.

Once the paramedics have deemed Jonah stable, he slides off the side of the ambulance and walks over to me, sitting beside me on the bumper. The night air feels heavy, as though it is trying to push me down into the earth, but the snow is stopping, and above me, the clouds are parting. I get a glimpse of a pale half-moon coming out to bathe the whole scene in its cold light.

"I know I can't ask you to do this," he says, "and I know it's not fair, but you can find them on the other side, can't you? Can you go find them and bring them back?"

Pressing my lips into a line, I drop my head. I suppose I have done it many times before, but the memory of it makes my fingertips tingle with a chill that does not come from the night air. I may not be capable of doing it again, but it is more than that. Crossing to the other side is what Leonard did. All of these bad things happened because Leonard was trying to choose the people who lived and who died, no matter the consequences. Could I do the same thing? Should I do the same thing to bring Shiloh and Miles back?

I cannot be like Leonard. I cannot choose.

But is it choosing if I am returning a soul to the body that it belongs to, anyway? I honestly do not know, but not bringing them back when I am capable of doing so feels the same amount of wrong. I raise my eyes to the sky, blinking back tears as they build on my eyelids like dewdrops on spider webs.

"I cannot reach across the veil," I say. "But if their bodies remain alive, they may be able to find their own way back to them, and once that happens, I will make sure they both come back."

"Will she know how to get here?"

"Shiloh is determined," I say, clinging to this truth like it's a lifeline. "She is the most determined person I have ever known, and she will be with Miles, who is clever, so if anybody can figure out how to come back, it is the two of them together."

Jonah buries his face in his hands. I lean my head on the side of the ambulance. Out there, beyond the veil I cannot cross, Shiloh and Miles must be so afraid, but at least they are together. I hope I did not lie to Jonah. I know they will find a way back if they can. I simply have to hope that they find a way back soon and that their bodies will be waiting for them when they return. Because I will surely not make any bad things happen if I simply bring two more people back into their own bodies, will I?

FRANCESCA

Jonah, are you all right? My father is bringing me home and I could not find you anywhere at the hospital. Did you go home?

Francesca Russo

Missed FaceTime Call (3)

FRANCESCA

Jonah, please respond to me. I am very worried about you.

JONAH

I'm fine

BETHANY CITIZEN

**Mass Hysteria Incident Leaves Dozens Hospitalized –
Authorities Baffled**

Published: 6:28 AM EST January 7, 2020

BETHANY — Town officials are struggling to explain a bizarre incident that occurred late Monday night, when dozens of residents were found wandering near the Hudson & Sons grain processing plant.

According to Sheriff Ernest Oleson, nearly fifty residents, including the elderly and children, were discovered in a disoriented state, unable to explain how they arrived at the location. Many were still wearing their nightclothes despite the snow and sub-zero temperatures.

"We're investigating what appears to be a case of mass hysteria," Sheriff Oleson told reporters.

The strange incident began when multiple 911 calls reported unusual behavior throughout town, with some residents claiming neighbors were walking through streets despite the blizzard. Ten people remain in critical condition following apparent falls at the facility, and more are presenting with frostbite.

Dr. Emily Martinez, who treated several patients at Mount Keenan Memorial Hospital, suggested carbon monoxide poisoning might explain the collective disorientation.

"We're testing affected individuals for elevated CO levels," Dr. Martinez said. "The symptoms (confusion, memory gaps, and headaches) are consistent with exposure to an airborne toxin."

Amanda Nichols, 22, a nursing student who was among those found at the scene, has no recollection of traveling to the facility.

"Last thing I remember, I went to bed early because I was coming down with a bug," Nichols said. "Then I woke up in the snow performing CPR on someone I'd never met before."

Harold Thompson, 58, who operates Thompson's Hardware on Main Street, was also among those affected.

"People are saying I was out there in my pajamas, but I don't remember a thing," Thompson said.

Environmental scientists from Ohio State University are testing soil and water samples from the area. Preliminary reports suggest no obvious contaminants, though testing continues. Meanwhile, the Food and Drug Administration has taken samples from the local bakery, whose owner, Ethel Mood, was one of the people found at the scene. A spokesperson for the agency said, "It felt for all the world like one of those medieval things where people go temporarily crazy from contaminated flour."

Mount Keenan Memorial Hospital reports that most affected individuals have been released, though some remain under observation. Psychological counseling is being offered to all those involved.

SEE ALSO: "Carbon Monoxide Safety: What Every Homeowner Should Know" (Page 4)

Weather bulletin, Mount Keenan area, January 8th 2020: The record low temperatures and snowfall experienced around the town of Bethany have now eased. All major roads have been cleared and reopened.

FRANCESCA

Hello, can you please respond to my
messages so I know you are still alive?

I do not want to be dramatic but I am very
afraid.

JONAH

Yep, sorry.

BETHANY CITIZEN
Sheriff Oleson Arrested Following Assault
Published: 1:17 EST January 10, 2020

BETHANY — Ernest Oleson, 47, was arrested Tuesday on multiple felony charges including assault and battery, child abuse, and official misconduct following an incident at the Hudson & Sons Grain processing facility last week.

The arrest comes after photos surfaced on social media showing evidence of alleged long-term abuse of his teenage daughter. The images were anonymously posted on a community Facebook group page.

"These are serious allegations that we're investigating with the utmost care," said District Attorney Leroy Burke. "No one is above the law, especially those who are sworn to uphold it."

As well as multiple accusations of historic abuse, Oleson allegedly assaulted his daughter at the grain processing plant when on duty during the night of the incident locals are now referring to as the "Bethany Blackout." Sheriff Oleson said that he was disoriented like other victims at the scene, but witnesses claim that he is lying, and police transmission records show him talking clearly to colleagues. Multiple witnesses, including Joshua Hudson, 42, the owner of the facility, have provided statements. Hudson claims he recovered security footage of Oleson physically assaulting his daughter.

Oleson's daughter remains in critical condition at Mount Keenan Memorial Hospital following injuries sustained during the incident.

While the investigation into Oleson's conduct continues, Detective Cornelia Vaughn will serve as interim sheriff.

"Our thoughts are with the Oleson family during this difficult time," Vaughn said in a written statement. "I urge our community to respect the family's privacy as the judicial process moves forward."

Oleson's attorney, Caleb Caldwell, issued a brief statement denying the allegations. "Sheriff Oleson has served this community with distinction for over twenty years. We look forward to addressing these unfounded accusations in court."

Oleson is being held at the York County Detention Center with bail set at $250,000. A preliminary hearing is scheduled for January 27.

YORK COUNTY FAMILY COURT

CONFIDENTIAL CASE SUMMARY - JUVENILE DIVISION

CASE: In the matter of MAXWELL ERNEST OLESON (Minor)

CASE NO: JV-2020-0199

DATE: January 10, 2020

<u>SUMMARY OF PROCEEDINGS:</u>

The court has determined that continued placement in emergency foster care is in the best interest of the child. The mother, Heidi Oleson, was present with counsel. The father, Ernest Oleson, remains in detention and was represented by his counsel.

<u>FINDINGS:</u>

• The mother's difficulty maintaining employment raises concerns about whether she will be able to provide a stable environment for the child

• Nothing indicates that the mother harmed the children, but evidence points to the fact that she failed to protect her son and daughter from their father's documented abuse

• On the night of the Bethany Blackout, the child was one of the many people found at the grain processing plant. The mother has no recollection of him leaving the house, and the child has no lasting physical injuries

• The father is ineligible for custody consideration due to pending criminal charges

• The court recognizes that the mother maintains a bond with the child and expresses concern for his well-being, but she requires significant intervention and support before reconsideration of custody

• Divorce proceedings between parents are ongoing (Case #DC-2020-3802)

431

<u>ORDERS:</u>

The child will remain in his current foster care placement (Wilson family)
• The mother is granted supervised visitation twice weekly (2 hours per session), contingent on her compliance with mental health treatment
• The father has been denied visitation privileges during criminal proceedings
• The mother must undergo a mental health evaluation and adhere to prescribed treatment, including compliance with therapy and medication management, as verified by a licensed provider before custody is reconsidered

NOTES: Guardian *ad litem* reports that the child is adjusting well to foster placement but experiences anxiety regarding his sister's condition

NEXT HEARING: Placement review scheduled for April 10, 2020 at 9:00 AM
cc: Jade Carter (Case Worker)
Samantha Singh (Guardian *ad litem*)
Legal counsel for all parties

CONFIDENTIAL - NOT FOR PUBLIC DISCLOSURE

FRANCESCA

It rained a lot today.

It made that warm dusty smell rise up from
the road and I thought of you.

JONAH

…

Because I smell like wet pavement?

FRANCESCA

Because it was a nice smell and I wished
you were here to smell it with me.

JONAH

Oh

Well thanks

You doing good?

FRANCESCA

Yes.

I am eating an orange.

JONAH

Nice

FRANCESCA

Have you ever noticed how oranges taste
different when you eat them by yourself?

JONAH

No?

FRANCESCA

When somebody peels one for me, it is
sweet, but when peel one for myself, it is a
tiny bit more bitter.

Perhaps I am not good at peeling them.

JONAH

This is for sure in your head

FRANCESCA

Many things are.

What have you been liking to eat lately?

JONAH

I promise I'm eating if that's what you're fishing for

FRANCESCA

I was not fishing for anything.

I only want you to remember to eat because eating is very important.

JONAH

I'll go ask Fred to peel me an orange

FRANCESCA

Good idea.

I miss you.

Do you have time to talk on the phone right now?

JONAH

Sure thing Franks

MOUNT KEENAN MEMORIAL HOSPITAL
PATIENT STATUS REPORT
PATIENT: OLESON, S.
DATE: 01/29/2020
STATUS: Day 23 post-fall. Remains in a deep coma (GCS 7). Prognosis uncertain.

NEURO:

Spontaneous eye movement observed intermittently
No purposeful tracking or response to verbal commands
No motor response to pain stimuli

INJURIES & RECOVERY:

Traumatic Brain Injury (TBI): Contusions noted on initial imaging, with evolving patterns of injury.
Spinal: No gross spinal cord injury noted.
Skeletal: Right femur fracture, ORIF performed on 01/08. Healing progressing.
Lungs: Initial pulmonary contusions improving. No current ventilatory support needed.

CURRENT MANAGEMENT:

Neurological monitoring for signs of improvement or deterioration.
Physical therapy (passive ROM) to prevent contractures.
Nutritional support via NG tube.
MRI scheduled for 02/04 to assess for chronic ischemic changes, anoxic injury progression, and structural damage resolution.

MOUNT KEENAN MEMORIAL HOSPITAL
PATIENT STATUS REPORT
PATIENT: ZWEERING, R.
DATE: 01/29/2020
STATUS: Day 23 post-fall. Remains unresponsive (GCS 5).
Prognosis uncertain.

NEURO:

Withdraws from pain stimuli.
Pupils sluggish but reactive.
EEG shows stable activity with mild fluctuations.

INJURIES & RECOVERY:

Lungs: Pulmonary contusions resolving. Chest tube removed,
breathing stable on room air.
Facial: Lacerations sutured. Swelling reduced.
Dermal: Right foot frostbite debridement performed. No active
infection.

CURRENT MANAGEMENT:

Neurological monitoring for signs of increased responsiveness.
Nutrition via NG tube.
Passive range-of-motion therapy.
MRI scheduled for 02/05 to assess injury progression.

From: bethanycommunitychurch@gmail.com
To: prayerchain@googlegroups.com
Subject: Updated Prayer Requests – February 5
Date: 02/05/2020 9:14 AM

Dear Prayer Warriors,

Please keep these community members in your prayers this week:

• Shiloh Oleson - Entering one month in a coma at Mount Keenan Memorial Hospital. Prayers for healing and for her brother Max. Her father's court appearance is scheduled for Tuesday.

• Officer Randall Zweering - Also entering one month in a coma at Mount Keenan Memorial Hospital. His parents and colleagues appreciate the continued support and prayers.

• Ethel Mood - Is still recovering from her knee fracture during the Bethany Blackout.

• The families of our departed community members and public service personnel. May they find peace and healing.

Prayer service continues Wednesday evenings at 7 PM.

Blessings,
Pastor Michael

43

JONAh

I run down the empty road. No music. I used to tell myself it was punishment, like maybe if I made running miserable enough, I'd earn the right to feel okay later, but now the sound of my feet slapping pavement makes me feel like I'm getting somewhere. Not geographically, obviously. It's a loop. I pass the same busted mailbox three times before I even break a sweat. But something in me believes I'm moving forward.

Yep. I know. The running surprised me too, but it's the only thing that makes my brain shut up these days.

I run through a crosswalk, glancing down the empty side street even though I already know no one's coming. My lungs burn from the damp air, but it's a good burn. Not the someone-please-help-me-because-I-swear-I'm-really-dying burn I was getting three weeks ago when I started. The weather has finally stopped trying to murder everyone. February's still cold as hell, but that otherworldly freeze that turned everyone into walking icicles has finally packed its bags, leaving regular winter misery now, which means a whole lot of slush.

Running was my social worker's idea. Six months ago, I'd have laughed her skinny ass out of the room for suggesting I work out, but hitting rock bottom has a way of making even the most ridiculous option worth trying.

I'm not above admitting that I wasn't doing good. I stopped eating. Barely slept. I knocked out when I finally got too tired in weird places, like school hallways or bus stops or pretty much anywhere except my actual bed.

As for my head ... well, let's just say it got loud. Loud enough to scare me, which is why I found myself dragging my sorry ass to my social worker's office three weeks ago to do the one thing I swore I'd never do.

She just about had a coronary when I asked for help. Sat there with her pen hovering over her notepad like I'd sprouted wings and a halo.

"What changed?" she asked, barely able to contain her smile.

God, what didn't?

Going to the hospital every day and watching the only two people who ever gave a damn about me hooked up to machines that breathed for them. Spending all my time thinking about what they were doing on the other side, wondering if they'd ever be back, or obsessing over how easy it'd be to join them. But I still felt uncomfortable telling my social worker any of that. I knew I had a choice. Either get my shit together or end it all for good, and I've been through too much crap to go out like that.

Because Shiloh will wake up.

So I embraced all the stuff I used to make fun of. I run three miles every morning before anyone else is stupid enough to be awake. I meditate. Less than I should because it makes me feel like a new-age soccer mom or, God help me, my own mom. I've started eating real meals, not just whatever I could steal from vending machines. My English teacher almost collapsed when I turned in a paper early. No more skipping. No more half-assing. I'm twenty-nine days sober, which is the longest stretch since I was fourteen. But no more thoughts about checking out early.

And no more foolery. I want those thoughts to be done for good when Shiloh comes back.

The sun still hasn't bothered to start rising by the time I turn onto the edge of my road and stumble to a stop, bracing my hands on my knees for a couple of seconds, staring up at the house. I still can't bring myself to call it my house because I'll only be here for another two months. My phone rings. I smile. Only one person calls me this early.

I answer the FaceTime audio call, sitting on the front steps and kicking my legs out in front of me. "Hey."

"Good morning." Francesca's voice sounds clearer these days. Stronger. "How was your run?"

"Fine." I probably shouldn't be so negative. I'm trying to be better about that. "Pretty good, actually."

"I am happy to hear it."

I can hear the smile in her voice, and I know she genuinely is happy to hear anything I tell her. After her dad dragged her back to Columbus, she started texting or calling me every day. I got a feeling she's checking to make sure I'm still alive, even though she'd never admit it. Doesn't matter to me. I'm glad to hear her voice. She's kind of weird, but she's so much stronger than me, and listening to her talk about the good things she's finding in her life helps me try to pay attention to the things that are happening in mine, which is good for me.

"How far did you go?" she asks.

I glance at the cheap digital watch Fred gave me after I started this whole running thing. It was nice of him. I may not like being forced to live with them because they're not Moe, but I got to say, they're growing on me. "Three miles."

"That is quite a lot farther than I could run," she says, and I snort. She's not wrong. "I am rather tired this morning. I stayed up quite late last night making a painting for my art class."

I lean back on my arm, wincing as a stab of pain runs down my fingers, and then I bring it back in front of my body. "What's the painting of?"

"The elephant I saw standing in the field on the other side one time. It was running through a big field that seemed to stretch out forever, and it was swinging its trunk like it weighed nothing at all. The way the light caught in its wrinkled skin made shadows pool in the creases like tiny rivers of darkness, and the bristles on its back looked like paintbrushes dipped in gold." She pauses. "Can I tell you something?"

She always says that, like I've ever told her no. "Go for it."

"I keep hoping that Shiloh and Miles are in a good place like that."

She says it like they've found their final resting place or some shit. I grit my teeth. "They're not over there hanging out with elephants."

"I know it may not be elephants, but—"

"They're coming back."

She says nothing. I got to force myself not to hang up the phone. I know she's said over and over again that she can't go to the other side to find them, and I'm not a moron, but our agreement was that as soon as they showed up, I'll call her, and she'll bring them back into their bodies as long as she's in good enough physical shape to do so.

I need to stop talking about them. Or my brain will go places I don't want it to. Places I try so hard to keep it out of.

"You got plans today?" I ask. "Other than school?"

"I believe Richie would like to watch a movie this afternoon, so I will do that," she says, and I roll my eyes at the sound of that asshole's name. At least he's being nice to her nowadays. "Do you?"

"Just the hospital."

She goes quiet for a couple of seconds.

"Jonah," she says, and I get the feeling I'm about to get a lecture. "You must try not to let the bad things win."

I hear her, I do, but it's hard to feel like I'm winning at anything when my girl and best friend are in the hospital and I'm out here running at six o'clock in the morning.

"I need to go," Francesca says. "Richie has agreed to drive me to school and I am beginning to prefer his company to that of my father. I will talk to you tomorrow morning, alligator."

I smile, pausing at the bottom of the stairs to say, "By the light of the moon, raccoon."

She giggles, a sound I've heard more often lately. Then hangs up.

Fred's making pancakes when I walk in. The kitchen smells like butter and coffee, which kind of rules. Moe's always smelled like stale dog and diapers.

The three boys are fighting, but they're always fighting about something. At least they're using inside voices. That's something of a miracle.

"Hi, Jonah." Fred casts a glance over his shoulder. "You hungry?"

I grab a plate, returning the high-five of one of the kids on my way over. "Starving."

Cindi shuffles in, still wearing her bathrobe. She blinks at me. Can't blame her. I've been living here for almost five months and these past couple of weeks are the first time I've been functional before seven.

I hitch a ride to school with Fred and the other kids. School is ... school. I actually ask a question in history, which seems to give Mr. Wallace a minor stroke because he stammers for a good couple of seconds before answering me. I take notes in chemistry because focusing on that is easier than focusing on the empty desk next to me. The cafeteria is as loud and depressing as hell, but after morning classes are done, I go in and grab a granola bar from the lunch line before slipping out the side door to the elementary school.

The chain-link fence separating the high school from the elementary yard is rusted in places, the metal flaking away like bad skin. I keep to the edge so none of the teachers think I'm creeping and spot Max right away. He's by himself over by the swings, scratching the dirt with a stick. I never see him with friends. I wonder if he had any before any of this happened.

I whistle. His head snaps up, those big eyes of his scanning the playground before landing on me. He drops the stick and bolts across the yard, sneakers kicking up wood chips as he runs.

He crashes into the fence and curls his fingers through the links. "You came."

"Course I did." I crouch to his level, trying to ignore how my knees scream. Guess I'm getting old at seventeen. "I come every day, don't I?"

He nods, but I know he still doesn't trust it. Shiloh's gone. His mom gets visiting hours, and his dad—well, good riddance, but the kid's got every reason not to believe in permanence.

He sits down across the fence from me, picking up a dead leaf and ripping off the stem. I try not to stare at the long scar stretching from under his eye down his cheek. He got it that night he was possessed. Shiloh would lose her mind if she could see it but, luckily, it's the only injury he got.

"Jessica made goat cheese sandwiches again." He wrinkles his nose, and I have to swallow the lump in my throat because his face looks just like Shiloh's. I know his foster parents because Moe knew them. They're sort of uptight but good people. They bring Max to visit Shiloh every Saturday, but Mrs. Wilson's healthy food kick is the bane of the poor kid's existence.

"Tragic." I pull the extra granola bar I grabbed from the cafeteria out of my pocket. "Want this?"

His eyes light up as I slip the bar through the fence. You'd think I handed him gold instead of that crumbly crap.

"Did you see her yet today?" he asks, voice dropping to a whisper.

"After school. But I brought that book you picked out yesterday for her."

He fidgets with the wrapper of the granola bar. "Do you think she can hear it?"

He asks some version of the same question every day. I give the same answer even though I know it's not true.

"Yep. I think she can."

The recess bell rings. Max winces and glances back at the school building, then turns to me.

"Tell her I'm being brave," he says. "I finished all my math worksheets, and I'm taking good care of Bill even though

Jessica is scared of bugs and doesn't like the crickets I feed him."

"I will." My voice is rougher than I want it to be. "Promise."

"And say hello to Bessie for me."

"Yes, sir."

I go to the shelter every few days to see Bessie. Her eyesight is getting worse, and the arthritis is hitting her front elbows hard, so nobody has come to adopt her yet. I sneak her a strip of jerky through the links when the animal control lady's not looking.

Max stands up and goes to run to his class line, but stops like he's remembering something. He sticks his hand through the fence. Mine meets his automatically. We tap knuckles twice, then flip to palm slaps, ending with the finger wiggle that makes him giggle every time. Then he's off, dinosaur hood flapping behind him as he runs. I watch until he disappears inside before heading back to my own school, cutting through the back field so no one sees the way I have to wipe at my eyes.

The rest of the day drags. I'm halfway to the door by the time the final bell rings. The hospital visiting hours start before class gets out, and I have to catch the bus to get there. The hospital smells nasty. Like antiseptic and death covered with a veneer of fake lemon. The reception desk nurse has stopped asking me to sign in. She nods as I pass, her eyes soft with pity, which makes me want to hurl because she doesn't know what I know. She doesn't know that Shiloh is going to wake up. She doesn't have to pity me.

I go left at the nurses' station, right at the water fountain, then straight past four closed doors to Room 302.

The door is cracked. I don't go in. Just stand here like a

creep looking at Officer Zweering's mom, who's asleep in the chair.

Miles looks exactly like he did yesterday and the day before that, since he has basically turned into a wax figure. The breathing tube is gone now, a small mercy, but there's still a mess of wires trailing under his blankets, monitors flickering quietly like they're bored. His face is less swollen than it was, though the bruising is a sick yellow-green, and the left side is a patchwork of taped-up cuts and stitched lines. One eye is still swollen shut. One of those possessed bastards broke his eye socket.

The nightstand is cluttered with police crap. A toy cruiser. A Bethany PD mug. All of it brought by this girl who's way too pretty to be a cop but usually shows up in her uniform. I thought about leaving a book or something, but none of that crap means anything. Especially since Miles isn't here to see any of it.

I don't need Zweering's mom to see me here, so I tap my knuckles against the doorframe once before continuing down the hall to Room 307.

Shiloh's room hasn't changed since yesterday. Same beige walls. Same window with a view over the parking lot. A couple of days ago, one of the nurses taught me how to braid her hair. It took a couple of tries, but I have to say, I did a better job with her hair than she did with mine.

I drop my backpack and slide into the chair next to her bed, leaning my forearms onto the rough sheets.

"Hey, Scooby," I say, feeling stupid as I say the words. I know Shiloh isn't actually here. Her consciousness is somewhere far away on the other side. Somewhere with Miles. Somewhere with elephants, if Francesca's paintings mean anything, but I talk to her anyway because what the hell else am I supposed to do? "Max says hi. He wants you to know he's taking good care of that damn gecko, and the thing sounds like it's in better hands than it was with us."

Just in case ... I reach for the ghost glasses I keep in my bag, my fingers shaking like an idiot as I slip them on. The room is empty. So I fold up the glasses again and try to focus on breathing.

How long does it take to get back from the other side? Ella Ruggles's creepy dead sister found her way back enough times to drive Ella completely nuts. Francesca found her way back in, like, one morning, so either they're taking their time and playing with elephants like Francesca said, or something is wrong.

Something had better not be wrong.

I read the book Max chose about the gorilla that solves crime aloud to Shiloh, feeling progressively more ridiculous with every talking animal I voice. I'd never do this for anyone else. But for her? For Max? I'd read the entire children's section of the library out loud.

The nurse said it would be good for me to do these things to keep her brain working. Something about neural pathways and brain stimulation. I don't get how that works, but I guess there's still something going on in her head because no one has pulled the plug yet. After I get done reading the book, I take out a pair of earbuds.

"Okay, Shiloh's brain," I say, moving her hair out of the way to put both earbuds in. "I got your daily dose of whores and sad orphans."

I hit play on my phone and the first notes of Les Mis crawl out from the earbuds, all strings and melodrama like the soundtrack to the world's most pretentious funeral. I turn down the volume. I wouldn't want her to come back deaf on top of everything else.

I got no idea what broke inside her when she took that

fall. Something major enough to kill her on impact, which is ... well, a whole range of possibilities I don't want to list, but I got to hope Francesca's resurrection trick can patch her up. There has to be some healing power in that. Every dead body Leonard hijacked was damaged enough to kill it in the first place, and he still puppeted those meat suits around. Leonard had Francesca bring souls back into literal *corpses*, for crying out loud, but I guess those poor bastards needed benmjöl pumped into them just to keep them shuffling around for a couple of months. They were basically walking pharmacy experiments with expiration dates.

Jesus, I hate this musical. I know all the songs now. Could probably hum the entire soundtrack in my sleep. I find myself listening to it a lot because it makes me think about her.

I can sort of hear the notes through her earbuds because I'm sitting so close to her head. I close my eyes for a second, letting it wash over me, but when I open them again, her eyes are still closed.

"Hey, if you wake up right now, I'll dress up like that creepy innkeeper with you for Halloween this year."

Nothing.

"Come on, Scoob." My voice cracks. "I'm running out of bargaining chips here."

Still nothing. I sigh and rest my forehead on my arms, the music filling the silence with someone else's tragedy instead of our own.

The sun crawls across the window, a rectangle of light that inches its way across the floor tiles. One of the nurses, Julie, brings me a cup of lukewarm coffee without me asking, which is nice of her, and gives me enough energy to power through my homework.

The Les Mis overture loops for the second time. I could sing that first song from memory. God help me.

I should drag my ass back to Fred and Cindi's, but the thought of leaving here makes my tired head want to do something stupid like cry. A hand lands on my shoulder.

"Hey." Julie's voice is gentle but firm. I didn't even hear her come in. "Visiting hours ended an hour ago."

I rub my eyes, nodding. Les Mis has stopped. My phone is dead. Great.

"Sorry."

"Five minutes," she says. "Then you have to go. Dr. Reynolds is doing rounds early tomorrow."

I nod, not trusting my voice. She pats the mattress, smiles at me, and walks out the door.

I slump back down, my forehead pressing against the cool metal rail of Shiloh's bed.

Five more minutes.

My eyes close again. I'm not exaggerating when I say I've been sleeping like crap because every time I close my eyes, I see her falling. I see Miles collapsing. I see their bodies hitting the ground over and over again like a highlight reel of the worst moments of my life. I need Shiloh. I never got nightmares when I had her to hold on to.

Something touches my shoulder.

"I'm going," I snap. "Give me—"

But the room is empty. The door is closed. No nurse is hovering.

I scan the shadows. That touch—it wasn't a nurse.

But I felt it.

Oh my God, I've spent over a month waiting for this, but now that it might be happening, I can't breathe. I literally can't do anything but sit frozen like a moron while my brain screams at me to move.

It could be some other ghost. Some asshole haunting the hospital and playing a practical joke on me, but I upend my backpack to get the glasses. I almost stab myself in the eye as I jam the brass things on my face to find Shiloh hovering at the foot of her bed.

She looks exactly like she did that night. Her hair's tangled from the wind, that teal and black jacket I always loved is unzipped enough for me to see her T-shirt under it, but she's totally see-through, and this thin white haze surrounds her like she's being projected from some ancient film reel. Her pointed toes float inches above the floor.

I'm hallucinating. I have to be. I've been sleeping like crap. I've wanted this too much.

But to be sure, I take off the glasses and rub my eyes. My hands shake as I put the glasses back on.

She's still there. Hovering in the same place, watching me with those eyes of hers that I'd only seen in my dreams for the last month.

And smiling.

44

FrANCeSCA

I draw a tiny star in the margin of my notebook. I have already drawn quite a few of them and I am well on my way to creating an entire miniature galaxy, which is good because anything would be more interesting than listening to Mr. Drubich's attempt at an interesting history lecture.

"Francesca?" Mr. Drubich says, and I jump at the sound of my own name. "Can you tell us which president implemented the New Deal?"

Everybody turns to look at me, which is not my favorite thing in the world as it makes it rather difficult to think.

But this time I am lucky because the answer comes to me. "Franklin D. Roosevelt."

Mr. Drubich smiles as though he is glad that I am paying attention to him. Admittedly, I was not paying much attention to him at all, but history has always made sense to me. Perhaps because I have spent so much time with those who lived it.

Mr. Drubich returns to telling us all about President Roosevelt's economic reforms. I am about to go back to drawing my tiny stars when I notice Elliot watching me from two chairs away. Her hair has changed color from a couple of days ago and is now a deep blue that makes me think of the deepest parts of the ocean I have only seen in photographs, and of strange fish with lights dangling in front of their noses.

She raises her hand in a small wave, which immediately makes me lower my eyes back to my notebook. Wait a minute. What am I doing? She is being friendly toward me, so I need to be friendly as well. I lift my eyes to wave back, but she is looking down at her notebook again.

So much warmth rises to my cheeks that it is quite a miracle that my face does not melt clean off. I suppose I am not accustomed to anybody paying attention to me unless they either needed something from me or were about to be mean to me, but unless Elliot is planning to cut all of my hair off for a cruel joke, I do not think she would have offered to dye my hair if she did not want to be my friend. Evangeline told me in no uncertain terms that she wanted me to at least try to live, and I would not want her to be disappointed with me if all I had to report was watching movies in the living room with Richie while eating microwaved dinners on a tray when I see her again.

I am not feeling as sad about Evangeline not being here as I was in the first couple of days after I came home. I suppose it is because I know I will see her again. I may need to wait some time, but the comforting thing about time is that it is guaranteed to pass, eventually. Perhaps I do not need to be quite so alone while I am here.

So when class ends, I wheel myself toward Elliot's desk before she can leave, stopping behind her as she stands up.

"Elliot?" I ask, and she spins around to look at me like she was not expecting me to be there. "I like your hair."

Elliot's eyes widen before her face relaxes into a smile. "Thanks. Remember I offered to dye yours too? That invitation still stands, if you want it."

I hesitate. Before everything that happened in Bethany, I would have declined because my white hair was something that made me look like a soul. It acted as a marker that I did not belong in the world of the living, but perhaps if I accepted that I must stay around for a little while longer, then I could change that little part of myself as well.

"I would like that." I am surprised by how much I mean it. "Thank you."

Her smile grows. "How about Friday night?

"Actually, would tonight be possible?"

"Tonight?" Elliot's eyebrows lift, but her smile doesn't falter. "Yeah, sure. My mom's working late, so we'll have the bathroom to ourselves and she won't get mad at me about the smell of bleach. Actually, we won't have to use bleach on your hair because it's white already." She scribbles her address on a torn piece of notebook paper and hands it to me. "Come over around six?"

I nod, carefully folding the paper and tucking it into my pocket. An odd sensation spreads through my stomach like a collection of butterflies has decided to hold a dance competition there. I have never been invited to another person's house for a social reason before, but if this is what Evangeline meant by truly living, then I suppose now is as good a time as any to begin.

I am quite surprised by how quickly Elliot is able to change my hair. In her bathroom, she mixes dye chemicals and talks more quickly than I have ever heard another person speak before, and I have to focus quite hard on remembering everything she is saying. Her mother is a nurse. She tells me she has a cat with six toes named Socrates, whom I will not be able to meet until he becomes accustomed to my smell and feels comfortable enough to venture out from underneath the couch. She dreams of becoming a marine biologist despite never having seen the ocean.

I choose small pieces of myself to share with her as well, such as my newfound enjoyment of painting. I have never spent a prolonged period of time with another person who is living and breathing and my own age before other than my friends in Bethany, and apart from not talking about all the dead people I know I am not entirely sure how to behave.

"Are you nervous?" Elliot asks, noticing my silence.

"A little." I watch her snap on a pair of green plastic gloves that make her hands look like they belong to an alien creature. "I have never done anything quite like this."

"Changed your hair? Or hung out with someone after school?" Her smile is teasing but kind.

"Both, actually."

She pauses, the mixing brush hovering over the bowl. "Really? Well, I'm honored to be your first, then." A blush creeps across her cheeks. "That came out weird. I just mean, you know, that it's cool. You being here."

"It is quite cool." The slang feels strange but fits on my tongue, as though I am trying on someone else's shoes and finding that they fit.

She begins applying the blue dye. The chemical smell is sharp, but there is something exciting about it that makes me not notice the headache it is giving me, and when Elliot finishes rinsing it out, she turns my chair around to the mirror. I can hardly believe it. My curls have turned the same beautiful shade of blue as hers. It makes my eyes stand out against my pale skin, and for the first time in months, I do not immediately think of all I have lost when I look at myself.

"So?" she asks. "What do you think?"

I tell her I love it. Richie comes to pick me up in his car when we are finished, and I smile all the way home.

At nine o'clock that night, I am lying on my bed, still running my fingers through my hair when Shiloh's iPod buzzes. The screen displays Jonah's name, and my heart does a peculiar flip in my chest like a small bird attempting its first uncertain flight. He hardly ever calls this late.

I answer the FaceTime call so hastily that it is a wonder I do not drop the device. "Are you all right?"

The tiny whirl spins for a couple of seconds before Jonah's face fills the screen. He is grainy in the bad light.

"They're here." His smile cuts from one ear to the other. "They came back."

I sit upright so quickly that my vision blurs around the edges, the entire world falling away as though someone has pulled the floor from beneath me. "Who is—"

"Shiloh and Miles." The connection catches up, and Jonah grins down at the screen in high definition. He is outside, I believe, because there are shadows on his angular face. A streetlamp casts yellow light onto his black hair. "I was at the hospital and I felt something touch my shoulder. I thought it was the nurse kicking me out, but it wasn't, so I put on the ghost glasses, and there she was, standing there at the foot of her bed, looking at me like—" He wipes his eyes. "Francesca, they made it. They're *back*."

My heart pounds like a frantic drum that echoes in my fingertips and temples, and it is my turn to smile as I clutch the phone in both hands. Oh, goodness, I *knew* they would come back. All this time worrying that they were lost forever in that gray expanse on the other side, and now they have found their way home. I want to dance around my room and let out a cry of pure joy, but my legs do not work and my voice catches in my throat like a butterfly in a spiderweb.

"Are you absolutely certain?" I ask.

"Are you serious right now? Do you think I'd make up something like that?" A wet laugh escapes him. "Miles is his old self again. He doesn't look like an off-duty cop anymore. I'm not going crazy. I can't believe they're here."

His voice catches on certain words. He is crying. Jonah Weatherby, who would usually rather set himself on fire than show his emotions, is crying.

Until he pauses. "Hold on, what did you do to your hair?"

I laugh, touching the strands as if to show him. "I made a friend at school, and she dyed it for me."

"It looks rad as hell." He stops walking and stares down at the camera. "So, when can you come? Can you get here tonight?"

I glance at the clock on my nightstand, its red numbers glowing like tiny embers in the darkness. I would like to, but it is nearly nine o'clock and far too late to ask Richie to drive me all the way to Mount Keenan without asking questions, but... I close my eyes, pressing my fingers against my temples where a drumbeat of worry has started. Richie may have made his peace with me, but he has no reason to like my friends. But they have found their way back after crossing the veil—how miraculous, how beautiful, how impossibly brave

of them to navigate that strange world and find a path home
—so I do not want to wait.

What if they cannot stay until morning? What if the other
side decides to reclaim them before I can get there? I believe
they should be all right for one night. I have restored the
balance, after all, and Evangeline stayed with me for months
without fading back across to the other side, but Bethany has
always been a strange place, where the rules of both sides
bend like reeds in the wind, and I cannot be truly certain that
they will be safe until morning.

Jonah may not be able to come pick me up, and I certainly
cannot drive, so Richie is my only option.

I tell Jonah that I will call him if I have a problem and then
hang up the phone, sliding off my bed and reaching for my
sweater. I am not entirely sure how we will be able to access
both of their rooms now that visiting hours are over, but I am
sure Jonah has a plan for that. He always does.

I wheel myself to Richie's room, knocking hard on the
door.

"What?" Richie calls, sounding annoyed.

I open the door to find him sitting on his bed in basketball
shorts and an oversized T-shirt, eating a bag of potato chips
and looking rather startled to see me. His eye patch sits on his
nightstand, and his empty eye socket is on display. I like it
quite a lot more than the patch because it is less distracting,
but I believe he is going to get fitted for a permanent
prosthetic eye soon that will be designed to match the one he
has left which I believe will make him feel better about the
whole situation.

"What's wrong?" He removes his headphones, setting
them down beside him.

"I need your help," I say. "I ... need to go to Mount
Keenan. Would you be willing to drive me?"

Richie stares at me, his remaining eye studying my face like I am a mathematics problem he cannot solve. Once, such scrutiny would have made me wish I could shrink, but I meet his gaze, and a strange understanding passes between us, as fragile as a soap bubble but just as real.

He runs a hand through his disheveled hair. I prepare myself for rejection, but instead, he surprises me by saying, "Okay."

The drive feels quite long, headlights illuminating the empty road as his ancient truck rattles beneath us. We have been driving for over an hour, the radio playing softly between us, and neither of us has said a word. I continue looking at him, feeling as though perhaps I should say thank you again for driving me, but I have already said that, and there are only so many times one can say the same thing before a nice thing becomes uncomfortable.

I am glad when we finally pull into the hospital parking lot, the building rising before us like a strange castle with its windows glowing yellow against the night sky. Richie finds a space near the emergency entrance and stops the engine.

"Thank you," I say, "for driving me."

Richie shrugs. I go to open the door and he helps me with my wheelchair, unfolding it beside the passenger door. He helps me into my chair with a gentleness that feels entirely new between us. He knows Shiloh and Miles are in here somewhere, and that Jonah is here as well. He looks around as if searching for the people who cost him his eye, but there does not appear to be any anger in him anymore.

I am never entirely sure what to say around Richie, and there is quite a lot of silence, but he and I have been spending quite a lot of time together between him driving me to school every morning and asking if I would like to watch movies with him after or even during dinner. I have not forgotten about all of the times he has called me Psycho Sis, or how he entertained a relationship with Ashley Christensen knowing how mean she was to me, but I do believe in his own way he is trying. I would quite like to have a good relationship with Richie if I am going to stay in this world, so this could be how we eventually get there.

"Come out when you're done," he says, already turning back toward the driver's seat. "I'll be right here."

"Thank you."

He gives an awkward half-wave before climbing back into the car, pulling out his phone and slumping down in his seat.

I wheel myself toward the entrance, my heart pounding as the automatic doors slide open. I do not make it far past the doors before a powerful feeling spreads through my chest, and my smile grows too big to continue.

Jonah sits in the corner of the waiting room, which is otherwise empty except for one old man who has fallen asleep in a green-backed fabric chair in front of the television. Two souls shine like beacons on each side of Jonah, as though they are human shapes carved out of pure light, and Jonah is wearing the ghost glasses so he can see them. Shiloh floats above the chair beside Jonah, her spectral form glimmering with that peculiar light that only souls that have spent quite a lot of time on the other side possess. She pokes Jonah's shoulder. He tries to grip her hand, but cannot grasp her, even though it does not stop him from trying. Miles hovers on the side of Jonah, leaning against the wall with his arms crossed instead of falling through it, which I know from experience is something only powerful souls can do. He smiles at Shiloh and Jonah, like he could look at them for a long time without getting tired.

I cover my mouth with my hand as a laugh bubbles out of me. Shiloh sees me first. Her eyes widen, and in a flash, she is moving, rushing through the air with such speed that the air temperature drops several degrees as she grows closer.

"Oh my God, your hair!" she says, and I laugh because my hair feels like a silly thing for her to be talking about with all the serious things we have to discuss.

"I am so happy to see you," I tell her, wiping the tears that have somehow escaped down my cheeks. "I was afraid ..."

Shiloh reaches out to touch my face like she wants to wipe my tears away. "I'm dead and I'm not crying. If anyone should be a mess right now, it's me."

I laugh. There is a new energy about her. Perhaps she is simply excited, or perhaps I am not accustomed to seeing Shiloh not being sad.

She twists around over her shoulder. "Miles, come over here. Stop being weird in the corner. Francesca's here and you're acting like you're at a middle school dance."

"I was giving you a moment." Miles glides over in a motion that seems both graceful and clumsy at once. He offers me a small wave. "I like your hair. It's very ... blue."

"Wow, you're so observant," Shiloh teases. "Next, you'll tell us the sky is blue."

"It is on this side. I've missed it." Miles smiles. There is something different about him as well. He also looks happy, but the difference runs deeper than that. It is almost as though he is older, or perhaps like he knows things I do not, as if the other side has made him wiser by showing him things he had not seen before. Perhaps it is because he spent some time in the body of someone who was older than him. I had forgotten what it feels like for Miles to look my age, but he certainly does not feel it. There is a greater sense of maturity about him.

I wonder what they got up to on the other side. I wonder what they have seen. So many questions burn on my tongue at once that I do not even know how to begin, so all I can do is stand there smiling at them.

"You pull it off," Shiloh says. "The blue."

I smile even wider, my heart feeling like it might burst with happiness. "A girl at my school helped me."

"You made a friend?" Shiloh says. "Who are you and what have you done with Francesca?"

Miles chuckles. "It's an improvement from setting people on fire."

Shiloh smacks him on the arm, but I cannot help it. I snort with laughter.

Jonah walks over to us with his hands in his pockets, his face oddly vulnerable in a way I have never seen before. He watches Shiloh through the spirit glasses like she might disappear if he blinks too long. His eyes look watery, and I notice how he keeps swallowing hard.

Shiloh sees him and leans in closer to ask me, "Is it true he came to the hospital every day?"

I nod.

"He told me he's started running," Shiloh says. "Is he kidding?"

"He goes every morning before school."

Shiloh shakes her head, but her smile grows. "Who the hell is he?"

He is somebody who loves her very much. I am about to tell her this when Jonah catches on to what we are saying.

"Are you guys talking about me?" he asks, and I realize he can only hear my half of the conversation.

I laugh as Shiloh floats right in front of him, her face so

close to his that if she were solid, their noses would touch. Jonah's composure breaks, a tear escaping down his cheek before he quickly wipes it away. Miles smiles at them, and the moment feels so intimate that I almost want to look away, as though I have accidentally peeked through someone's window, but it is difficult not to watch when they all look so genuinely happy. I suspect there is one thing that would make them even happier. I decide to wait a moment before bringing up the reason we are all here.

"So, Jonah, how do you propose we get to their rooms since visiting hours have ended?" I finally ask, my wheels squeaking slightly as I adjust my position.

"I got a plan." Jonah grins, glancing at Shiloh and Miles through the spirit glasses, then back at me. "What do you say, guys? One more time for old times' sake?"

45

FrANCeSCA

Jonah leans in close, his breath tickling my ear as he whispers his plan to me. I try to keep my expression blank, but I cannot stop a smile from creeping onto my face. His scheme is not exactly comforting, but at least it does not send terror shooting through my veins like our previous adventures did, so for me, that is practically love.

I force my face to stay still when Shiloh and Miles vanish through the waiting room wall, laughing together from the empty hallway. Some electronic beeps come from the direction they disappeared in. A door slams. Then another. Something metal clatters to the floor as though a cart of medical instruments has been pushed over, and I do everything I can to try to look normal, turning to look in the direction of the noise like any normal person would. The man beside the television remains asleep.

Casting a strange look around, the nurse at the reception

desk stands up to investigate the sound. Jonah and I look at each other, and I bite my lip to stop myself from dissolving into laughter.

As the nurse half-jogs across the waiting room, Shiloh appears in the mouth of the hallway, flying alongside the running woman and unclipping her ID badge from her pocket. Shiloh swipes her hand across the badge, and the card skids across the floor to us. Jonah bends down as though he is tying his shoelace, and palms the badge so smoothly that even Evangeline would be proud. Shiloh has gotten good at this. Spending time on the other side has made her quite powerful, as she could never affect things in the real world before.

Miles presses the elevator button before the nurse can come back. The doors slide open with a ding that feels impossibly loud in the quiet room.

Jonah pushes my wheelchair forward with such speed that my stomach lurches, and I let out a surprised yelp as we careen across the lobby and into the elevator. Once the doors close, he lets out a laugh that is so jubilant that I cannot help but join him, my own giggles spilling out of me like bubbles.

It is not difficult to reach the ICU using the ID card. Shiloh and Miles rejoin us upstairs and fly out ahead of us, creating distractions to pull any nurse's attention away and clearing a path for us to go right through. Jonah enjoys this far too much and makes sound effects as he maneuvers my chair through the hallways, humming a tune that sounds suspiciously like a theme song from a movie I watched with Richie not too long ago that had lots of car chases in it, and I cannot stop smiling the entire way until Jonah stumbles to a stop in an empty hallway lined with closed doors.

I crane my neck up to look at him. "It is a good thing you began running to prepare yourself for this moment."

He grins down at me. "Glad to be of service."

Miles soars over our heads like a streak of light, hovering near the closed door in front of us. Shiloh floats beside him, her light casting tiny dancing shadows on the polished floor.

"So?" I look between them. "Which one of you would like to go first?"

Shiloh glances at Miles, and something almost imperceptible passes between them, a look that contains an entire conversation. The air around me goes still. They are keeping a secret. Does Shiloh think I cannot tell?

I am not the only one who notices.

"What's wrong?" Jonah asks. "Why are you looking at each other like that?"

"Nothing's wrong," Miles says quickly. "It's … well, there's someone I'd like you to meet, and it's important to me that you stay calm and hear me out. Especially you, Jonah. This is one of the reasons it took us so long to get back."

So many days waiting. So many nights staring at the ceiling wondering if they were lost forever, and they could have returned home sooner? I almost want to ask if they saw Evangeline over there, but the words die on my tongue.

"We would have been back a lot sooner if we didn't have to go find this guy," Shiloh says.

What guy? Who could possibly be more important than coming home?

Jonah looks at me, as if wanting me to translate for him because he cannot hear them, but I cannot take my eyes away from Miles as I say, "Who is it?"

Miles glides through the door by way of reply. I suppose he will not tell me and I must find out on my own. Jonah glances over his shoulder to make sure nobody is coming, then opens the door and pushes me inside.

I glance around the room for a couple of moments, my

eyes quickly settling on the bed, and I realize this is Miles's room. The body on the bed that was once bulky and muscular looks thin and pale against the white sheets, hands resting at its sides, but it is not the body that catches my attention. It is the translucent figure standing next to it beside the bed.

I gasp. Jonah immediately stiffens behind me. The figure has a face I know well, but not because I have ever met him before. His posture is straight. His uniform appears pressed. His badge catches the dim light in a way that reminds me of stars reflecting off still water, and his eyes hold no accusation or suspicion, only a quiet understanding.

Officer Randall Zweering.

He dips his head. I struggle to wrap my mind around him being here. Miles's soul was pulled through the gate, but Officer Zweering's body …

Oh.

Oh no.

The pieces snap together in my mind with terrible clarity. This is why Miles was delayed. This is why he and Shiloh keep looking at each other with those heavy glances.

Seeing this version of Officer Zweering, I do not understand how anybody could have ever mistaken Miles for this man. They may have had identical physical characteristics, but Officer Zweering's eyes are sharp, with not an ounce of fear in them, whereas Miles hardly ever ceased looking unsure.

"This is Francesca," Miles says to Officer Zweering, gesturing at me. "She's the one I told you about."

Officer Zweering runs a translucent hand through his hair in a gesture that reminds me so much of Miles that my chest aches. "You're the girl who sees ghosts," he says. "I spent a lot of time not believing that was possible, but I guess I was wrong." His eyes go to Jonah. "I was wrong about a lot of things, and I'm sorry."

Jonah's fingers tighten on the handles of my chair, talking only to me when he says, "What's happening right now?"

I open my mouth to answer him, but Officer Zweering continues.

"I'm still trying to wrap my head around all this. Your friends filled in some gaps, but honestly, it sounds like something from a horror movie that I wouldn't even believe, though it's hard to argue when you've experienced the things I have."

"You're going to have to get your job back," Miles says. "I, uh, was a terrible cop. Oh, and you might have some explaining to do to your friend Lindsey."

Surprisingly, Officer Zweering laughs, but the weight of what they're planning crashes down on me. I know exactly what Miles is going to say before the question forms on his lips. I can see it in the way his form hovers slightly farther from his borrowed body than it should, in the respectful distance he maintains, in the resigned acceptance that softens his eyes.

Miles exchanges a glance with Officer Zweering before looking back at me. "So what do you think, Francesca? Do you think you could bring him back?"

I knew these words were coming, but they still knock the air from my lungs as if I have been pushed down a long flight of stairs. "Miles—"

"I know." His smile is so kind it hurts to look at. "But it's okay."

It is not okay. I cannot watch another person disappear from my life.

Jonah steps out beside me as if he is only catching on to

what is happening. "No." He looks at me. "Francesca, you're not going to leave Miles over there. For this guy? Are you kidding?"

"I do not have the right to make judgments," I say, and besides, I do not believe it is fair to judge Officer Zweering. I did not know him as a person. He was trying to be good at his job.

I want to reach for Jonah's hand, to anchor him somehow as he slips into something bad. Shiloh must see it as well because she glides over to his other side, hovering right beside him but not touching him, for her hands will bring only cold. Miles offers his friend a sad smile.

"You're coming back." Jonah glances at me, as if wanting me to tell him I agree with him, but I say nothing. My tongue feels like it is stuck to the roof of my mouth, like when I eat too much peanut butter. He whirls back to Miles, pointing at Officer Zweering's spectral form. "I'm sorry, but this guy was an asshole, and he died doing exactly what he signed up for. He wouldn't have been at the labyrinth in the first place if he weren't stalking me. His body was open because his own choices killed him. It wasn't anything we did."

Officer Zweering presses his lips together but says nothing. The air between them crackles like static electricity.

"I died because of my choices too," Miles says.

But Jonah cannot hear him. Tears gather in my eyes. They blur my vision until Miles becomes a smudge of light.

"Please tell him I'm going to be okay," Miles says. "I promise. Shiloh and I found these lakes over there that I'm super psyched to go back to. Did you know there's a way you can travel through time to visit the same places in different eras? I have the entire world to explore. The other side is much more than what you said, Francesca. Some parts of it are bleak, but the other parts … I can't wait for you to see them."

The certainty in his voice causes my chest to constrict until I can hardly breathe, like someone has wrapped their hands around my lungs and squeezed. Another goodbye. Another soul choosing to cross over rather than stay in this world. I wonder why I had not seen any of the good parts on the other side. Perhaps because all of the souls I crossed over to retrieve had not deserved or chosen to be in them. Or perhaps you only get to reach that part of the other side once you die for real.

"I'm not going to be gone," he says. "I can come visit when I find gaps to get through, and I'll see you all again when it's your time to join me."

Yes, he will see us again, but not for years and years. Not until we've lived our full lives without him. Not until we have forgotten the sound of his voice. Not until we have moved on with our lives and Jonah has learned to live without his best friend. Again.

I am crying openly now, tears running down my cheeks and salt stinging my tongue. Jonah has gone completely still, his face hardening into something that reminds me of a statue. Shiloh reaches out to curl her hand around his wrist, and he sucks in a breath between his teeth as he stares down at where her hand is on his arm.

"I've had a long time to think about this," Miles says, "and it's what I want to do."

I swipe at my tears with the back of my hand. So many tears, and for what? I cannot undo what happened that first day when Miles died, the day he turned on the steps of my trailer and I crept into the morgue to find his original body and replace him inside of it. I had not known that he was dead. Or that I had to bring him back right away to give him a chance to recover.

I glance back at Jonah, who takes a step away, his jaw setting hard as Shiloh remains close to him. Miles glides across the room to join him. I wheel myself closer to the hospital bed, looking at the large body lying on it. The monitors beep, tracking a body that has been waiting patiently for its soul to return, although I had not expected it would be this one.

I raise my eyes to Officer Zweering. "Are you ready?"

"As I'll ever be." He glides over to Miles and shakes his hand awkwardly, trying hard to make contact rather than pass one soul through another. "Thank you."

I close my eyes as Officer Zweering comes back to hover above his own body. I breathe out a sigh, reaching for that place inside me where I remember how to do this like I am finding a familiar muscle I have not used in months. I lay my hands flat on the broad chest, and my arms tremble as I guide Officer Zweering's soul back into place. It slips into his body with a sound I feel more than hear, like a gentle whoosh of something arriving, displacing what was empty air. Goosebumps rise on my skin as the connection takes hold. It used to take such an effort, but not this time, because it is right. I am restoring the old order.

I sit back in my chair, my breath coming in little gasps as the world spins. I grip the armrests to steady myself.

"Did it work?" Miles whispers, his voice sounding farther away though he hovers right beside me.

I … am not sure. I lay my head back onto the fabric of my chair as Miles stares at Officer Zweering. The machines beep like tiny birds chirping at each other. The rhythm speeds up. A smile forms on Miles's mouth, as if he knows from this that I have succeeded. It may be some time before

Officer Zweering wakes up, as his body will need time to remember him. The heart monitor may alert the nurses, and there is at least one more soul I must put back inside its rightful body today, so I ask Jonah to push my chair out of the room.

In the hallway, Jonah checks both directions before pushing my wheelchair toward Shiloh's room. His fingers grip the handles so tightly that his knuckles have gone as white as seashells, and his breath comes in small hitches behind me like he cannot quite remember how lungs are supposed to work. I can tell he is angry. He has taken his ghost glasses off as if he does not want to see Miles, who is following behind us, flying low to the ground below me on his stomach like one of those flat fish.

"Do you think Jonah will be mad at me forever?" Miles peers up at his friend. "I don't want him to hate me."

I keep my voice soft so Jonah cannot hear me speaking. "He will understand in time. I promise he already knows it was a brave thing you did."

Miles closes his eyes for a second before he nods and falls back behind the chair where I can no longer see him. I wish he would stay where I could see his face, at least for now, because soon he will be gone.

In Shiloh's room, all four of us pause around her bed, hesitating as we stare down at her body. Compared to Miles, her body looks much smaller, with tubes snaking into her nose to breathe for her and her leg encased in a white cast decorated with signatures I cannot read from here. There is a child's drawing of a dinosaur made with a red marker.

I have not seen her since right after her fall. I had been so focused on bringing her back that I had not properly considered what state her physical form might be in after falling from such a height. Her chest rises and falls in a mechanical rhythm, the air pushed in and drawn out by machines rather than her own will.

I raise my eyes to her. She is staring at her body with deep creases on her forehead.

"Shiloh," I say, and she lifts her eyes to look at me. "Your body has survived a major injury. Are you absolutely certain you want to return to it?"

She does not hesitate. "I have to try."

"I simply want to make sure you understand that there might be ... complications." My voice catches on the last word. I remember my own body in those moments after I returned to it. How foreign it felt, how the simplest movements required concentration, and I was not injured like she was. "You may need medicines to manage the pain. You may need help to relearn things your body once knew how to do without thinking. You may not be able to remember things. Are you sure you would like me to proceed?"

Shiloh nods. "I mean, worse case, the body rejects me and I have to go spend eternity at the lake with this guy, right?"

Miles smiles at her. "I'm going to make you write so many poems."

I breathe out a sigh and I wheel myself to the head of her bed, positioning my chair where I can easily reach her. I center myself, trying to find the trembling energy that is making my head dizzy and tamping down on it.

It is like my mother said. I am not my own, and I was bought at a price.

Everything comes at a price.

A memory comes to me. I raise my eyes to Jonah and smile.

"Do you remember that time you told me I needed to stop bringing people back from the dead, and I told you that perhaps you should all stop dying?"

Miles laughs. Shiloh smiles, and I glimpse the tiniest tug at the corner of Jonah's mouth.

"You did not listen very well," I say.

I reach a hand toward Shiloh's floating form. Instead of reaching for me, she rushes toward Miles, pulling him into a big hug. Their forms press together. They do not quite pass through each other, but blend at the edges in a way that living bodies never do. Their energy glows brighter where they touch, their forms seeming to strengthen rather than diminish each other, and it reminds me of what Evangeline told me once. Some souls never truly lose each other once they have connected. Space and time and even the veil between worlds cannot sever such bonds.

"Do you promise you're going to be okay?" Shiloh asks.

Miles nods, smiling sadly as she makes no move to let him go. "I wouldn't have chosen to do this if I didn't think I would be."

"I'm going to miss your voice."

"I'm pretty sure there's still a video of me from freshman year debating whether a hundred chickens would beat one car-sized chicken in a fight. It's somewhere on YouTube. You know, if you get desperate."

Shiloh laughs through her tears. She holds Miles for a moment longer, and when she finally pulls away, she wipes at her eyes with translucent fingers.

"You better come visit me," she says, her voice firm despite the tremor running through it.

Miles nods, his smile sad but certain. "I promise."

"I'll see you on the other side."

"Not for a long time."

"In the scheme of eternity, it'll be soon." Shiloh turns to me, her light dimming as though preparing herself for what comes next. "Ready?"

I reach a hand toward her. She hesitates for a heartbeat, glancing back at Miles one more time before closing her fingers around mine. I flinch at how cold they are.

I close my eyes, reaching for that strange power that flows through me. It comes more readily than it did a few minutes ago, rising from somewhere deep in my center and spreading outward like it knows exactly where to go. A shudder passes through me as I guide Shiloh's soul like I am attempting to direct water, but I know how to do it now because I understand this feeling. I know it, and I am in charge of it. I blow a long breath as I press Shiloh's soul back into her sleeping body.

As soon as I feel the connection, I open my eyes, my fingertips tingling with pins and needles like they do after holding them in snow for too long. The room seems to swim around me, the edges of things blurring like a watercolor that has been left in the rain. My blue hair falls in sweaty strands around my face. I push it back with trembling hands.

"Did it work?" Jonah has come up beside me. He leans forward, his knuckles white where they grip the metal railing of Shiloh's bed, his eyes never leaving her face.

I stare at Shiloh. I can feel Miles and Jonah on either side of me, looking at her from two different sides of the veil, as if I am Ms. Ruggles's cling wrap that separates the worlds. Miles hovers right above the floor to my left, his ghostly form casting a soft bluish glow on Shiloh's skin. Jonah stands on my right, his body so tense I can almost hear his muscles straining, his breath fogging slightly from being so close to Miles.

Perhaps she will not wake up. Perhaps the damage to her body is too great, and I have sentenced her to another prison, this time made of flesh.

I whisper a silent wish. That this can be one good thing I do. Only good. With no secret costs I could not have foreseen.

Everything is still as if the world is waiting. Even the air seems to hold its breath.

Perhaps this time, the universe will be gentle.

Perhaps this time, a lost soul can come home without breaking something else.

Perhaps sometimes, only sometimes, small miracles can be granted without demanding payment in return.

I am still wishing when Shiloh opens her eyes.

Epilogue

Shiloh

I side-eye Miles, who's hovering next to me. "Are you absolutely sure you want to do this?"

Miles nods. I'm bad at lip reading. I catch maybe six words out of ten on a good day, but I don't need to read lips to understand what he's saying now.

I'm sure.

I swear there's something more mature about him. Maybe it's all the time he's been spending with those poets on the other side, but he has this quiet confidence about him that almost makes me feel too young to be hanging out with him. Him showing up yesterday was the first time I'd seen him in a month. I felt the drop in temperature when I was at the kitchen table doing my homework and rushed to get the ghost glasses from my room. But when he told me through our game of charades what he wanted to do, my stomach dropped to the floor.

"What am I supposed to say?" I ask. "'Hi, Mr. and Mrs.

Barot-Renaud, I know you hate me since I broke your son's heart, and then he died trying to save my brother, but guess what? He's here, want to see him?'"

Miles glares at me. I stare at the gray house in front of us. This feels like such a bad idea. I'm so scared that if it doesn't go well, Miles will be crushed, but I owe him enough that I'd put on a hat and dance the cha-cha for his parents if he asked me to.

With trembling fingers, I let myself through the picket gate and approach the front door. The toe of my left sneaker drags a little through the dry leaves. One of the reminders from my swan dive off the grain bin. Dr. Buchman says I'm lucky I can walk at all. Lucky I only had to relearn how to walk instead of, like, breathe. Lucky my speech only slurs when I'm tired instead of all the time now. But he's right. I am lucky. Lucky to have a friend like Francesca, that's for sure. Even on the worst days when my leg won't cooperate or when I can't remember what I had for breakfast, I don't take anything for granted for one second because I'm still here.

I stop walking in front of the door and push my hair behind my ears, noticing for the hundredth time how it's still growing out unevenly from where they shaved patches to put in the ICP monitor. Jonah says it looks badass, like an undercut. He says I should get a tattoo there so that when the hair grows back, it'll be a memory, but I don't need any more memories of those days. I could have woken up bald and I wouldn't have cared.

Miles flickers next to me like a dying lightbulb, his anxiety making him more transparent than usual.

"You're going to blow the porch light if you don't chill," I hiss.

He glances up at the light and glides backward so he's behind me. Before I knock on the door, I glance over my shoulder at him. "Will you come say goodbye before you go back?"

Miles smiles at me, nodding. I reach over my shoulder. It takes a couple of seconds, but his fingers tighten around mine, burning with a cold so intense that I can only take it for a couple of seconds before I have to let go.

I take off the ghost glasses and snap the frame in half at the bridge. I slide one lens into my pocket and drop the other into the paper bag. I'm not about to give up my only line of connection with my best friend, but this is the only way his parents will be able to see him.

The doorbell echoes through the house. My stomach lurches as footsteps approach from inside.

His mom opens the door. Her brown hair is tied back in a braid, and there are dark circles under her eyes that weren't there a year ago. She freezes with one hand still on the knob.

"What are you doing here?"

I glance past her into the house. I can't see Miles's dad. It's a Saturday, so theoretically he should be home, but Miles once told me that sometimes he goes to the college on the weekends to catch student performances. Or maybe he's inside cooking. It sure smells like something is cooking.

I remember the words I planned. "I have something for you."

"We don't want anything from you."

Right. Why would they? What was Miles thinking, asking me to do this? Me being here is going to hurt them.

I can feel Miles behind me. His presence feels like a pressure against my back, nudging me forward when every instinct screams at me to run.

I grip the paper bag so hard the corner rips. "I know I'm the last person you want to see, but this is about Miles."

"How dare you?" There's so much venom in those three

words I almost step back. "A whole year without a word, and you show up on my doorstep to talk about my son?"

She's right. I wasn't there for his funeral. I was in jail while they lowered his original body into the ground, and I was relearning how to put one foot in front of the other while they were still trying to figure out how to live their lives without him. As far as they know, I don't care about Miles, so what gives me the right to be here now?

"I'm sorry." It's not enough. "I know this sounds crazy, but Miles is here, with us, right now, and he wants to see you."

Her expression goes blank. Of course it does. I sound like I should be in a padded room.

"You should leave."

"Please." I hold out the bag. "Please look through this. He wants to see you."

For a second, I think she might slam the door in my face, but she doesn't. I suddenly realize she's holding back tears, and maybe deep down I'm confirming something she already suspected. She takes the bag with fingers that shake as badly as mine and pulls out the lens, which looks ridiculous. One half of a broken pair of glasses with a temple still attached. For a second, I see it through her eyes: a crazy girl who barely survived a suicide attempt standing on their porch with a broken piece of eyewear claiming their dead son is with her, and all she has to do is look through the magic lens and she'll see him. She must think I've completely lost my mind.

I want to walk away now. Run before she uses the lens, but I can't leave it like this. There's so much I need to say to her. So much I want to tell her, but no matter what I say, nothing will bring back her son. Still. I can't just say nothing.

"I'm sorry," I say. "I never meant for any of this to happen.

Miles is ... he was the best person I know, and he loved you so much. He still does."

I turn away before she can react, my feet carrying me down the steps and onto the path.

"Good luck," I whisper, knowing Miles can hear me even if I can't see him anymore. "You got this."

The gate clicks behind me. I hope she puts the glasses on. What if she thinks it's a trick? What if she throws the glasses away? What if this is the last chance Miles has to say goodbye, and I screwed it up by being the worst possible messenger?

I didn't want him to stay dead. I begged him to come back with me, screaming at him on the other side until I could literally not make a sound anymore to let Francesca bring him back inside his body, but he made up his mind. He said he'd rather go to his parents on his own terms, as himself, when he was ready. Not try to convince them that he was still Miles in a different body.

I hated him for it. Not because it was wrong, but because it made me sad, and it still does. I don't care what's right. I want him alive.

But he does seem happy. He doesn't regret it. I wish I felt that sure about anything. I'll go to where he is. Eventually. He just got there earlier than I did, but from what he tells me, there's a whole lot of living he has yet to do in the world of the dead.

I'm almost to the stop sign at the end of the road when a sob comes from behind me. I glance over my shoulder to see Miles's mom standing on the porch with one hand clasped over her mouth, the other gripping the lens to her face.

I force my feet to keep moving, wiping the tears that are pooling on my eyelids. She used the glasses. He can say hi to his mom, even tell her all the things that happened after he died, but I can't get rid of the pain in my stomach because he deserved a better friend than me, and a better ending than the one he got. At least he can be with his parents now, some of the time. They'll know he's watching over them. I mean, it's like what Francesca has said all along, right?

No one is ever really gone.

Except for Leonard. That asshole is gone for good.

I'll hear how it goes from Miles when he comes to tell me, but I have a feeling I won't be seeing him for a couple of days.

A school bus rumbles past me, kicking up a bunch of dead leaves. It's still early September and warm today, like summer is still holding on. After last winter, I'll never take for granted what it's like not to be cold. The sun beats down on the back of my neck and reflects off the leaves, which are starting to turn yellow and orange. It's amazing how a place can hold the memory of so much darkness and still look so beautiful in the sun. I heard a musical quote like that once.

Someone's burning leaves. The smell reminds me of when Max and I used to jump in piles Dad raked up for us. Before Uncle Jim died and Dad became a monster. Before he tried to kill me.

I grab the top of a fence, digging my nails into the wood and closing my eyes. *Breathe in for three seconds. Hold for five seconds. Breathe out for seven seconds. Like Miles taught me.* It helps. I'm getting better. I still get nightmares, but sleeping on the phone with Jonah helps, and I'm not sprinting to the bathroom to hurl my guts out in the middle of the night anymore. I can walk past the police station without my stomach twisting into knots most days, although I still haven't been past the Sheriff's Department. Sometimes, the trains clank over at the loading station by the grain bins. Jonah and I have walked past it a couple of times from the main road out of Bethany, and I see the grain cars and the new metal of the repaired ladder glinting in the sun. Closure, he calls it. Most days I can even look in the mirror without seeing the girl who almost died in that silo.

Small steps. That's what everyone keeps telling me. Healing happens in the spaces between the hard days.

I focus on putting one foot in front of the other. Mrs. Jenkins is arranging flowers on her porch, and I say hi when I pass by. In the main part of town, I wave at Ethel through the bakery window, and she runs me out a chocolate chip cookie and wraps me in a hug before sending me on my way. She remembers nothing from that night, but she's seen the Facebook photos of me. Everyone has. Nobody in this town talks about what happened that night. It's like people think if we all pretend hard enough, we can erase the night when half the town went crazy and tried to murder each other.

I eat the cookie on the bus ride and stare out at the endless fields of corn rolling past. It's yellow, healthy, and free from any blight, just like normal. I hated living here for most of my life, surrounded by corn and people who I thought liked Dad so much that they didn't care about what he was doing to us. But since he's been gone, the fields have stopped feeling like they were trapping me. I actually like living around people who are strong enough to heal and care about each other and come together after such a tragedy. Even if their coping strategies are to pretend it never happened.

The bus drops me off in front of Walmart in Mount Keenan, only a couple of blocks from our apartment. It's the apartment Mom rented last fall when she first decided she was going to leave Dad. The apartment that we finally moved into. Our home. A completely perfect two-bedroom apartment at the edge of some kind of business park that smells like microwave popcorn and has Max's action figures scattered everywhere, but that has no bad memories anywhere.

I force myself to climb the stairs like I do every day instead of taking the elevator because it's good for my leg, and I fumble with my keys as I reach the door. The second I get it open, the best voice in the world yells my name from the other room.

"Shiloh!"

Max slams into my legs and throws his arms around my waist so hard I almost topple backward. I drop to my knees with a slight wince to return his hug.

He looks up at me with those big brown eyes, his face deadly serious. I try not to stare at his scar. Francesca told me how he got it, when the soul was trying to claw its way back into his body, but I'm grateful every day that's the only scar he's walking away with. The ghost didn't take him from me. Remembering makes me hug him tighter.

"Bill threw up his cricket," Max says.

"He threw up his cricket?" I repeat, slightly confused.

"I think he's dead."

I choke on a laugh. God, Max is obsessed with that lizard. I was glad that Officer Zweering never asked for him back.

"What makes you say that?"

"I poked him, but he didn't move."

"That doesn't mean he's dead."

"Kelly at school said her lizard died, and they had to flush him down the toilet."

"We're not flushing Bill down the toilet."

I can barely contain my smile as he drags me through the door to where Bill is sitting on his rock under the heat lamp. He blinks, which is pretty lucky. Bill blinks on a calendar basis. Crisis averted.

But Max is still concerned. "Can geckos get pneumonia?"

"I don't think so."

"Dad has pneumonia. I heard Mom talking on the phone about it."

I tense at the mention of Dad, but Max's face shows no emotion. Just states it like any other fact. Max doesn't know about what Dad did to me, and somebody took the photos down from Facebook when I was in a coma. God knows how they got there in the first place, but I'm glad they aren't there anymore. I'll tell him when he's older. Once he finally trusts that Dad is not coming back.

"Bill doesn't have pneumonia," I say, steering us back to safer territory. "How about you just let the poor guy sleep?"

I go back to the door to take off my shoes and lock the door. Force of habit.

"Mom?" I call. "You home?"

"In here!"

I find her cross-legged on the floor of her room, in the middle of three open photo albums. She looks up at me and smiles. Her blonde hair is tied back in a low ponytail, and she's wearing a bright yellow T-shirt that's almost the same color she painted the walls.

When I first woke up from my coma, Mom didn't have custody of either of us. Max was still with his foster family, and I was technically a ward of the state, but by some miracle, they put me in the same home as Max after I was discharged until Mom could prove herself to the courts. I think almost losing me helped her. She had Max to live for, of course, but with both her kids so obviously needing her ... I don't know, but something changed. I remember sitting in that courtroom when she finally got provisional custody. Her hands were shaking so much she could barely sign the papers.

A case worker still drops by to check how things are going, but Mom looks happy now. She goes to therapy twice a week. She's coming off the tablets she's taking under medical supervision. She got a job at this boutique downtown, which she seems to like, and the two of us—well, things aren't perfect, but every day, I trust her a little more, so we're moving in the right direction.

I gesture at the albums. "What's all this?"

"I found them when I was unpacking our books," she says. "They're my high school yearbooks. Want to see?"

"Your fashion choices from the 90s?" I drop down next to her. "Yes, please."

Max comes around behind me and wraps his arms around my neck. He points at a picture of a teenage girl with crimped blonde hair and way too much blue eyeshadow, standing cheek-to-cheek with two other girls. "Mom, is that you?"

Mom laughs, covering her face. "Look at that hair! Oh God, what was I thinking?"

I pull the album onto my lap, checking the date to make sure it's from before her senior year and I'm not going to get any jump scare pictures of a younger Dad in here, before flipping through the pages.

I find a picture of her at a school dance and stop. In the picture, Mom is standing with a lanky boy and wearing a long yellow dress. The same yellow dress I wore to my own homecoming dance last fall that I destroyed when I blew Leonard's brains across the back wall of his trailer. I close my eyes for a second, focusing on my lungs expanding so I can push the memory away.

Then I look more closely at the boy. My mouth drops open.

"Oh my God, Mom." I jab my finger onto the picture. "Is that Call-Me-Bill?"

Mom looks confused. "Who?"

"Vice Principal Medina." I tap the photo again. "Bill Medina?"

Mom smiles and nods, like it's the most normal thing in the world. "Bill asked me to homecoming sophomore year."

"You *dated* him?"

"No." She laughs. "Oh God no, but he had such a huge crush on me—this was before I went out with your father—but he was a nice boy."

Maybe she should have married him instead of Dad. I need to keep joking about it so I can stop being so scared.

Dad got five years in jail for what he did. We don't visit. Sometimes, we take flowers to Uncle Jim's grave. I know Dad used to do that, and it was one of the few things I respected him for. Jim was Dad's younger brother, and Mom once said that Dad used to protect Jim. Sometimes I wonder what Dad had to protect Jim from. Dad's parents are seriously weird. I know that much.

Mom is still looking at the picture of her and Call-Me-Bill, her face all dreamy. I choke on nothing.

"*Mom.*"

She looks up. "What?"

"Don't even think about it."

"I'm not. I was just reminiscing."

"Good," I say. "Because you can't date Call-Me-Bill."

"I will not!"

"I'd rather get detention every day for the rest of high school than have you date Call-Me-Bill." I laugh through the words. "I'd rather pull out my pinky nail with a pair of pliers than have you date Call-Me-Bill."

Max giggles.

"Heidi Medina," Mom says. "It has a kind of musical ring to it, doesn't it?"

I make a gagging sound. Mom assures me she was only

kidding, but I swear her eyes linger a second too long on that picture.

I spend twenty minutes with Max waiting for Bill the gecko to blink again, and eventually he shuffles off his rock and goes off to lie somewhere else. We make mac and cheese for lunch and spend the afternoon building this huge blanket fort in the living room. Mom lets us use her comforter and even crawls inside to watch an episode of that dinosaur show Max loves with us.

I nap through one episode and then crawl out of the fort to do my PT exercises when Max watches the next. Just after one, my phone vibrates, and I snatch it up so fast I almost drop it.

JONAH

Will be home at 6, wanna meet me at the park?

I smile at the screen. Jonah is good about texting, even when he's at work. After he aged out of foster care in April, he moved out of the temporary home, dropped out of school, and got a job with a construction company he's still working at now. It's not what he wants to do for the rest of his life, but it pays well. He got his GED over the summer and volunteers at a recovery center two days a week in the hopes that they will give him a full-time offer once he's made enough money to get himself started. He's busy, but I see him every weekend and every day of the week he can make it.

I lean back on the chair, typing back:

only if u shower first

He sends me a GIF of Shrek taking a mud shower. I can barely concentrate on homework with how excited I am to see him, but I manage to at least get my English paper started by the time my phone vibrates again around three. This time, the text is from Francesca.

It's a photo of a painting hanging on a brick wall. The painting looks like a bunch of random brown and green smears with what might be a yellow circle in the middle.

I quickly take a picture of our blanket fort and type:

Francesca replies with a video of herself. I smile just seeing her face, which has changed so much in these past months. Her hair is now dyed a deep purple. She's wearing this shimmery silver eyeshadow that makes her eyes look bigger, and she has dark lipstick on that makes her look years older than she is. Her flowing black top has bell sleeves that billow around her as she rolls her wheelchair with one hand.

"Please tell Max his fort-building abilities are superior to these paintings," she says into the camera. "I came to this gallery today because it was *supposed* to have an interesting theme, but there is certainly a line in modern art that separates the paintings of ducks that have a deeper meaning from simply paintings of ducks."

Elliot comes around next to Francesca and drops her head into the frame, sticking out her tongue. "Hi, Shiloh!"

Francesca laughs. The video ends. I smile at the screen.

I've tried telling her a million times that this Elliot girl has the biggest crush on her, but Francesca laughs it off and says they're just friends. I give it a year before it turns into something. Elliot is obsessed with her.

I send back a quick 'modern art is stupid' before putting my phone down. It's so good seeing Francesca living this whole new life. She started hanging out with Elliot more this spring, and Elliot introduced her to her friends, and before long she was part of this big friend group of artsy girls who like to go to galleries and smoke weed on top of bridges and go see indie movies. They all think Francesca is some kind of wise, ethereal figure, which she sort of is. I don't understand it, but she's so happy. She says she doesn't smoke weed because of her own experience with foolery and benmjöl, but she knows Jonah well enough not to look down on people who do, even though Jonah doesn't smoke anymore. He doesn't drink either. He made that promise to me in the nursing home and hasn't broken it. Not even once.

I'm planning to go to Columbus to visit Francesca for a weekend in October. That would mean leaving Max alone with Mom for two nights, and I don't know how I'll feel about that, but if things keep going the way they have been … I'm feeling good about my chances.

Max and I clean up the blanket fort and eat an early dinner that Mom makes. Just before six, Max goes to put on his shoes and I tell Mom where we're going. She gives me a knowing smile. It's annoying how she's gotten better at this whole being a mom thing, but she just tells me to be careful.

The park is a twenty-minute walk from our place. It's nothing fancy. Just a grassy field, some basketball nets, and a small pergola covering some picnic tables. It's pretty crowded since it's a warm Saturday night, and I immediately spot a familiar face on the basketball court. Officer Zweering runs up and down one of the courts in a gray Bethany PD T-shirt, playing one-on-one with a girl wearing a matching police tee. She fakes him out with a crossover that has him stumbling, and they both erupt with laughter before she sinks the shot.

I remember his apartment. The weights. Richie tied against the radiator. Zweering lives a few streets over from here, and I learned over the summer that he works out here regularly because I see him here all the time. I never talk to him, though. I don't know the guy.

Our eyes meet across the court. The scars on his face have healed about as much as they ever will, turning to white lines across his cheek. His smile wanes. He gives me a small wave before grinning at the girl and going back to the game.

It still freaks me out a little, watching him move around in that body. It's weird seeing Officer Zweering smile with Miles's face or laugh with Miles's mouth, but the body never belonged to Miles. Not really.

I spot Jonah at a picnic table. His back is turned to us. He's using the table as a backrest with one arm draped over the top while he stares out at the courts, no doubt looking at what I just was.

Max breaks free from my hand. "Bessie!"

The big white dog snaps her head up at the sound of her name, perking her ears as her cloudy eyes struggle to find the source of the sound. Jonah turns around. A huge grin spreads across his face when he sees Max charging toward them. He pockets his phone and stands as Max reaches the dog.

I try to play it cool, but my feet are already carrying me toward him and, in seconds, I'm running. He lifts his arms just in time to catch me. I crash into his chest, and his arms lock tightly around my shoulders, crushing me against him. My own arms wrap around his waist as I bury my face into the curve of his neck. He lets out a low laugh. He smells good. Clean. Like soap.

He pulls back just enough to smile down at me, his hands still resting on my shoulders. I reach up and push the damp black hair out of his eyes.

"Hey." He brings his rough palm up to hold my face for a second, his touch sending a tingle through my entire body. "God, I missed you so much."

He leans down. Max clears his throat, staring up at us with a big smile on his face.

"Can I take Bessie to the field?" he asks.

Jonah loosens his arm from around me, but doesn't let go. His shoulders are broad now. He's gotten way stronger from hauling bricks or whatever they have him doing at work, and he's still running every day. He hasn't been able to convince me to go with him yet. He's working on it. "Stay where we can see you, okay?"

"And don't let her pull you," I add. "Remember last time?"

"I'm stronger now." Max flexes his skinny arm to prove it. "See?"

Then he runs away, talking in a high-pitched voice to encourage Bessie to go with him.

Jonah gives me that crooked smile that makes my stomach do a flip. "I'm sorry. Where were we?"

I tilt my head up at him. "I think you were about to kiss me, but don't let me put ideas into your head."

"No," he murmurs, leaning down. "Wouldn't want that."

His lips meet mine. Soft and real. There's something steady in the way he kisses me, something that settles the noise in my head for a second. His hand's still at the back of my neck, his thumb brushing against my skin. When we pull apart, he doesn't look away. His eyes lock on mine, all open and full of feeling in that way nobody else gets to see. Just me.

Getting to this point wasn't easy. After everything that happened with the foolery, it took months before I let him touch me without some part of me remembering his hands around my throat. I wouldn't even let him hold my hand. I wanted to so bad, but I'd flinch every time he moved too fast. I hated myself every time I saw the hurt flash in his eyes, but he never made me feel bad about it. He'd go quiet for a couple of seconds before changing the subject to something funny.

It was Max who changed things. One morning not long after we moved into the apartment and I was pouring milk over my Cheerios, he looked me dead in the eye and said, "Is Jonah your boyfriend again or what?"

I told him no. Saying no felt wrong, but so did calling Jonah my boyfriend, especially since no label even began to cover how important Jonah was to me at this point. I could see how hard he was trying. He changed everything to get those thoughts under control. His promises hadn't been empty. They were real.

The next time I saw Jonah, we were here, at the basketball courts, watching Max try to learn how to dribble from some older kids. After the game, Max begged me to let Jonah come over to see our new apartment. I hesitated, glancing at Jonah. He gave me a small smile that said *ball's in your court*.

I found myself saying sure. The three of us made microwave popcorn and watched *How to Train Your Dragon* on the couch in the living room. Max crashed halfway through. When the movie ended, I carried him sleeping back to the room we shared, and when I got back to the living room, Jonah was still on the couch.

I went to sit back next to him, pausing for a second before

deciding to leave a foot of space between us. The credits were still rolling. He leaned his head back and gave me a lazy smile.

"He go down good?"

I nodded, resting my elbow on the back of the couch, unable to pull my eyes away from his. This boy who had to shoulder so much. This boy who had lost so much and had pulled himself up on his own. He was still showing up for me. Still here.

I didn't even think. Just rested my hand on his arm.

Jonah went still. He knew as well as I did it was the first time I'd touched him since that night with the ghosts. His eyes never left mine as I shifted toward him on the couch.

I was sitting close to him now. Close enough for our legs to brush up against each other, with the glow from the TV lighting up one side of his face. I grabbed his hand and threaded my fingers through his. His palm was warm but rougher than I had remembered. He didn't move.

The TV switched to black, then went back to the browsing page. I had so many things I wanted to tell him, but before I could even open my mouth, he jumped in.

"I got to say something," he says. "I don't want you to say anything. I just want you to listen."

The intensity in his eyes made my breath snag. I nodded, squeezing his hand to let him know I was listening. He swallowed hard before continuing.

"I love you," he said, and I tightened my grip on him as the words fell between us like something precious and fragile. "I love you more than I've loved anything else in my life. You're the best thing that has ever happened to me, and I know I messed up with the foolery, I know, but I'm ready for this now. I wasn't ready before, but I'm ready now. You can count on me."

My lip wobbled, but I bit it hard. I wanted to say something back, but I couldn't find any words, so I gripped his hand so hard it almost hurt.

"You're the only thing in my life that makes any sense," he continued. "We've been through so much, you and me, but I'd go through it all again, Shiloh, every second, if it meant I could end up with you. I know you don't trust me. I'm so sorry for what I did to you, but I swear I got it under control now. I'll spend the rest of my life proving it. I don't care how long it takes. I'll be here, and I'll be loving you every second, until you're ready."

I could feel the tears running down my face, but I couldn't bring myself to look away from him. Jonah. The boy who had been my friend through the biggest horrors of my life. The boy who loved me enough to teach me that I could be loved, and that I was not something unworthy or broken. The boy who did the hard thing and came back to me. He was mine, and I knew, like I knew my name and how much I loved Max, that every single part of me was his. Saying I love you didn't feel like enough for what I felt for him.

"Jonah." I wiped my eyes with my free hand, tasting salt on my lips. "I'm ready."

I leaned even closer, but his hand came up to my shoulder to keep the space between us.

His eyes searched mine, his mouth open and breathing. "Are you sure?"

He was giving me an out, a chance to back away if this was too much. But for the first time in months, I didn't feel that familiar jolt of fear. So I nodded.

His eyes dropped to my lips for a fraction of a second, then raised to mine like in question. I nodded again.

He moved slow, so slow, like I might bolt if he moved too fast. His hand came up to my face, his thumb brushing across my cheek so lightly it almost tickled. My breath caught somewhere in my throat as his fingertips traced along my jaw, and I noticed it was shaking. He tilted my face up, guiding me toward him with the gentlest pressure, and when his lips finally touched mine, the contact was barely there. Just the softest brush, like he was giving me one last chance to change my mind. I didn't want to change my mind. I wanted him. I wanted … this. I pressed forward, my fingers curling into his jacket.

A small sound escaped from the back of his throat, and he smiled against my mouth. I knew then that whatever happened next, whatever ghosts or monsters or average everyday horror came for us, I'd be okay, because I'd face all of it with him. And I have. Every day since.

"So I have to talk to you about something," Jonah says, his voice pulling me out of the memory. He sits back down on the picnic table, facing Max who is waving a stick in front of Bessie's nose.

Oh no. Nothing good ever follows that sentence. But I force myself to play it cool. "What's up?"

His fingers tap against the wooden picnic table. "So, you know Drew and Sean?"

"Your roommates who I see multiple times a week?" I grin at him. "Yes, I know them."

"Well, Drew asked if I wanted to re-up the lease with him for next year."

"Sean's moving out?"

Jonah nods. "Drew's girlfriend is moving in, so they're taking the bigger room, which means the rent's getting split different."

I nod, waiting for him to get to the point, watching as he runs his hand through his hair.

"I've been thinking …" He looks at me, and there's

something vulnerable in his eyes that makes me forget to breathe. "What if you moved in with me next year?"

The world goes still. I blink at him. Did I hear that right?

"You want us to live together?" I ask.

"In the spring. After you graduate. If your mom and Max are okay by then." He pauses. "I know it's a big step, but I want to wake up next to you every day. I want that crappy apartment to be ours. I want you, Shiloh. All in."

My brain races to catch up as I try to wrap my head around what he's saying. Jonah and me. I have never lived with anybody but my family. I'd thought about the future with Jonah before, but not like this, in such a real way … getting to wake up next to him and his choppy hair every morning? Seeing him every day because he'd come home to the same place I also lived in? The idea hits me like a bolt of electricity, and for a second, I can't even breathe because picturing it feels so good.

Until I drop right back to the ground.

"What about Max?" The words jump out of my mouth before I can even process what Jonah's suggesting. Because that's my default. It's always been my default.

Jonah's eyes shift to where Max is playing with Bessie in the field. "The apartment isn't far from yours."

Right. Mom still has custody. I couldn't take Max with me even if I wanted to, and she's actually trying now. She's going to therapy. Getting counseling.

But the thought of not having Max under the same roof makes my stomach clench. Every day, I wake up and make him breakfast. Every night, I tuck him in. Who would check if he did his homework? Who would make sure he brushed his teeth?

"I can't leave him," I say, the words sounding hollow even to me.

"You wouldn't be leaving him," Jonah says gently. "He could stay with us on weekends. I'd watch as many episodes of that dinosaur show with him as he wants."

I try to laugh, but this is too serious. Weekends. Not every day. Not enough.

"But I can't afford—"

"I've been saving," he cuts in. "I can pay for us both until you find something."

I stare at the dirty concrete under my sneakers. I'd be leaving Mom when she's finally getting her life together. Uprooting Max when he finally has something solid. But this would also be more than six months from now. Could things feel different by then?

"You don't have to decide right now." His fingers find mine on the table. "I just wanted to put it out there."

His voice is casual, but he knows what a massive deal this would be for me. Jonah's giving me an out. Like he always does.

The pressure behind my eyes builds, and I blink hard against it. In the field, Max throws a stick for Bessie, who can barely see it but tries to chase it, anyway. She stops in confusion halfway across the grass, her tongue lolling in the warm evening. Her time is passing. My time is passing, and Max is growing right under my nose. I've spent so long protecting him that I've never stopped to think about what I want. Not beyond getting through the next day, or the next one of Dad's episodes, but Max is safe now. He doesn't need me the way he used to.

I did my job.

Taking a deep breath, I let myself picture it—Jonah and me in his apartment. Our apartment. I could get up early and make coffee before going to the animal shelter. I liked doing community service there. Maybe I could get that grouchy old officer to hire me full-time. Jonah would come home covered in dirt but I'd still fling myself into his arms anyway the second he stepped through the door. Max would visit on weekends. He could bring his homework and I'd still help him, at least until I stopped knowing enough to be able to. By the time he hits high school, maybe Mom will be solid enough that I wouldn't worry every time I drop him back off.

I'd still be there for all of it. Just differently. But just because it'd be different doesn't mean it'd be bad.

"Yes," I say, the word coming out strong and clear.

His eyes widen. "Yes?"

"Yes," I say again, and I smile so hard my cheeks hurt. "Yes, I want to."

The smile that breaks across his face cuts dimples into his cheeks. He laughs, cups my face in both hands, and kisses me.

As our lips press together, a cold breeze rustles through the grass. The air around me drops at least ten degrees and goosebumps rise on my arms. I know that feeling.

Jonah pulls away enough to talk. "You feel that?"

I nod. You don't go through what we did without developing a sixth sense for this kind of thing. My hand reaches for my pocket, going for the ghost glasses before I remember I gave half to Miles's parents and I left my half in the apartment.

I try to ignore the prickling sensation crawling up my spine. I hope it's Miles, here to tell us how it went with his parents since he promised to visit me after, and not some other random ghost. I guess I'll have to wait until I go home and get the glasses before I can find out. I feel weird knowing Miles could be watching us right now when we can't see him.

But hey, there are worse people to be haunted by.

A Note from Claire

Thank you from the bottom of my heart for reading this entire series. I can't tell you how much it means to me that you stayed on this adventure through all five books and are reading this right now. Thank you for loving the characters. Thank you for staying up late just to read another chapter and find out what happens. I read your posts on social media and every email you send me, and it brings me so much joy that you love these books like I do and that I get to share this world I love so much with you.

If you have a second, I'd be so grateful if you'd consider telling your friends about the books and leaving a review to help more readers discover the series. Word of mouth is the best kind of marketing, so if you know anyone who you think would enjoy this adventure, you'd be my hero if you helped me spread the word.

Resources

Even though *They Fall* is a work of fiction and to my knowledge nobody knows whether ghosts are real, the characters in this book deal with many challenges that teens and their families deal with in real life. If you or someone you care about needs information, resources, or someone to talk to, here is a short list of resources that could help.

SAMHSA's National Helpline
A free, confidential, 24/7, 365-day-a-year treatment referral and information service for individuals and families facing mental and/or substance use disorders.
1-800-662-HELP (4357)
https://www.samhsa.gov/find-help/national-helpline

The National Domestic Violence Hotline
A free, confidential hotline available 24/7 for anybody who is

experiencing domestic violence or questioning aspects of
their relationships.
1-800-799-SAFE (7233)
https://www.thehotline.org/

PACER Center's Teens Against Bullying
A website run by PACER's National Bullying Prevention
Center created to help teens learn about bullying, how to
respond to it, and how to stop it.
https://pacerteensagainstbullying.org/

National Suicide Prevention Lifeline
The Lifeline provides 24/7, free, and confidential emotional
support to people in suicidal crisis or distress.
1-800-273-TALK (8255)
https://suicidepreventionlifeline.org/

RAINN National Sexual Assault Hotline
A 24/7 hotline that connects individuals who have
experienced sexual assault, or who know someone who has,
with a trained staff member in their area.
1-800-656-HOPE (4673)
https://www.rainn.org/about-national-sexual-assault-
telephone-hotline

Acknowledgments

This book was challenging to write. I had never written an ending before, so I felt immense pressure to get this one right because I wanted to do right by both the characters and by you. It took a long time for me to feel happy with how this one played out. I was able to get it to this point because of some people I'm immensely grateful for.

The people I want to thank first for this book are my beta readers. I was struggling with this one hard, and getting to talk through all the parts of it that I was unsure about helped so much. Your comments transformed this early draft into the version of the book I'm happy with. So, from the bottom of my heart, thank you to Anshul Singh, Hector Torres, Taylor Rees, Candie Johnson, Cathy Shaner, Raemonah Nicholas, Lindsey Soich, and Elizabeth Day. You have also all been my hype people for so long, and I'm just so grateful I get to share my books with you.

Next, I want to extend my heartfelt thanks to Perry Iles.

Thank you for helping me bring this series to life and editing over half a million words for me in this universe. I'm so happy to have gotten to go on this journey with you.

Everybody on my ARC team—thank you for meeting every book in this series with enthusiasm and for helping me make each launch such a fun and exciting event.

Mila, thank you for the amazing cover designs, for being so great to work with, and for understanding my visions for each cover.

Of course, none of this would have been possible without the love and support I've gotten from my family. You are my bedrock and the foundation of my life. I love you so much.

Tristan, my love for you is the beating heart of Shiloh and every one of these books. I'm so proud of the person you are and think you're just the coolest. I'd burn the whole world down, too, if you were kidnapped by an evil circus dude. So, you know, try not to do that.

Mum, you made me grow up believing there was nothing I couldn't do and gave me this deeply instilled confidence in myself. I look up to you so much. You made me believe I can really do this, and I'm forever grateful for that.

Papa, thank you for being my cheerleader and for teaching me to believe in myself like you have always believed in me. I'm so grateful for how much time you spend watching my videos and talking to me about my books. You give the best pep talks and are always the person I turn to when I feel like I can't hack it, and you give me the confidence or perspective I need to keep going.

Andrew, I remember telling you about this ghost book that I had barely started writing on the night we met. Thank you for being my daily sounding board, the person I turn to if I run up against a problem or have a question about the logic of a scene, and also for laughing with me through this whole process—like two weeks ago when I was convinced I had misspelled acknowledgments in every single published copy of all of the books but it turned out to just be the British spelling. I love going through life with you. By the time I publish my next book, our wedding will have already passed, so this is my one chance to say this in a book I published: I can't wait to marry you!

I want to shout out my four-legged family members (Koda, Mocha, Kingly, and Jack), who kept me sane during the past four years of publishing these books and encouraged me to go on walks or get out from behind the computer.

None of this would have been possible without you, reading this right now. So thank you.

And remember, trying to bring people back from the dead will always end poorly. Please don't try any of this at home.

Claire Fraise is the author of paranormal thrillers about sinister spirits and the brave ghost hunters who bring them down. She won the Grand Prize at the 2023 Writer's Digest Self-Published Book Awards for *They Stay*, and has written four more books in the completed series. When Claire is not sitting behind her computer writing about murder, you can find her hiking in the mountains, on the back of a horse, or teaching her rescue Chihuahua that it's not nice to bark at people. Even though it goes against every introverted bone in her body, she is on social media. Connect with her on YouTube at Write with Claire Fraise, Instagram and TikTok at @clairefraiseauthor, or visit her website at clairefraise.com.